The Witness Tree

For Debbie – Enjoy the journey to 1805 cherokee Territory.

Denise Weimer

by
Denise Weimer

SMITTEN
HISTORICAL ROMANCE
LIGHTHOUSE PUBLISHING of the CAROLINAS

THE WITNESS TREE BY DENISE WEIMER
Published by Smitten Historical Romance
An imprint of Lighthouse Publishing of the Carolinas
2333 Barton Oaks Dr., Raleigh, NC 27614

ISBN: 978-1-64526-062-2
Copyright © 2019 by Denise Weimer
Cover design by Elaina Lee
Interior design by Karthick Srinivasan

Brought to you by the creative team at Lighthouse Publishing of the Carolinas (LPCBooks.com):
Eddie Jones, Shonda Savage, Robin Patchen, Pegg Thomas, Stephen Mathisen, Barbara Curtis

Library of Congress Cataloging-in-Publication Data
Weimer, Denise.
The Witness Tree / Denise Weimer 1st ed.

Printed in the United States of America

PRAISE FOR *THE WITNESS TREE*

The Witness Tree is a fascinating blend of history, adventure, romance and spirituality. The story grabbed me on the first page and kept me reading to the last with its authentic history and beautifully drawn characters. Denise Weimer's knowledge of the Moravian people gives the story extra depth. If you like historical fiction that opens up new worlds to you, you will love reading *The Witness Tree*.

~Ann H. Gabhart
Bestselling author of *The Refuge*

Again the gifted author Denise Weimer has woven memorable characters with superb storytelling. Having lived in Tennessee, learned of the Moravian ways, and studied the Cherokee culture, I can attest that Weimer truly captured the sights, sounds, smells, and spirit of the missionary life in the wild Indian Territory. I was touched by the characters' struggles and successes, and I'm sure this wonderful story that will move your heart.

~Susan G Mathis
Author of *Katelyn's Choice*

Sensitively written and brilliantly researched, *The Witness Tree* opens a whole new world to readers. The characters, based on actual historical figures from the early 1800s, become alive on the page, thanks to the skillful word-crafting of author Denise Weimer. Engaging and heart-rending, *The Witness Tree* transports readers to another time and place when Moravian missionaries followed a call to share the Gospel with Native Americans of the Cherokee Nation. This novel brings history alive in all its romance and harsh realities. A must-read for historical lovers. A must-read, period.

~Elaine Marie Cooper
Author of *Love's Kindling*

Denise Weimer has crafted a beautiful tale of faith and romance in this unexpected intersection of Moravian and Cherokee culture. Great attention to period detail, a heart-melting love story, and illumination of a lesser-known era make this a story that fans of historical fiction should not miss!

~**Shannon McNear**
RITA® finalist and author of *The Cumberland Bride*

The Witness Tree is a beautiful story of what growing love really looks like. The theme of determining God's leading, while not always understanding why things happen as they do, truly resonates. Having a bit of a Moravian background, I was both intrigued and enlightened by Denise Weimer's research and story-telling. I don't know of other books in Christian fiction that have dealt with this little-known aspect of Moravian missionary and Cherokee history. Denise brings it to light with accuracy and heart-wrenching detail. Her writing just keeps getting better.

~**Naomi Musch**
Author of Selah Finalist *Mist O'er the Voyageur*

The Witness Tree is a fascinating story detailing the Moravians' establishment of a mission to the Cherokees in Northwest Georgia early in the nineteenth century. John and Clarissa Kliest's Moravian marriage, selected by lot, and their journey from Salem are only the beginning of the challenges this arranged marriage faces. All the characters have depth, displaying good and flawed qualities. Adventure, romance, suspense, as well as insights into the history and events of that period keep a reader's interest throughout.

~**Janet Grunst**
Author of *A Heart Set Free* and *A Heart For Freedom*

Denise Weimer made me a spectator first, and then a participant, as I traveled with Clarissa and John into a compelling melding of cultures enhanced by the beauty of the Appalachian region. I truly enjoyed *The Witness Tree* and the emotional journey of its interesting characters.

~Debra E. Marvin
Multi-published historical romance and mystery author

Acknowledgments

Many talented and knowledgeable individuals have graciously lent their expertise to the process of *The Witness Tree*'s publication. I can't begin to say how much I have learned from my agent, Linda S. Glaz of Hartline Literary, and Smitten Managing Editor Pegg Thomas. You have both opened so many doors for me. Thanks are also due to my keen-eyed general editor for this project, Robin Patchen. I'm so glad I got to work with you!

Much appreciation to the staff and Friends of the Chief Vann House State Historic Site for the wonderful tour and the questions you answered.

Please see my Author's Note regarding the real history behind *The Witness Tree* and the timeline changes I made to accommodate the story.

My novels would scarcely get to my agent, much less the public, without the behind-the-scenes efforts of my launch team. The ladies who helped with *The Witness Tree* volunteered their time as beta readers (Adriann Ansel, Carrie Hayes, and Emma Pressley) and blogger/reviewer influencers on social media (Jasmine Augustine, Becky Dempsey, Michelle Fitzgerald, Lori Parrish, Crystal Scott, and Julia Wilson). You are a priceless blessing to this author navigating her path in the great big publishing world.

Reader, thank you for investing your time in this story. All reviews are deeply appreciated, and I would love to connect with you on social media. I hope you enjoy *The Witness Tree*.

DEDICATION

To my husband and daughters:
Thank you for understanding when I need quiet "writing time."
And to my parents:
You will always be my most important beta readers and
influencers. Your sacrifices and support have allowed me to do
what God has called me to do and what I love third best to
Him and you!

CHAPTER ONE

Salem, North Carolina
Late August, 1805

"You have received a marriage proposal."

At Susanna Stotz's whispered words, Clarissa Vogler almost dropped her paintbrush into the carpet of lush grass. Her heart thundered with so much excitement it was easy to act surprised. "I have?"

Susanna nodded.

She couldn't see the middle-aged woman's face because of the way she stood, blocking Clarissa's light as she painted the women at work in the garden of the Single Sisters' House. But Susanna could read Clarissa's expressions with ease, so she widened her eyes. "Who asked for my hand?"

She wasn't supposed to already know the answer to her question. In their faith, a man ready to wed told his choir helper— his spiritual advisor—followed by the elders. They counseled and prayed, then, based on biblical principles, consulted the lot—slips of paper in a jar that read *yes*, *no*, or were left blank, indicating the encouragement to wait. Only if the lot offered a *yes* from God did the intended bride receive a proposal.

"Brother Kliest."

Clarissa pressed her fist to her chest, barely noticing the dampness of the paint smudges on her apron. She closed her eyes. *Yes*. The name of the man who promised her freedom.

"The proposal pleases you?" Susanna asked.

Clarissa's breath whooshed out in a rush of admission. "It does."

Many single sisters did not wish to marry. The communal

lifestyle of the Moravian Church gave unwed women independence that those in the outside world only dreamed of. But ever since Daniel—a joiner who did carpentry and cabinetwork in the Single Brothers' Workshop, but also an aspiring painter trained at the prestigious Nazareth Hall in Pennsylvania—had hinted at a shared destiny, Clarissa had dreamed of a different kind of freedom. One where she could explore her art in the outside world.

Other sisters spoke of rapturous devotion to their Savior. Clarissa loved God, but until she met Daniel, only painting had transported her above the strict monotony of Salem. But she had a problem.

Rather than replying, Susanna clasped and unclasped her hands in front of her navy, empire-waist dress—a gesture that, for her, betrayed an unprecedented amount of emotion.

Nervousness lashed out and curled around Clarissa's middle. She wet her lips and rested her brush in a jar of water. "Do you not approve?"

As Clarissa's choir helper, Susanna *must* approve.

Susanna bit her lip. "'Tis complicated. Why don't we sit over there, where we can talk?" She tilted her white-capped head toward a bench.

"Very well." Clarissa removed her brush from the jar. After drying it on a rag, she laid it alongside her English boxed set of watercolors and rose to follow Susanna.

The shady spot where they settled provided some relief from the late-August heat. Clarissa dabbed the back of her neck with her handkerchief. "Please tell me what troubles you, Sister Stotz."

"I am concerned whether you are ready for the changes this marriage could bring." Susanna leaned forward but pressed her lips together as if too much information might escape.

Why couldn't Susanna be direct? During their *Sprechens*, or Speakings, times when Clarissa could discuss any moral or theological struggles before taking communion with the congregation, Susanna communicated with a lot of body language and carefully orchestrated silences intended to bring about confessions. Clarissa often resisted such manipulation—well-intended as it may be—but today it was all she could do to hold her peace.

Clarissa followed Susanna's pointed gaze toward the new boarding school next to their dormitory. "You mean my teaching?"

"You've done a wonderful job instructing our pupils these last two years, even though our classrooms in the Single Sisters' House have been overcrowded. I know how excited you are to begin the first year in the new school."

Clarissa nodded. Scholars from across the southeast were already arriving for the fall term.

Susanna continued. "'Tis a great honor to instruct in not only reading and writing, but also the extra lessons in drawing and painting."

"Indeed, a great honor."

She was supposed to move from the house into the school next week. Daniel had timed his proposal so that she might move with him instead.

Her mind wandered to his dark, laughing eyes as he'd painted her miniature. She could even hear his voice, how he'd praised the drawings she'd brought him to evaluate as he'd completed likenesses of Clarissa and her siblings and parents at her father's house outside of town.

"You show great talent."

That brief and rare time she'd been allowed to interact with a single man—under her mother's chaperoning, of course—had been enough to form an understanding that when Daniel went to the elders to request a wife—a wife who would one day accompany him to study under the master painter, Thomas Sully, in Philadelphia—he would request Clarissa.

Susanna mistook Clarissa's daydreaming as wistfulness. She patted her hand. "A proposal by Brother Kliest is also a great honor. There is not an eligible man more highly regarded than he."

Clarissa blinked, barely catching her brows from shooting up.

She'd never heard Susanna speak well of any man, married or not.

Susanna's cheeks colored. "For his many contributions to the community, of course."

Clarissa nodded. Contributions? Daniel? At best, he made an adequate woodworker, even though many in the community considered his artistic aspirations selfish when Salem so needed another joiner. He must be more respected as an emerging artist than she'd realized. Or was Susanna not so oblivious to the opposite sex as Clarissa had imagined?

"I believe he requested you because of all that you have in common."

"I can see why he might have thought that."

She must remain vague. Meetings between single men and women, including interactions as innocent as the passing of journals on painting techniques accompanied by little notes such as they had done, were forbidden. The elders even took pains to direct traffic across the square that lay between the Single Sisters' and Single Brothers' Houses so that the sexes did not unnecessarily cross paths. Why, the oldest members recalled the days when married people still lived in separate choirs, only coming together for marital relations once a week or so, as the church had functioned in the mid-1700s under Count Zinzendorf.

Susanna squinted at her. "As promising a proposal as this is, I can imagine it would pain you to give up your position at the boarding school."

"I realize only single sisters can teach." She had prepared herself for this. A small sacrifice for future potential.

"That is normally the case."

"What do you mean, 'normally'? Do you have reason to think the elders might allow me to continue?" At this possibility, Clarissa's mask of composure slipped. "Perhaps with the advanced art scholars?"

She'd be leaving for Philadelphia as soon as Daniel's correspondence with Sully resulted in an invitation, but Susanna wouldn't know that. The elders were more likely to approve Daniel taking a wife if he opened a joinery shop first. So there would be time in the interim, perhaps six months, even a year. Some of the girls she'd taught in the past couple of years showed promise.

The ribbons of Susanna's pointed-front *haube*, the white cap most younger women had begun to discard as unflattering, danced across her shoulders as she shook her head. "Given how quickly Brother Kliest needs to move forward with his plans, there might be scholars, but not the ones here."

"What do you mean?"

"Oh dear." Brow furrowing, Susanna chewed her lower lip. "I thought you'd already heard the news about Brother Kliest."

Clarissa shot to her feet in uncontainable exasperation. "What news? Sister Stotz, you are not making any sense."

Rising also, Susanna took Clarissa's hand. "Sister Vogler. You have been offered not one holy opportunity, but two. Brother Kliest has been called to go to the Cherokees, the Indians just south of Tennessee. The elders only wish to send married couples. And the wife they wish to send is you."

Clarissa's arms went numb. She couldn't even feel Susanna holding her hand. "Daniel Kliest, to go to the Cherokees?" She couldn't think of a more ridiculous combination.

Susanna's eyes rounded in twin pools of horror. She clasped a hand over her mouth. "Not Daniel. *John*. His older brother. *John* Kliest has asked for you."

❧　❧

John Kliest. Clarissa could picture him as she hurried up Church Street past the sanctuary that had replaced the old *Gemein Haus* five years ago. Everyone recognized the man trained to succeed his father Frederick as Salem's surveyor and bookkeeper, but few knew him.

Daniel's older brother had spent many months traveling until he'd become the building supervisor. In that capacity, Clarissa had glimpsed him over the last year, measuring and inspecting at the site of the new boarding school. Whenever she'd beheld John's imposing form, she'd cut a path around him. The wildness he'd picked up from his journeys to the Cherokees four and five years ago still clung to him—in his quick, restless movements and the way he gazed at the horizon. A man like that did not always act within the ordered boundaries of their society. Such a man was to be avoided.

Clarissa had no wish to talk to anyone until she made it to her father's house, with one important, secret stop along the way. The heat and the incline of the hill forced her to pause outside the doctor's residence. She leaned forward and pressed a hand to her chest.

The door of the imposing brick home opened, and Dr. Samuel Vierling ushered a customer out of his apothecary. He caught sight of her and called out from his steps. "Sister Vogler, are you all right?"

"Quite all right, Dr. Vierling. Simply catching my breath."

The middle-aged physician chuckled. "My family may enjoy living atop this hill, but my patients give me many complaints." He gestured toward his door with the elaborate arch of tracery above. "Were you coming to see me?"

"Oh no. Just on my way to visit my mother, er, the long way around." Clarissa stumbled over her answer, well aware that the good doctor would find it confusing that someone complaining about exertion would be going out of her way. No one knew she and Daniel exchanged messages using the witness tree that marked the corner of Salem's property. She smiled, waved, and started walking again. "Have a lovely evening, Dr. Vierling."

The physician raised his voice a notch. "I hope the effects of the cowpox vaccine I administered last month did not prove too severe for you."

She swiveled with her face schooled into a patient and respectful expression. "In truth, 'twas not as bad as the inoculation itself. And it seems to have been effective."

"Yes, I am seeing more influenza than smallpox, after all. Be safe, Sister Vogler."

Clarissa did not miss Dr. Vierling's frown of concern. Doubtless, he thought she should not be leaving town alone.

Martha Vierling began to play one of Count Zinzendorf's old hymns on the pianoforte as the doctor closed the door. Clarissa relaxed with a sigh, and Martha's sweet voice followed her up the street. *"Gottes Führung fordert Stille ..."*

Following God demands our stillness.
Rushing to employ our powers,
Even with the best intentions,
We confuse God's will with ours.

God is in control, even if I don't feel it. Even if I don't understand what is happening. I must hold onto that.

At the top of the hill, a line of evergreens separated travelers from God's Acre, where the departed Moravian faithful of Salem lay under flat stone slabs. Above the cemetery, Church Street intersected the east-west road that ran north of town. The witness tree stood at the juncture of this road and another lane that looped south. Some forty years earlier, Frederick Kliest's axe had marked it as such with three slashes on its trunk. That and the knot on the back had made it a perfect place for Daniel to leave Clarissa messages.

Even more shocking than John's proposal had been the news that followed it. Susanna had also revealed that Daniel had left town. The burning ache in Clarissa's chest told her Susanna must have been mistaken. She hurried forward, sped by the sure knowledge that Daniel would not have abandoned her. Not now. At least, not permanently. Not without communicating his plan.

As the tree came into view, so did a figure. Clarissa froze, palm returning to her chest. Daniel?

No. The man walking toward her was taller, more solid, his
closely trimmed, dark beard speckled with gray that somehow did
not make him look older. John Kliest. He might be a good ten
years ahead of Daniel, having passed thirty, she guessed, but his
unlined face and intense blue eyes indicated an untamed energy
that Daniel, even while painting, had not possessed.

He recognized her a second later, for he, too, stopped and
stared. "Sister Vogler."

His first words spoken to her. He bowed. None of the heat that
seemed to be affecting Clarissa colored his face.

"Br-brother Kliest." Now she was stammering too?

Laugh lines danced around his mouth. He took a step toward
her, watching her as one watches a doe in the woods. In fact, he
clutched the tiger-striped maple stock of the Rowan long rifle
he'd commissioned her father to make some years ago. He was
probably the only man in their pacifist community to own such a
gun—presumably as protection from wild animals when he was off
surveying. But he did not carry his surveying instruments today.
Had he been hunting, perchance?

"Headed to your father's?"

"Yes."

John's gaze darted to a spiral of the blonde hair she found so
hard to keep under her cap. "Might I accompany you? This isn't
the best path for sisters to travel alone, being outside of town." His
narrowing eyes questioned why she did not take the usual route
between the Single Sisters' House and the gunsmith's.

"My parents might be more alarmed if I arrived in your
company."

"I don't think so, Miss Vogler."

The way his tone dropped sent tingles to her toes. And he called
her "miss," not the more proper "sister."

He studied her reaction as if gauging whether she'd yet been
told of his proposal. A dozen unasked questions jockeyed in her
throat. *Why did you ask to marry me? Was it only because twenty years*

ago, Father visited the Cherokees himself and convinced the congregation to set up a mission? So now you have some thum—*stupid—idea that I should go as well? What about Daniel? Where is he, and did you know of his intentions toward me? Did you push him out of your way?*

But these were not things a Moravian lady asked a bachelor, marriage proposal or no. These were things Clarissa must learn from others. She would give nothing away until she knew more. And she couldn't check that tree until John was gone.

She clasped her hands together. "Such things are not done, Brother Kliest. But I thank you and bid you a good day."

That smile danced around his lips again. He tipped his hat. "Until next time, Sister Vogler."

Next time?

Biting her lip, Clarissa hurried past him, indignation sweeping her.

He was confident he would be accepted. Because he'd achieved status in the community? Because the nobility of his calling to be among the *Pilger- und Streitersache*—the church's pilgrims and militants for Christ—would trump anything his younger brother offered?

As soon as John disappeared from sight, Clarissa crumpled on a fallen log. She loosened the strings of her bonnet in an attempt to calm her panicked breathing. She looked back at the witness tree. She already knew the knot would be empty.

The elders had agreed with John's plans, and the lot had been consulted. It must have said *yes,* or the proposal would not have been made. And a proper lady never refused a positive answer from the lot, because even though she *could* do so, the lot represented the will of God.

CHAPTER TWO

John Kliest strode with unfaltering steps toward the tavern, intent on breaking two expectations of the church tonight.

The brick wall of the main level lacked windows. The elders did not want congregation members peering in at the "strangers" in Salem on business who were fed and housed by a Moravian married couple at the inn. They certainly did not encourage members loitering, listening in on the gossip while sipping brandy or beer.

The elders also did not like secrets. In Salem, nothing was secret. From the bickering of rival potters to how often a man knew his wife, all was to be aboveboard and accounted for so that sin could not take root.

Despite this, John was meeting his friend, Peter Keller—recently arrived from Pennsylvania—at the tavern … to discuss secrets. Under the circumstances, the elders would understand. Peter and his new wife, Rosina, were staying in one of the first half-timbered homes built in Salem. But since it was now used to house married church members visiting from other settlements, a large family from Bethlehem shared their lodgings. And Sister Clarissa Vogler had yet to announce her answer to his proposal—though her response on the road this afternoon told him she'd indeed received it. Yes, plans involving all of them were best kept quiet … for now.

John greeted the tavern keeper in the walk-up bar of the central hallway. In the guest room to the left, noisy travelers lined long tables for the ordinary meal—the standard, inexpensive supper. Sprinkled with only a few patrons who conversed over tables set with muslin cloths, the gentlemen's room to the right offered the more intimate setting John sought. As a lad of sixteen in 1791, he had glimpsed President George Washington at supper during his solitary visit to Salem at the very table where Peter now stood.

The tall, red-haired man clasped John in a half-embrace. "Brother, I've taken the liberty of ordering us cider."

"'Tis good, although after these last few days, were I a drinking man, I'd imbibe something stronger."

"I am eager for an update." As John leaned his weapon against the wall, Peter held a hand up. "Whoa! Should I be prepared for some sort of uprising?"

John chuckled. "When I saw Brother Vogler yesterday, he invited me to bring the piece back to be serviced and engraved with my initials before leaving for the Cherokee Nation."

"I shall be glad you carry it, especially on that stretch between Tellico and Springplace." Peter sat forward, his florid face eager. "So 'tis settled, then? You're to accompany us?"

He took a deep breath, inhaling the pungent scent of the oil lamp that cast flickering light into the darkness outside the window. "Only if Sister Vogler will have me. My brother left this morning for Philadelphia, but the lady has only just received the news. Despite the fast-approaching date of our journey, I fear she is not the type to be rushed."

Peter nodded. "'Tis a big decision, one she must bring before the Lord."

"And, apparently, her parents."

"How do you know that? Was she at their home when you went?"

"I met her on the road on my way back." *After I stopped to check the tree.*

Once, several months prior, John had seen Daniel leave a folded paper in the knot of the big oak their late father had marked as a surveyor. He'd assumed only a person outside their community would agree to such assignations, yet his concerned questioning had yielded no answers. Now he knew the recipient had been Clarissa

Vogler. His hunch that Daniel would attempt to communicate one last time had proved correct, as evidenced by the note resting in his coat pocket.

Peter's mouth—which had popped open at John's last statement—snapped shut when the hired worker approached to inquire as to their dinner choice. He restrained his questions until the man had departed with their orders. "How did she seem? Favorable?"

John chuckled with regret. "Not so much. I offered to walk her to her parents' home, but she would have none of it."

"You did say she seems a woman of propriety, which is much to be valued."

"Mayhap, although I go only on glimpses of apparent devotion during services"—not that he had been watching her, of course— "and her reputation as an excellent teacher."

"The two qualities which recommended her to the elders as a missionary wife—the wife without which, I may remind you, you shan't be going to the Cherokee Nation."

John grimaced as he sipped his cider. "The notion hangs like an albatross around my neck." He'd often questioned the reliability of the lot as an indication of God's direction. Now his fate was subject to something far more capricious—the whims of a woman.

"Trust me, Brother, no one understands the frustration of unsatisfied *Zeugentriebe* more than I."

The "desire to witness" had settled on Peter three years prior, after he'd paid a resupply visit to the Steiners, the middle-aged couple who had begun the Springplace mission adjoining Chief James Vann's plantation at the turn of the century. But the lot had denied Peter since, as it had denied John when he sought to return on a more permanent basis after accompanying the Steiners to help them break ground. When John had taken Daniel to school in Nazareth, the two men had analyzed the possible reasons for this. Neither had found an acceptable explanation … until the elders suggested both men should take a wife. Peter had wed Rosina, a teacher from the Bethlehem Girls' School, only last month.

"When I heard you and your new wife were the couple commissioned to join the Steiners, I knew it was time to try again."

"And I am glad you did, but you can see why the Unity Elders' Conference would stipulate Sister Vogler's participation. After all, the Steiners have made clear that the Cherokee language proves their biggest obstacle. Sister Vogler is uniquely qualified, given not only her talent with languages but also the knowledge about the Indians her father undoubtedly shared."

John grunted and tore a piece of the crusty loaf the servant had brought them. He'd like to think his skills with level and compass might come in handy, too, but he only said, "Martin Vogler did admit that he'd taught Clarissa the Cherokee words he'd picked up, even though she was quite young, because he wanted to remember them."

"See?" Peter punctuated the air with a knobby finger. "She will make the most valuable member of our party. All I can say is, pray and give the woman the time she needs to come to peace. I can assure you, it will be worth it."

John intercepted the subtle twitch of Peter's eyebrow. A trace of the man's smirk remained as he reached for his earthenware mug. "I take it marriage sits well with you."

"Ah, yes, my friend. Don't believe all they tell you in the Single Brothers' Choir."

John smiled. "Rosina seems the most sweet and sprightly of ladies. Her skill with botany will be an asset in Springplace too."

"Certainly more than that of a humble hatmaker."

"Mayhap the Indians will replace their headdresses with top hats."

Peter laughed loudly as their mutton chops arrived.

John tucked into his steaming vegetables. "Jesting aside, your strengths are spiritual, not economic. I've never known a man more devoted to the Lord's cause than you, Peter."

"Except perhaps yourself."

Convicted by his friend's generosity, John shook his head. "No. You have a genuine love for the Cherokee people that is truly amazing on such short exposure. What I have is a push to chart the unknown that has never let me rest."

Peter grinned, resting his knife on the edge of his plate after he finished sawing into his meat. "You should accompany Lewis and Clark on their way to the Pacific Ocean."

"That would be amazing, but perchance we'll have our own adventure … if I can woo a wife." The muttered tail of John's statement almost got drowned out by clinking silverware and a bark of laughter from a diner across the room.

"On that note, a word of advice?"

"Of course." Peter might be roughly John's own age, but John considered him a spiritual mentor.

"I know you said you think Sister Vogler would only respond to your brother's overtures because of her interest in the art world. Tread carefully, though. Daniel was not without his assets. Despite their limited interaction and the boundaries set by the church, he may yet have engaged her more tender feelings."

Staring at his green-trimmed pearlware plate, John nodded. He did not want to tell his friend it wasn't sadness he thought he'd glimpsed in Clarissa Vogler's eyes—it was fear. And maybe a bit of anger. Even if she agreed to marry him, it would be a long time before she knew him well enough to realize he had her best interests at heart.

❧ ❧

Clarissa had still lived with her family in town, attending the school for Moravian girls through her twelfth year, when John Kliest commissioned his gun. But the house where the family had moved so the mill on Tar Branch could generate power to bore and rifle gun barrels held no memories of John. Rather, Clarissa pictured Daniel here, even though the light of evening rather than morning stole into the parlor. He had stood just there, behind his easel, while he positioned her by the window. Her mother had sat in the corner, her eyes too focused on her silk-on-linen sampler to notice the way Daniel's lingered on her daughter.

Why had Daniel not at least left a goodbye note? Something to explain why he had gone?

"Clarissa." Anna Vogler interrupted her reverie. Clarissa stood frozen in the middle of the braided rug, gazing into nothingness. Her mother waved to the settee. "Please sit down."

Clarissa settled, then scooted over when her father sat next to her. As always, the scent of wood shavings and varnish came with him. She cradled and sipped her tea. Why couldn't Father have accompanied her brother and cousin back to his shop? Wasn't he always saying he couldn't leave his apprentices unsupervised, even his own son and nephew? But the scowl on his face said he had no intention of his wife dismissing him as she had Clarissa's younger sisters to clean up after dinner.

Placing his mug aside, Father cleared his throat. "We may now speak of Brother Kliest's proposal."

"You were not surprised when I told you before dinner." Clarissa lowered her tea, clasping both hands around the cup. "I assume the elders came to you this morning."

"Actually, we were summoned to them yesterday."

"Yesterday?" That was not normal. Elders preferred to involve parents as little as possible in the proposal process, only delivering news once a decision had been reached.

"Because of the missional call, the council wished to consult us *before* going to the lot. They needed information on your qualifications to teach Cherokee children."

"And you recommended me."

"Of course. You are an excellent teacher, and I assured them I had shared everything I remembered from my brief visit to the Indians in 1784."

Clarissa swallowed, placing her tea on the table beside her. How she and her siblings had basked in those hours at their father's knee, gathered around the fire while he told them of his adventures. They'd been awed by his stories of crossing the Blue Ridge Mountains in waist-high snow and how he'd journeyed on even when his guide had fallen ill. They had laughed when he'd told of his struggle to keep a straight face while eating sour hominy in front of his watching hosts.

The community reverenced her father for having preached to the Cherokees and forged an understanding for future contact. She'd gladly spent hours writing down every word he remembered in the Cherokee language, never dreaming her childhood fascination would one day threaten the marriage and life she coveted.

She glanced at her mother. "Did you not think of the hopes I had shared with you, about studying painting in Philadelphia?"

Mama's gentle face crumpled with regret. "'Twas but a youthful fancy, Clarissa."

"No, 'twas not. You said yourself I had promise."

Mama shook her head. "Women—even Moravian women—do not become artists, except for those like Rosina Keller who draw their flowers and herbs or teach like you do in schools. And you *can* teach, my *liebling*."

"But why teach girls art if they can't paint what they want? And certainly, why teach Indian girls such things?"

"Because in doing so you impart the love of the Savior to them." Father's firm statement squashed any selfish argument. "I did not protest Daniel Kliest lending you his art books because they helped you instruct the boarding scholars, but your mother allowed unhealthy fantasies to flourish between the two of you. It was *leichtsinn* … carelessness."

"But I cared for Daniel! How could you agree for me to marry another—especially his own brother?" Clarissa tried to contain her angst in the twisting of her handkerchief, but her voice rose in a manner that betrayed far too much emotion. Moravians did not marry for attraction but for practical purpose. Her father was right. How many times had she failed to confess to Susanna before communion how she'd daydreamt about Daniel?

Her father dismissed her sentiments with a brash wave of his hand. "Bah! How can you care for a boy you saw a few times whilst having your picture painted? I rue the day I commissioned him. Elder Schneider was right. 'Twas vanity."

Clarissa lowered her gaze to her hands clasped in her lap. No one knew about the notes she had exchanged with Daniel, not even her mother. They were innocent, simple updates about Daniel's plans for the future—though they made it clear she was part of those plans. But her father would never understand.

"I could see a future with him. We had so much in common. He would have opened my world."

"The world *is* open, foolish girl." Her father's sharp tone and red face caused Clarissa to sink back on the cushion. "You have been offered the noblest calling a Moravian woman can hope for— the whole reason our forefathers came to America. To spread the Gospel message to the heathen. And you would turn up your nose at it because of some *Regungen*"—he appeared to struggle against lapsing into his native tongue, windmilling his hand as he spat out the English meaning with disgusted emphasis—"*fleshly feelings* toward a boy not even established to take a wife? Enough!"

"Martin." Mama spoke his name, softly chiding.

Tears fell from Clarissa's eyes, but another question wrenched from her aching chest. "Please just tell me what happened to him. Why did he leave?"

Her father straightened. "I told the elders it was best he go on to Philadelphia because I feared he would divert you from your true calling."

"My true calling." She whispered the words as she realized what he meant. Not painting but recording the Cherokee language. Was that what she'd been called to do? Live among a foreign people? In a foreign land? There must be some mistake. Even though the church held mission work above all else—the many trades in their settlements had been established to support it—she'd always known she was not cut out for the wilderness. She thrived in the order of ringing bells and evening prayers.

Clarissa scrambled for some way out. "Brother Kliest—John— could not have known Daniel intended—"

"He did not know. He asked for your hand in good faith, for a good cause. You should be honored." Father grabbed his earthenware mug and took several swallows of the contents, which were probably lukewarm at best.

A shuddering sob worked its way from Clarissa's middle, and she buried her face in her handkerchief. Her mother reached across from her wing chair to touch her free hand.

"Daniel did care for you, my *liebling*—"

"Anna." Father's warning cut off whatever Mama had been about to say, but Clarissa drew a spark of solace from her statement.

"But we must put that in the past," Mama continued. "The important thing is, the Savior's approbation has been given through the lot to John Kliest. Your father is right that he is a highly regarded and capable man. The elders agreed for him to accompany the Kellers only if you wed him, and your assignment will be only for a short time."

Clarissa raised her head. "I don't understand."

Clunking down his drained teacup, Father spoke again. "A few years after my trip, our apostle to the northern Indians recommended our missionaries learn the language of the Cherokees and hopefully write it down. Yet everyone who has since dealt with the tribe finds their language impossible. You, my dear, would be commissioned for this task while your husband applies himself to building and surveying in the area."

"And once it is written down?"

Mama squeezed her hand, appealing to Clarissa's need for security. "You would return to Salem, where your bridegroom holds a position of considerable standing."

"And he can only go if I go?"

The first pang of sympathy for John Kliest struck Clarissa.

She'd heard he had asked twice in the past few years to return to Springplace. He must want that very badly indeed if he was going to all this trouble. But how could she marry such a forbidding man? She could barely tolerate being in his presence. Yet at the same time, he attracted her. That intensity of barely leashed energy caused her to tremble inside the way she did when a storm came too near.

"That is right." Mama nodded. "The elders understand this is a big decision for you. Since you and Brother Kliest have not spoken before, they have consented for the two of you to walk about town tomorrow, if you are willing. Hear the man out, Clarissa. See if his words do not set a fire in your bones as they did ours."

The man made her lose her breath, her thoughts, her perspective. Clarissa feared the fire he'd set in her bones would little resemble a missional fervor and might even exceed the bounds of church-sanctioned propriety between husband and wife.

Oblivious to her discomfort, Father rubbed his hands together. "I admit, he had me hankering to go off into the wilderness again, even at my age."

"Oh, you shall not be leaving me with this smithy full of gangling apprentices in their *bedenkliche Jahre*, those difficult years," Mama declared, though her tone hinted at fond teasing.

Her parents' camaraderie touched the ache in her heart, and Clarissa gave a faint smile. She had to look at things realistically. Daniel must have learned too late that his own brother had taken her name before the lot. Even if he had felt pressured to leave, she couldn't blame her father. She couldn't blame John. God's will through the lot trumped all. She must wish Daniel well and see what she could construct from the pieces left to her.

Clarissa blew and dabbed her nose, then sat up straight. Her parents had found love through the elders and the lot. Perhaps so could she. "I will hear the man out."

CHAPTER THREE

John waited for Clarissa on a shady bench on the main square. One of the potters emerged from his workshop with a bucket and headed for the public pump that provided water from the town's log-bored pipes. Not wanting to engage in conversation, John hopped up and paced.

What would he say? How would he act? How, in a mere two hours, did one court a woman in such a way as to produce an outcome favorable to the rest of his life?

John stopped, removed his broad-brimmed hat, and ran a hand through his hair. He knew what the elders would say—that God's will had already been revealed in the lot and he needed to stop supposing he had to convince Clarissa Vogler of anything. He just needed to give this to God.

But he'd tried to do that very thing once before and look what had happened. He'd been left shamed and rejected. The memory cued a rush of anger at the position the elders—and yes, God—had put him in. Rather than allowing John to devote himself to his spiritual calling, they'd weighted him with an impossible challenge. One couldn't trust one's emotions to a woman. He didn't want a wife, but he needed to woo one.

He slapped his hat against his leg. Best he approach this like a business proposal. With kindness and reassurance, he'd convince Clarissa that she'd find a life with him both adventurous and fulfilling. He'd be much safer to treat this like the partnership it was rather than a romance. He'd also be much less likely to scare her off.

He could care for her without losing his head again. Was not true love to seek the well-being of another? Marrying him and traveling to Indian land near Georgia and Tennessee was in Clarissa's best interest. And since love could be commanded, did the Bible not show that love was a choice that may or may not include one's feelings? Did not Moravians believe in marrying for higher purposes than passion or even emotional attachment? Yes, that was the right way of things.

John stood straight when he caught sight of the young woman in question, clad in a flowered dress and a navy bonnet. She couldn't look sweeter or more appealing. *Partnership*, he reminded himself.

Clarissa's arm twined through her choir helper's like a clinging vine. When the women caught sight of him, he couldn't tell which one turned a deeper shade of red.

He approached, clasping his hat before his chest. "Good afternoon, sisters."

As though she were the would-be bride, Sister Stotz lowered her lashes. "Sister Vogler, this is Brother Kliest. I leave you two to get acquainted. Brother Kliest, please deliver our sister back to us for dinner."

John bowed. "I will, Sister Stotz."

The choir helper whisked herself away, leaving John and Clarissa standing almost toe-to-toe in awkward silence. Sudden panic engulfed John. Who was this petite blonde creature in front of him, with her smooth skin and fluttering hands? He'd hardly spent any time around the fair sex. Only once had he imagined he knew a young lady well enough to discern the inner workings of her mind. He'd been proven vastly mistaken. And he was supposed to make this one his *Gehülfin*—his helpmate?

Clarissa's eyes came up to his, not blue or green like one might expect from the color of her hair, but dark brown, like a doe's, and just as vulnerable. As if she were asking him a question. Pleading for him to help her. How could he do that?

God?

His arm went out, seemingly of its own accord, because *he* would not have reached for her, surely. She sucked in a tiny breath as his fingers descended her muslin sleeve. She did not turn her palm over. He did not expect her to. She just looked at his big, rough fingers resting on the back of her hand. But by some providence, the unexpected touch built a bridge.

John cleared his throat. "Thank you for agreeing to meet me. Thank you for considering my proposal."

"The honor is mine, sir."

"Will you walk and talk with me for a while?"

Clarissa nodded. "Where shall we start?"

John tipped his head toward a red-trimmed building on Main Street, with its unique combination of pink stucco on the first story and brick above. "I've been smelling the tempting goods from the bakery while I've been standing here. Care to go in?"

"Inside? Together?" Clarissa's eyes rounded.

In hopes that a jest might set her at ease, John allowed a teasing grin. "Aye, unless you prefer to go to the back door and request hard cider."

Sure enough, she plopped her hand over her mouth to stifle a giggle. Clarissa's gaze descended to his smile, making John suddenly conscious of the slight gap between his front two teeth. Her smooth cheeks turned pink again. John thought her embarrassment had more to do with being caught staring than the questionable history of the bakery, but she covered any emotion by asking, "You do know why the elders had Brother Butner take over?"

"Because the single sisters once had to purchase bread from the single brothers unchaperoned?"

She nodded again.

"I'm not sure 'twas much of an improvement for town morality, are you?"

Clarissa laughed, the sound twisting John's insides and filling him with unexpected elation. "No." So word *had* made it to the single sisters that Thomas Butner sold spirituous libations to the male youths of the town. "I believe the Butners prefer farming to baking. Perhaps we better buy our breads while we still can."

"Agreed."

Gesturing ahead of him, John fought the unreasonable urge to offer his arm as they crossed the street. What was this strange sense that he needed to offer her a physical barrier of protection? She had not agreed yet to his proposal, and even if she had, married Moravian couples refrained from showing public affection.

Opening the door of the shop, John inhaled the aroma of baking bread that wafted from the domed oven on the side of the building. After a few minutes of browsing the wares under the watchful eye of Mrs. Butner, they selected a bag of lemon cookies made in the famous Moravian, wafer-thin style.

"Oh, this does make me long for the Christmas spice cookies, and the sugar cookies with their butter and nutmeg. I start to think of them as soon as the weather cools off. Ugh." Clarissa waved a hand in front of her face as they exited the bakery as if to shoo away the late summer humidity.

"Christmas is my favorite season too." He refrained from pointing out that should things go according to plan, they would celebrate the Savior's birth together this year ... in the Cherokee Nation. "There's a bench on the square. Shall we sit there?"

Once they had settled in the shade, John opened the bag and offered Clarissa a wafer. She took one and nibbled.

John knew the onus of starting the conversation fell on him. "Please tell me about yourself, Sister Vogler."

She paused and looked up at him. "What do you know?"

"Not nearly enough."

He meant it sincerely, but she must have thought he was flirting, for she dropped her gaze. "You must know something, else you would not have asked to wed me." He did not respond quickly enough, for Clarissa lowered her hands to her lap, still clutching half a wafer. "Or ... did the elders suggest me?"

"'Twas ... a mutual decision." John hadn't wanted to go into the details of the succession of his meetings with the council—some of which had included Daniel and her father—but she deserved a bit of background. "You probably don't recall, but I visited your home a few times when you were quite young."

The golden-brown eyebrows knit together as she gazed over his shoulder, presumably into the past. "I do recall. You joined us for supper and asked many questions of my father about the Indians."

"What a boorish dinner guest I must have seemed." John laughed.

Relaxing again, Clarissa finished her cookie. He offered her another. Eating with her felt intimate somehow, and rather awkward, like taking one's first communion.

"We did not mind. We loved Father's Indian stories. But you did frighten me a bit."

"Frighten you?"

"I thought you quite grown up." She narrowed her eyes. "You had this restless energy about you."

John kept his face impassive to avoid interrupting, but his mind skittered down a rabbit trail. She'd probably never envisioned him as a potential future mate. And now? He bore little resemblance to his charming, smooth-faced brother. Did she find the gray in his beard repulsive? He folded the cookie bag closed as she resumed.

"'Twas almost as if you might bolt up from the table and make for the frontier at any moment. You … have it still."

He smiled. "You have me pegged already, Sister Vogler. After hearing your father's stories, I knew what I was meant to do. I helped select, survey, and begin the mission at Springplace, and 'tis not in my nature to leave something unfinished."

"And to finish it, you must have a wife."

Her flat intonation, the barest downturn of the corners of her mouth, hinted at a need for reassurance. Of course, she must not feel like a commodity traded at the community store. "You were not chosen without careful reflection. That is what I was intending to say." What he wouldn't say was that when the elders had asked him if anyone in particular came to mind, Clarissa's face had risen before him without a moment's hesitation.

"Because of my father's teaching."

John shifted on the bench. Would she be the sensitive sort whom he had to coddle? He'd thought her firm and purposeful. Was she expecting some sort of declaration of admiration? He'd wade into those waters, but only ankle-deep. "Yes, but also because I know you are an excellent teacher, one for whom languages pose no difficulty. The elders were aware of your spiritual devotion, leading us to agree that you might find it an adventure to help teach the Cherokee children at the mission while recording their language."

"An adventure? In truth, Brother Kliest, trekking into the wilderness near Georgia is not the sort of adventure I had in mind."

No. Rather, she would have mapped her adventure among art showings and wealthy merchants into an urban wilderness that lured innocent young women to their demise. But it was best that he did not let on that he knew about that. "You will have the opportunity to do everything at Springplace that you are doing here, and as you have been told, we will only be there so long as it takes to master the language."

"I can take my paints?"

"Of course! On one of my trips, my companion drew portraits of the various chiefs at council—Doublehead, The Glass, Bloody Fellow—and they loved it."

"Such names!" A slight shudder passed through Clarissa's slender frame. "They sound fearsome."

John hastened to reassure her. "The Cherokees have changed much since the wars in Kentucky and Tennessee. The peace agreements put Indian agents in place who have started teaching the men to farm rather than hunt for sustenance, and the women to weave and sew. We go to the Upper Towns, which are much more progressive than the Lower. And by Lower, I actually mean more western than southern." He paused with a searching glance, measuring her knowledge of geography.

Clarissa nodded. "My father told us that as the Cherokees have given up land, they have moved south from Tennessee. But that the Lower Towns occupy more of western Georgia and dip south into Alabama."

"That is correct. The Upper Cherokees extend fairly far down now, a good bit south of Springplace. The land I surveyed for the mission was purchased from a farmer named Brown and adjoins the plantation of Chief James Vann."

"A plantation? A real plantation like those outside Salem?"

"Much like those. Vann raises race horses. He has almost a hundred. He even owns slaves, though I find that a conundrum."

"Yes, for a people who are oppressed to oppress others ..."

John caught Clarissa's gaze, encouraged by their point of agreement. Eager to paint an inviting picture, he continued. "The land is the most beautiful you shall ever see, hundreds of acres both cultivated and wooded, with deep rivers and mountains on the horizon. Peach and apple orchards. Vann and his wife"—he'd caught himself before he said *principal* wife—"dress like we do and speak English. Last I heard, they were constructing a brick home as fine as any in Charleston and Savannah."

Clarissa gasped. "Truly? I must say, that does not align with the picture my father gave me. He talked about the natives dwelling in log huts and using sweathouses. The women working communal fields while the men spent every winter away at the hunting ground."

"Most of them do still dwell in log cabins. Vann and some of the other Upper Cherokee chiefs lease land to the government for postal roads. They run ferries, mills, and trading posts. Vann is considered fabulously rich."

"I see. So this is the man who is supporting the mission. And he wants us to teach the children about God?"

John bit his lip. He wouldn't dare tailor the truth. "The chiefs were less interested in us sharing the Gospel and more interested in us providing housing and clothing and instructing their children. 'Tis still a noble purpose, helping the Cherokees not only peacefully coexist with the settlers but apply skills that will allow them to thrive as their old way of life dwindles. They don't realize yet that we offer an even more valuable gift than that, the truth of God's love for them. But as the missionaries are allowed religious instruction alongside reading and math, in time, they will understand."

"I see."

She did not see. There was so much more he needed to tell her, but there was little time before she needed to decide. That was why John felt this increasing pressure to sway her with the positives.

"And you believe that recording the Cherokee language will help with all of this."

"Yes!"

Without thinking, John reached for her hand. Eyebrows fluttering up, she withdrew, but not before that telling blush stained her cheeks. Indicating awareness or distaste?

While Moravian women were trained to pay no heed to the brethren, on his travels, other women had often followed him with their eyes. As a youth, their interest had flattered him. So much so that he'd once allowed the power of that attraction to draw a stranger close. Miss Benson had found him so irresistible she'd declared her intentions to adhere to his faith. Look where that shaky foundation had landed him.

Now, he might hold no illusions of romantic courtship, but an unexpected fear that Clarissa might compare him unfavorably with his brother constricted John's chest. He certainly did not want the woman to whom he'd proposed to find him completely unattractive. And why did he keep feeling the strange urge to touch her? He thought he'd mastered such impulses. It must be his zeal for the mission before them.

"Forgive me, Sister Vogler. I do get passionate about this. Just imagine what a difference it would make for the Cherokees to read and write in their own language, including—eventually—a translation of the Bible."

"Oh, that would be amazing." She spoke on an awed exhale.

"'Tis hard to imagine not having the Word to live by."

"I can see Springplace becoming the center of future outreach to the Upper Towns, then, hopefully, the Lower. A growing community, maybe like Salem itself. And then, other communities, where the Indians can absorb economic and spiritual truths."

"So we would be like building blocks of such a community. I think I can see how we'd both be useful to such a purpose."

"Purpose. Yes." Now she spoke his soul language, her faraway gaze indicating that she'd begun to grasp the vision. John leaned forward, but Clarissa's eyes narrowed on him. "It would only be for a short time? This mission to the Cherokees?"

John hesitated. "That is the agreement. We will remain with the Kellers, who will travel with us to Cherokee Territory, and the Steiners, who started the mission, until we complete our assignment." When she became accustomed to her new home, immersed in the work, acquainted with the people, she'd understand his desire to help plan and build future communities. Maybe then they could request permission to stay.

An apologetic grimace twisted Clarissa's face. "Good, because I am woefully inadequate in the face of storms and snakes and savages."

John attempted to smother a smirk by rubbing his hand across his beard. "I will be with you to face all of those dangers, although I believe you will find them overstated." He liked the thought of protecting her, guiding her, teaching her. Would she be as good a student as she was a teacher? "And I believe you will be moved as I was by the beautiful country and the beautiful people."

"Perhaps ..."

He hastened to fill the void her wistful statement revealed. "Have you not dreamt of leaving Salem? Traveling to a new and exciting place? Doing something meaningful for God?"

"Yes," she whispered, and sadness clouded her expression.

Thinking of Philadelphia again, no doubt. Dabbling with her paintbrush under Daniel's admiring eye.

He spoke with conviction. "Sometimes, our destiny doesn't look like we think it will." John held out his hand, palm up. "Will you come with me, Sister Vogler ... Clarissa?"

It was a huge presumption, speaking her Christian name, but she did not chide him. Biting her lip, she lifted her hand, and for what seemed like an eternity, held it in the air above his. Then she rested her delicate fingertips against his rough ones. "If you will go very slowly, John, I will."

CHAPTER FOUR

D id he understand that she was asking him to go slowly in all areas? That he—that *this*—frightened her? Even the smallest touch of John's callused fingertips felt foreign, forbidden. After a lifetime of being taught to look away, purify one's thoughts, subject unspiritual emotions to fact and truth, it seemed as though she must now heave some mental lever and bond almost immediately in spirit and body with this man.

Right when Clarissa risked falling prey to panic, a smile flashed over John's face that took her breath away, and he answered. "Go slowly. I can do that."

The laugh lines, that tiny gap in his teeth, his blue eyes intense upon her! Coupled with the rasp of his thumb as it stroked once across her hand, these things created a sensation akin to pain in her middle. Taking a quick breath, she pulled her hand back to press her stomach.

Daniel had been ... uncomplicated. Somehow, she'd sensed that she could control him, and that had given her security. The future she'd planned with him had given her security. With this man, she felt no such thing.

"There's something you must know," she said on a shallow breath.

"What is it?"

"My father said that when you went to the council, you had no knowledge that your brother intended to ask for my hand."

John grew very still. "When I first approached the elders, I did not, but you did, it seems."

She'd expected defensiveness, maybe even anger that she dared question his integrity, but the flash of something behind his eyes—

fear?—relaxed the anxiety clenching her chest enough for her to continue. Clarissa nodded. "I cannot begin our marriage with a secret. I met Daniel when he painted our family portraits. He helped me with my art. He knew how much I wanted to travel to Philadelphia to study under Thomas Sully, as he intended to do."

"And you could only go as his wife."

"'Tis true."

"Were you … fond of him?"

Clarissa dropped her gaze. Despite her desire for a clear conscience, she couldn't quite bring herself to confess about the notes. Since she'd burned them all, John couldn't be assured of their innocent content, and such behavior would bring her character into undue question. "I feel sure I would have grown to be."

"And now … can you let that go? I can assure you I did not step in front of my brother in an attempt to obtain your hand."

"Thank you, and … I must let it go. He is not here. You are." She shoved aside a stirring of panic. Daniel wasn't coming back for her, or he would have contacted her by now.

"Clarissa, I tell you this not to place blame, but to ease your mind. When the elders … learned of Daniel's interest, they did not find his situation conducive to taking a wife."

She nodded. She did not have to ask why John had hesitated. He might not want to accuse Martin Vogler, but she already knew her father had shared his poor opinion of Daniel with the council.

She had also wondered how they would live while Daniel studied in Philadelphia, but he'd assured her there were ways. He always had his joinery to help make ends meet. "But a call to missions is the best reason to marry."

"Yes. There is much we could say on the subject of my brother, but wisdom, I believe, would guide us to silence. Shall we let the past be past and focus on our future?"

That was exactly what everyone had counseled her. Wanting to agree, Clarissa tilted her head, but when she remained silent, John asked with only a hint of impatience, "Something else troubles you?"

"I fear to speak it."

"Sister Vogler, please." John touched a finger to her chin, turning it up. "Do not fear anything about me."

Surprised by his consideration, Clarissa held her breath. Could it be possible for John Kliest to be tender? Loving? She found it difficult to entrust her deepest thoughts and feelings to anyone, especially a man, but she forced herself to speak. "It is just that … in my art, I find deep satisfaction. A lightening of burdens. Even a joyful sense that I am doing what God intends."

"I would not begrudge you that. That is how I feel about this mission."

"I am relieved you understand. I have always seen painting as part of my future—not just teaching it but exploring it myself." She paused, trying to make an inquiry with her eyes that felt too bold to put to her tongue. Married women were expected to focus on their families, their joint callings with their husbands.

A faint smile laced John's lips. "Sister Vogler, I don't have a decade on my younger brother without the travel and connections to show for it. I have built homes for the best German merchants in Pennsylvania and surveyed land for some of the wealthiest strangers—some of whom know artists more accomplished than Thomas Sully. If God leads us back to Salem, I can secure my wife an opportunity to further her art."

Confusing emotions tumbled through Clarissa. Realization that God could have replaced a small fortuity in her life with a bigger one. Misgiving over the phrase "if God leads us back to Salem." Anxious excitement at hearing him speak the words "my wife." But in truth, she could not have asked for a better response. A small smile trembled on her lips.

"Satisfied?"

Clarissa nodded.

"Good. Remember, this is to be a partnership. You can bring anything to me at any time."

"And you must do likewise."

"Then shall we take a turn about the square, and I will tell you all about myself?"

All about himself? What vanity! Clarissa's mouth fell open until she spied the slight twitch of one of John's eyebrows. "You jest! But 'tis exactly what I would like. You have been so many places, and I have so many questions about the mission."

"We will have lots of time on the trip. 'Tis likely to take a month."

John helped her to rise but quickly tucked his hand behind his back. Clarissa envied the strangers in their habit of strolling arm in arm. She wouldn't dream of initiating such a thing, even though that limited contact might provide a comforting illusion of familiarity.

She did not have to fret long, for they had no sooner reached Main Street than John called out and waved to a couple entering the community store. "Brother Keller! Good morning."

The lanky, ginger-hackled man waved back with a broad grin, and the neatly dressed sister at his side glanced their way with her brows raised. Clarissa knew all the residents of Salem, yet these visitors, though they wore the understated garb of Moravians, were strangers to her.

"Is this the missionary couple from Pennsylvania?" She tilted her head toward John to inquire in a low voice. "The ones with whom we'll be traveling to Springplace?"

"Indeed. Brother Peter Keller is already a good friend of mine. Come, let me introduce you."

John guided her across the street with a hand hovering near her back. Though he didn't touch her, the gesture ignited hot tingles on her skin. She flushed, then reminded herself that she was engaged now. She would soon be a married woman. Still, she felt as though she stood outside her own body, observing a different person as John introduced her to Peter Keller and his bride, Rosina.

"You have much in common with Sister Keller, Sister Vogler." John stepped so close he bumped Clarissa's arm. She zoomed back into her own body in a flash. "Both of you have been teachers, and you're both skilled in drawing."

"Oh, but I hear you are far more creative." The willowy, dark-haired woman reached out to press Clarissa's hand. "My mind is scientific. I am most interested in capturing the flora and fauna in print and learning their many uses."

"Then this will work out perfectly." John smirked, cutting a glance at Peter. "Sister Vogler can teach the Cherokee children reading and writing, and Sister Keller math and science, while Brother Keller and I go fishing and hunting."

"Wha—" Peter Keller's question ended on a puff of breath, a laugh, and an enthusiastic thump on John's back. "She has agreed to take you, you ornery old man?"

"Shh!" John pretended to shush his friend, while heat invaded Clarissa's face again.

With her basket bumping Clarissa's skirt, Rosina leaned close to whisper, "Congratulations. I am so happy to have another woman along for the journey. Another white woman, that is."

Clarissa knit her brow. She'd opened her mouth to ask Rosina what she meant when Peter spoke up, gesturing to the store in front of them. "We were just going in to see if Bagge's has what we need. Come with us!"

"Yes, you can help me pick out books and fabric and sewing supplies and—well, just about everything." Rosina tugged on Clarissa's arm.

Clarissa's head spun, and she could feel the stares of passing matrons on the street. She hadn't meant for anyone but John to know of her decision until word could pass through the proper channels—Susanna to the elders. Now, if she were seen shopping with John and the Kellers, the whole town would know by evening prayers! She craved quiet time alone to process this stunning chain of events, but if news spread, the sisters would flock to her room tonight like so many novices at Catholic confessional.

"I'm sure they won't have all we need." Brother Keller winked at his bride. "But hopefully they can get in what they lack by our departure next week."

"Next week?" The question squeaked out of Clarissa's constricted throat before she could stop it. "I thought we were leaving next *month*!"

Brother Keller stared at her with a slack jaw. "Why, next week *is* next month, Sister Vogler. Did not Brother Kliest make clear our timeframe?"

"No … I … thought we agreed not to rush her." John glanced at her, then back at Brother Keller.

Rosina squeezed Clarissa's arm as if they were best friends sharing a secret. "You shall be married within a couple of days, Sister Vogler. 'Tis so exciting. Do say we may come to your betrothal love feast. In the Cherokee Nation, we'll have to rely on each other. I daresay we shall be like the closest of families."

Families? The rising humidity of midday denied Clarissa the oxygen she needed. She was leaving her parents, siblings, everyone and everything familiar, to go to Indian Territory with people she barely knew and a husband she would wed in two days. What had she agreed to?

❦ ❦

Clarissa had always found comfort in the traditions of the church, but deprived of the support of her mother and Susanna, a sickly mixture of abandonment and panic swirled in her gut. Sister Holland, the matron of the Married Persons' Choir, had assumed her spiritual oversight and now sat beside her in the meeting hall, back ramrod straight.

Across the aisle, Brother Holland sat with John, who wore the swallowtail black coat of civilian men with the dark waistcoat and pants typical of their sect. Only his white linen shirt and necktie broke the austerity of his costume. He looked straight ahead, so serious she wondered if she had imagined that when they'd met two days before, he'd sought to put her at ease. Even teased her.

There hadn't even been time for the engagement love feast Rosina had suggested, which might have given Clarissa a chance to get to know her groom better.

Had Brother Holland lectured John on his duties as a husband in as much detail as Sister Holland had lectured Clarissa about hers as a wife? Clarissa cringed to imagine it. And there was more to come. Tomorrow, she would endure further intimate discussions with the Hollands in the company of her new husband. One's transition to the Married Persons' Choir occurred with the same invasive oversight as did any major step in life. Only their imminent departure for Springplace would curtail the extensive standard teaching.

At least the love feast scheduled for this evening would delay the wedding night, if only by a few hours.

Clarissa jumped when Sister Holland touched her elbow. John and Brother Holland were standing. The minister had invited them forward for the joining, blessing, and prayers.

As the congregation behind them stirred, Clarissa rose. She permitted herself one quick glance toward her mother, who wedged Clarissa's wiggly youngest sister beneath her arm. Mama nodded. Clarissa could do this. But her heart thudded, and her legs trembled as she approached the altar.

John's gaze swept her in her borrowed wedding dress, a white muslin round gown with golden-brown embroidered trim. Did he think her pretty? If only he would smile at her. Was he having second thoughts?

As they knelt in front of the minister, Clarissa's breath came in short bursts. She couldn't give herself to a man who only wanted a bride so he could go to Indian Territory. But then John's pinky finger inched over on the rail until it brushed hers. And he left it there as they repeated the traditional vows. Clarissa forced herself to slow her breathing, her heartbeat. He was aware of her, and he cared about her needs, her feelings. For this moment, that was enough.

Finally, he reached for her hand to place his mother's silver ring on her finger. His hands were warm as her eyes met his. She attempted to return his gaze with confidence, but the might-have-been tugged her inside out. Why couldn't he be Daniel, eager to whisk her off to explore her dreams in Philadelphia? Instead, she faced a horizon of unknowns, all fearsome.

The Hollands led them out of the meeting hall as the trombone choir played. In the private room off the sanctuary, Sister Holland reminded Clarissa of her next step. "'Tis time to change your ribbon to that of a married woman. This signifies a moment of grave reflection, and as such, Brother Holland will offer prayers asking for the grace needed in your new situation of life."

Clarissa's fingers went to the pink strings at her chin that tied her *haube*. When she opened her eyes after the prayer, Sister Holland held the blue ribbon that would show Clarissa was married. The woman began to sing "Because Your Heart Is with Us, We Do Not Lack for Blessings," and Clarissa worked the ribbon of her girlhood loose.

Sister Holland quirked her head as she accepted Clarissa's emblem of the Single Sisters. "I have seen many a bride grow emotional at this moment. No one would fault you for shedding a tear, my dear."

Clarissa darted a glance at John and offered a brave smile. "I'm fine." Maybe not fine, but numb. She dreaded the moment when her cocoon of numbness would burst.

"Bear in mind, even though our time together has been short, Brother Holland and I are here to support you during this transition. 'Tis best to process the feelings that lie behind these symbolisms and allow the gravity of the moment to settle upon us."

Considering what lay next, Clarissa couldn't help a tremor sweeping over her. John must have noticed, for to her surprise, he stepped closer to her, almost blocking the insistent matron from view. He took her hands, and she forced her gaze to his.

His answer was to Sister Holland, but his warm eyes were

focused on Clarissa. "I believe we are both aware of the gravity of the moment."

Clarissa tried to remind him with her expression of his promise to move slowly. *Please protect my heart.*

Sister Holland sniffed, satisfied. "Then, in keeping with tradition, 'tis time to share in the first kiss."

John placed a hand on Clarissa's waist, drawing her close. He smelled of wool, soap, and a new scent uniquely him. He leaned down toward her and stopped when mere inches separated them, then whispered something the Hollands, who were sharing their own kiss, wouldn't hear.

"I choose you, and only you, forever."

If Clarissa's heart had not melted over the changing of her ribbon, it did now. All the fear, the doubt, the unwanted hope for a tender emotion she could not name, surged into her body and mind, jangling her nerves and leaving her heart pounding. She tilted her chin up. John's parted lips touched hers so softly, so briefly, it could barely be called a kiss.

His words and his gesture did not match. Clarissa's face flooded with shame. She had been right. She was no more than a ticket to his precious mission.

Thinking of giving herself to a man who might use her in such a way, she wanted to burst through the door into the meeting hall and beg her mother to take her home.

CHAPTER FIVE

John gave a quiet sigh of relief when Brother and Sister Holland released him and Clarissa to the care of the Kellers. The couple had been a bit too opinionated for John's taste. His friend would be far less invasive. In fact, Peter seemed to sense Clarissa's tension, for as they entered the tile-roofed cottage on the north side of Main Street, he invited them to join him and Rosina in the small parlor for drinks. The dancing shade of a poplar tree just outside cast relaxing shadows, while a cooling evening breeze played with the muslin curtains.

Rosina hurried in with a pot of aromatic herbal tea. "I don't mean to be ungracious, but I'm glad the family who stayed here with us for the past week left."

"My dear, you love children." Peter smirked as he took his cup from his wife. "Oodles of them."

"I do, but their close proximity is hardly conducive to the peace and privacy sought by newlyweds." As she poured the steaming liquid into cups for herself and Clarissa, Rosina's face turned bright red. Peter's laugh only deepened the color. "Oh, you shush. What I mean is, the Kliests could not have stayed with us had the other room remained occupied."

"Of course," Peter said, though amusement still danced in his eyes.

Clarissa accepted her cup with thanks.

"My special brew, comfrey and peppermint." Rosina winked on the side she probably supposed only Clarissa would see, but John noticed, and heat crept from his own collar. Did she not suppose he knew such herbs calmed nerves, a good prescription for an anxious bride?

Oblivious, Peter crossed one leg over the other. "I am glad you could stay with us now. We might as well get used to each other since it will be close quarters in Springplace."

"We're grateful." John cut a glance at Clarissa, expecting her to protest or at least ask for more details about those *close quarters.* He had mentioned the cabin-sharing before, hadn't he? At least dropped it in with a lot of other information?

She folded her hands, a frown of concern flitting across her forehead. "Please, tell me more about what to expect at the mission. I find I do best when I'm prepared."

Sipping his tea, John tried to appear casual and relaxed. "Brother Keller can best speak to that since he visited more recently."

"You started the place from scratch, right, John?" Peter glanced at Clarissa. "My pardon, Sister Kliest, but your husband and I go way back. Even in mixed company, it makes me want to laugh when he calls me 'Brother Keller.'"

Pausing in stirring honey into her cup, Rosina leaned toward Clarissa, the expression on her pretty face eager. "Oh, *can* we use our Christian names? And let the men use theirs? It would be so much more comfortable."

Clarissa lifted the corners of her lips, though she shifted back in her seat. "Of course."

As Peter's wife smiled in satisfaction, John answered his friend. "There was nothing there but about ten acres of cornfields and some run-down shacks when we arrived. After marking the bounds of the old Brown plantation on which the mission is located, I helped Brother Steiner fell trees for the first cabin."

"Thankfully, there are several now"—Peter glanced at the women—"new, as Brown's were not only falling down but flea-infested."

Clarissa shuddered. John couldn't blame her. She was accustomed to comfort, if not luxury. While Moravians believed in simple living, the sturdy and handsome German construction of their brick buildings towered fortresslike above the surrounding countryside.

She must not think that Springplace would feel completely foreign. John prompted his friend for reassurance. "In addition to the new cabins, they have a kitchen, a separate bake oven, a barn, and a cabin for the children who board at the mission rather than with Vann, right, Peter?"

"Yes. With a limestone spring only feet away."

"I've had my husband tell me all he knows of the plants that grow there." Smiling at Clarissa, Rosina rubbed her hands together. "I cannot wait to explore along the banks of the Conasauga River." 'Tis under three miles from Springplace. I plan to document all the flora and fauna. And of course, we shall take our pupils for botanical study. In Bethlehem, we enjoyed the most exciting rambles on the mountains and even moonlit transits across the ferry. 'Tis nothing like an excursion to aid a student's education."

Peter smiled indulgently. "You can tell my bride was born with a sense of adventure."

Lucky Peter. John hoped some of Rosina's enthusiasm would rub off on Clarissa.

Rosina grabbed Clarissa's hand. "We shall explore it all together!" When Clarissa gave a polite nod before gently withdrawing, Rosina did not seem fazed. "Peter says the soil is red but very rich. They grow most of the things we do here."

"'Tis fortunate the Steiners have the garden flourishing." John added another drizzle of honey to his tea and stirred. "We lived for the first months on corn bread, eggs, and coffee."

"Oh, no one will go hungry on my watch." Rosina waved a hand, apparently gazing into a rapturous future that conveniently excluded drought, storm, pestilence, and theft by the very Indians to whom they would minister. "I plan to cook all our traditional German dishes, as well as some Cherokee recipes. I want to try that soup they make. What was it called, Peter?"

"*Ga-na-tsi.*"

"Yes. *Ga-na-tsi.* Of beans, corn, and hickory nuts. Does it not sound delicious?" Rosina leaned toward Clarissa again.

Peter gave a chortle. "You will not be cooking. You and Sister Kliest shall be teaching every morning. And in the afternoons, your time will be taken up with instructing the girls in European handcrafts."

Clarissa stared at him, giving a slow blink. "Then who *will* be cooking?"

'Twas a fair question. John looked to his friend.

Peter unbuttoned the top of his waistcoat. "The church is purchasing and signing into my guardianship an African woman to help relieve you sisters of the hard labor."

"Whaa ..." Clarissa's question trailed into nothingness. Her teacup clicked on its saucer, and her face paled.

John's stomach plummeted. Moravians were encouraged to flourish by their own economy, and while the church board occasionally purchased slaves for larger projects, he'd never dreamed they would send one to the Cherokee Nation with their party. He spoke into the silence. "We can manage without a slave."

"Tell the women that after we are there a week. Sister Steiner is getting up in years. Word of the mission spreads monthly, and more chiefs bring their children for instruction."

"You cannot be all right with this." John pressed his back against the cushion of his wingchair and splayed his hands on his knees. "I might expect a Salem man to accept this decision without question, but you, Peter? A Pennsylvanian? A Christian?"

Peter shook his head. "'Tis not my decision, John. The board is firm. The woman will be transferred to our oversight in a few days."

Rosina pursed her mouth over her tea, blew, and sipped. "If it makes you feel better, Brother Kliest, we hear she is being purchased from a bad situation indeed." She lifted a shoulder. "'Tis just the way of things."

John glanced at Clarissa. Her lips parted as though she wanted to speak, but instead, she shifted her focus to John. She seemed to be waiting for him to do something about this unnerving news. Even though they had barely touched on the issue of slavery, he read on her face that they shared the same mind. He cleared his throat and turned to Peter. "I know many think so. Slavery has been with us since biblical times, but that doesn't mean the Bible condones it. Personally, I have always seen a contradiction in Christians, especially missionaries, owning slaves."

"What would you suggest, then?" Peter's lips pinched. Not a question, really, judging by the way he folded his hands and squared his shoulders.

"I would have pressed for a freedwoman who would be paid a wage."

"Well, 'tis too late for that now." Rosina drew herself up. "And I think it will prove a blessing for her to serve at our mission. She may even come to know Christ."

Clarissa responded in a quavering voice. "I doubt that will be the case when she witnesses hypocrisy from those who are supposed to serve as examples to her."

"Clarissa." John spoke her name in warning.

Tears glistened in her eyes as she rose. "If you don't mind, I am tired from the day and wish to ready myself for bed."

Rosina remained sitting, blinking like an indignant owl. "'Tis the room to the right. Sister Holland has prepared it for you."

"Thank you. Good night, Sister Keller. Brother Keller." With that formal address, Clarissa turned for the door.

"I shall bid you good-night also." John offered a hasty bow before following her into the bedroom.

He closed the door behind them. Clarissa stood with her back to him, surveying the chest of drawers, rope bed with folded quilt, and simple chair. Her shoulders lifted with a deep breath.

He touched her back, and she jumped.

John kept his voice at a whisper. "I am glad we agree on the issue of slavery, but we must take care not to alienate my good friend and his wife—our partners on this journey."

Clarissa whirled to face him, pleading. "Can you not go to your 'good friend' in private and set this right?"

"How am I to do that? You heard him." His voice remained low, but emotion laced his words. "The decision was not his."

"Yet how can we possibly tell Indians of freedom in Christ with a bondswoman in tow?"

Taking in Clarissa in her distress—a pulse ticking in her soft throat, her chest rising and falling, her fingers twisting that soft, almost sheer material of her dress—John worked to balance his admiration for her convictions with his frustration over the position she was putting him in. He also battled an insane urge to pull her into his arms and kiss her, and not the silly whisper-soft touch he'd limited himself to at the ribbon-changing.

"There's nothing I can do to change the situation, so I shan't be vexing Peter by hounding him further."

Clarissa balled her fists at her sides and squeezed her eyes shut. A tear slid down one cheek.

"You truly care that much?" He stepped closer, lightly chafed her sleeves with his hands. "Shh, now. One of the secrets of getting along in life is not bashing one's head on brick walls."

Her swimming brown eyes opened. "We are supposed to be knocking down those walls, John, but we cannot do so hand in hand with racial superiority."

Her use of his name weakened his resolve, but he did not want to examine the truth in what she said. In his line of work, he dealt with many different types of people. Slave or savage, rich or poor, he got along by treating them all the same ... and not thinking too much about society's prejudices. "By that same principle, I urge you to not judge Peter and Rosina. They are good people."

"Don't you see? This could doom the mission to failure."

"Yet writing them off before we even leave would surely reap the same result." He waited for her to see reason, and a moment later, her shoulders slumped.

"Very well. I will try to be friends with the Kellers. 'Tis obvious you admire them."

"Thank you."

Chin tucked and lips compressed in resignation, Clarissa moved to splash her face with water from the pottery basin.

"'Tis stuffy in here. I'll crack the window." John did so, then tugged off his coat and hung it on a peg. When he began unbuttoning his waistcoat, Clarissa froze with the towel to her face and stared at him. "What?"

She looked away. "Nothing."

Of course. She'd probably only seen her father and his apprentices, her relatives, in their shirtsleeves while at work in their shop. John slowly finished unbuttoning his vest before sitting on the bed to take off his shoes. Clarissa stood near the window, watching him, even the golden light from the lamp unable to chase the pallor from her face.

He patted the feather mattress next to him. "Come here."

She did not move.

"Please."

When Clarissa perched on the bedspread, John reached for the blue string of her *haube*. His pulse raced. To think, he had the right to claim such a treasure. "May I?"

She nodded, the muscles in her throat shifting as she swallowed.

He pulled and untied the strings, then removed her head covering. Clarissa wore what looked to be a wealth of hair in a tight bun. "Will you take it down?"

Another nod. She tugged out a number of metal hairpins. Golden waves spilled over her shoulders. With them came a sweet, clean fragrance that twisted John's middle into a knot tighter than her former coiffure. He licked his lips, looked away.

"It's beautiful." It was an honor to see but a danger to touch.

"Thank you."

After a deep breath and a silent command to focus only on her face, John turned to her again. "The same color as the trim on your dress." Now, why had he said that? Mentioning such an inane detail was certain to make her uncomfortable.

Sure enough, Clarissa's eyes widened. "You also looked … very nice."

She had found him attractive? And was willing to admit it? John stood in a hurry. "I suggest you remove your gown so that you don't suffocate tonight. I will sleep on the floor." Jerking out of his waistcoat and tossing it onto the chair, he reached for the quilt at the foot of the bed.

"But 'tis expected—"

He raised his chin from refolding the material longways. "A week ago, you had never even spoken to me. You thought you would marry my brother. Under the circumstances, I don't care what the church expects—*I* do not expect anything from you right now except respect and willing partnership."

Amazingly, Clarissa persisted in her breathless protest. "The Hollands will ask for a report in the morning. If not tomorrow, they will want assurance that things have been … *finalized* before we leave for the journey."

"I will take care of it."

Her jaw firmed, lifted. "I may be naïve, and uncertain, but I have been taught my duty—"

John snapped his face toward her. "Speak to me of your duty when you don't look like a doe at the wrong end of my rifle."

Were those tears springing to her eyes again? It made no sense. He'd given her a freedom few women had. She ought to be grateful. By morning, he'd be paying the price for his own generosity.

She blinked rapidly, her lips trembling. His choir helper's remonstrance concerning the use of gentle words with women came back to him. John tried softening his tone. "Please don't fret. There is no need for hurry."

Clarissa nodded. Finally, she whispered, "Thank you."

He sighed. At last, she seemed content. As John arranged his pallet on the floor, she reached for a hairbrush from her bag. With crackling strokes, the bristles purled through those long locks, releasing that maddening, sweet fragrance. He faced the other way, the ache of his shoulder protesting the bearing of his weight against the wood floor, but then he heard something else. Sniffles.

Why was the woman crying? There'd been no doubt of the fear in her eyes five minutes ago. And she had no way of knowing that by not demanding intimacy, John was negotiating time for himself as well as for her. Desire would not rule him ever again. Certainly not when his wife remained a practical stranger who dreamt of his brother.

Despite Clarissa's earlier words about knocking down walls, some walls were good … necessary for the marking of boundaries. Too many disputes arose with free range and the assumption of good will. If they could build a marriage on the respect and partnership he'd asked for without allowing emotion to lead them, they stood a much better chance of success.

CHAPTER SIX

T he covered wagon swayed with the motion of the Yadkin River ferry. Clarissa peeked out at swirling waters and, beyond that, the purple-hazed tops of the Blue Ridge Mountains. The teamster, Jacob Hartman, steadied the anxious horses. On the shore behind them, Peter and Rosina waited with their hostler, wagon, and animals.

The docking ferry lurched, causing the hanging lantern overhead to swing wildly. Clarissa grabbed it and eased herself back onto her trunk-seat amid rope, farming implements, and boxes of books and household supplies. The African woman who had shown up with Peter the day of their departure placed a hand on her abdomen, even though she did not stir from her reclining position on the wagon bed. Clarissa's suspicions about the slave's physical condition grew.

"Are you all right, Pleasant?"

A soft grunt was the only reply.

As the ferryman secured the floating raft, Clarissa said, "Perhaps if you walk a bit, you would feel better. I know I'm going to." She wanted to get ahead of Rosina, who had walked most of yesterday beside John and Clarissa in the front of their party since Peter had ridden behind on horseback. She also wanted to get away from Pleasant, who was the least aptly named individual she'd ever met. But sympathy caused her to stifle this desire.

Pleasant lifted her turbaned head, a tear tracking from one eye.

Clarissa touched her shoulder. "You must be so uncomfortable. When are you due?"

"I doan know what you mean." Pleasant shrugged away from her.

Clarissa stifled a sigh. She couldn't force the woman to confide in her. "I will give you some rest, then."

Once the teamster led the wagon onto solid ground, Clarissa stuck her head out the back and called to John after he bid a good day to a post rider and a frontiersman who had crossed with them. Her heartbeat stuttered when he glanced her way. He looked more frontiersman than Moravian himself in a long osnaburg hunting shirt, which he wore belted over leather breeches. His powder horn and shot pouch hung from a leather strap.

"I wish to walk a while," she told him when he came over.

"Again? We'll start to climb in elevation almost immediately."

Had he noticed that she'd tried to hide a limp by the time they'd stopped at a small inn yestereve? "Then I shall go as far as I can. I shan't slow you down."

Leaning on his rifle, John glanced at the pitiful form balled up inside the wagon. His strong fingers closed around Clarissa's as he helped her down, muttering in her ear. "You can't avoid them the whole trip."

His breath stirred the fine hairs on her neck, the unfamiliar and oddly personal sensation making her take a tiny step back. She cocked her head. "Avoid who?" Still clasping John's hand, Clarissa injected innocence into her tone. "Must I be avoiding someone to wish to walk with my husband?"

John pulled his hand away. "Even I can see you are still not natural with Sister Keller." He turned to watch the ferry as it tugged toward the other side of the river. "It puts a strain between me and Peter."

"I am natural. I told you we made amends about Pleasant. Sister Keller assured me it would not have been her choice to bring a slave." When John did not respond, Clarissa brushed her linen skirt over her petticoats. She studied the tips of her boots. "Perhaps my natural state is just not as ingratiating as Sister Keller's."

"She only wants to be your friend." His tone chiding, John led her away from the wagon and the sharp ears of Jacob Hartman, who kicked back on the wagon seat with a strand of jerky. In a field where the shrill chirping of crickets swirled above the sounds of the river, John uncorked his canteen and offered it to her.

"Thank you." Clarissa took a sip, then handed it back. Could she share her reservations about Rosina with John, or would he reckon it unwarranted criticism? She brushed her fingers over the tops of the yellow wildflowers. "She will be my friend, though I wish she would allow it to develop over time."

"Aye. Over time. That is the way." His blue eyes focused on her face, narrowing into a squint.

Clarissa took the statement as an opportunity to vent the unease that had been building inside her. "When she acts as though I am her bosom companion, it makes me uncomfortable."

"I think 'tis just her personality. Enthusiastic." John stepped in front of her and waved as the post rider spurred his mount toward the Blue Ridge and the Great Wilderness Road, leaving a trail of dust.

"Well, it feels—I don't know … manufactured. Especially when she treats Pleasant as she does. I don't mean to speak ill, but … have you noticed?"

Clarissa studied her husband, unable to read his expressions well enough yet to determine if he'd picked up on the same overly kind yet condescension-tinged manner Rosina assumed with the slave. Her attitude toward Pleasant provided only one clue, true. But it supported Clarissa's suspicion that the other woman's piety ran no deeper than the morning sunburn she'd acquire if she didn't keep her bonnet strings tight.

If there was anything Clarissa couldn't stand, 'twas self-righteousness. With disingenuousness a close second.

John took a long drink and looked out to the Yadkin, tracking the progress of the second part of their group. "The bondswoman does seem to prefer our wagon. 'Twould be my guess that Sister Keller takes her silence as insolence."

Both John's defense of Rosina and his interpretation of the

situation darted a pain to her chest. Clarissa shook her head. "'Tis not insolence, mark my words. The woman has been ill-used. Abused. Probably by her last owner. Who knows if she was forced to leave children behind in Bethania? And even in her middle age, she soon will add another."

"What?" John lowered his canteen, and a drop of water dripped unheeded off his chin.

"Well, I guess I shouldn't be surprised that you failed to notice if Sister Keller did not either. Her rounding middle?"

"She is a raw-boned woman, 'tis all."

Clarissa shook her head. "No, 'tis not all. A babe will be born on this journey."

John gasped. "You must find out when." Eyes wide, he made a shooing gesture toward the back of the wagon.

"I tried talking to her, but she does not wish to share anything. No, I shall walk a ways. Perhaps she will open up later if shown patience and kindness." Clarissa put her hands on her hips, subtly stretching. Moisture she couldn't inconspicuously wipe trickled down under her stays and shift with the same steady progress as the ferry. She wanted to reach the shade ahead before Rosina joined them. "Shall we go?"

Motioning to the teamster, John nodded, replaced his canteen, and followed her back to the road. His next muttered comment showed that he was still focused on the impending birth. "Surely, she cannot be that far along. We must make it to Knoxville, or at least to Abingdon, before she goes into labor."

Clarissa tossed a grin over her shoulder. "I shall be sure to give her those instructions."

His eyebrows lifted. "Would you prefer to attend the birth?"

That notion hadn't occurred to her. Clarissa shrank back. "I am not qualified for such a task." Although, no doubt, Rosina was.

"As I thought." John made a sound of irritation, removing his hat and running a hand through his hair. "Afterwards, our travel will be greatly slowed. I should warn Peter." He glanced back to where his friend attempted to lead snorting horses from ferry to land.

"You should *not* tell him until I can ascertain details."

He gave a grim chuckle. "They did not bank on an infant, I can lay odds on that. The woman will be out of commission for quite some time. And what if she has a girl?"

Clarissa let her mouth fall open. "First of all, what do you mean 'if she has a girl?' If she has a girl, the child will be just as loved and cared for by the Lord, and therefore by us, as if she had a boy."

"Of course. I did not mean—"

"And second, the woman has a name. 'Tis Pleasant."

When John's eyebrows disappeared under the brim of his hat, instant regret filled Clarissa. She never dreamed she'd talk to her husband like that, even if she did not know him. *Especially* when she did not know him. The many challenges of traveling with virtual strangers with whom she did not see eye to eye was already taking a toll on her composure.

Then, the unmistakable sound of Rosina's call added to her frustration.

Clarissa hurried ahead, acting as if she did not hear her. Hot tears pressed behind her eyes. Where did these strong emotions come from? Clarissa had always applied the Scripture that bade one's responses to be given with grace, seasoned with salt. Lately, the salt was taking over. She must get hold of herself.

It took several minutes before she realized the creak of wagons and jingle of bridles did not follow her. She looked back to find Peter still in conversation with the ferryman. Halfway between him and Clarissa, John stood with Rosina, his arms crossed over his long rifle and a mocking grin on his face. How far would he have let her walk ahead by herself? Ach, the exasperating man!

Part of the exasperation lay in the fact that Clarissa's eyes had returned to him again and again yesterday. She couldn't help but notice his confident stride, the way his common shirt hugged his broad shoulders and tapered to trim hips. Did he have to be so attractive? Noticing a man was a new thing indeed, and unsettling. Especially when the man did not seem to notice her.

Rosina's attention turned from John to her, and she fluttered a hand. "Ho! Wait on us, Clarissa!"

It seemed she had little choice unless she wanted to face ruffians and wildlife unaided. Grateful for a few more minutes to compose herself, Clarissa waved back, shifting her weight off the blister forming on her right foot. She was pretty sure the thin place she'd noticed in her stocking last night had turned into a hole.

By and by, the party started moving. When they caught up, John's grin remained in place and focused on her.

She pressed her lips into a contrite smile and ducked her head.

"I'm so happy to be entering the mountains." Rosina spread her arms, a basket dangling from one of them, as she inhaled. "The air is cooler already. I'm sure to find some unique plant specimens along our way. Maybe some ginseng."

"These aren't the mountains proper, just the foothills," John told her.

"We won't cross today?" Clarissa snagged a long grass and shredded it as she walked.

"Not until tomorrow. We shall overnight at one of the small towns yet on this side."

"Will there be an inn?" Clarissa hadn't enjoyed sharing a bed with Rosina, but the crowded sleeping arrangements had removed the expectation that she lodge with her husband. She did not think she could bear another night of him lying on the floor, as he had done the whole week in Salem. While she appreciated John's sensitivity in giving their connection time to grow, Sister Holland had indicated that husbands desired intimacy more than their wives. If John did not want that, he must not find her attractive—or want her at all, as she had suspected, except as a stepping-stone to his spiritual calling. A humbling prospect indeed.

"Perhaps." John shrugged as if it did not matter to him. "One always runs the risk an inn might be full."

Or full of bedbugs. Clarissa scratched a red bite on her arm.

Rosina tilted back her head, releasing a dreamy sigh. "'Twould be exciting to sleep out under the stars. Do we have many more large rivers to cross?"

"The New River, near the forks of the Holston. Then we can pass a day or so in Abingdon. From there 'tis about a week's journey to Knoxville."

Rosina wrinkled her nose. "Nothing to get excited about. Peter told me Knoxville was nothing but a rough-and-tumble town full of criminals and tippling houses."

"That may be true, but the Methodists are having a revival in those parts." John grinned at them. "I hear when the Spirit moves in their meetings, things get pretty interesting. Perhaps we could stop in and see what all the fuss is about."

"I'd rather not." Rosina lifted her chin, turning her gaze on the forest.

Finally, something the woman was not keen on exploring! Clarissa spoke softly. "I would not mind attending a revival."

John cocked his head, studying her. "I dare say you would not."

Rosina shifted her basket to the other arm. "I wonder if that tree has dropped any of its chestnuts. They make a fine substitute for coffee."

"In the wilderness, 'tis good to be prepared." John voiced his agreement in an overly enthusiastic tone.

Clarissa shot him a glance, indignation burning in her chest. But then he kept watching Rosina, like one watched a pot of soup for the first bubbles. Dare she hope he wished Rosina otherwise occupied for a few minutes too?

"Please, go on ahead." Rosina waved them forward. "I will catch up."

As Rosina circled back to the tree in question, Clarissa hastened to clear any misunderstanding with her husband. "John, I wanted to say … I'm sorry I let the situation with Sister Keller and Pleasant affect me so."

"'Tis understandable. You have been thrown into a change of circumstance you never would have expected only a few weeks ago, among people you don't know yet. We all require time to adjust."

At John's unexpected generosity of character, Clarissa tucked her chin. "Yes, but I needn't have spoken to you in such a manner. You made clear that you wished for respect above all else."

He studied her a moment, grave. "I can see that when you believe in something, you do so with all your heart. I admire that." John shifted his cumbersome weapon to rest across his shoulders, his eyes scanning the woods ahead. "But I try to remember that *people* are more important than causes. If you offend a brother, he will not listen to your views."

"But if we must always walk on eggshells, who will speak for the downtrodden?"

"We will, in the proper timing." John smiled, then winked at her. "I believe you do possess some *Zeugentriebe* after all."

The suggestion surprised her, alleviating any potential embarrassment from John's gentle admonition. She'd never considered her strong feelings about social oppression to be *Zeugentriebe*—tied into a call to missions. Perhaps she would prove useful on this journey after all.

And perhaps if she and John went about things in opposite ways yet arrived at the same destination, they were not as different as she had imagined. She'd thought him fierce, standoffish. But today he showed her, if not affection, the ability to be kind. The moment his finger touched hers on the altar flooded back into her mind. Clarissa smiled, allowing warmth to fill her.

When she remained silent, John reached over to bump her arm. "Please, when I am the one in need of grace, remember what I said about needing time to adjust."

She laughed. "I will try."

A sudden urge to reach for his hand swept over her, so powerful it caused her to gasp in a quick breath. She was weighing the meaning of this unwelcome compulsion when Rosina returned, eager to show them the chestnuts in her basket. The gushing botanist interrupted her own recitation of their uses with a glance toward Clarissa's hem. "Why, Clarissa, are you favoring your right foot?"

"My shoes are rather new, is all."

"Oh dear," Rosina said. "I thought everyone knew not to wear new shoes on such a journey."

John's frown underlined Rosina's concerned tone, making Clarissa feel like a foolish schoolgirl. *Not when they are the only pair one owns*, she wanted to retort, but she bit her lip. Kindness.

"You should return to the wagon." Rosina scowled at Clarissa's feet. "Tonight, I can make you a poultice for swelling."

"I don't have any swelling, just a blister on my toe. 'Tis nothing." Fixing her eyes forward, Clarissa firmed her mouth.

If Rosina could flit along beside John with her basket of magical herbs, Clarissa could too. Besides, sympathy or no, she possessed no desire to return to Patience's oppressive silence in the wagon. 'Twas stuffy enough on the road. Even though Rosina praised the cooler air and had yet to break a sweat, Clarissa drew out her handkerchief to wipe her brow. She unbuttoned the top hook of her bodice and fanned a hand in front of her face.

"Here, my dear." Rosina dug in her basket and brought out a dark-green, waxy frond. "A magnolia leaf. Works wonders."

"Thank you." Clarissa tried to keep the grim tone out of her statement, but judging by John's cocked eyebrow, she failed. She needed a lot more practice in responding to Rosina's patronizing with grace. She fanned with the leaf in silence.

By the time they reached a small creek, Clarissa's feet ached. She sighed in relief when Rosina asked to stop—not to rest, of course, but to gather plantains and watercress leaves.

Peter nodded in agreement. "'Tis a good place to water the horses and eat a bite ourselves."

"All right." John tilted his head as he watched Clarissa collapse on a fallen log. "You should soak your feet in the water. Let me help you down to the creek."

"Thank you, I don't need help," she said, but when she started to rise, the top of her boot scraped her blister like the firm swipe of a tanner's fleshing beam. She stopped, catching her lip between her teeth.

John hurried over to cup a hand under her elbow. "You needn't feel guilty for taking a rest. Sister Keller should return with something useful for that blister."

Clarissa sighed. "Undoubtedly."

With a laugh, John escorted her to a flat rock overhanging the bubbling brook. When Clarissa cast an uncertain look back toward the road, John placed his body between her and the men. "They will be busy with the horses. Just ease off your shoes."

Clarissa waited a moment, but John did not leave. Instead, he swirled his canteen in the creek. With little choice, she undid her laces, but when she went to pull the right boot, it did not budge. "Maybe it *is* a little swollen."

John reached down and tugged the leather strings until the tips came within half an inch of the first holes. Then he angled the boot off. Clarissa gasped. Not only was there now a hole in her cotton stocking, but a red ring of blood stained the edges. Before she realized what he was doing, John swooped beneath her petticoat and loosed the hosiery from the garter just above her knee. He rolled it down and off her foot, not pausing until he gently lowered her leg into the water. Only then did he look up at her.

"We'll get you moccasins in Abingdon."

The hot flush of her cheeks seemed to bring him awareness. Clearing his throat, he reached for the other boot, but Clarissa drew her foot under her hem. "I can do it. Thank you."

"Very well, I shall go help with the team. You stay here, and we'll bring you some food."

"You don't have to wait upon—"

John's warning look cut her off. As he climbed back to the road, Clarissa frowned. Wonderful. All it took to make her look helpless was a pair of boots.

Rosina soon arrived, chattering about her finds and bearing a tin plate with bread, salted pork, and apples to share. After thanking her, Clarissa ate quickly. She was surprised at how hungry she was. Watching minnows and water bugs dart about in the shallows, she swirled her feet in the current.

"How are you doing, Clarissa?"

"My foot feels better now, thank you. Perhaps if I wrap my toe—"

"Of course, we can do that, but that isn't what I meant. I meant with you and Brother Kliest. I don't mean to pry, but since we have no choir helper and shall have to rely on each other at Springplace, I feel obligated to inquire about your *Herzenszustand*—your heart's condition."

Really? Now Rosina wanted to be her choir helper, her *chorpflegerin*? For her to bare the secrets of not only her heart but her marriage? "Brother Kliest and I are well."

"Are you certain? I thought I sensed some tension between you. As though maybe something was … off."

When Clarissa rose, Rosina looked up at her.

"I don't mean to pry," she said again, "but my husband is concerned about Brother Kliest."

This couple married only a month longer than they were talking about them, sharing concerned observations. "A new marriage is bound to have adjustments, and … this"—she waved her free arm to encompass the surrounding forest—"is certainly an adjustment." She paused, but Rosina only stared at her with bright, round eyes, innocent and blank. Of course. Rosina and Peter had no adjustments. Only bliss. Glancing up the creek, Clarissa gathered her boots. There. Another rock, a better height for putting her shoes back on, in peace. She heaved a breath. "If you will excuse me …"

"Well, yes." Rosina's tone sounded hurt again.

Clarissa heaved her weight up onto a higher rock to begin her climb.

Rosina yelled. "Clarissa!"

Gunfire accompanied by a puff of smoke exploded overhead, and Clarissa screamed as a long, squirming form flew into the air inches in front of her. A snake with brown diamond markings writhed headless across her bare feet. She shrieked and shuffled backward, stumbling into Rosina's outstretched arms. The horrible sense of the creature's dry skin touching hers sent a shudder from head to toe.

And still, the thing flopped to and fro in the dirt.

John ran down the hillside, double-checking the accuracy of his aim with a satisfied grunt. "Copperhead." He reached for Clarissa. "'Tis dead. Shush."

But she couldn't stop sobbing, her nerves as frayed as the spine of the snake.

John pressed her head into his chest. He smelled of powder, sweat, and leather, but when his arms came around her, she went limp. He held her, one hand stroking a soothing rhythm on her back. "Hush now, you're all right."

How long since she'd been held like this? A memory rose of her father comforting her after a hawk had eaten her kitten. In such moments, feminine self-sufficiency was overrated.

"Goodness. We should get her back to the wagon." Rosina spoke behind her. "I've got her boots. I can make a tea for hysterics."

That did it. Clarissa drew back, bracing herself on John's arms. "I am *not* hysterical!" If he would hold her up long enough for her shaking to stop, she could show him she was capable of composing herself.

But he did not give her that chance. The world tilted as her husband picked her up and carried her up the hill. Clarissa protested, struggling to cover her bare feet with her skirts as staring faces turned their way, but John strode ahead. Pleasant climbed out of the wagon, making room for him to deposit Clarissa in the back.

Rosina slid in after. "Don't worry, I can tend her," she said to John.

Pleasant joined them in the wagon, face wreathed in an odd little smirk. Trapped with the two women, Clarissa swiped angry tears with the back of her sleeve. The last thing she'd wanted was to be rendered helpless and needy. But how could she protest without causing further offense?

Pleasant, however, finally had something to say. "That dance you was doin' down there"—a full grin broke out over her dark features—"jus' like the kind they do at the slave quarters. Maybe even better!"

CHAPTER SEVEN

John backed out of the doorway of a closet-sized room at the
Abingdon, Virginia, inn, where he'd just deposited a moaning
Pleasant on a dirty, striped tick. From the narrow hall, he could see
Rosina tending Pleasant and Peter stowing a load of their most
valuable supplies under a spare bed in the adjoining chamber where
Clarissa waited. Peter came to peer over John's shoulder.

Raising a tin cup to Pleasant's lips, Rosina did not look at them
as she spoke. "Gentlemen, no need to hover. I feel quite up to the
task until you return with a doctor. The specimens I gathered in the
mountains will come in handy."

"Are you sure you can't oversee the delivery yourself?" Edging
past John, Peter frowned at the writhing slave. "The cost of a
doctor comes very dear."

John had been right in predicting his friend's displeasure over
the inconvenient pregnancy, but he guessed Peter's current frown
originated as much from Rosina's insistence in walking ahead
with John the past two days as from the dent to his pocketbook.
John wanted to tell him that he appreciated a break from Rosina's
endless questions about Springplace as much as Peter did. Besides,
his own wife had grown more irritable by the day, as her healing
feet prevented her from walking with them.

Rosina stared at her husband with lips parted. "The cost will
prove even higher should complications rob the elders of their
investment."

No further need for discussion there. John turned and tucked
his knuckles into Peter's midsection. "Let's go."

Clarissa came to the entrance of the next room, twisting her
hands in her skirt. "What shall I do?"

"Stay with the supplies. Under no circumstances let them out of your sight." The fourteen-inch walnut case containing his precious circumferentor—commonly called a surveyor's compass—was among the boxes. Should he bid Clarissa to guard it with her life? No, his instructions had been clear. Instead, he added a more practical tip. "And if you want to guarantee a place to sleep tonight, guard the bed too."

Clarissa's gaze darted to a rope bed at the far end of the open chamber, where a white-bearded old man emitted a high-pitched snore.

John lifted one corner of his mouth. "I don't think he shall give you any trouble, but in case of emergency, call out the back window. We will hear you in the hostelry."

Peter nodded in response to her wide-eyed stare. "One of us will remain in earshot."

"Very well. I saw a mail slot on the east wing of the tavern. I will start a letter back to Salem apprising them of our progress. I can finish it with an update of a happy birth." Clarissa painted her face with a brave smile.

Satisfied, John followed Peter down the stairs that led to the tavern and then out the back door to the stables. Pleasant had been moaning and groaning half their journey. Doubtless, the dramatic woman was still hours away from delivering her child. He had time aplenty to help with their wagons and horses before going in search of a doctor.

❦ ❦

Clarissa's quill scratched looping letters with the same artistry she dedicated to her *Frakturschriften*, the ornamental breaking of letters in German script style. Drawings and special sayings, or *Spruchbänder*, accompanied the swirling text. The technique represented breaking the artist's self-will.

She paused and looked up. If she were to create a *fraktur* drawing now, what would it say? Matthew 16:24? Jesus' own words: *If any man will come after me, let him deny himself, and take up his cross, and follow me.*

It had been all she could do to pinch her lips shut and not complain to John about being jostled those endless miles in the wagon with the groaning Pleasant while Rosina gleaned the facts about their destination Clarissa longed to learn. The unknown ahead mocked her. She had thought herself quite good at self-denial, but she'd begun to realize that the carefully ordered life of Salem had not tested her the way the unstructured wilderness would. Clarissa shivered with the sense that her own *fraktur*, breaking, was only beginning.

"Sister Kliest."

The hiss from next door brought Clarissa to the hallway. "Yes?"

Rosina looked up from wiping Pleasant's brow. The woman panted and twisted on the bed. "I grow concerned. Her labor seems to be progressing faster than I anticipated."

"I am sure the men will be back soon with a physician."

"He may not arrive in time if you are right that she had other children."

"Why don't you ask her?" Eyes wide, Clarissa nodded toward the writhing form.

"She doesn't like talking to me. Why don't you look out the back window and see if you can get anyone's attention?"

"Fine." After checking the main room to make sure no one approached their belongings, Clarissa hurried to the window. The view below revealed only a scrawny rooster strutting across the dirt yard. "I don't see anyone. I thought you felt competent, Rosina."

"To assist, not deliver this child. I am trained in botany, not midwifery. I need help!"

"John told me to stay with the supplies. I'm sure 'twill be but a minute."

"It had better be."

Clarissa bit her lip at Rosina's muttered statement. She couldn't help but wish the men were present to witness the capable sister's befuddlement.

In the main room, the snoozing traveler had flipped to face her, but his eyes remained closed. Deep breaths flowed from gaping red lips in the snowy beard. Poor thing. If Clarissa could hardly bear the rigors of travel, how must this old man struggle on the Great Wilderness Road?

Returning to the small desk at the foot of the bed she dreaded to sleep on, she dipped her quill in the ink pot. *We had anticipated a week's worth of travel from here to Knoxville, but now our pace will be slowed by the arrival of the slave Pleasant's infant.*

"Oh no!"

Rosina's cry made Clarissa pause again. She sounded truly distressed this time. Had she deigned to check the laboring woman's progress?

The harried sister appeared at the door, gasping. "'Tis coming! 'Tis coming! You must go for the doctor."

Clarissa slid the quill in the holder, darting a glance at the sleeper, who snorted and shifted to his back. "But I don't know where to find one."

"The tavern keeper, he must know. Or a midwife. Anything. Anyone. Just hurry."

"I cannot leave the parcels!"

"I will watch them. I will watch both rooms if you will just go."

Clarissa hesitated but a moment. A loud moan from Pleasant launched her into motion. "Stand there, in the hall." As she slipped past, she pointed to the spot on the floor where she expected to find Rosina when she returned.

Her heart beat fast. She hurried down the narrow stairs, drawing curious and interested stares from strange men with her descent into the foyer.

※ ⁊

John led the physician through the front door of the inn and bumped into a familiar figure with blonde curls escaping her day cap. He braced his wife by the forearms.

"What are you doing down here?"

Clarissa indicated the rotund, greasy-haired man at her side. "The innkeeper agreed to accompany me to the physician's office. Is this him?" Her wide brown eyes assessed the elderly professional in black behind him. Said gentleman bowed.

"I told you I would fetch him. Why did you not stay upstairs as instructed?" John's gaze traveled over Clarissa's shoulder to a pair of rough-hewn onlookers tippling beer on a hallway bench. One of them lifted a mug to him.

Clarissa pulled her shoulders back. "Pleasant is delivering the child as we speak. Please, we must hurry." She turned and led the way up the creaking steps.

Rosina's cries for assistance reached them at the head of the stairs. John followed his wife down the hall while the doctor pushed into the small chamber. Clarissa peered inside.

"I have him, but I need you to cut the cord," John heard Rosina say. A moment later, an infant's lusty cry and Rosina's triumphant laughter indicated success. His estimation for the woman's abilities rose another notch. "It happened so fast, practically all I had to do was catch the baby."

"May we see?" Clarissa strained on her tiptoes.

"Yes," Rosina said, "just a moment."

As busy shadows shifted in the birthing chamber, a shaft of evening light in the main chamber fingered the stack of supplies still resting under the bed. He'd worried for nothing.

Only when Rosina appeared in the door with a bundle in her arms did John realize the middle-aged innkeeper waited behind him. The man's crusty face turned childlike with wonder when Rosina folded back the blanket.

"Why, he is light as cream skimmings!"

Clarissa's eyes met John's. Indeed, she had been right about the abuse Pleasant had suffered.

Rosina beamed. "Isn't he handsome? The mother seems to

not care by what name the child is christened, so I have selected Michael."

"I reckon you earned the right to pick," the innkeeper said.

"Aye, good work tonight, Sister Keller." John nodded to Rosina. Her practical skills and quick thinking would prove valuable on the frontier. "Do you need anything else?"

Rosina's soft face glowed in the candlelight. "Thank you, I think the doctor will have everything we need. There is a trundle bed, so I will stay with Pleasant to care for the child."

John couldn't suggest the innkeeper leave his own premises outright, but he could offer a hint. "Well, sir, it would seem we are of no further use. Sister Keller has things well in hand."

With a swish of skirts, Clarissa departed to the other room. The tavern owner lingered in the hall as if hoping for another glimpse of the drama playing out in his inn, but John followed Clarissa. She had sat at the desk, back straight, and was tapping the quill against the blotter with more force than was necessary.

John stood in the door a moment, uncertain of whether to address the tension he sensed in the room. He shifted his weight. "Was it inappropriate of me in some way to congratulate Sister Keller on a job well done?"

"Certainly not." Clarissa did not look at him.

"Then what is the matter?"

She drew a deep breath, then released it slowly. "Nothing is the matter."

John decided to spare himself further discomfort. "You are right. Nothing is the matter. I returned with the doctor as promised. The baby is born thanks to Sister Keller, and the valuables are safe thanks to you." He just then noticed the rest of the room was empty. "Where is the old man who was sleeping in here?"

Clarissa shrugged. "I suppose he went down to get dinner."

With a sinking feeling, John ducked to look under the bed. A wave of icy fear raced into his chest. "My compass. 'Tis gone!"

"What?" Clarissa shot to her feet, the quill she held loose in her hand dripping ink onto the floor.

He shifted the remaining boxes and crates, then spun to survey the periphery. "That old man, he must have taken it while you were downstairs!"

"Sister Keller said she would watch both rooms."

"I asked *you* to watch this room."

"She was the one who insisted I go for a doctor. What was I to do?"

"Truly? You would place the blame elsewhere?" Panic made John's response razor-sharp. "Do you have any idea how valuable that compass is? 'Tis a Chandlee original from Virginia, the most advanced available."

"Well, if you had *told* me what was in the box, I might have kept it with me."

Why was she standing there all self-righteous, defending herself as if *he* had done something wrong when her carelessness had just sacrificed his livelihood? John wanted to shake her for her impudence, but tracking down the culprit took precedence.

When he stepped into the hall, he found the innkeeper waiting, eager to involve himself. "What may be the trouble, young man?"

John couldn't speak fast enough. "The elderly traveler who was to share our room has disappeared, and I believe my surveying equipment is gone with him. We must mount a search."

"You're in luck." The man's bushy eyebrows waggled like those of a thespian on stage. "Just so happens, the sheriff is downstairs having dinner."

He put a hand on the innkeeper's shoulder. "Good, let us consult him."

※ ※

Two hours later, John carried a spluttering candle down the hallway and into the common chamber. He supposed Peter and the teamsters constituted three of the forms now recumbent on the dusty ticks. John placed the candlestick on the tiny table by the bed where Clarissa lay against the wall and sat to shuck off his shoes.

"You did not recover it?" she whispered as he stretched out on his back.

The cold heaviness of despair laid on John's chest like one of the flat slabs in God's Acre. "No. There was no sign of the old coot."

A sniffle. Had she been crying? Good. She'd come to understand the full extent of their loss in the days ahead when the lack of his equipment rendered him incapable of adding coin to their limited purse. "Is there nothing we can do, then?"

With a grudging sigh, John related what he'd learned. "The sheriff has been tracking a man fitting the description I gave for a while now. He takes items of value from lodging establishments along the Wilderness Road and pawns them in Knoxville."

Clarissa's voice grew breathless with exasperation. "Well, what is the plan to catch him?"

"He and a deputy rode out after the thief. Perhaps they will apprehend him or spring a trap in Knoxville."

"Yes! We will pray fervently it will be so."

"I told the sheriff we shall lodge at Chisholm's tavern in the city, but I don't hold much hope." He failed to disguise the weight of sorrow in his voice. "My father gifted me with that circumferentor before he passed."

"John ..." Clarissa reached for his hand, attempting to twine delicate fingers through his.

When he pulled away, she shifted so that her tantalizingly soft form came into contact with his shoulder. No, she would not comfort him, not when she was the cause of his loss.

A man's first night sharing a bed with his wife ought to be memorable. Well, 'twould be memorable, all right. John would have a hard time forgetting how angry and heartsick he felt at this moment.

"I'm sorry," she whispered.

He turned over and blew out the candle.

CHAPTER EIGHT

Clarissa doubted she could feel more miserable. On the inside, at least. The wagon sheltered her body from heat and rain, but her companions grieved her heart. Pleasant couldn't help her condition, but she did not seem happy about the birth of her son. Of course, given the tragic and possibly even brutal circumstances of his conception, could anyone blame her?

'Twas not likely the slave would overcome her bitterness to bond with her son either. Not the way Rosina kept the two apart. As though she considered Pleasant incapable of caring for the child, Rosina tended to both with a martyr-like zeal while little concealing the fact that she shared her husband's impatience for the necessary delays in travel. Worst of all, she insisted on traveling in Clarissa's wagon. She probably preferred to keep hers neat and tidy. So she imprisoned Clarissa in a space so crowded with people and supplies she could hardly move.

Not that John wanted her walking ahead with him, anyway. And not that she could have, since the birth and the theft seemed to have made him forget his promise to buy her moccasins in Abingdon.

Yes, the worst of her heartache came from his silence toward her. He was polite, not punitive or petty, and the faraway look in his eye told her he genuinely suffered from the loss of his equipment. She couldn't imagine how she would feel if someone took away her paints, her charcoals, even though they weren't a keepsake from a parent. Yet when she tried to tell him this, he shrugged her off. Nothing she could say would make it better. With great cost and time, they might replace the equipment, but it would never be the same as the set his father had given him. And he did blame her.

Not with anger, but worse … with a resignation that hinted that he regretted his decision to wed her.

She couldn't remember ever praying so hard for anything—even a chance to go to Philadelphia—as she had for the recovery of that compass over the last ten days.

As they approached Knoxville, John climbed up next to Jacob Hartman on the wagon bench. Her curiosity overcoming her shame, Clarissa peeked out between the two sets of broad shoulders.

"Why are we still stopped?"

"Got a little traffic jam." Brother Hartman nodded ahead. Clarissa gaped at a herd of cattle completely filling the street, lowing, tossing their horns, urged on by the whips of buckskin-clad drovers mounted on prancing horses.

Rosina rose up on her knees behind Clarissa, the baby swaddled in her arms and her nose wrinkled. "What is that terrible smell? Livestock?"

"Well, they are not helping," Brother Hartman said with a chuckle, "but I imagine what you smell are the nearby tanneries."

"Ugh." Rosina sank down as the wagon lurched forward. "'Tis hard enough to breathe back here as it is."

Clarissa gripped the beam supporting the canvas. "Is that where they are taking those cows? To a tannery?"

"No, I reckon those are bound over the mountains to South Carolina." Brother Hartman tilted his head toward the east.

"I've never seen so many people."

Finally, her attempts to engage her husband's attention paid off. John nodded. "White's Fort became a town with the land lottery about fifteen years ago, and it just keeps on expanding. It has grown a lot since I was here last. Lots of folks use Knoxville as a jumping-off point for the trail west."

Clarissa nodded, though John, still facing forward, would not see. "Is that a newspaper office?"

"It is. There is even a college here." He turned to offer her a brief smile.

Feeling encouraged that maybe falling off the edge of Tennessee wouldn't seem so terribly far from civilization after all, Clarissa admired frame houses and churches and what appeared to be well-stocked stores. "We can replenish some supplies before leaving."

She had said the wrong thing, reminded John of what he could not replenish. His bearded face turned impassive, and as Rosina complained that Clarissa was blocking any breeze, she retreated to her seat. Only when the wagon lurched to a halt in front of a tavern that looked slightly better than the last five they had stayed at did Clarissa move to the back of the wagon, eager for escape.

But she stayed put when two riders on horses drew up behind them.

One of them called out. "Are you John Kliest, by chance?"

"Yes! I am he." His tone surprised and maybe hopeful, John jumped down from the bench.

The dandier of the two men, who wore Hessian boots, dismounted, looping his stallion's reins around a hitching post. He strode forward to shake John's hand. "Sporting good luck. I thought it might be you, so I followed you through town. You Moravians are easy to spot. Well, not you so much, but … the others."

"How can I help you, sir?"

"Sheriff Link Williams. I got word from Abingdon that you parted unwillingly with some personal property during your stay there."

Clarissa gasped. She leaned forward against the back of the wagon until it clicked and almost came loose. She righted herself as John answered.

"Did you apprehend the thief?"

"Sheriff Johnson's men tailed him all the way to right outside Knoxville, where they found him with this."

The second man approached John with a walnut case. He started to hand it over but snatched it back, casting a wary glance at the sheriff. "Perhaps 'e ought to tell us what's inside."

Speaking in a clear, firm tone, John did not lower his hands after his initial reach for his equipment. "A surveyor's compass with a silvered dial and an eight-point fleur-de-lis. If you look closely, you can read 'G. Chandlee, J. F. Kliest' engraved on the southern quadrant."

When the lawman surrendered the case, Clarissa's eyes flooded with hot tears. She sat back on her heels, whispering, "Oh, thank you, Jesus. Thank you."

She startled when a hand touched her back. Rosina. But more importantly, when she wiped her eyes, her husband's gaze met hers. He nodded and smiled.

Joyous relief faded to sadness. Rather than return the gesture, Clarissa tucked in her trembling lower lip and turned away. Things might be all right in John's mind now, but Clarissa's bore more reservations about their marriage than ever. The distance they had to travel before they could become a real couple made the vast journey to Cherokee Territory seem like a stroll around the square.

❧ ❧

They rested a couple of days in Knoxville before making the thirty-mile trip to overnight at the Tellico military blockhouse. Watching the teamsters drive the wagons out of the sixteen-foot palisade the next morning left Clarissa with an empty feeling. The good road ended here, on the bluff overlooking the Little Tennessee River at its junction with Nine Mile Creek. The wagons would return to Salem, and the Kellers and Kliests would continue south with pack mules and a couple of horses secured by letters of credit from the officers at the fort. The rest of their belongings would be shipped later. An Indian guide with the appropriate name Goingback now took the point position on the trail.

Waiting on the Kellers to get free of the tangle of people at the fort gate, Clarissa stepped to the side of the path. The heavy morning mist, which hung over the eerie French and Indian War ruins of Fort Loudon on the South Carolina side of the river, promised the onset of autumn. Picturing the painting she would make of the scene if given the opportunity, Clarissa tried to focus on the bright splashes of yellow, red, and orange waving from the early-turning maple trees. But she shivered with a sense of foreboding she could not shake.

"'Tis like a point of no return, is it not?" John paused beside her, leading two of the pack mules tied together. Unlike Clarissa's darker sentiments, his tone carried an undercurrent of excitement.

"You love this, don't you?"

"I have to admit, the end of civilization quickens my heart."

"And stops mine." Not meeting his gaze, she rolled a spiny sweetgum ball under her moccasin. The soft shoes and apology he'd tendered in Knoxville had cracked but not removed the protective shell around her heart.

"I told you, 'tis like a village at Vann's place."

Clarissa twisted her lips. "A very small village."

"We will make it our own."

John reached out to squeeze her fingers, giving Clarissa a brief infusion of his confidence. With a faint smile, she pulled her hand away and hid it in the folds of her skirt.

She wanted to picture the future the way he did, but when their relationship remained so tentative, how could she? Especially when he acted as if nothing had happened. Was that his normal way, freezing someone out in anger, then expecting them to forgive without any discussion or explanation? It wasn't Clarissa's way. And it wouldn't have been Daniel's either.

With this aching chasm between her and John, 'twas harder than normal to shoo away lingering thoughts of his brother.

Clarissa's cheeks burned in the resulting flash of self-recrimination, but John seemed oblivious. He followed Goingback as the Kellers rejoined them. He tugged his two pack mules forward and studied the stream of travelers headed for the ferry and the fort. "Right now, I'm more worried about those going into Tellico than those going out."

"What do you mean?" It had seemed a secure place, complete with parade ground and portholes. Even now, soldiers watched them from the tower on the northeast corner. She would feel much safer staying.

"You know how Captain Buttler told us they were preparing to host a council?"

Clarissa nodded. "He said there will be an agreement for a postal road to run from Tennessee into Georgia."

"Yes, men like Vann support leasing land to the government for its construction. Basically, they will widen the trail we are using now."

"That sounds like a good thing. What's the problem?" She drew closer to her husband, walking ahead of Rosina. The woman fiddled with Michael's blanket and cooed his praises to Peter, who brought up the rear on horseback, with a spare mount in tow. Rosina's insistence on carrying the baby while Pleasant rode one of the pack mules irked Clarissa—and she struggled not to show it.

"The problem is, other Cherokees are considering signing away rights to the Cumberland Plateau, their richest hunting ground."

"But you said the Indians are learning farming instead."

John rubbed a hand over his whiskers and tilted his head. "There are still many who oppose parting with the land."

"Chief Vann?"

"Yes."

"Will he be attending the meeting?"

"He will. In fact, we may meet him on the road."

Clarissa's curiosity stirred at the prospect. She wanted to attempt a little mixed-language conversation with their paid guide now. Clad in Indian leggings and moccasins and a European coat and hat, he walked but a horse-length ahead of them, never looking back. All she had gotten out of him so far was his name in Cherokee, "*u-tsv-dv*." The strange combination of consonants already made her fear the elders held an unjustified confidence in her linguistic abilities.

She tucked a stray curl under her bonnet and lengthened her stride to match John's. "If Vann is as influential as you say, maybe he will be able to retain the Tennessee lands."

"He is very influential, but so is his greatest enemy from the Lower Cherokees, Doublehead. Doublehead has long held out against the white man's incursion. In fact, he was the one at the council I attended in 1801 who protested that the narrow trails were already wide enough for the white people to find the red man's land. He was so set against us starting a mission that, after he finally agreed, he asked me for a bottle of whiskey for helping the proposal go through."

Clarissa's brows shot up. "And now he wants to sell the land? What changed his mind?"

John rubbed his thumb against his forefinger. "Same thing that usually changes men's minds."

"Money?"

"Bribes, if the rumors are true."

"Is that why Vann doesn't like him?" She was beginning to admire their host even before meeting him. "He suspects Doublehead of dealing under the table?"

"That is the current reason, yes. But their enmity goes way back." Switching hands on the lead for his mule, he shot her a sideways look.

"Tell me. I want to understand what I am walking into."

Her misgiving stirred when John hesitated. "I don't want to alarm you. The wars between the Cherokees and the settlers ran fierce only a decade ago."

Prepared to wheedle more information from her husband, Clarissa's steps almost stumbled when Goingback slowed his pace, then turned to face them. When he spoke, his dark eyes glittered. "Doublehead is Babykiller."

"What?"

"All Cherokee know, he kill sister of Vann's wife that he married. And kill her unborn child. And he kill babies in war Vann try to save."

Clarissa's lips parted, and she turned to John. "Is this true?" She did not know why she was asking her husband, a Moravian from North Carolina, when a Cherokee man had just related this information with great earnestness, but she needed his confirmation.

John gave a nod, his lips set in a straight line in his beard. "Goingback speaks of the massacre at Cavett's Station in Tennessee. A settler and his family tried to surrender, but Doublehead and his Muskogee allies killed them the minute they opened the door. Vann was said to have grabbed one boy and put him on his saddle, but Doublehead took his axe ..."

When her husband's voice trailed off, Goingback supplied the ending, complete with emphatic gesture. "Smash in skull."

Clarissa closed her eyes against the images. She shuddered, wondering how much the Cherokees could truly have changed in just over a decade. "I hope we never meet this Doublehead."

"He is not welcome on Vann land," Goingback said firmly.

John seemed determined to redirect the conversation. "But as speaker of the Lower Towns at national council, his words hold great weight."

The feathers tied in Goingback's hair fluttering in the breeze, he scowled at the trail ahead. "Men who eat flesh of enemies greatly feared."

Clarissa's mouth dropped open as a sizzle of alarm raced through her. "What do you mean?"

"'Tis starting to rain." John took hold of her arm, slowing her pace to allow the guide to continue ahead of them. He nodded toward Rosina, who handed Pleasant the baby, then accepted Peter's help up onto a horse. "You may wish to join the women and ride a while. You can use a canvas to stay dry."

She lifted her chin. "'Tis but a drop. What I wish is to talk to Goingback. There are many words I could learn from him. Is that not my duty, my reason for this mission?" Surely, he would not keep her from that small satisfaction, mistaking her for such a coward that she couldn't tolerate a couple of tall Indian tales.

"The Indian was hired to guide us, not instruct us. The rain will slow us enough." John squinted up into the sky, from which drops fell in earnest now. His hand on her forearm tightened. "We need to pick up our pace if we are to ford the Hiwassee before dark."

Clarissa tugged her arm away as the hurt that had built up since the theft of the compass bubbled over. "Then why did you bother to buy me these moccasins in Knoxville?"

"I don't wish to quarrel with you." John's lips thinned, then he lowered his tone. "Please, Clarissa."

"Fine." She whirled and stalked back to Peter, who helped her mount the horse he'd been riding. She'd tried to connect with John despite the continued sting from his paltry apology. Yet he made it clear at every turn that he did not value her enough to desire any meaningful communication.

Though her heart still ached an hour later, Clarissa was glad she hadn't argued further. The early October skies, which had continued to spit on them, finally opened in a massive deluge of rain that caused the banks of the Hiwassee to overrun. The oiled cloth protected her for a while, but the mist soaked her clothing and seemed to settle into her very bones. And those bones ached from the endless jostling of the horse.

Clarissa wondered how Pleasant endured. The slave woman rode slumped over her mount with her baby cradled in a sling on her chest. Funny how Rosina had returned Michael to his mother the first moment toting him proved an inconvenience.

Determined to reach the river before nightfall, the men allowed only the briefest of stops. They ate dried beef, bread, and nuts in the saddle. Clarissa told herself there must be an inn or a farm they could stay at on the other side of the river. She yearned for a change of clothes, a crackling fire, and a hot meal.

Yet when they reached the Hiwassee, no homestead, no ferry, and no store awaited them. Rain resumed a steady tempo, plunking loudly on the waxy green leaves of rhododendron and mountain laurel and the colorful foliage of the serviceberry. The party halted at the banks of the river, and she waited, teeth clenched against her shivering, while the men conferred.

"How shall we get across?" Clarissa called as soon as John approached.

He squinted up at her, water streaming from his hat brim. He had to raise his voice to be heard above the rushing of the water. "Normally, we could all ride across, but Goingback thinks with the water this high it is too dangerous. He will take you women across in a canoe he located just down the bank, and Peter and I will take turns with the horses and mules." He held out a hand to help her down.

Clarissa glanced at the swirling gray waters and then at the loaded mounts. "They will be afraid with all that weight on their backs. Might it be less dangerous tomorrow?"

John frowned. "Trust me, Clarissa."

Only with reluctance did she dismount, giving a comforting pat to the rain-slickened neck of her tired mare.

Rosina's voice rose from the horse behind them. "Pleasant should go with Sister Kliest, and when we know it is safe, I can follow with the baby."

Clarissa and John both turned to stare at her. John's brow arched, and Clarissa's chest expanded with relief that her husband finally saw through the woman. Clarissa lifted her chin. "That will not be necessary, Sister Keller. I will go alone to make sure it is safe for all." God help her.

John signified his support with a squeeze of her hand. "We can fill the rest of the canoe with supplies on the first run."

His approval made her flush from head to toe, despite the chilling rain. Within minutes, the men had the canoe loaded, and John helped her take her seat. He touched her arm as Goingback prepared to shove off.

"I will be riding right beside you."

Clarissa nodded and clung to the sides of the flimsy craft,

gasping as the nose surged forward. Goingback paddled hard against the current.

"First time canoe?" he asked.

"Yes." Many first times on this trip. And many more ahead.

Blinking the water out of her eyes, Clarissa searched for John's form on his dark mount. There he was, coming alongside them. A towline stretched behind his horse to one of the pack mules. He held the reins loosely, allowing the horse to pick its way deeper into the river. Water surged over the side packs, and the animal neighed. Sudden panic clawed Clarissa's chest, and she turned her head, unable to watch her husband's struggle against the elements, and unwilling to examine her reaction to it.

Halfway there. The man behind her was much stronger than he looked, back bent into the force of his paddling, not making a sound. *Jesus, please get us to safety.*

As a party of several riders intersected the swollen waters from the south, John let out a cry. She whipped around to find her husband bending low over the horse, struggling to hold on. Behind him, the mule froze in the swirling river. Clarissa's hand flew to her mouth. Would John be swept downstream?

"The girth! It tore. I can't hold the pack."

"Let it go!"

The answer came from the other side of the river, from a man clad in a European greatcoat now a fourth of the way out.

The saddle pack spun away on the current. To Clarissa's astonishment, the approaching rider steered his mount downriver to intercept it. At the same moment, John recognized him.

"Vann!"

Goingback started chuckling.

Water flew on either side of the chief's mount, then the horse plunged in to swim. Clarissa stared, open-mouthed, as the man reached wide to grab the saddlebag before it disappeared into a deep eddy.

"Is that really James Vann?"

"Yes. Only one Vann."

For such expert riding, Clarissa had expected admiration. What she did not expect was the fear that tinged Goingback's reply. But Vann was the hero of all the stories, wasn't he? Yet part of her was relieved that he'd be continuing on to Tellico and not joining them.

When finally she stood on the bank, dripping wet and trembling, John's arm around her in a squeeze of congratulations, James Vann emerged from the river. Water sluiced down his coat and both sides of the tossing neck of his black stallion. He dropped the leather saddlebag at their feet.

"Good to see you again, John Kliest." He lifted his hat. "And this must be your new wife."

CHAPTER NINE

Four times now, John had lit an ember on his char-cloth with his steel striker and flint, but the jute—unraveled cording, teased and shaped into a bird's nest—refused to catch flame.

He sat back under the rock overhang and stifled a growl. "I fear the kindling is too damp."

"But 'twas in your box and crossed the river in the canoe." Clarissa's big brown eyes pled for comfort.

The women had taken turns changing their outer garments behind a canvas, bent over at the back of the small, cave-like maw in the earth John remembered on the south side of the Hiwassee. They'd been lucky to find it unoccupied by man or beast. Still, Clarissa had been none too pleased to learn no tidy accommodations awaited them in this stretch of wilderness. The ladies had been unable to divest of their wet undergarments, and John guessed that was what was causing his wife's continued shivering.

John blew out a breath and tried to calm himself. Naturally, it would be the one time Clarissa needed a fire that he couldn't start one.

Goingback appeared at the entrance of the overhang, sounds of his arrival camouflaged by the damp, pungent decaying leaves. He dropped a skinned rabbit and squirrel along with the butt of his flintlock on the ground before sliding inside, silently doubling the pressure on John.

Rosina seemed to sense his anxiety as he leaned over to try again. "Sister Kliest, let us cut the meat up while he works. We can add those onions and potatoes from Tellico to the pot for a nice stew."

John muttered between breaths to coax the latest ember into a flame. "Or we may just have onion and potato soup."

Clarissa laid a hand on his arm as she shifted around behind him. She probably did so to balance herself, since the presence of six adults necessitated elbow-to-elbow closeness. But he chose to think she meant it as reassurance, especially when she whispered, "You can do it, John."

A minute later, the spark took. A cheer went up. Afraid to get too hopeful, John warned them. "Best get that stew on fast. I don't know how long the few sticks we found will burn."

"Well, now! I looked far and wide for that bit of dry kindling," Peter protested with mock offense.

They had all done their jobs, the kind of teamwork that warmed John's heart. Now they sat back and listened to the rain while feeding the fire and letting the meat cook. Unfortunately, smoke quickly filled the small cave, causing them to choke and cough.

Rosina waved a hand in front of her face. "I don't know which is worse, the damp or the smoke."

To John's surprise, Clarissa laughed. They all laughed. Except Pleasant, of course.

"We've almost made it." John shifted toward the cave opening for a breath of air, splaying his hands on his knees. He preferred damp trousers to being unable to move. "We will be at Springplace by nightfall tomorrow."

"The Steiners will have our beds and a warm meal ready." A longing glint lit Clarissa's eyes. "I bet they will plan a love feast for the day after, with a *Singstunde*."

Rosina clasped her hands together. "Mm, I can just taste the cinnamon buns."

John smiled, thankful for the camaraderie between the women, but he did not want Clarissa to get her hopes up too much. The rustic cabins were nothing like the fine brick houses to which she was accustomed. And how would she respond to the slaves and Indians who loitered around the mission looking for handouts? Stealing? The unwritten code of conduct differed vastly from the ordered propriety of Salem.

The fire lasted long enough to mostly cook their stew. They devoured every morsel, even though the meat was a little red and the vegetables a little crunchy.

Peter lit a lantern when the fire went out. "Finding the space to lie down in here will be the trick. We shall be like logs in a row."

Somehow, he and Rosina ended up on the inside. Goingback took his place at the rim where he could keep an eye on the animals picketed under the pines outside, leaving Pleasant to break the space between the two couples. The damp, cool breath of evening licked John's back as he faced his wife.

She shivered despite her blanket, and he longed to provide her with a soft mattress, dry clothing, and a roaring fire.

"Only one night," he murmured.

When she nodded and turned her face into his chest, John drew back in surprise.

Clarissa took his flinch as displeasure. "You are still angry with me." Her voice was barely a whisper.

It took him a moment to realize what she'd said. "Why would I be angry?"

"I tried to be brave on the river today, to please you."

Her admission pierced John with compassion. She wanted to please him? "You were very brave." He chuckled. "And you did not give me the tongue-lashing I expected about this cave."

"Well, I will if we pass a house tomorrow a quarter mile down the road." He could hear the smile in her voice.

"I assure you, there is nothing for miles."

"Then I accept the cave. And I thank you for the fire."

"I wish I could have made it last longer." When she pressed against him, his mind hurried to other ways he could feed a fire. Hardly an acceptable thought when Goingback's musket nudged the back of his leg.

"If you are not angry, would you mind putting your arm over me?" Clarissa convulsed in a deep shiver.

She did not have to ask twice. He might not have wanted a wife, but now that he had one, he wanted to show her he could protect her. And the tension over the compass had showed *him* 'twas better to remain on good terms with the wife he had.

John pulled her against him, relishing her softness. The simple embrace did wonders to dissolve the tension between them that had somehow lingered, even though John thought they had made amends in Knoxville. Perhaps this was a good time—as they entered the Cherokee Nation—to ensure harmony. "I told you I was sorry for becoming upset over the compass."

"Yes, you told me. In as few words as a man could muster."

Had there been accusation in her tone, John would have taken offense. But he heard only sadness. She needed more—more words, as his choir helper had warned him women did. "I know it was not all your fault. We should have kept a brother in earshot as we promised, and Sister Keller ..." He dropped his voice another notch, leaning so close the fine hairs above her ear caught in his beard and tickled his nose. "After insisting you run for a doctor, she should have caught that baby with one hand while reaching 'round the corner to keep the other on my compass."

Clarissa gave a snort of a laugh that made Pleasant turn over. Away from them, thankfully. And thankfully also, Clarissa did not heap further recriminations on Rosina. But she did ask, "You know what made me leave our things and go for the doctor?"

Panic? John wanted to suggest that but instead said, "What?"

"I thought of what you said about people coming first. Pleasant and her child were more important than the equipment."

Conviction stung John's conscience, followed by a rush of pleasure that Clarissa had taken his words to heart. "You were absolutely right. They were."

Clarissa sniffled, wiping a hand across her face. "I wanted to do the right thing, so when you did not think I had, I was heartsore for days."

That meant she cared. John fought the urge to defend himself.

"Clarissa, this is the moment." Admitting the truth hurt.

"What moment?"

"The one when I need grace."

Clarissa breathed a little laugh. "Yes, it is." After another moment, she spoke again. "I forgive you."

"Thank you." He placed a thumb on her temple, hoping the touch would comfort her.

"When you weren't talking to me, I felt so alone on this journey."

The darkness made honesty so much easier. No wonder the choir helpers lectured newlyweds on the privilege of sleeping beside their spouses. "I would never leave you."

"There are more ways of leaving than in body."

Her words convicted him again. "You are right."

John had been left in body before, something Clarissa could not do. But she could leave in spirit, couldn't she? If they started too fast, without a firm foundation, and she discovered she would have preferred his brother, after all? Why would he set himself up to repeat that sort of betrayal?

"Is that why I cannot get close to you?" She shifted, tilting her face up to him.

"You are pretty close right now." He squeezed her waist. This cave gave him an excuse to touch her in ways he'd been telling himself contained an emotional risk. And he was liking it. And wishing they were alone.

Clarissa placed one of her small hands on his chest. "There is a wall around you, John Kliest. I don't know who put it there or what you are afraid of, but I am not leaving, in body or mind."

He knew what she needed then because he needed it too. He tucked his head to hers and, for the length of a heartbeat, sealed her mouth with his. Her soft lips firmed under his, and he instantly wanted more.

Clarissa gasped.

John held his breath, preparing himself for her to pull back. "Still afraid of me?"

"Yes." She wove her hand into the wet hair at the back of his neck, sending both warmth and shivers down his body, and she whispered against his mouth. "But I have seen sides of you that I did not expect—good and noble sides—and that gives me hope."

❧   ❧

Golden-orange rays of setting sun bathed the valley that nestled Springplace and James Vann's Diamond Hill plantation the next evening. Along the roadside, winged sumac blazed crimson in its rays, and sweet shrub, yellow. An arrow of squawking geese flew overhead as John stopped to put an arm around Clarissa. He wanted to witness her reaction.

She breathed an exclamation of delight as she surveyed the chief's stately brick home fronted by double white columns and surrounded by fields of cotton and corn. "'Tis beautiful," she murmured, then shot a glance at Goingback. "Beautiful. *U-wo-du-hi?*"

The man grunted. Perhaps John had been right when he'd encouraged her to ride rather than allowing her to walk alongside their guide as he had today. Clarissa's endless questions must have drained the stoic Indian.

John pointed to where a copse of trees obscured the cluster of buildings he'd helped to construct several years prior. "The mission lies just there, near the spring."

"I can smell the smoke from the evening cooking fires." Clarissa sighed in anticipation.

Goingback grunted again, his nose tilted skyward. "Not cooking. Funeral pyre."

John glanced at him, a spiral of unease filling his middle. Whatever Goingback thought, John couldn't allow him to frighten away Clarissa's sense of welcome. And he didn't really want to know either. Not at this moment. "No, she is right. I can see the smoke from the cabins." With a tug to the pack mule's lead, he also urged his wife forward with a gentle nudge to her elbow. "You will find the chimneys are different here—wooden, unattached from the cabins, and lined with clay—but surprisingly efficient."

"Are those orchards I see ahead?" Rosina had dismounted her horse and appeared beside them, holding Michael.

John wondered that Pleasant didn't protest her baby's frequent abduction, but then, maybe she'd rather not be reminded of the unwelcome addition to her life. Clarissa steadied herself on his arm as they descended the hill, and the sharp tip of guilt speared him. God keep him from not recognizing his own blessings.

The clearing of Rosina's throat prompted him to answer her. "Yes. Orchards. A paradise, is it not?"

The wild beauty of the land he remembered filled John with a sense of rightness. Finally, he was where he belonged. And thankfully, the glowing faces of the women indicated they shared his joy, though whether it was at being there or from relief at the end of their journey, he couldn't tell.

Rosina jostled the child when he whimpered, allowing him to suck her finger. Between her dark hair and the boy's light skin, no one would guess she was not his mother. "Peter told me they grow peaches, apples, pears, plums, and quince. But mostly peaches."

"'Tis true." John's enthusiasm spilled over into his voice. "They have a blood peach called the black plum peach of Georgia that is the best I have ever tasted."

"Too bad we missed the harvest." Clarissa studied a row of slave cabins ahead, brow knit. He had told her that Vann owned slaves. Maybe she just hadn't expected so many.

"Oh, but we will be here next year." Rosina smiled.

"You can try some kiln-dried. And, of course, there's always peach brandy." John winked at the women, then turned his attention to a group of children who ran out from the log homes. Crying out greetings, they clustered around Rosina.

"How sweet." Clarissa's face softened. "They want to see the baby, Sister Keller."

Rosina, who at first had snatched the child high as if protecting him from wild dogs, bent and lowered her bundle. She turned back the blanket. "His name is Michael."

When a half dozen small fingers poked the child's face and hands, Rosina snapped back to scarecrow status.

One little boy pointed at John and said something that—due to a thick, foreign-sounding dialect—he couldn't understand. Reading his blank expression correctly, Clarissa translated. "He says we must be the new missionaries." She bent down to the child. "Yes, we are. Will you come see us tomorrow? I might have some sugared corn in my bags."

Forgetting the infant and freeing Sister Keller to escape, the children began a frenzied dance around Clarissa. She laughed, holding up her empty hands. "I have nothing with me now. Come tomorrow."

John stared at his new wife in amazement. With these raggedy slave children, she was as natural as he'd ever seen her. If she proved as comfortable with the Indian children, little doubt would remain as to her calling.

She turned to him. "Can the slave children come to our school too?"

He shook his head. "The agreement was to teach the children of Upper Town chiefs. You will have enough on your hands learning their language."

Clarissa sighed as parents sitting in the open doors of the cabins called their offspring home, allowing the missionary caravan to proceed. "Maybe someday."

She stared over her shoulder with obvious regret until John took her hand. He did not care that Moravian couples were not supposed to show affection in public. This was an important moment, and she needed to feel his support.

They passed stables, a blacksmith shop, and a corn crib. His feet ached, and his clothes hung stiff and scratchy after yesterday's soaking, then the smoking they had gotten in the cave. But his heart felt as light as the sun-kissed clouds skimming the sky. After

Clarissa's heart-warming admission that she could see a future with him the night before, he'd kissed her again—slow and sweet. Then he'd asked her to face the other direction and held her loosely, not giving way to passion, because it was neither the time nor place. But it had been a promise of the fulfillment of the foundation they were building. Now, he couldn't wait to hold her in his arms again … in their own bed.

"Will we call at the house?" Clarissa stared at the white-trimmed brick mansion crowning the rise as they passed it.

"Tomorrow. 'Tis almost dark, and the mistress will be settling in for the night." John felt certain the poised Peggy Vann would make a good impression on Clarissa. "Though I look forward to seeing your reaction to the inside of the house."

"I look forward to it as well." Clarissa's gaze riveted to the Cherokee men loitering on the porch of Vann's store. Dressed in a colorful combination of traditional and European garb, they smoked pipes while a group of boys played marbles in the dirt. She spoke over the lowing of animals from the pens behind the tavern as the party turned east toward the mission. "Though I admit I am content to wait until tomorrow to explore. This is indeed a big plantation, if not a small town. Tonight, I want only a hot meal and soft bed … and maybe a bath." She cast John a shy glance.

Might he interpret that in a hopeful manner?

The cluster of clapboard-roofed cabins surrounded by gardens, orchards, and woods offered a welcome sight indeed. Light poured from an open door as William and Louise Steiner hurried to greet them, dogs barking and chickens scattering. William's wirehaired northern hunting beagle, Snoot, nosed about their shoes and skirts. John bent to pet the dappled head.

The Steiners looked the same as John remembered, if a bit thinner for running the mission on their own for several years. Sister Steiner still wore her *haube*, dark dress, and apron. She hugged the women while Brother Steiner embraced the men.

"Praise God," Sister Steiner said. "We are so thankful you are here!"

"And we are so glad to be here." Face crumpling in an expression of grateful relief, Rosina touched the older woman's arm.

"I can imagine, my dear." Sister Steiner clapped her hands together. "And how fortunate the timing of your arrival. One of the Indians brought us a turkey this afternoon, and I made apple tarts! We will call the children who board with us to help unload your things, then we shall have dinner and evening prayers. But first, would you like to see your cabin?"

The light of anticipation that had built on Clarissa's face extinguished with the last, singular word. "Cabin?" She repeated it so softly Sister Steiner strained forward to hear.

John's stomach sank.

"Yes, dear, 'tis right over here. Your own husband helped build it, and a fine job he did too." Sister Steiner gestured ahead of them, leading the way across the swept-dirt clearing. "After the men left, we used it to house the loom and spinning wheel, but we have moved those to our home now."

John trailed Clarissa toward the eighteen-by-twenty log building. He did not need to peer inside, as the women did, when Sister Steiner opened the door. He knew what it looked like, with its table and fireplace central and a storage loft overhead.

"We shall light the lamps and get a fire going in no time. We have added two beds, and you see, you shall be quite snug when you draw the muslin partition I sewed." Sister Steiner lowered her voice to address the ladies, although John could still hear her raspy whisper. "Brother Steiner and I will host each of you couples one evening a week for dinner and a visit, to give the other the needed privacy."

John avoided looking at Peter, but he couldn't ignore the congealed expression on Clarissa's face. She attempted to match Rosina's enthusiastic appreciation with her own nod and smile, but obviously John should have been clearer about the cabin sharing. He might pay the price for that.

CHAPTER TEN

As Brother Steiner concluded the baptism of Pleasant's son, Michael, with a lengthy prayer, Clarissa stifled a yawn. What frightful irreverence! She opened her eyes to find her husband glowering at her. Well, 'twasn't as if she could help it.

Last night the feather mattress had welcomed her aching body in a soft embrace, but her limbs had remained taut as John had undressed in the semi-dark. When he'd lowered himself next to her, every nerve ending in her body went on alert. After lying with him in the cave, she'd longed for his nearness. The brush of his hand on her cheek and the masculine scent of him made her breath short. But all that battled with her ire.

How had he not made it clear that they were to share a cabin with the Kellers? Yes, Clarissa was accustomed to common sleeping rooms, but as a single woman! 'Twas something entirely different and terribly awkward to have one's brand-new spouse beside you and another newly married couple just on the other side of a thin partition.

So when John had tangled his fingers in her hair, Clarissa had whispered Sister Steiner's reminder. One night a week of privacy.

When his fingers fell away, Clarissa had murmured a hasty explanation. "Do you not see how uncomfortable this is, with the Kellers just there, when we have not yet—"

"I would not have pressed you." The short reply had been followed by John turning away. Not much later, he quietly rose and left the cabin despite Clarissa's whispered protests.

For hours, she'd waited for his return, her heart aching to set things straight, but eventually she must have drifted into a fitful slumber. At dawn, she'd awoken as John dressed, a pallet on the floor attesting to his place of rest.

Now, his eyes seemed to challenge her: *You think* you're *sleepy?*

But this was not the time to address their marital challenges. A whole day lay ahead, a Sabbath day. She needed to focus on God's work and the people who would be part of her future.

Now, at least two dozen slaves pressed against the walls of the Steiners' cabin and stood in the clearing outside, attentive and respectful during the service. The pupils sat on the floor. Sister Steiner had introduced them at the morning litany. Three boarded here at the mission, taking lessons and sleeping in their own tiny cabin right next to the Steiners': Tom A-ca-ru-ca, son of Chief Chuleoa; Sam Hicks, nephew of Big Half Breed; and Charles Hughes, known as Charlie, son of Whitetree and Elizabeth Hughes, who was a relative of Vann. Assessing the restless energy of the boys, Clarissa struggled to imagine how the Steiners had kept up with their physical, emotional, educational, and spiritual care unaided to this point.

She guessed Tom to be around eight, and Sam and Charlie to be ten or eleven years old. Sam's dark eyes lit with respect and eagerness whenever they fixed on the adults. Sister Steiner had confided that he was their most promising scholar, and Tom, the most miraculous. His father, Chief Chuleoa, had been one of the most vocal opponents of the mission school before the day he'd shocked them by showing up to enroll his son. Charlie, however, perplexed Clarissa more. Darker in complexion, he held his wiry frame stiffly, as though perpetually on the defensive.

James Vann's children, Sally and Joseph, known as Joe, respectively eight and seven years old, rounded out the roster but resided in the big house.

Standing behind Sally and Joe with the faithful slave she'd introduced as Caty, Peggy Vann clasped her hands in front of her fashionable drop-front dress. The light-skinned, dignified young woman had not been what Clarissa had expected. Curiosity piqued, she hurried to Peggy's side when Sister Steiner announced 'twas time to fetch the food from the kitchen for the love feast.

"Would you and your lovely children like to help us carry the coffee and buns?" Clarissa smiled at Sally and Joe. They smiled back. She hoped the mistress of the plantation would see her request for what it was, an invitation to get acquainted rather than impertinence.

Peggy's expression reflected brief surprise—but Clarissa quickly learned 'twas not for the reason she feared. The woman spoke in a low voice, her words halting. "Sally and Joseph are not mine. Sally is of Jennie Foster, and Joseph of Nannie Brown."

Clarissa blinked rapidly. "I … see." Who were these people?

"But I would be happy to help. I wish you welcome at Diamond Hill."

"Oh, 'tis a lovely plantation. I know you are proud." As the men and children scrambled to arrange tables and benches in the cabin, Clarissa followed Sister Steiner out the door into a bright autumn midday, Peggy at her side.

"Proud, yes."

Most of the discussions about Springplace had included only James. Clarissa should have asked more about his marital history, his children. She'd been so overwhelmed with her own new marriage. Coming in, she'd known only that Joe was the favored son of James. These other women must have been wives of Vann who had died, and Peggy must be his new bride, although Clarissa guessed the woman to be fifteen years younger than her husband. 'Twas not unusual. Why, just over a decade lay between herself and John.

Clarissa decided to test out her theory. "Are you … newer here, then, as well?"

"Not new, no. I married at fourteen."

"Fourteen?" Clarissa gasped.

Waiting for them by the open door of the log kitchen, Sister Steiner placed a hand on her shoulder. "Peggy is principal wife, the only one who remains at Diamond Hill." Louise's face warned

Clarissa to leave the subject for another time.

"Of course. Pardon my many questions," Clarissa said to the mistress. "'Tis just that I am eager to get to know you."

Peggy smiled, revealing perfectly even, white teeth. "As am I. After this, you come to see my house."

"Oh, I would love to."

Perhaps she might make an unexpected friend in Peggy. Whatever her circumstances, Clarissa felt drawn to her. But her mind spun as she poured steaming black coffee into earthenware mugs and Peggy set them on a tray. Of course. She should have realized the Cherokees' practice of plural marriage would extend even to a progressive chief like Vann.

"You come to house. Pray." Peggy fixed her dark eyes on Clarissa, then Sister Steiner. "This we need after what happened."

Clarissa looked between the two women. "What happened?"

Sister Steiner pressed her lips together before answering. "I hate to sully this Lord's Day with the tragic tale, but if you are to visit the big house later, Sister Kliest, I suppose you must know."

"Please tell me." Clarissa's heart felt as though it turned to wax, especially when Peggy placed one of her delicate hands on Clarissa's sleeve.

"We were robbed. Almost killed."

"Here? Who would do such a thing?"

Sister Steiner answered. "Several of the Negroes. White men assisted them, one a former overseer. Chief Vann still has men investigating and searching for other potential accomplices. Some have been taken into custody, while others ..." Her voice trailed away as she placed some of the sweet buns they had baked early that morning in a basket.

The fragrance of cinnamon and mace and the scent of strong coffee, so welcome moments before, curdled the contents of Clarissa's stomach. Criminals with a vendetta against their hosts remained at large? "What did they take?"

Removing the lids of the coffee pots, Sister Steiner paused.

"Thirty-five hundred dollars."

Clarissa blinked in surprise. A small fortune!

"From under the bed where I slept. And guns and other things. I was not supposed to wake up." Peggy's hand fluttered to touch Clarissa's arm again.

"Mrs. Vann was understandably shaken," Sister Steiner said. "But for now, we should focus on the love feast. 'Tis the Sabbath, and we will give thanks to the Lord for sending us the Kellers and the Kliests."

"Yes, your presence makes things better."

Peggy's hopeful statement failed to shake Clarissa's sense of unease. She assisted Sister Steiner in filling the coffee pots without comment.

Rosina appeared at the door, two of the boarders at her side and her face bright. Envy of her well-rested state made Clarissa quirk her mouth to one side as the other woman offered her assistance. "Can we help carry things? Everyone is ready."

After they served those gathered in the Steiner cabin, slaves included, Clarissa slid onto a bench beside John. Her conversation with Peggy had reminded her how little she knew of this new place and how much she wanted someone strong by her side. She offered him a tentative smile, and relief flooded her when he returned the gesture.

He leaned close to whisper. "I am proud of you for approaching Mrs. Vann. I thought you would like her."

"She is lovely. She has invited us to the house after the feast. Will you come?"

John dipped his head. "Did she tell you of the robbery?"

"Briefly."

"I just heard as well. Brother Steiner did not want to overload us last night as we arrived."

"So, you will come?"

He squeezed her hand under the table. "Of course."

Clarissa's heart swelled.

Brother Steiner took his place by the hearth. Raising his voice, he spoke in English rather than the German the missionaries preferred when no outsiders were present. "We welcome you today to our Sabbath love feast. It is our custom to break bread together in the tradition of Acts Two, and today we express special gratefulness for the Lord's protection and provision for the Kliests and the Kellers on their journey from Salem. In a moment, the brothers will share some of the adventures they faced." He paused to grin at John, who nodded his agreement. "But for now, let us give thanks for this bounty before us."

Clarissa closed her eyes at the prompt to pray in unison. The missionaries and students joined together. "Come, Lord Jesus, Our Guest to be, And bless these gifts, Bestowed by Thee. Amen."

The prayer comforted her, as did the familiar roll and coffee, but none so much as her husband's shoulder pressing against hers. Did he have no idea that his mere touch opened a pit in the bottom of her stomach? Gazing around at the unfamiliar faces speaking unfamiliar dialects, Clarissa relished John's nearness more than she feared it.

After the love feast, Sister Steiner and Pleasant cleaned up in the kitchen while Peggy, Caty, Sally, and Joseph escorted the new arrivals to the big house. The children ran ahead as the adults took a path past the mission spring. Fresh water bubbled up between rocks, tempting Clarissa back on a later day for a solitary toe-dipping, while Rosina admired the crimson Virginia sweet spire and yellow spicebush that made the setting so welcoming.

John pointed to a tall, golden-leaved poplar ahead. "That tree marks the corner between Vann property and the old Brown plantation."

"A witness tree?" Clarissa raised her brow as she glanced at him.

His slight frown betrayed some discomfort. "Yes. You will find it inscribed with the date of my survey."

She nodded and looked away. Her pulse matched the tempo of the woodpecker hard at work somewhere overhead. His expression, the way he looked at her … 'twas almost as if he knew about the notes she had exchanged with his brother in the Salem witness tree. Daniel would not have told him. Would he? And she'd been so sure Daniel would not have left town without telling her, yet there'd been no message.

As they cut through the orchards, she attempted to pay attention as Peter named the varieties of peaches and apples he'd helped plant on his last visit. John pulled one off a nearby tree and tossed it to Clarissa.

She turned it over in her hands. "Why, this is the largest apple I have ever seen."

Peggy smiled at her surprise. "*Cullawhee.*"

"*Cullawhee.*" Clarissa bit into the fruit, and the explosion of flavor made her eyes pop open wide. "It tastes like autumn."

She munched with appreciation as they climbed the hill to the main complex. The house loomed to their right, facing a circular drive. Clarissa tossed her apple core toward a burned patch in the middle of a small field behind the double stables and corn crib.

When she started to fall behind, John took her arm. "The house is a work of art, don't you think? Chief Vann hired a brick mason from Virginia and a carpenter from Tennessee. But bricks, nails, hinges, boards—all were made right here on the plantation."

Clarissa drew a breath to express her admiration, but Rosina spoke first. "It's astonishing, really, like civilization looming up out of the wilderness."

Peggy nodded. "Many stop here. Cherokees camp on the land all the time." She pointed to a hewn-log structure connected to the rear porch by a brick walkway. "Cookhouse lies behind. And root cellar must be entered from outside. You come, you ask … all we have is yours."

Clarissa marveled at her generosity. But then, when one's husband was the richest man in the Cherokee Nation, one could afford to share. "Your husband owns such a huge plantation."

"Cherokees use land, but not own." Peggy swept her hand to

indicate the fields and gardens surrounding the house. Then her eyes brightened. "But we own horses. Many horses. You like to ride?"

Clarissa spluttered at the humorous picture of a Moravian woman galloping across this wild country on a spirited steed. "I have not had much occasion, I suppose." Something told her that her limited time riding in their slow supply caravan from Tellico could not qualify.

John laughed. "But perhaps she could learn." Leaning closer, he murmured in her ear, "Then you could accompany me if I go out surveying."

Warmth stole over her cheeks as Rosina giggled and Peggy nodded and smiled, opening the door. A rush of cool air swept through the house from the already-open door on the other side of the hall. Clarissa wandered into the foyer, her neck craning and her mouth dropping open. Her eyes followed a floating staircase that rose three stories, its only support the wall.

"'Tis amazing, is it not?" Drawing up beside her, John patted the rail. "I wish I could say I had designed this."

"I have never seen anything like it."

Peggy showed them the fine furnishings and the twelve-foot ceilings in the dining room and parlor with obvious pride before they mounted the staircase. Her mood seemed to change as her hand slid along the banister, her voice lowering. "The white men wanted my husband dead. They gave Solomon, one of the slaves, a rifle to kill him. If he had been home ..." She shuddered.

"Why would they want to kill Chief Vann?" Clarissa asked.

"My husband has many enemy. He is hard man."

Recalling her impressions at the Hiwassee, Clarissa attempted to fit the puzzle pieces of James Vann together. "We are thankful neither of you were harmed."

Peggy opened the door to a bedroom, and a young, white woman stood up from a chair where she'd been knitting. "This is Miss Crawford, daughter of our former overseer."

Everyone bowed. When no further explanation or introduction was offered, Clarissa's gaze rose to John's, inquiring. He gave a slight shake of his head. Why was the daughter of a *former* overseer staying here, and why did he not want her to ask?

The attractive blonde girl resumed the motion of her darning needles while Peggy went over to the bed and lifted the quilt. "Under here was the chest with money."

"I heard it was found in the woods, with one dollar left inside." Peter propped his hand on his hip.

Peggy nodded. "That is true. A cruel joke on us. My husband was so angry." Her eyes glittered with something that looked not like anger, but fear. Fear of the criminals who had threatened her safety?

Rosina swept forward and laid a hand on her arm. "It could have been so much worse."

"Yes. I sleep deeply, but that night, I woke. And this is what I see." Peggy reached for a large stick propped against the wall. Rosina stepped back as she swung it upward and bent toward the bed. "A dark face leaned over me. Hot breath on my skin. The man said, 'If you make a sound, I beat you with this.'" Peggy's face twisted in a snarl that Clarissa supposed mimicked the intruder's.

"And yet he did not." John stepped forward, closer to Clarissa. Did she look as uneasy as Rosina? Her husband's gentle gaze seemed to relax even Peggy. "That is not a coincidence, Mrs. Vann."

"I make not a sound."

"You were very brave, but I think 'twas more than that which stayed the robber's evil plan. Even though perhaps you did not sense it, God turned those men away from your bedside."

Peggy's shoulders slumped, and her grip relaxed. The stick fell and rolled under the bed. Clarissa's heart softened with compassion when tears filled the young woman's eyes. "If I could believe in such a God ..."

"But you can." Clarissa moved closer, and she and Rosina took Peggy's hands at the same moment. Clarissa felt the presence of

God in the room more strongly than she ever had at the Home Church in Salem, stealing her breath with His power.

The tears spilled and fell down Peggy's cheeks. "I live in such fear here, in this beautiful house." She whispered so low only the women would hear her.

Clarissa's heart wrenched, and she glanced behind her, sensing the need for the men to step away. They were backing toward the door, but a clamor sounded outside, men yelling and dogs barking. Miss Crawford jumped up and darted to the window. Her hand shook as she moved the curtain to peer out.

She spoke in an equally shaky and breathless voice. "They have Solomon! In chains."

John and Peter followed her to the window.

"What will they do to him?" Clarissa asked Peggy.

The fire in Peggy's eyes faded, and she turned away, not bothering to wipe the tears streaking her cheeks. "He need justice for what he did, but I never want to see again what was done to the last slave they captured."

John's gaze sought Clarissa's at the very moment she could not veil her horror—the very moment she remembered the strange words of Goingback and the burnt patch where she had so casually tossed her apple core.

CHAPTER ELEVEN

An hour into their afternoon corn picking, a rustling stalk parted to reveal Peter's face. "Are you ready to tell me what that was about this morning?"

John wrestled another head of Indian corn from its nesting place and plunked it into the canvas bag hung across his torso. "I'd rather not."

He'd been dreading this moment since he and Peter headed through the cool October drizzle to the near field while their wives and the Steiners conducted lessons.

That morning in the cabin, the early arrival of a group of Indians had caught them unawares, causing Peter to stick his head past the partition a bit too soon. He knew Peter wouldn't let the awkward moment pass.

John moved down the row, but Peter cut through and followed him. "I would suppose. A pallet on the floor? I picked up some distance between you and Sister Kliest this week, but are things that bad?"

"No, things are not that bad." John fought down the desire to tell his friend 'twas none of his business because he knew spiritual concern rather than idle curiosity motivated the questioning. "Look, I know 'tis the Moravian way to scorn secrets of any kind, but 'tis a simple arrangement between my wife and me that need concern no other."

"'Tis not natural, John. And when winter comes and the cold hovers on that hard floor, I daresay you will agree with me."

"Look, we will have it worked out by then. Clarissa is just … uncomfortable about sharing a cabin."

"She?" Peter's eyebrows rose almost to meet his ginger thatch of hair. "I would wager you are the less comfortable one."

"Ha-ha." He added no mirth to the sounds. "Shall we just say things have not been as Clarissa pictured them?" A voice whispered in John's head. *Or as you painted them?*

Peter plucked ears behind him, and they worked back-to-back. "That business surrounding the robbery was a shock to us all. The poor Steiners. I'm glad we are here to support them."

"I told my wife that I did not remember Vann being so monstrous—volatile when drunk, yes, but ..."

"It sounds as though he has changed." Peter turned, lowered his voice. "Brother Steiner told me in confidence that this summer he was called up to the house to find the man writhing in pain. He claimed a creature had crawled in his ear."

John's brows rose. "Did he find anything?"

"How is one to determine such a thing?" Peter shrugged and brushed the dampness off the shoulders of his coat.

"Do you think he is losing his mind?"

"I don't know. Brother Steiner speculated that it could be some imbalance, either mental or physical."

"Or spiritual." John grimaced.

He hated to feel this way, but their host's struggles took the highlight off his own. Then again, wasn't Vann and the world he created the reason for his own struggles? Both terrible and beautiful, life here, but Clarissa's withdrawn demeanor told John that the recent crimes and Vann's violent retributions were eclipsing the beauty she'd glimpsed upon their arrival. If only she would let him encourage her. But the shared cabin and constant interruptions kept her walls intact.

"You are discerning, my brother. The atmosphere here can be troubling." With a twisting and a sloshing sound that scattered droplets from the ears, Peter resumed his corn picking. "Vann grows increasingly cruel to his slaves, his guests, even his wife. Other days, he can be the most charming man you have ever met."

"He needs Christ."

"Yet Brother Steiner says he shows no more interest in spiritual matters than he did when he invited us here."

"Maybe we can start with Peggy Vann. She showed an openness that day in the house."

"She did, but Brother Steiner believes 'tis through the children that God will most likely work."

John paused and lifted his hat from his forehead, pushing back his damp hair. "And our wives seem to be making connections with them already."

Since learning of the inhuman slave execution, Clarissa had focused her attention on the children. After lessons and luncheon every day, she followed Sam Hicks around with a notebook in her hand, asking the Cherokee words for everything she could point to and writing down the phonetic spellings in English. 'Twas a start for her syllabary, she explained.

Despite the ache he felt over Clarissa's withdrawal, John couldn't help but be proud of her skill. But he could hardly brag on his own wife. He was preparing a compliment for Rosina's skill as a teacher—she had taken the children on a "march" along the borders of Vann's plantation, collecting botanical samples—when mention of the women appeared to jog Peter's memory.

"This situation of sleeping on the floor," he said. "This evening will be your first time alone in the cabin while we sup with the Steiners. Perhaps that will allow things to resolve."

The same hope had jockeyed in John's mind, but the moments this week that he'd found Clarissa gazing at the horizon with the look of an animal caught in a trap had caused that hope to wither. She hadn't said it, but he sensed he'd disappointed her. Deeply. Maybe at least they could talk tonight.

"John!"

His name came not from the man behind him, but from a terrified female voice at the mission. Clarissa. John dropped the corn and ran, Peter behind him.

As he cleared the head-high stalks, he saw his wife running.

Not toward him but behind a big black man who strode away from the complex toward the plantation house. The limbs of a petite white woman straggled from the slave's arms, swinging like a ragdoll's. His heart almost stopped when, still some fifty yards distant, Clarissa grabbed up her skirts, darted in front of the pair, and planted herself in their path.

"Stop!" Clarissa placed her hands on her hips. "I will not let you take her in this manner." A quaver in her voice betrayed fear behind her attempt to speak with authority.

John pounded up to the unfolding scene. "What is going on here?" He heaved for breath, his gaze darting from Clarissa to the massive slave. At the fear in his wife's face, he placed a hand on her elbow. "Are you all right?"

"I am, but Miss Crawford is not. She is—*wounded*." Tears gushed out of her eyes and ran down her cheeks. "She was a guest in our home. And this man barged in and took her."

John's gaze shifted to the unconscious woman.

Peter, already breathing hard behind John, gasped. "Christ have mercy. Sweet Lord, have mercy."

The girl's hands and feet were disjointed, swollen to twice their normal size. How she had made it to the mission, John could never guess. He drew his shoulders back, his eyes flicking back to the black man. "Did you do this?"

The fierce-looking field hand became instantly contrite. "Naw, sir! I never dare lay a hand on a white woman, 'cept to carry her back home, jus' like Massuh Vann told me."

"Please." Clarissa put a hand on John's arm. She nodded toward a big tree a few feet away, asking for a private moment.

"Stay right there." John shot a threatening look at the slave while Peter stepped in front of him.

"He's not going anywhere."

"Naw, sir, but please hurry. I don't want the massuh after *me*." The man shifted Miss Crawford's weight, causing her to release a low moan.

As soon as he and Clarissa stood apart from the others, John asked in disbelief, "*Vann* did this?"

She nodded. "Or had it done, according to Miss Crawford."

He hadn't even realized Vann had returned from Tellico. The master certainly wasted no time dispensing his *justice*. "What happened?"

Clarissa drew a shuddering breath. "I was teaching in the children's cabin, and I saw someone hobble by, into our house. I followed because I knew it was a woman. I was concerned because Sister Steiner told me how some of the Indians like to … steal."

John nodded, prompting her to continue.

His wife was holding her composure by a thread. "I found her … hiding under the bed. She begged me … she begged me to conceal her, John. Said that Vann suspected she had taken part in the robbery, but that she was innocent. What he did to her …"

When Clarissa bowed her head and sobs racked her body, John cupped her chin. "And then this man came?"

"He dragged her out, and she f-fainted. Her poor hands and feet. She is just a child. Oh John, do not let him take her."

Her trusting plea wrenched his heart. At that same moment, the slave's deep voice rose from the discussion he must have been having with Peter. "I got to take her back, or she not be the only one punished."

Resolve stiffened Clarissa's spine, and she darted back to them. "No. She is a free woman, not a slave. She sought sanctuary with us."

John searched out Peter's expression. His friend's grim countenance answered his query, but he translated for Clarissa. "We are not in the United States of America. We are in Cherokee territory, and James Vann is the local representative of tribal law."

Clarissa gasped. "But she is white, not Indian. That authority cannot extend to her."

Peter stepped forward. "It can if she has chosen to reside in his home."

Clarissa's chest heaved. John could see her mental wheels turning as she sought another solution. The slave started walking forward.

"No! No." Clarissa jerked into motion, attempting to cut him off again. "This is not justice, this is evil."

With a glance toward the big house, John reached for her arm. When she fought him, he held her back and leaned close to whisper a strident warning in her ear. "We are on his land. Would you like to join her?"

Clarissa's body went slack, and her face drained of color. Anguish at eroding her sense of safety pierced him, but her recklessness forced him to make her aware of the danger.

"We are here by our host's invitation, and we must none of us get on the wrong side of him." Peter's words underlined the realization dawning in her eyes.

Clarissa's spine stiffened. Her shoulders squared. She balled her fists, and her eyes shot fire between them. "Cowards! You are both cowards!"

Before John could stop her, she ran down the hill toward the mission.

Peter jerked his head in that direction, indicating John should follow his wife. "I will go up to the house and see what I can do. Maybe I can talk Vann down from killing the poor girl. This deeply grieves us all, John. But you know the whole project is at stake."

John found Clarissa in their cabin, a hand on the mantel, bent toward the embers of the morning fire as sobs shook her body. When he touched her shoulder, she whirled to face him.

"Are we not here to stand up to evil?"

"Peter has gone to talk to Vann. The Steiners have been able to reason with him before."

Rather than being mollified, she spat back a disgusted response. "Reason? With such a demon?"

"Clarissa, we face not one demon, but a whole host. We win not by charging into the first fight we find, but by planning, wisdom, and prayer. A slow, steady siege."

"So if Brother Keller is not successful, we just let that poor girl be tortured?"

"We need to be praying right now, not arguing. That is where our power lies." Tears pricked the back of John's eyes. He tried to reach for her hand, but she pulled away.

Clarissa firmed her quivering chin. "Yes, we should pray, but please let us do it separately. I need to be alone right now."

The disappointment, the disillusionment, in her eyes made him feel like the smallest man on earth. Did she not realize how much he wanted to be that strong savior who rushed to rescue those in danger? To earn her admiration? He couldn't walk away and leave her to such a misguided judgment of his motivations—of himself. "In this case, rash actions could lead to disaster. James Vann is the most powerful man on the Upper Towns council. If we cross him, no one will come to our rescue. At best, we would be evicted, the mission ended."

She pressed a hand to her stomach as if to hold back the sobs. "What kind of world have you brought me into? What kind of monster is this man?"

"The kind who does not know the Lord. The kind who is in bondage to liquor and who has lived in darkness his whole life. Remember, these same Indians we break bread with today would have scalped us only a dozen years ago. Do you think their brutal customs die easily?"

"You told me these people were civilized, different from when my father visited. But 'tis *unecht*, false. The worst kind of falseness. Just a veneer, bricks and European clothing coating unspeakable cruelty."

"Yet not so unlike that tidy revolution in France that now has Bonaparte gobbling up Europe."

Clarissa fell silent. He'd struck a chord.

He continued, trying to drive his point home. "Cruelty knows no skin color. European or Indian—any freedom without God leads back to bondage. 'Tis why we are here, Clarissa. Think of those children out there"—John pointed to the cabin door—"and tell me this opportunity is not worth preserving."

"You should have been honest with me. Instead, you lured me here"—she flung an arm wide, her face twisted with disdain—"with charming words of beautiful sunsets and noble callings."

"I am sorry if I did not prepare you." Despite John's effort to keep his response even, sarcasm and condescension leached in. Clarissa's accusations stung. How could she not understand, nothing was more important than this work? John tried again to modulate his tone. "I told you, things were not like this when we visited. Maybe Vann just showed us one face. But lure you? If I did, 'twas, yes, at least to a noble calling. Unlike the sordid temptations of Philadelphia which would have ruined you had the elders not disapproved my brother's request."

"What?" Clarissa's whisper punctured the silence that fell after his statement.

What had he just said? In his defensiveness, had he mentioned the letter?

She prompted him, her eyes wide as a startled doe's. "Your brother's request. I thought he was offered a living in Philadelphia because my father wanted him gone. That Daniel did not even know of your proposal. Do you mean he spoke to the elders?"

This was not a conversation he wanted to have now. Maybe not ever. Yet, he would not be dishonest. "I told him they were in favor of me wedding you. It was then that I learned of Daniel's intentions. I had him come to the meeting with me the next day."

"He spoke for me. He asked for my hand?"

The muscles in John's stomach contracted like the claws of a steel trap. "He revealed that he already had an appointment with his choir helper to discuss the matter."

"And they sent him away." Clarissa clasped her hands over her mouth and turned to the side. "Because you were older, more established, more respected. And on this *noble* mission. Did he stand a chance?"

"He stood a chance." John's tone came out flat. *The letter, tell her of the letter*, his flesh clamored. But he couldn't hurt her like that.

He reached toward her. "I'm asking you to trust the elders, the lot."

She shrugged away, not meeting his gaze. "Right now, I believe we would have fared better without them."

Her words penetrated.

She wished she had not married him.

His heart throbbing with pain, John turned and walked toward the door. He paused in the threshold. With her back to him, Clarissa reached for her easel and paints. What had she once said? Painting was the way she escaped?

The only way she *could* escape him now.

CHAPTER TWELVE

When John received an invitation from a chief who lived some thirty miles south on Oothcaloga Creek to map his community, Clarissa welcomed the reprieve. The fact that The Ridge was a friend and fellow former warrior with Vann, a man who shared Vann's disdain for Doublehead, made his request a command. So John took a horse and a pack mule bearing his equipment and provisions for a day's travel, and Clarissa waved him off with a heavy heart. Heavy with guilt, because her relief overshadowed any sadness at his departure.

The night of the incident with Miss Crawford, the Steiners had counseled with them while the Kellers had benefitted from the empty cabin. Of course, the Steiners had supported John. They'd encouraged Clarissa that the signs of growth they observed in Peggy, the children, and some of the slaves outweighed Vann's irrationality. In fact, they argued, did not that very irrationality prove the desperate need of these other people? If they challenged Vann directly and failed, the light in Springplace would go out.

Clarissa had capitulated, especially since Peter had returned from Diamond Hill with the news that Miss Crawford had been spared. But something hardened in her spirit. She would apply herself to her assignment, record the Cherokee language as quickly as possible, and insist on an immediate return to Salem.

Of course, John had sensed the gulf widening between them. He hadn't raised any important subjects in the week following, and he'd spent each night in their shared bed, at her side to avert further questions, but stiff, not touching her. She caught sadness in his gaze, but the fact that he'd allowed the elders to shove Daniel aside in his favor left a bitter taste in her mouth. He had misled her about so many things. How could she trust him again?

Clarissa did not dare tell anyone the deeper fears that weighed on her heart, not even Sister Steiner, who clearly sympathized with her struggle to adjust to Springplace.

For the first week after John left, the relief allowed her to release the tension, the unmet expectations she'd carried since her sudden marriage. But sometime during the second week, Clarissa became aware of an emptiness. The air chilled her more. But that could just be the deepening of autumn. She felt disconnected to everyone around her. But that could be because she still did not know them well. She could not, however, explain the sense that someone had lifted an emotional—and maybe a spiritual—cloak from her.

She felt it even now, sitting in the afternoon sun on the porch of the Steiners' cabin, and shivered.

"*U-yv-tla?*" asked Sam from beside her.

"Yes. Cold." Faithfully, Clarissa recorded the syllables in her little book. "There's that *yv* sound again. How can I differentiate it from the *ye* sound when I write it as one letter?"

Thwk.

Now, there was an interesting sound. Clarissa stood as Charlie Hughes rounded the corner of the boys' cabin with Joseph Vann. Both clutched seven-foot cane blowguns in their hands. She got their attention by waving and calling out. "*A-ni-tsu-tsa!*"

Joe looked her direction. "*V-v?*"

Clarissa practiced the language as much as possible, but she doubted she'd ever get used to the Cherokee nasally word for *yes*. "You should not be shooting those darts near the houses."

Charlie gave her a sullen look. She had every suspicion that he encouraged the misbehavior of the younger boy, even though the exalted Chief James Vann, Joe's father, certainly provided a far worse example.

"Tell them to go hunt squirrels." Sister Steiner spoke from inside the cabin, where she stood over Rosina and Sally Vann as they worked at the loom.

Rosina craned her neck around the corner. "My husband will return from the blacksmith soon and can set them to something useful."

Clarissa gestured from the boys to the color-speckled forest and firmed her voice into a command. "*U-di-le-ga ... sa-lo-li!*"

Sam stifled a snicker with his wrist, and Joe burst into a guffaw, but at least the two troublemakers made their way toward the woods.

Hands on her hips, she whirled to face her prized pupil. "What?"

"You just told them to heat squirrels, not hunt squirrels."

"Oh." Admitting her mistake with a laugh, Clarissa sank back onto the bench. "Yes, the heating comes after the hunting. So ... as I am doing so well with basic words today, and you don't seem to like to talk about concept words and emotions, let's try something different. Spatial words."

Sam studied her as if she'd spoken German. Putting out her hands, Clarissa reviewed right and left, then made a point of placing her book on the bench beside her. Quirking his dark brows, Sam again offered the word for left.

"No." Clarissa moved the book to the other side.

He gave the word for right.

"No." She shook her head and patted her leg, then his, then pointed at the book. "Between."

"Ah! *A-ye-li.* Between."

"Oh yes. Good, Sam." Clarissa snatched up the leather volume and scratched that down. They proceeded to work on behind, beside, above, before, and below. As words filled her page, she warmed inside at last. "We're making great progress."

"Can I go hunt now?" Sam's wistful question stole Clarissa's satisfaction.

"But we have so much more we can cover."

"The boy does need his exercise." Sister Steiner loomed in the doorway, winding a ball of yarn around her hands. "'Tis not good to always ask him to work while the others play."

Clarissa sighed and closed her book. "Very well. Let's see if we can find them." He cocked his head at her, but she didn't need to explain that she suspicioned the sneaky duo could stand some checking up on. Standing, she gestured Sam ahead of her.

They had not gone far when a yell reached her. At the edge of the clearing, the hunters darted toward the woods. Sam's face brightened. "*Si-qua!* They have hit a hog!"

Clarissa's mouth watered. They had not had meat since the side of beef Peggy donated to celebrate their arrival, due to the Cherokee predilection for allowing their animals to forage. She'd asked a couple of Vann's slaves to catch one for them but to no avail. She hitched up her skirt to join in the hunt. But no. The blowgun arrows were too small to bring down a hog—and vexing enough to cause it to turn on the boys. She yelled to Joe and Charlie to stop.

Charlie turned toward them, his face mutinous. Pointing, he gave an exclamation in Cherokee which Sam translated.

"He says they must track it."

Clarissa drew up in front of him and placed her hands on her hips. "No, you will not. Such an arrow will not fell that beast. 'Twill only make it mad. You should have called for help so it could be caught. We needed meat, and all you have done is driven it away." When Sam gave her a blank stare, she rolled her hand impatiently. "Tell them."

"Uh …"

Charlie did not wait for Sam to process the string of strident English. He lunged for the cover of the trees, but not fast enough. Clarissa grabbed his collar and jerked him back. "Oh no, you don't." As he struggled, she snatched the blowgun out of his fist and shoved it at Sam. She propelled the miscreant before her while she threw a command over her shoulder. "Come, Joseph."

Vann's son trotted along after them, back to the Steiner cabin. She marched Charlie straight inside and announced to the startled Louise, "Someone does not like to listen. Instead of hunting squirrels as he was told, he shot a hog and was going to chase it into the woods even when I bade him not to. Perhaps he would rather join Sally at the loom."

Sally whipped her head around so fast that the ribbons in her hair fluttered, eyes round at Clarissa's suggestion.

Sister Steiner pursed her lips and corralled all three boys on the porch. "Master Joe, you may go home. I hope you will not think you must copy bad behavior from anyone because they are older than you."

She spoke of Joe's father. Clarissa nodded.

As the generally amiable younger child took his blowgun and retreated, Louise pressed Charlie and Sam onto the bench. "And you two can wait here for Brother Keller."

Sam piped up. "But I did not do anything—"

Sister Steiner's raised brows squashed further protest. She turned to Clarissa, whose rumbling stomach fixated on the barbeque she'd imagined for a brief, wonderful moment.

Running a hand over the curls escaping her day cap, she couldn't keep a complaint from escaping too. "'Tis ridiculous that we are said to own eighteen hogs, yet I have not seen a chin hair of a single one in the two weeks since our arrival."

"I suggest you take a deep breath, Sister Kliest. You can use it to read Spangenberg's *Idea Fidei Fratrum* to these boys while they wait."

Solemnity settled with the mere mention of the bishop's theological treatise in German. Why did Clarissa feel she might as well be sitting on the bench beside Charlie?

※ ※

The next afternoon, Brother Keller occupied the boys with a project in the workshop. Since Rosina continued Sally's weaving instruction, Clarissa decided to seek out Sister Steiner to see if she required any help. She needed to stay busy. Guilt over her estrangement from John gnawed at her even when he was away—

along with an unexpected concern for his welfare.

She changed into her work dress in the cabin, musty with the lingering scent of the morning's fire and quiet except for the cawing of a crow on a limb outside. Clarissa tied on her apron and stepped close to the bed to touch John's empty pillow. She'd always loved time alone to reflect. Why this sense of loneliness, as if she was missing something—someone—important? Had a man she did not even love taken up residence in her heart? Despite the things he'd done to hurt her?

Her eye fell on John's small trunk at the foot of the bed. What would she do if he did not return from Oothcaloga? She would be free. Free to go back to Salem, to her teaching, to her painting. Maybe even to Daniel. But somehow, the notion pierced her with sadness.

Why would I feel such a thing?

Clarissa knelt in the sunlit dust motes and lifted the cover of the trunk. 'Twasn't her business, but she craved some reminder the man was real. She lifted a white linen shirt to her nose. Inhaled. Closed her eyes. 'Twas as if he stood beside her. Her stomach twisted with the memory of his kiss. She'd wanted quite a bit more of that before misunderstanding wedged its ugly self between them. When he returned, would they be able to work things out? She wanted to forgive him, but could she trust him? What else was he hiding from her?

Clarissa sorted through other articles of clothing. Books. A bunch of envelopes bound by twine. She weighed them in her hand. No. She would not overstep that boundary of privacy. She put the letters back but left the shirt lying on John's side of the bed. Just because … she might want to sniff it again tonight before she fell asleep.

She pulled the partition closed and hurried across the dirt yard.

In the kitchen, Sister Steiner was poring over her smudged German cookbook while Pleasant nursed Michael on the side porch. According to what Clarissa had observed, feedings were the only time the baby seemed safe from Rosina's interference, and even that probably would not be so if Rosina had any say about it.

Sister Steiner straightened as Clarissa entered. "I am thinking of roast butternut squash tonight and a good corn pudding." She broadcasted her next question to the porch. "What do you think, Pleasant?"

"Mmph." The indistinguishable mumble constituted the slave's reply.

Clarissa reached for a basket on the table. "I can gather the squash."

"That would be lovely, dear." Sister Steiner leaned closer and lowered her voice. "Rosina believes Pleasant is lazy, but I tend to think that at her age, the birth took it out of her."

Or maybe the woman simply craved time alone with her child. The baby fussed as Pleasant ended his feeding. A smile stole over Clarissa's face as she glanced at them. "I agree. I am happy to help."

Sister Steiner crooked an eyebrow at her. Taking Clarissa's tenderness for wistfulness? "You must be at odd ends with your husband gone."

She turned her lips up. "I am doing all right."

"Well, while you are out there, you might as well gather the last of the pole beans."

Her hearing amazingly improved, even over the baby crying, Pleasant commented from the porch. "She gonna have to fight that Indian woman for 'em."

"What Indian woman?" Clarissa whisked out onto the porch to see what Pleasant saw. Sure enough, a woman with long black braids was bent over the waning vines at this end of the garden. Swinging her basket on her arm, Clarissa took a step off the porch. "Why, she can't do that! There were just enough for us to cook up tonight."

"Sister Kliest." Sister Steiner's firm tone arrested her. "The squash can wait. Come into the kitchen, and let's fix a cup of tea. Pleasant, why don't you walk Michael a bit until he settles down?"

"Yes'm." Sounding content to be dismissed, the slave woman sauntered off toward the trees, leaving Clarissa to look askance at the older sister.

Louise sighed and led the way back into the kitchen. Placing the kettle on the stove, she gestured toward the bench by the table. "Please sit."

Clarissa felt like the sensitive Sally must when she received a rare scolding. Best to address the awkwardness head-on rather than cower under it. "Sister Steiner, I fear you are displeased with me lately, although I don't know why."

"Not displeased." She uncovered a loaf of pumpkin bread and transferred it to the table. "Concerned."

"I have taken to heart the words you and Brother Steiner shared with us last week. I am devoting myself to the cause, to the children."

"Yes, you are working hard ... too hard, I fear. You always have that notebook in hand."

Clarissa sighed. "I have written down hundreds of Cherokee words, but I don't feel I have scratched the surface, partly because Sam does not seem able to relate the phrases for bigger concepts. Emotional concepts. Spiritual concepts." Frustrated by all she had yet to grasp, she waved her hand above the table, almost knocking off the candlestick.

"It will come. You need to allow yourself time to adjust, to rest."

Clarissa let her hand fall. "I am simply eager to make progress."

"But might that eagerness cause you to come across occasionally as ... impatient?"

"Impatient?" Clarissa cringed. "I don't think so ..."

Sister Steiner set a pearlware plate containing a block of fragrant tea in front of her. She added the tin holder that propped up the cones of sugarcane. "Your relations with everyone here are new—fragile. You are still learning so much. 'Tis not all bad, like what we dealt with last week ... just different. For instance ..."

"Yes?" Clarissa prompted Louise when she paused to pour the hot water.

"The Indian lines between sharing and stealing are different than ours. Money and horses and personal possessions, yes, those are the same. But food—produce of the land—since land is only tended, not owned, they see no wrong in helping themselves. Whether we like it or not, we dare not speak against it."

"I see." Clarissa took her mug, chipped off a larger-than-normal chunk of the pressed, dried tea leaves, and placed them in the bottom. "Doing so alienates them?"

Louise nodded, settling to prepare her own brew. "Another one we must correct without alienating is Charlie Hughes."

"Charlie? Why?"

"You must not have heard that his great-uncle is Doublehead."

"What?" Clarissa gasped. A chill ran down her spine.

"Yes. His mother, Elisabeth Hughes, is a relative of Vann, and that is why he is here. As you know by now, the Cherokee clan is matrilineal, which means the mother's side of any family holds greater weight in making decisions. But Charlie is also full-blooded Cherokee, unlike the other children, which makes him feel inferior."

"I had noticed that, but I did not know about Doublehead. John—Brother Kliest, I mean—told me about the enmity between Chief Vann and Doublehead. He sounds like an even more frightening man than Chief Vann."

"So you can understand why no ill reports of our mission must reach him. He would not hesitate to make enough trouble not only to withdraw Charlie but to close us down."

"Of course. Thank you for telling me."

Sister Steiner sipped her tea. "There is much to learn here, Sister Kliest. I would like to be your *chorpflegerin*, if you will allow. Your spiritual and practical mentor in this strange wilderness where we find ourselves. We must hold to the precepts of our faith if we are to not only survive but thrive."

Thrive? Here? Clarissa could not imagine such a thing, but she nodded. Louise reminded her of her own mother in some ways, a support she greatly missed. "I would be honored."

"Then as such, might I ask if there is something deeper troubling you than these momentary irritations?"

"I … ah …" Clarissa sat up straight, heat creeping up from her collar. Had Rosina told Sister Steiner about the week that John had slept on the floor? In fact, had she been relating every lapse Clarissa made to the older woman? Rosina's retreat from trying to advise and encourage her suddenly made a lot of sense.

Adding to Clarissa's suspicions, Louise prompted her with a statement, casually delivered as she sliced pumpkin bread. "When I am at odds with Brother Steiner, all else falls into disarray."

A vague admission wouldn't hurt anything. "Well, as you know, Brother Kliest and I have not seen eye to eye on some of the challenges we have faced."

Sister Steiner nodded, using her thumb to lift some crumbs that fell to the table. "I hope you have set aside your anger toward your husband over the situation with Miss Crawford, Sister Kliest. As we discussed, not only would Vann simply have sent someone else to take her, but the slave would have suffered repercussions. And the mission as well."

"I do realize my husband considered the … long-term plan." Even if she still did not completely agree with it.

"Good, because nothing except your relationship with God, and I do mean nothing, is more important than your relationship with your husband. Even the work we are doing at this mission. Although … I will be the first to admit that words are our most powerful tool for pushing back this darkness. Specifically, the Word of God."

"I understand, Sister Steiner."

"Despite our disagreements, Brother Steiner and I have had to learn to work as a team these past several years. 'Twas not easy at first, mind you. But with God's help, and patience, and honesty—"

"But that is just it. He has not been honest." The words fell out of Clarissa's mouth before she could stop them. How had Sister Steiner exacted such a confession in a matter of minutes, when she'd managed to remain close-tipped with Susanna for years? It must be the light of wisdom shining in her eyes.

"How so?" When Clarissa hesitated, Louise reached across the table for her hands. "I cannot help you if you are not honest with *me*."

So Clarissa found herself relating everything—her sense of betrayal that John had painted a false picture of life at Springplace and concealed the fact that Daniel had asked for her hand. Her fear of being no more than a part of John's plan to return here. Her fear of a future that not only lacked love, but also lacked the fulfillment of her dreams.

Sister Steiner remained calm while Clarissa talked, only sitting forward when Clarissa drew to a conclusion. "I know John is my husband now, and I must respect him, but I keep struggling with one major thing. How could John use his superior position, his superior calling, to elbow aside his brother's claim? He did not seem to have the slightest remorse."

"For one thing, that claim had not been established by the lot."

"Daniel was not allowed to go to the lot. The elders judged him unfit and sent him away."

"Are you sure that was the way of it?"

"Well, yes." Clarissa chewed her lip, trying to remember if she'd forgotten any important facts that John had related. Then fear hit her that she spoke out loud. "But what if there is more that he has yet to tell me?"

Sister Steiner frowned and opened her mouth, but a cry of greeting and the barking of the hunting beagles froze her in place. "Perhaps another group of Indians passing through?" She stood.

"Oh dear. They will want to be fed, and we haven't enough beans."

Louise swung around with a finger raised to scold her but

paused when she saw Clarissa's teasing grin. "Aw, you! We don't have enough beans, but I am glad you are beginning to focus on the right things."

"I'm trying." Clarissa laughed and followed her to the door.

"We shall talk again about your marriage. You can count on me to pray. And I ..." Whatever she beheld from the threshold caused her to lose her train of thought. "I cannot believe it. Speaking of answered prayers!"

"What?" Who had come? An elder to tell them they had made a mistake in sending Clarissa to the Cherokee Nation? Or at least a slave who had finally caught and slaughtered a hog? Clarissa edged up behind Sister Steiner. Only a middle-aged Indian couple dressed like homesteading farmers and an adolescent girl with long black braids approached across the clearing. "I don't understand. Who are they?"

"Chief Little Rock, his wife Du-a-i, and their daughter Dawnee." Louise sounded breathless.

Seeing as how there seemed to be a lot of chiefs in the Cherokee Nation, she wasn't sure what was so important about these people. "Why are they special?"

Sister Steiner wrung her hands together. "Because Dawnee's older sister, Dawinzi, was a student here last winter, and she died while in our care."

"Died?" Clarissa gasped.

"Yes, of a mysterious fever. I can only trust that their visit means what I hope it means."

Sister Steiner waved and hurried forward with an expression of mingled joy and hope. A minute later, Clarissa froze as—*boom!*—a rifle shot silenced the barking of the dogs.

CHAPTER THIRTEEN

Certain she would find someone lying dead in the yard, Clarissa ran outside. Sister Steiner stood frozen with her hands in the air. The Indian family approached from the right, while to her left, in the turnip patch, Brother Steiner did a victory dance that looked quite native in origin. He held up a creature whose head dangled wildly at the end of a long neck and let out a delighted cackle.

"Roast goose for supper!"

Basket overflowing with green beans and a couple of small pumpkins, the Indian woman Clarissa had almost accosted earlier now hurried over to accost Brother Steiner. She talked rapidly, pointing at his rifle, though Clarissa could only make out a few of her words.

Sister Steiner composed herself and, ignoring the sideshow, greeted her guests. She hugged the willowy, light-skinned woman in calico and bowed her head to the man, who wore an unusual turban with a feather fixed on the front by a silver brooch. A variety of silver bangles danced on his arm.

"Chief Little Rock. Du-a-i. Dawnee. Welcome. What a joy to see you again." She gestured to Clarissa. "This is Sister Kliest."

The girl named Dawnee, who must have been eleven or twelve, fixed shining dark eyes on Clarissa. Her face lit with a smile. She might have been the most beautiful child Clarissa had ever seen. Clarissa nodded at the trio. "*Si-yu.*"

They responded in unison. "*Si-yu.*"

As if following her hand that seemed to move of its volition, Dawnee stepped forward and fingered one of Clarissa's curls. "*Gi-ni-tlo-yi da-lo-ni-ge-i.*"

"Looks like—" Clarissa searched for the translation of the

second word, while Du-a-i whispered her daughter's name in a chiding tone. "Oh, 'tis all right."

"Gold," Du-a-i said with an appreciative smile. "She too curious."

"I am curious too." Clarissa grinned at Dawnee before glancing back at her mother. "You speak much English?"

"A little. We have English neighbor."

The strident tones of the garden invader followed Brother Steiner into their midst, even though the woman had stopped near the border of sunflowers. Probably unwilling to sacrifice her bounty.

"Why is she still scolding you?" Clarissa asked.

Chief Little Rock grunted, nodding as he listened to the woman. "Shooting goose in garden ruins rifle."

As if that made perfect sense. Just one of the many unique superstitions she'd heard since arriving here, from the Cherokees and slaves alike.

"Which I am entirely willing to risk for the rare taste of meat," Brother Steiner said with a grin. Shooing the dogs away as he placed his prey on a nearby patch of grass, he bowed to the party of visitors. "'Tis honored we are to welcome Chief Little Rock. I hope you will not be too offended to sit at our goosey table tonight?"

The chief pushed his daughter forward. His noble, impassive face fascinated Clarissa. She itched to run and fetch her charcoal and paper. "Dawnee help cook."

"Oh, so you *will* stay?" Sister Steiner clasped her hands under her chin.

"Yes. We will stay." Du-a-i's smile illuminated her humble face.

"Well, let's get cooking!" Sister Steiner fetched the fowl and led the women across the yard while her husband ushered the chief to their cabin for a drink and a smoke.

"Where did you travel from?" Clarissa asked the newcomers, then tried a Cherokee version of her question.

Holding her hands out as if she were measuring something,

Dawnee attempted to answer in English. "Half ... half ..."

"Halfway?"

She nodded. "Halfway to Hiwassee."

So they had likely passed this family's farm on their journey down from Tellico.

"Are you passing through to Oostanaula?" Sister Steiner named the village where many Upper Cherokees held meetings. She stopped at the chopping block, positioned the goose's neck on the stump, and reached for the nearby axe. With a matter-of-fact swing of the sharp blade, she divested the goose of its staring head. As she went for the feet next, Clarissa hurried to the kitchen.

Inside, Pleasant—with Michael asleep in a sling—cleaned the squash Clarissa had never picked from the garden.

"Oh, thank you for getting those. I know you have so little time with your sweet baby." Clarissa paused to skim Michael's curly head with a gentle finger. "He's so sweet."

"Humph. When he sleepin', not fussin'." Pleasant made a face as she tucked her chin to survey her son, conflicting emotions etched in the lines by her mouth and brow.

"He loves you, even when he's fussing." Clarissa offered her paltry encouragement, hoping against hope that a vision of a richer future might begin to replace the pain of the slave's past. "And Pleasant, if you ever find Sister Keller's attentions too much—"

Pleasant turned her back, *thunking* through the squash with her sharp knife. "I help you with something, Sister Klies'?"

Clarissa stifled a sigh. Pleasant didn't know she could trust her. At least not yet. "I need the plank Sister Steiner likes to use to prepare meat. Brother Steiner shot a goose."

Pleasant nodded her head toward the corner. Clarissa grabbed the board and an extra knife. As she hurried back out, the slave tucked a burlap bag over Clarissa's arm. "Them feathers goes everywhere."

The small gesture of thoughtfulness halted her, warming her heart. "Thank you, Pleasant."

Pleasant hardly ever spoke, and when she did, it was often to argue with Rosina and—occasionally—even Sister Steiner. Clarissa paused in an attempt to meet the woman's dark eyes. Pleasant looked away as she had been taught, but Clarissa wanted her to know that she did not expect her to. *Perhaps if we express some appreciation, it could make her burden a little easier.*

Back at the chopping block, another unexpected sight awaited. Sister Steiner stood over her goose carcass, tears streaming down her cheeks. She couldn't wipe them away with her bloody hands.

"What in the world?" Clarissa hurried forward. Placing the board and bag on the ground, she reached the corner of her apron to her mentor's face. "'Tis just a goose, Sister Steiner."

Sister Steiner laughed. "Oh, 'tis not the goose. Du-a-i has just told me that she and her husband wish us to take Dawnee into our school."

❧ ❧

After dinner, Sister Steiner lined the children in front of the mantel and led them in the singing of three hymns, one in German, one in English, and one in Cherokee. Du-a-i wept through all three. On the bench behind the table that still held the remnants of coffee and sweet buns, Clarissa leaned across Dawnee to offer the woman her handkerchief.

"Are you *ha-wa*, all right?" she whispered.

Du-a-i nodded and wiped her face. "Dawinzi. I remember."

"Songs remind her of my sister," Dawnee said. "When she come here, always sing."

Sister Steiner took the Indian woman's hand, explaining to Clarissa. "Du-a-i knows we do not sing like the Indians do, for merriment, but to praise and pray to God."

Sam Hicks stepped from the shadow of Sister Steiner's skirt. He'd been on hand through the dinner to act as interpreter when each party's understanding of the other's language failed. Now, with a steady gaze, he addressed Dawnee's mother. "God sees and hears all things and knows even the thoughts of our hearts. And those who love Him will after this life be received into heaven."

Clarissa drew in a quick breath. His diction might indicate memorization, but his face revealed all earnestness. No wonder the child had so quickly found a place in all their hearts.

He switched to Cherokee, while Du-a-i sat nodding and dabbing with Clarissa's handkerchief. When he finished, she squeezed Sister Steiner's hand. "I wish I live here, to hear more *go-we-li u-ha-ge-dv*." More Holy Book.

"Oh, me too." Sister Steiner bent down to hug her. "You must come more often."

"This why we bring Dawnee," Chief Little Rock stated. "To learn good things."

"And we will teach her good things." Smiling, Clarissa squeezed Dawnee's shoulder. The child had insisted on sitting next to her at dinner.

"But where will she live?" From a bench over, Rosina glanced at the three boarders, whose eyes had followed the winsome young maiden during the meal. "We cannot put her in the boys' cabin."

"Well, our small loft upstairs is chocked full of supplies," Sister Steiner said, "but I think we can make room there."

Dawnee's small hand closed around Clarissa's arm. When she looked down, the child stared at her with bright, inquisitive eyes. Dawnee couldn't know that she was married—newly so, at that—or that they shared a cabin with another newly married couple. She only knew she wanted to stay with someone to whom she had, for whatever reason, attached herself.

Du-a-i noticed her daughter's hopeful expression. She gave a little laugh. "Dawnee like English. Very curious. Want to *be* English. You look English."

Rosina cleared her throat. "We are actually German, of course."

Clarissa ignored her, turning to Dawnee. "Oh no. You must never be anything but what you are. I am *u-da-tli*, married, but if you wish, you may stay with me until my husband returns."

Dawnee nodded vigorously. Clarissa thought her heart would burst. The beauty John talked about … maybe she was seeing a glimpse in this moment.

Later that night, she got another glimpse. While the chief and his wife bedded down at the Steiners', Clarissa showed Dawnee into her side of the cabin. The fire Clarissa stirred up on the hearth illuminated John's shirt lying on the bed, where she'd forgotten she'd left it. The girl pointed to it and uttered a string of Cherokee that Clarissa could not follow. When she shook her head and shrugged, Dawnee asked, "Hu-sand? You miss?"

Like many, Dawnee struggled with the English consonants absent in her native tongue, like the "b" in "husband."

"Yes. He will be back soon."

"You glad?"

Clarissa opened then closed her mouth. Would she be? Her faith, her conscience, demanded the truth. He was her husband. She wanted to respect and admire him, yet every time she had begun to, he had disappointed her.

Thankfully, Dawnee did not wait for a reply. She clasped her elbows and made a rocking gesture.

"Baby? No." Clarissa felt her face heat. "New husband." She pointed to herself. "New wife."

"Ah." The child sounded like a prophet of the ages as she rattled off another string of Cherokee. She closed her statement with firm assurance. "New now. But you glad later. You will love. And have baby too."

Where was her book? Her quill? And Sam. She just might go get Sam out of bed to translate the gaps. For she'd found the person who could share emotional and spiritual phrases from the Cherokee language.

Clarissa placed John's shirt gently back in the trunk and patted it before closing the lid. She climbed into bed and pulled the quilt up under her chin, battling down a strange new sense of excitement. Was this what John felt when he viewed a mountain range? An obstacle one conquered in land-eating strides to reach the peak and see what lay on the other side?

When Dawnee jumped into bed with a running start and laughed uproariously as the luxury of the feather mattress engulfed her, Clarissa started giggling too.

🌿 🌿

Dawnee's presence meant that Sally lingered at the mission longer each day. The older girl treated Vann's daughter as if she were the same age, including her in her work and playing with her as well. Everyone seemed drawn to Dawnee. Her zest for life was contagious, her curiosity boundless. In fact, as Rosina and Clarissa helped the two girls set up to make cornhusk dolls outside the barn one afternoon, Tom, Sam, and Charlie kept loitering around offering to help. Finally, Clarissa set them to work bringing the dried husks from the stall and placing them in buckets of water to soak.

A servant from the big house—dressed much more nicely than the field hands—knelt on a blanket, cutting bits of cloth. Peggy had sent her to assist, along with the supplies they were using for the dolls—material, buttons, and twine. She had plenty left over from sewing projects even though she farmed out her own dressmaking to a local white woman. Beside her, Dawnee and Sally laid strips of husk softened in the boys' water pails and dried by Rosina into stacks of four.

Clarissa stood over them, hands on her waist. They didn't need her help, but she couldn't miss out on the fun. Suddenly, it struck her. "That golden autumn glow, it highlights your faces so beautifully. I'm going to get my paints."

A sense of inspiration filled her that had been missing since Salem. The last time she had painted after her quarrel with John, it had been out of anger. Now, as she hurried to the cabin and returned with her supplies, she breathed deeply of the woodsmoke-scented air. The murmur of voices working in cooperation, sprinkled by giggles from the children, warmed her heart. Clarissa opened her paints with joy.

"These will make the best gifts for the slave girls," Sally said in Cherokee.

"'Tis kind of you to think of them." Rosina surveyed their supplies. "That means we need double the amount of piles we have now. Boys, can you soak another batch?"

"I will!" Charlie jumped up from where he'd been squatting, looking over Dawnee's shoulder.

Clarissa wasn't even sure he'd understood all of Rosina's request, but she liked this new, helpful attitude. "Thank you, Charlie. *Tsu.*" She pointed to the bucket to make her meaning clear.

He nodded and scurried over.

As the boys brought more husks and the girls twisted and tied them into the shapes of people, Clarissa made her first strokes. She outlined the girls first, then dabbled in the yellows and reds to capture the warm light behind them. Pleasure filled her, relaxing her limbs, slowing her heartbeat until Rosina looked up and commented. "I wonder what is troubling the dogs down the lane."

A minute later, a rustling in the bushes nearby made everyone pause. With a furious snorting, a dark shape shot from the underbrush and headed straight for their scene of domestic tranquility. The girls screamed. The slave and Rosina attempted to pull them away. The hog ran with a blowgun arrow protruding from its haunch, while the boys ran toward it yelling challenges about who could catch it first.

Clarissa leapt to her feet. "No, boys!" Her approach attracted the maddened animal toward her easel. It darted between the slender legs, sending her wooden paint set and pad flying face-first into a nearby mud puddle, before streaking across the clearing and into the orchards beyond.

"Oh no! Oh no!" Clarissa stood frozen, afraid to assess the damage. She glanced back at the children to make sure they were all right.

Charlie spread his hands wide and said with an expression of exaggerated innocence, "Was not me!"

"I can see that."

She could also see a flash of better-than-average clothing as a familiar figure emerged from the woods across the way. "Joseph Vann!" The figure disappeared. "You come back here!"

Clarissa took off down the lane that led to the main road, intending to give chase through the patch of woods if necessary, but a horse and rider, a mule, and the Steiners' passel of tongue-lolling hunting dogs obstructed her path. She shaded her gaze to view the rider. "John!"

As her husband swung off his mount, her heart surged with an emotion not unlike the one she'd experienced upon opening her paints. He looked so solid, so handsome, even with his beard untrimmed and his clothes rumpled. She hesitated but a moment before throwing herself into his arms. "I'm so glad you're back."

Clarissa felt his lips press against her temple. "I missed you." She turned her face up toward his, meeting his bright blue eyes. She caught her breath at his expression. Intense. Longing. "I found I could not stop thinking..."

Would he kiss her? Her knees wobbled, then his gaze turned toward the lane behind them. Dawnee stood there, holding Clarissa's paint set.

"Who is this?" John released her. "And what mischief have I interrupted?"

Reluctantly, Clarissa took a step back, though she did not want to release that forearm, hard with muscles. "This is Dawnee, daughter of Chief Little Rock and Du-a-i. She came to school here while you were away. As to the other, you might guess who is behind the mischief."

"Joe Vann?"

She nodded and squinted into the woods, though the little villain was long gone. "He shot a pig, and this time hit it. It ran through our doll-making setup."

John frowned. "He was warned. His behavior must be addressed."

Clarissa nodded but turned to greet Dawnee with a smile.

"This hu-sand?" The girl's shy gaze assessed John.

"Yes. This is my husband."

"That is good. He make you happy, but ..." Dawnee's pleasant expression slipping, she held out the box of watercolors.

Clarissa gave a cry. "My paints!" The blue and green—broken. And the yellow and red, which had been wet, were now blackened with mud.

What about the pad? She hurried toward the barn, where the women were reorganizing the doll-making supplies. Dawnee and John followed, leading the horse and mule.

"Sorry about your painting." Sally held out Clarissa's pad, her expression a mixture of confusion and regret. Regret Clarissa understood, but confusion?

The loose-bound book flapped in Sally's grip, two of Clarissa's paintings visible. She took it, her stomach dropping. Mud swirled the depiction of the girls she'd just started. No matter; she hadn't gotten very far. The other painting, the page behind it, had not been damaged. And it explained Sally's confusion.

"Who is that?" Sally pointed. "He scary."

Clarissa covered the painting in question as fast as she could, but not before John glimpsed it from behind. She knew he'd seen it by the gravel in his tone when he answered. "It's no one, Sally. Just something Sister Kliest should never have drawn."

CHAPTER FOURTEEN

So many things had become clear to John on the journey back from Oothcaloga. Things he and Clarissa needed to focus on to succeed in both their mission and their marriage. Yet his wife's painting challenged both, and within minutes of his return. How could Clarissa have been so foolish?

After assigning the strangely eager boys to stable the horse and mule, John instructed Clarissa to follow him back to the cabin. She collected her supplies with a grim face and went to whisper something to the new Indian girl. John strode across the clearing, too frustrated to wait. Besides, he wanted to wash off the road grime.

He paused at the partition to their side of the cabin. A child's doll lay on his side of the bed. A soft-gray wool dress hung from his peg. What had been going on here?

John threw his coat and waistcoat over the evidence and snatched off his shirt, then used the water in the wash basin to cool his temper. God had spoken to him clearly about that temper over the past couple of weeks. He could not blow it within the first hour back at Springplace.

Clarissa's voice entered the cabin before her, calling out his proper title. "Brother Kliest? I've brought Dawnee to—" She stopped at the partition, her eyes rounding as John turned, water dripping down his face and bare chest. Scarlet color crept over her cheeks, visible even in the dim light. She shoved a palm toward the slight figure behind her, turning the child away. "You can come back later for your things." After a shuffling, Clarissa said, "Thank you, just put the easel by the door."

Stifling a surge of pleasure that the sight of him partially undressed affected her, John toweled off. Slowly.

Clarissa turned back to face him, eyes downcast, hands clasped around her sketch pad. "I suppose you are angry with me."

He crossed the room and stopped mere inches in front of her, allowing his height and state of undress to unsettle her. Because maybe if her confidence was shaken a bit, she would listen. He waited until she looked up, those brown eyes startled.

"I meant it when I said I missed you, wife. 'Tis time we do something about that."

Her lips formed an adorable little O.

John yielded to the urging inside and, without otherwise touching her, bent to lock his mouth on hers. He closed gently on her soft lower lip, the pressure making his intentions clear.

"Oh!" Clarissa stepped back, putting a hand to her mouth.

John took hold of her loosely dangling sketch pad and held it up with a slight shake. "And aye, I am deeply disappointed in you. What were you thinking?"

"I—I painted it after Vann hurt Miss Crawford. It was the only way I knew to release my anger."

John studied the picture of their host, shaking his head. Clarissa's skill surprised him, but that made it all the worse. Because the likeness of the two sides of Vann, joined in one torso, looked all too real. On one side, the man in European clothing reached out with a noble and entreating countenance. On the other, the reddened face of a buckskin-clad savage twisted in anger and hatred, his hand clutching a brown bottle. The backdrop included a clear blue sky on one side and flames like those from hell on the other.

"What if Sally had recognized her father? What if she still does?"

Clarissa's features crumpled in fear and regret. "I would feel horrible."

"As you should. Again, you have created a situation that could threaten our work here. All we can do is ask God in prayer to cover the matter, and I will trust you to burn this later."

With another shake of the offending papers, John stepped

away—though to do so was torture—and opened his trunk. His best shirt lay on top where he'd left it, but his long, white linen necktie had fallen to the bottom. Of course. Impatient, John rummaged for it with one hand, his letters falling out of their twine before he finally located what he desired. He slid Clarissa's drawings in under his clothes, where no curious child would easily find them, and latched the lid.

Turning, he unfolded his shirt over his knee. He looked up to behold his wife blinking tears from her eyes. "I am sorry about your paints, but I think it best that you put them away for a while. Focus on what you came here to do."

"I *have* focused. I have worked so hard that Sister Steiner bade me to rest. And nothing brings me peace like my painting." She took a tiny step forward, but he did not have the patience to heed the plea in her voice. Why was she so set on a pastime, anyway?

"We can discuss that later. For now, we are going to see Vann."

"To see ...?"

John did not know when Clarissa had looked more alarmed—when he'd kissed her or right now. She wrung her hands as he tugged the shirt over his head. "I have letters for him from his friends, The Ridge and Charles Hicks."

"Is Charles Hicks our Sam's father?"

"Yes. He served as an interpreter at the meetings I attended when trying to get the mission approved. He is also the treasurer for the national council. He and The Ridge and The Ridge's brother, Oo-watie, allies of Vann, are the most powerful leaders at Oothcaloga. All are in their thirties and have young sons. They would love to see a mission school established there." Buttoning his waistcoat, John cast a quick glance at Clarissa, unable to hide his excitement. "I found a perfect location central to their farms."

Her face slackened. "I thought you went there to map the region as a courtesy, not to look for a future mission spot."

"I did. I have not said anything to them yet. I cannot ignore what I found, though. Clarissa, it's a community even more open to European ways and Christian faith than Springplace."

"But … I am just beginning to settle in here. Dawnee is helping me grasp and record aspects of the language I couldn't before. She is so intuitive, John … a real gift."

John paused to squeeze Clarissa's hand. "And I would not do anything to disrupt that. Well, except send her to sleep someplace else." He cast a slanted eye at the offending doll on the bed. It grinned back at him with its red-stitched mouth. "I know it has not been easy for you, this change. I want you to be comfortable while we are here. In fact, 'tis why I have already spoken to Peter about constructing our own cabin."

"Truly?"

His heart leapt when Clarissa's face lit. She wanted to be alone with him … or at least, away from the opinions of Rosina. He would take what he could get. Their own cabin would provide a space for their love to begin to grow, something else he'd clearly seen the need for during his time away.

"I want our marriage to feel real," he said, "and I want to give you space to work. I will speak to Vann about it this evening. We need to think of the future." He turned away to tie his stock and shrug into his black swallowtail coat.

"But … a future here, right, and not in Oothcaloga?" Clarissa asked in a faint voice. "And when we are finished here, you said we would return to Salem."

He faced her, fighting a sense of disappointment that a desire for creature comforts still ruled her spirit. "Are you not willing to go where God would have us go?"

"Of course, I seek to submit myself to God's will." Clarissa licked her lips. "But what if God's will is for us to return to Salem? Are *you* willing to do that?"

John placed his hands on her forearms. "I will go where He sends me."

"But you do not wish to go to Salem." As she spoke the soft words, her gaze drifted over his shoulder, out the window. As if she disconnected from him despite his touch.

In truth, 'twas as if she had read his thoughts. John might as well be honest. "After the potential I witnessed these past weeks for the spread of the Gospel among the Cherokees, no, I do not believe God will call us straight back to Salem. But who am I to conjecture?" He whirled and put on his hat with a cheer manufactured to override the visible hopelessness settling over his wife. "'Tis only for us to do our duty as it appears before us day by day. And now, that duty is to pay a visit to James Vann."

Clarissa's eyes flashed back to him. "Oh no." She stepped away. "I have avoided that place—that man—since we first arrived. You do not need me to accompany you."

"But I do, for you witnessed the events with Joseph."

She shrugged away from his attempt to take her arm. "No, John."

"I assure you, the chief will receive us with the utmost respect. He always does."

"Unless he has been drinking, or someone has filled his ear with tales, or he thinks someone has stolen something from him. Or all of the above."

"If that is the case, I will escort you home posthaste. I promise," he added when she pursed her mouth at him. John quirked his brow. "You cannot avoid him forever."

"Oh yes, I can."

Time to pull the figurative ace from his sleeve. "How can we move forward in our duties if we are ruled by fear rather than love? 'Charity shall cover the multitude of sins.' We must give a second chance to all people, Vann included. Show him the grace God shows us."

"I do despise it when you sermonize against me." Clarissa whirled and grabbed her bonnet from the peg. Tying the strings, she started for the door.

John stifled a chuckle as he tucked the letters from Oothcaloga into his breast pocket.

The November evening breeze nipped through his wool coat and sent the tails of Clarissa's pelisse swirling as she marched ahead of him up the lane. He was about to ask her to come back and take his arm when—upon sight of the house—her steps slowed. As he drew even with her, an expression of genuine unease lengthened her features.

"Perhaps I can just visit with Peggy."

John took her arm without asking, drawing her near with a shrug of his shoulder. "I will keep you close to my side. Do you not trust me to take care of you?"

Clarissa stared up at him with her wide, brown eyes, only fear and a sort of sad resignation registering there. Did she regret his return? He vowed to do his best to win her trust. To have her look at him with admiration, respect, and one day … love.

Inside the foyer, the scents of beeswax candles, roast beef, and cleaning wax mingled. They followed a black house servant to the parlor, but not before a scrabbling sounded on the stairs high above. He and Clarissa looked up to see a worried, youthful face peeking down from the banister leading to the third floor. Clarissa raised her brows, and John stifled a chuckle.

The door before them opened to reveal Vann in a fine, gray wool coat and dark breeches, smoking a cigar before a crackling fire. He stood at their entrance, his broad face expressing a warm welcome. "Brother Kliest, hello. Hello, Sister Kliest."

When Clarissa saw that only Vann occupied the room, she hung behind John rather than stepping forward to greet their host. Yet when Vann asked if they would take brandy, she popped out a startled reply. "No! Thank you."

John gazed at her, amused, before confirming her response in a more judicious manner. "No, thank you. But please, we do not mean to disturb your leisure." He waved at the wing chair Vann had occupied.

In turn, Vann indicated the sofa facing the fire. "Will you join me?"

"We would be honored. But first ..." John paused to withdraw the correspondence, holding the envelopes out to Vann. "I bring letters from The Ridge and Charles Hicks."

"Oh! I am eager." Vann took the offering and scanned the outsides before placing both envelopes on a nearby desk. "I had hoped you would come see me today. How are my *tso-ga-li-i*?"

John smiled as he lowered himself onto the settee, placing himself between their host and Clarissa, even though he caught not a whiff of alcohol. "Your friends are well, but I must confess, troubled."

"What troubles them?"

"Your mutual enemy. Hicks spoke much to me about the evidence he sees in the papers of Colonel Meigs that Doublehead has received bribes. That he has more than once sold Cherokee land to the whites."

Vann slammed a fist into his open palm. "This I suspect from the treaty councils I attend. At the last one, I drew my blade against him and would have run him through had others not separated us. His actions are against our law. Punishable by death."

Clarissa winced. John reached toward her under the folds of her skirt, touched her fingers. She quietly withdrew her hand. She was still upset with him. Because he'd asked her to put away her painting? Or because he'd made her come here? Both, probably.

"The Ridge says he will visit soon. Perhaps with his support ..."

Vann nodded, lifting his cigar to his lips again. "Yes, it is a matter for the council."

"There is another matter, closer to home, that we need to address with you."

"Oh?" Vann held out his box of cigars to John, who declined with a wave, grateful he no longer had to worry about smoking a ceremonial pipe.

"The matter of your son, Joseph."

To John's surprise, Clarissa broke in, sitting forward slightly.

"He is a bright child, and generally well-behaved, but I fear the older boys have encouraged him on a path to mischief."

"Path to mischief?" Vann frowned in confusion.

"Acting bad," John said.

"Who does this acting bad? The little *i-na-dv*, Charlie Hughes?"

John wasn't sure what an *i-na-dv* might be, but judging from Clarissa's flinch, it wasn't good. Still, he must keep to the matter at hand. "We do have some concerns about Charlie, but the latest incident, one of many, involved only Joseph." John went on to explain the boy's proclivity for blowgunning the pigs.

For a moment, Vann appeared to struggle to suppress mirth. Then he cleared his throat and answered in a grave tone. "It is not acceptable, his bad action. I will take him in hand."

John nodded. "Thank you, sir."

"Please, will you not be too hard on him?"

John turned to look at his wife in disbelief. Apparently, her concern for young Joe overrode her fear of the boy's father. He admired her for that, but he said only, "The chief has assured us the problem will be taken care of. That is what we came for."

Clarissa's throat worked as she swallowed, then nodded.

"But while you are here," Vann said, "tell me of the school ... you, Sister Kliest. All make good progress?"

"Oh yes. The boys excel in arithmetic, but the girls are better at reading English. We hope to begin their instruction in writing it soon."

"This is good. Dawnee, girl of Chief Little Rock, is she well?" Vann leaned back, the firelight glinting on the golden threads of his double-breasted brocade waistcoat as he blew out a plume of smoke.

"She is well. A joy to all. She is my biggest helper in writing down your language in English." Clarissa's body relaxed, and her face glowed when she spoke of the girl who had, it seemed, become her favorite pupil. How had this girl wrought such a change in so little time? "And I feel certain she will be my biggest helper in writing it in Cherokee too."

"In Cherokee?" Vann sat forward.

"Yes, sir."

"This I did not know you did. Like your … alphabet?"

"More of a syllabary." Clarissa paused, then switched to Cherokee that John couldn't follow for a few sentences. He raised his eyebrows in surprise and further admiration. She'd made even more progress while he was away than he'd thought. "But yes. That is the plan."

Vann grunted, brows beetling over his dark eyes. "This is not good plan."

Clarissa gasped, glanced at John. "But why not? 'Tis why I was sent to Springplace."

"To write our words in English, yes, but in Cherokee? Many will not approve."

"I don't understand."

Sharing her confusion, John broke in. "The words should be written in Cherokee so all the people learn to read them in their towns. Not everyone can send their children to our schools. Think how it will change things for all the people to read and write, send letters like the whites along the postal roads, and most importantly, read God's Word for themselves."

"Maybe have newspaper?" Vann lifted his pipe into the air like a question mark.

"Yes!" Clarissa smiled.

"I say it is good. My friends in Oothcaloga would say it is good. But there are those who would not, even in these parts. For certain, those of Doublehead's blood." Vann knit his brows again, fixing a meaningful gaze on Clarissa.

"You mean Charlie," she whispered. She raised her voice. "But why is this bad?"

Vann rose to stir the fire, and sparks popped and danced under his poker. "Long time ago, Cherokee man went to chiefs and said he wanted to make a book. They told him the Great Spirit first made a red boy and a white boy. To the red boy he gave a book, and to the white boy a bow and arrow, but the white boy came 'round the red boy, stole his book, and went off, leaving him the bow and arrow. So it is that an Indian cannot make a book."

Clarissa sprang to her feet. "But that is an old fable. It is not true, certainly not now."

"Some still believe. Some say if words are not spoken or sung, they have no effect. So no reason to write words. Still others say to do so is … how you say? … witchcraft."

John rose beside Clarissa as she drew in a sharp breath. In the firelight, her face blanched white, while Vann's looked almost as red and fearsome as in her painting. John placed a hand on her waist. "My wife does her work as the servant of God."

"And under my protection." Vann's features relaxed as he replaced the poker in its holder. "This I know. But others would not understand."

"Are you telling us to not make the syllabary?" Clarissa asked.

"I believe in your work. I want to see this day when Cherokees can talk in written words like whites." Vann settled back in his chair. "But for now, I would urge, work in quiet."

Clarissa nodded, tucking her hand in John's arm. Perhaps as a signal to depart, or perhaps she needed support. Either way, his heart surged in response. He squeezed her fingers but directed his attention to the chief, recognizing an opening to make his next request. "Would you allow another small cabin to be constructed for such a purpose? For Sister Kliest and me to live in, and for this writing of the Cherokee language?"

"When we are gone, you could use such a cabin for the schoolroom." Clarissa raised her gaze to John. Hopeful they would soon be gone? Hopeful they would convince their host?

Vann swept open his arm, shaking his head. "As always, you are welcome. The land is yours to build on as you will."

"We thank you deeply, Chief Vann."

"Yes, thank you." Clarissa produced what appeared to be a

heartfelt smile. John had known if he could only get her face-to-face with a sober Chief Vann, her respect for the man's many positive attributes would grow.

"Now, will you stay to dine?"

John expressed his appreciation again but made their excuses to Vann. He bowed. "We will leave you to your letters and your family."

When the servant showed them out, Clarissa stopped on the porch, taking deep breaths.

John offered a teasing grin, along with his arm to escort her down the steps. "You survived."

Clarissa raised her eyes to the heavens in a thankful glance. "Tonight, he was the angel Vann." When they had walked a distance from the house, she asked, "But how can God use such a conflicted man to further our mission?"

"The same way He used evil kings to further His goals throughout all of history."

"I am thankful it went as it did, but I must admit, Vann's warnings frightened me."

"We cannot let fear of one boy's opinion threaten such an important work."

"'Tis not just one boy." Clarissa withdrew her arm from his, leaving John feeling empty. "And I do not like hiding something from one of our students. It seems wrong. Charlie is just now responding well, showing interest in helping record the language, though doubtless because he envies the time Sam works with Dawnee and myself."

"Perhaps now that I am back and harvest is done, I can take the boy under my wing, begin teaching him how to apply his mathematics to surveying." John brightened with an idea. "I could use another helper in building our cabin."

Clarissa stopped, hopped in place, and lifted herself on her toes. She clapped with delight. "Oh, could you, John? That would be wonderful. I think it might help Charlie find his place."

This was the feeling he wished for between them. Maybe tonight ...

John stopped walking as the oddest sensation traveled from his feet upward, an unsteadiness, a looseness in his bones.

Clarissa had yet to notice anything amiss. "I must be honest, John. After what Vann said, I am not certain about continuing the syllabary." Her eyes widened, and she reached toward him. "What on earth is happening?"

"Not *on* earth. *In* the earth. I think this is an earthquake!" As the ground shook harder under them and the farm animals and dogs protested in a strange cacophony, John grabbed Clarissa's arm and led her away from the trees. They knelt together in the middle of the field. Clarissa's eyes grew so huge, he reached for her and, after kissing her temple, tucked her forehead under his chin.

"Does this happen often here?" Her breaths came quick, moist, and warm against his neck. More distracting than the shuddering ground.

John swallowed to steady his reply. "To my knowledge, almost never."

"Only as I was saying that perhaps I should not continue the syllabary?"

CHAPTER FIFTEEN

Their return to the mission found the chickens rushing about squawking, the hunting dogs cowering under the cabin porches, and a frantic tangle of exclamations in English, German, and Cherokee. And not just the children were speaking in Cherokee. Apparently, in their brief absence, visitors had arrived from the southeast: an Indian named Youngbear, his sister, and the sister's husband, a white man named George Coker. Everyone gathered in the Steiners' cabin. Dawnee ran to cling to Clarissa's side, while poor Sam struggled to keep up with translating the guests' rapid-fire questions.

"He wants to know if the earth is falling apart, if it is very old." Sam turned from Youngbear to his sister, who chattered in her native tongue and made fluttering hand gestures. "She says no, this is the work of a conjurer and a great snake."

"*Tla-no.*" Coker patted his wife's hand, shaking his head. "*Tla-no i-na-dv.*"

The woman began to weep.

"Please, everyone, have a seat." Brother Steiner's authoritative voice rose above the din. He gestured to the table, then glanced at Rosina, who was sweeping up the broken shards of a pearlware plate that must have fallen off the shelf. "You too, Sister Keller."

Sister Steiner agreed. "Yes, let us all talk sensibly about this. We can clean up later."

Clarissa took a seat next to the Indian lady and touched her arm. As Dawnee edged in next to Clarissa, leaving John to settle on the opposite side, she spoke to the woman in Cherokee. "My name is Clarissa. What is yours?"

"*A-we a-ni-di.*"

"Howanetta," Dawnee whispered in her ear.

"Howanetta. What a pretty name. Would you like some coffee, Howanetta?"

The woman shook her head. Tears still ran down her face, and her hands on her lap trembled. She said in Cherokee, "The earth never shakes like this. Is it because I married George? The conjurer says bad things will happen if we grow too much like the whites."

Her husband translated words Clarissa struggled to understand, but with a bitter sigh that showed his impatience. "I tell her not to believe that nonsense, but you think she listens to me?" He slapped his hand on the table, making the fringe on his hunting shirt dance.

"Your husband is right. This is not because of your marriage." Clarissa put as much emphasis into her voice as possible without further frightening the woman. She looked up, realizing that everyone was watching. She hadn't meant to become the center of attention, only to comfort Howanetta. She sought out Brother Steiner, but he gave a brief nod, indicating she should continue.

"I translate, Sister Kliest?" Sam asked.

"Yes, please, Sam. I fear some of these words may be beyond me in Cherokee." She reached for Howanetta's hand, focusing on her face in an attempt to calm her own now-jangled nerves. "The conjurer does not have power over the earth. God does. God the Father is Creator. He sustains the earth, but at times, He does allow things like floods or earthquakes or fires. Those things serve as reminders that we should seek Him."

"How do we find this God?" Youngbear's brows knit together beneath his colorful turban. "Is He the Great Spirit?"

"And what does He want from us?" Sam translated Howanetta's question right after her brother's.

"I told you about God," Coker said with a scowl and a sheepish glance around the room.

Youngbear frowned, crossing his arms. "I want to hear from missionaries. You act worse than Indians who never hear about Him!"

Clarissa's glance at John showed he was biting back a smile, not just of amusement, but of something else … pride in her. She smiled back, still holding her new friend's hand. She couldn't believe the concern and love that flowed through her for the stranger.

Brother Steiner interrupted before an argument could break out. "We would love to tell you about Him."

He shared how God the Father had sent God the Son, Jesus, to be born as a man and live among the people He had created, then to become the sacrifice for their sins. An expectant hush fell over the room. Brother Steiner spoke of how God wanted a personal relationship with His children. How the death and resurrection of Jesus opened the way for sinful people to live in harmony with God.

The fire gave an occasional pop, but no one moved. The faces of children, missionaries, and Indians alike focused on Brother Steiner. Dawnee laid her cheek against Clarissa's shoulder.

A sense of rightness settled over Clarissa, and suddenly everything made sense. These people were beautiful, and words were God's chosen tool to lead them to freedom.

Then why did a powerful urge make her fingers itch for her paper and charcoal?

※ ※

As Brother Steiner had Sam read aloud from *The Harmony of the Four Gospels,* John couldn't keep his eyes off Clarissa. The sweet, natural way she'd comforted and shared with the Indian woman testified to the fact that Clarissa had finally begun to grasp the vision of this mission. But then, her joyful look had faded to a frown.

Brother Steiner concluded with a prayer and began to answer the many questions of Youngbear and Howanetta. John stood to seek his wife, but George Coker approached around the end of the table.

"I reckon you're the one I am seeking."

"Me?" John extended his hand to the man. "I am John Kliest."

"The surveyor?"

"Yes."

"Then you're the reason we came. See, I bought land from Howanetta's family when I married her. I come from Franklin County, Georgia. I'm one of the lucky few whites to settle in these parts. I want to make it official-like, and I heard there was a missionary who had one of them special compasses who could measure off the parcel Youngbear sold me."

"I can do that, but I only today returned from Oothcaloga." John's gaze sought Clarissa's. He couldn't allow another diversion to his languishing marriage. "Is it something that can wait for a while? I have projects here."

He'd also promised Clarissa he would take an interest in Charlie Hughes. He and Tom were busy putting corn kernels into a cast-iron popper to hold over the fire. Glancing over his shoulder, Charlie tossed one straight into the flames and snickered. He rocked back on his heels and waited for the mini-explosion.

Coker cleared his throat loudly, drawing John's attention back. "We-ell,"—he drew the word into two syllables—"the land he's selling me is a little distance from his farm. There is an old cabin on it that I'm keen to fix up before winter." Coker shifted his lanky weight and rubbed a hand over the bristly, dark growth on his chin. "I would rather get things squared away so we can move in. We hoped you would come with us tomorrow."

"Tomorrow?" Dismay chiseled away at John's polite tone.

Coker jingled a leather pouch on his belt. "I can pay good."

The Ridge had thanked John for his services in a handsome manner, so money did not figure prominently in his mind at the moment. "I thank you for your proposition, but I will need to discuss it with my wife."

Coker persisted. "'Tis not far. Less than a day's ride, not even halfway to Frogtown."

"Thank you. I will discuss it with Sister Kliest and the other missionaries."

At that moment, Clarissa stood and darted out of the cabin. Where was she going? She did not need to be alone in case another tremor came. John excused himself to follow her. Besides, her departure offered the perfect opportunity to talk about Coker's offer. But to his surprise, Sister Steiner trailed him to the door and called after him.

She wrapped a shawl about her ample frame as she stepped into the chilly November night. "Brother Kliest, I would bid you to be patient."

"Patient? Why would I not be?" John rocked on his heels as an owl hooted from a nearby tree branch.

Who-who-whoo.

"Your wife has gone to fetch her sketch pad." What? After he'd specifically told her to stop painting?

But Sister Steiner continued. "Sister Keller told me what happened earlier, and I had already gathered from Sister Kliest that you were not overly fond of her art."

"I am not un-fond of her art. I simply think it can fritter away time better spent."

Sister Steiner crossed her arms over her bosom. "I do wonder if, in their zeal for your mathematical abilities, your instructors neglected the creative side of your education. You *have* heard of John Valentine Haidt?"

Eager to follow Clarissa and uncertain why this good matron detained him, John drew in a breath to answer, but the owl beat him to it.

Who-whoo!

They both laughed, and John relaxed.

"Of course." Every child in every Moravian settlement in Europe or America grew up intimately acquainted with Haidt's religious paintings. Several of them hung on the walls of the Single Brothers' meeting room in Salem.

"And you do realize our greatest response to the Gospel among the Cherokees has come when Brother Steiner and I have shown them Haidt's depiction of Jesus on the cross?"

He hadn't known that. But … "I know Clarissa is talented, but I doubt she is in the same category as a master painter."

"Not yet." Sister Steiner held up an index finger. "And she never will be if you do not believe in her gift. Yes. Her skill with languages is valuable, but one should never discount a calling which warms one's heart like painting does Clarissa's. She has asked Howanetta if she can draw her. The prospect has delighted a young woman who moments ago wept in fear."

John took the point. "Very well. I will not protest her painting tonight, but I still need to speak to her in private."

"About Mr. Coker's request?"

"Did you overhear him just now?"

"He was in the process of telling us his business when the earthquake occurred. May I make another suggestion?"

"Most definitely, Sister." Because she would, anyway. He may as well appear receptive.

"If you are of a mind to leave with him tomorrow, take your wife with you. In fact, I strongly encourage it."

"Why would Clarissa want to go?" John propped his hand on his hip. Sister Steiner had not been on their sojourn to the Cherokee Nation, or she would not think her idea so laudable.

"Because she needs to get to know her husband. And you need to get to know her. The Kellers are almost as newlywed as you, but they have not had the misunderstandings that you have had with Clarissa."

Misunderstandings? Which ones did Sister Steiner refer to, and how did she know this? John felt a flush creep up from his collar despite the brisk, windy night.

Seeing his struggle, Sister Steiner drew closer. "I have acted as Clarissa's choir helper while you were away. It is clear that you and she have much to talk about." Her face softened. "I can tell you this. Your wife wants to trust and love you, Brother Kliest, but those things cannot be forced. They must be wooed, with honesty and gentleness. Take the time to do that. 'Tis more important at the moment than anything else."

The truth resonated with John, spurring awareness and remorse. Had he been so set on surveying the path ahead for the mission that he'd failed to lay the groundwork for his own marriage? The look Clarissa had given him on the way to Vann's flashed through his mind. And the way she'd withdrawn her hand when he'd attempted to strengthen her with his touch. No, he had not been sensitive, and she did not trust him. John swallowed his pride. "You are right, Sister Steiner."

At last, with a nod and a slight smile, the older woman stood aside. Wanting to catch Clarissa while she was still in their cabin, John hurried across the clearing. A single light shone in the window. When he entered the door, he found Clarissa on her knees in front of the trunk. But instead of holding her sketch pad, she clasped a sheet of paper in one hand and an envelope in the other. Printed on the front of the envelope was the letter "C" written in his brother's swirly script.

She looked up at him, lips parted as a tear tracked down her cheek.

CHAPTER SIXTEEN

"Where did you get this?"

Clarissa's hand shook, and the numbness in her legs told her they wouldn't support her if she tried to rise. But she couldn't read her husband's expression by the light of the single lantern.

He stood frozen in the doorway. "From the hollow in the Salem witness tree." His voice was quiet, resigned.

The breath left her body, and with her skirts collapsing around her, she sank like a spent bellows onto the floor. At least he had not lied. "You took what was meant for me, read it, and hid it from me all this time."

"Did *you* read it?" John took several purposeful steps toward her as if to retrieve the letter she'd found loose in his trunk, right on top of her sketch pad. The hand of Providence.

Clarissa pulled it to her other side, hid it in the fold of her dress. He would not read it aloud, for she could not bear to hear the words again. Once had been enough. Her voice had no volume when she answered. "I did."

"Then you know why. I did it to protect you."

"When you took it from the tree, did you do *that* to protect me? Or yourself?"

John stopped, and his shoulders slumped. "Clarissa, I watched my brother grow up. He was doted on, his talents overblown by my mother. 'Twas as if she thought to make up for the place I had as my father's protégé. Daniel was charming but fickle. Driven by emotion and his own expediency. I feared what that letter might contain before I ever read it."

"It never occurred to you that Daniel might try to persuade me to wait for him?" Her words caused John to hesitate, but the fact that a frown rather than guilt appeared on his face caused her heart to sink. She turned the focus away from her own pain. "So you stole it. That day I saw you near the tree?"

After a second of hesitation, John gave a curt nod. "I wanted no loose ends. A clean slate with you."

"Is that what this is? A clean slate? Because it feels as if I've been shamed by not one brother, but two." Clarissa's heart squeezed as she thought of how Daniel had abandoned her and how John had deceived her.

John knelt beside her, his expression becoming alarmed as the detachment crept into her voice. "Wouldn't it have been better for you to have never read that? That—that glib way he bid you farewell, with no mention of any understanding between you?"

She swiveled to face him as a new thought wrought panic. "Do you think I made it up? Or that I imagined some attachment where none existed?"

"No! I just told you, I knew my brother better than you ever could have. Listen, Clarissa, there is more—"

"Hello, the house!" A light cast crazy shadows as two figures approached the open door.

Clarissa dragged a sleeve across her face and attempted to brace herself on the chest in order to rise, but John put a hand on her arm.

"Please, let us talk more as soon as possible."

"I cannot imagine I want to hear anything else. Why would I, when it could prove just as *unecht* as all you have already said and done to bring me here?"

"But you are right. Sister Steiner just said—"

"Brother Kliest? Clarissa?" Rosina stepped onto the threshold, interrupting John's rushed words. "Peter and I bring bundles of bedding for Mr. Coker and Howanetta. They are to stay in here, while—oh …" Her voice trailed off when she beheld them both on the floor. "Do we need to come back?"

"No. Please. Go ahead." Clarissa struggled to her feet and

attempted to brush down her skirts. As she did, she slipped the letter back into John's trunk. "I was just going back to the Steiners' to sketch Howanetta."

And to think, she had actually hesitated to use the gift God had given her out of fear of John's disapproval.

She grabbed her writing pad and charcoal and shut the lid while John rose beside her. She glanced at his expression, then turned away.

His regret had come far too late.

❦ ❧

Later that evening, Clarissa burrowed under her quilt while Howanetta nested on her pallet in front of their fireplace. Her brother occupied a similar position in the Steiners' cabin, while Dawnee had been relocated to the older couple's loft. The Kellers retired behind their partition. George Coker and John sat talking in quiet tones at the table, about what, Clarissa could only imagine.

At least one person was happy tonight. Howanetta had been delighted with her likeness. With great excitement, she had told Clarissa that Clarissa and her husband might travel home with them tomorrow in order for John to survey Coker's land. Clarissa had looked up in surprise at John, who watched her from across the room. He'd confirmed that, yes, they had been invited, but he would only go if she went with him.

"I have no intention of leaving you again so soon," he'd told her.

As if she would go with him after the secret she'd found in his trunk.

Something in Clarissa's spirit told her she was deflecting all her hurt onto John, when his motivations, if not his methods, had held her best interest. Daniel's words still marched across the back of her eyelids, telling her of the amazing opportunity the elders had offered him in Philadelphia if he would leave immediately. No mention of her at all. No mention of his determination to make her his wife and take her with him. Only the hope that God would direct her future path as well … one that obviously did not include him, though he'd lacked the courage to spell that out. Recalling his bright and casual manner, Clarissa cringed in humiliation.

Even if he had wanted to spare her the hurt Daniel inflicted, John had broken her trust twice. First, by taking the letter from the tree when for all he knew it contained Daniel's promise to return for Clarissa. And second, for keeping the truth from her this long. Better for her to have dealt with that hard truth and moved forward than to have carried this void of confusion.

When he finally crawled into bed next to her, she edged as close to the wooden bed frame as possible.

He whispered over her shoulder, his breath stirring the hairs at her neck. "I have been speaking with Mr. Coker. I told him I would not go unless a comfortable and private place could be afforded to us. He told me we can stay in the cabin he intends to move into next month. 'Tis central on the land I would be surveying."

"You can do as you wish, but I shan't be leaving my work here."

"Everyone agrees that we should both go." John laid a hand on her forearm. When she did not move, he said, "Clarissa, please turn and look at me."

"I cannot see you, anyway." But she did as he requested lest his voice rise any further. She instantly regretted it. He trailed his fingers from her temple, into her hair, down to her neck, then repeated the gesture.

"I don't need to see you to know that you are hurting, and part of that is my fault. I know I have gone about everything backward. You were right. I made decisions focused on getting here. I plowed where I should have tilled. I withheld when I should have given. That includes being honest with you. I should have showed you that letter."

"Yes, you should have."

"But 'twas true, I knew its content—the truth behind Daniel's leaving—would hurt you. I thought 'twould be better if you did not know. But now I see that it was more hurtful that I kept it from you. Will you forgive me?"

She took a shuddering breath, so afraid to trust again. Despite John's failures, 'twas difficult to hold at arm's length a man who lay inches from her, his words and gaze entreating her, his fingers stroking her brow.

"Please, Clarissa. 'Twas only because I care about you."

It must be true. What other benefit could he have seen in hiding his brother's rejection? Unless, of course, he didn't want to face her anger because he'd taken the letter in the first place. "How can I know there is not more you are concealing?"

This time, John took a deep breath. "Nothing like the letter, but there is more I should tell you about it. But please, let us do it face-to-face, not whispering with listening ears."

After a moment, Clarissa nodded. If she and John did not fix their marriage now, and he went away again, things might never be set right.

❧ ❧

Normally, the mountains looming to their north and the Coosawattee River flowing to their south would have captured John's attention. They saw fewer and fewer whites—and even fewer Cherokees dressed in European fashions—after they left the larger postal road at Ramhurst to head east on this Indian trail. But today, John's normal interest in his surroundings was diverted to his wife.

Clarissa rode in silence except when Howanetta spoke to her. The two managed to patch together an infrequent conversation in both Cherokee and English. From what John could tell, Howanetta told her about the farms and settlements they passed. Clarissa responded with genuine interest and warmth, but John sensed the sadness behind her smile.

He also sensed they had reached a turning point in their marriage, a point where it would either solidify or dissolve—if not officially, in the unseen but far more important ways. Interesting how God had allowed that letter to surface only minutes after sending Sister Steiner to help open John's eyes. Just to make sure John couldn't avoid the issue. He almost chuckled, thinking how the Almighty left no doubt as to His message. Everything must come out in the open with Clarissa, and John couldn't wait to finally be alone with her so that could happen.

The sun was beginning to inch toward the horizon at their backs when George Coker stopped and held up a hand. After a murmured conference with Youngbear, he told John, "This is where the land I will farm starts."

They had just crossed one of many creeks in the area. It gurgled noisily down from the mountains, running parallel to them from as far as John could see until it intersected the road they were traveling. Stands of hardwoods and rolling meadow lay between its border and the trail.

Coker rose in his saddle, shifting his weight. "This is the corner of the property, where the trail crosses the creek."

"And there is a perfect witness tree. Seems fitting to mark it, if we have time." John tilted his head toward a massive oak still clinging to its golden robe of autumn. "I would consider it a good start to our project."

Coker nodded. "I will wait with you while Youngbear rides ahead with the women. He can show your wife the cabin." Correctly reading John's expression, he attempted to reassure him. "The family lives nearby. Howanetta will set you up real good, and your wife will be safe there while we are out surveying."

John had explained earlier that he'd need both Coker and Youngbear to assist with the heavy chain links that measured off the land.

He glanced at Clarissa, whose eyes had widened. No way was he leaving her alone in a strange country with people he barely knew. "Thank you, but my wife will stay with me."

"We will practically be able to see the cabin from all points of the property. No need to drag her through the brambles."

John surveyed the lay of the land, his gut uneasy. He might be able to see the cabin, but could he monitor all approaches to the cabin? No, there were too many ways an unexpected enemy could sneak in.

"She stays with me," he said, "even if I do have to drag her through the brambles." When he met Clarissa's gaze, she rewarded him with the first genuine smile of the day.

He'd had his concept of boundaries all wrong. He'd thought to protect himself by keeping Clarissa outside them. But that wasn't how marriage worked. That was like saying he was giving himself to God but refusing any access to his life. A covenant in name only, without the sweetness of communion.

This union would not be complete with any distance between them at all.

CHAPTER SEVENTEEN

All day long, a voice had whispered in Clarissa's head that John would never have told her about Daniel's letter if she hadn't found it. Even if it had said Daniel would return for her. But something shifted when John said he wouldn't leave her.

The thought of finding out what that meant made Clarissa's knees wobble as she dismounted. She longed for rest, for the comforts of the cabin Howanetta described, but the firmness of her husband's jaw as he set about marking the witness tree indicated the same determination voiced in his promise to keep her near. She thought he'd merely reach for his axe, but John began to unpack practically everything the mule carried.

As he placed his circumferentor on a base with wooden legs attached, she wanted to ask why this couldn't wait until the next morning. But she bit her tongue and led her horse to the creek.

Howanetta sidled up and gestured between herself and her brother. "We go … cabin. Make ready. You need food?"

"Thank you, not tonight. Sister Steiner sent us plenty if there is a skillet to heat something in."

"Yes. Will be ready. Sweep. Start fire. George show you."

"Thank you so much." Clarissa offered an earnest smile.

As the Cherokee siblings went ahead down the path, Clarissa loosely tied off her mount and returned to John's side. Facing the witness tree, he peered down the compass arm through a sighting vane that consisted of a thin wire stretched over an oval. Then he removed a long, tubular, metal case from the pack mule.

Clarissa straightened from stretching her back. "What is that?"

"A Gunter chain." John directed Coker to take one end and stand in his previous spot while he walked toward the tree. "A full one runs sixty-six feet, but in the wilderness, we use a half chain … thirty-three feet, or fifty links. This distance, however, is only three-fourths of a chain." He paused to write in a notebook.

"Why do you have to do that part?" Despite her weariness, Clarissa infused enthusiasm into her voice to show him she was genuinely curious rather than complaining. Since math had always provided a challenge for her, she admired anyone good at it.

He looked up, a flash of pleasure lifting his brow and the corner of his mouth in a quick, surprised smile. His response grew louder as he walked back toward them. "I record the distance from the property corner to the witness tree, the taxon, the diameter, and the township information not only in my records, but on the tree itself."

"I don't know about that taxing stuff," Coker said, "but you goin' to put my name on there since there ain't no town?"

"I will include your initials, to be sure." With a grin, John hefted his axe and a wood chisel.

They followed him into the field, allowing the horses to munch on the high grass. It felt good to walk after such a long time in the saddle. To Clarissa's surprise, John cut two notches in the oak. "The witness tree at Salem had three." She said the words aloud, then flushed when she recalled the letter stowed in that tree that had brought her here.

John glanced at her. "My father preferred three blazes, but I always do two, one chest-high, and the other almost at ground level, in case someone fells the tree."

"That makes sense."

He used the tool he called a tree scribe knife to carve the necessary information into the blazes. When he stood, he smiled at her. "Thank you for being patient. I know that took a while, but I like to say there's no better starting point for tomorrow than one we make today."

Why did she sense he was talking about more than marking a witness tree? A man interested only in his own ambitions did not speak like that. A layer of weight lifted from her heart. The day of travel, of time to think, had been just what they needed to diffuse the heated emotions of the prior evening. Maybe they could talk now in a calm and reasonable manner.

George rubbed his hands together. "I couldn't agree more. Now let's get on down this path to some victuals and bed."

By the time they reached a cabin built in the same style as those at Springplace, only smaller, a plume of smoke wafted from the detached chimney toward the purpling sky. Inside, Howanetta had started water to boil in a kettle and placed both a small pot and a cast-iron spider over the coals. She insisted on helping Clarissa cut up the apples from her bag before leaving.

"I come with men in morning, bring eggs," she said with a wave.

Thanking her, John bolted the door after them. He latched all the windows and laid his rifle over the mantel. "I don't like staying in a place I haven't thoroughly scouted."

Clarissa glanced up from sprinkling cinnamon from her spice pouch onto the fruit and nuts. Sister Steiner had pressed a small cache of supplies into her hands that morning, including dried beans and a generous serving of cornbread, which she unwrapped. "I thought you were accustomed to camping in strange places."

"Not with a wife."

The statement made hope bubble up like the beans now in the pot. "I think we can trust Howanetta and her people."

"So do I, or I never would have brought you here." John knelt beside her, his presence far too close. "Clarissa, thank you for coming."

She nodded, unable to meet his gaze.

"I know I don't deserve another chance to make things right, and I don't blame you for being angry about the letter."

Clarissa recognized her opening, but she could barely squeak her question out past her constricted throat. "Why did you keep it, if you weren't going to show it to me?"

"Whether you believe it or not, 'twas not out of fear that you would be angry that I kept it from you. I told you the truth that I did it to spare your feelings. And after that … my hope was that you would come to love me, and Daniel would never come up again. But in case—"

Clarissa held up her hand, stopping him. She looked away, pretending the pause had to do with dinner. "Please. Let us wait for such talk until after we eat."

Her hands trembled as she wrapped a rag around the handle of the pot. John had hoped she would love him? That went against the voice in her head for sure and certain.

She served the beans over cornbread on their tin plates, then followed it with the apples. They ate in silence, not looking at each other in the flickering light. 'Twas strange to be there alone together. When Clarissa felt the hairs on her neck and arms tingle, it had nothing to do with the distant cry of a panther.

Suddenly John leaned forward. "You are so quiet. Did I say something else wrong?"

"I am just tired." Now that was a lie. Her nerves felt as charged as they had on their wedding night. Maybe more so. Clarissa busied herself with clearing the plates. "Would you like some chamomile tea? I could use some."

He reached out to grab her hand before she left the table again. "What I would like—what I could use—is for you to sit down and let me finish what I was trying to say earlier."

The air puffed out of her lungs in a small breath. "Very well." She sat. Her eyes widened when John reached into his waistcoat pocket and laid the envelope with the "C" on the table between them.

"I must have this out, Clarissa. There should be no more secrets between us."

She nodded, biting her lip.

"I was trying to tell you, in case your attachment to my brother came up again, this letter represented the only evidence I had that he left willingly." John stared into her eyes. "He had a choice to stay."

Clarissa gasped. "What?"

"When Daniel told me he had an appointment with his choir helper to ask for your hand, I requested that the elders allow him to go to the lot before me."

"You ... did?"

"Yes. They asked to speak to your parents, to receive a better understanding of the unusual situation. After that, the elders offered to pay for his travel and upkeep while he studied under Sully. Or he could go to the lot before me with the understanding that if God approved his marriage to you, he would remain in Salem and open a much-needed joinery shop."

Clarissa's breath came fast. The rough boards of the table blurred before her. "So he chose ... he chose ..."

John did not have to answer. Daniel's letter had told her what he chose. "I never wanted to reveal that part of the story, but now I find that, selfishly, I want your loyalty more than I want to spare you the pain of my brother's rejection. And of course, I did promise to tell you everything."

The rejection dissipated in the light of John's revelation. "You want my loyalty? And you said earlier that ..." She brought her trembling fingers to her lips, where the hope he'd expressed lodged and refused to come out. *That you would come to love me.*

John shook his head, not with disagreement but with regret etching lines by his mouth. "I realize I have given you every reason to dislike me and have no right to hope for anything else. I showed ill judgment and ill temper on our journey. I disagreed with you about standing up to Vann. I discouraged the thing you love most, painting. And most of all, I kept this from you when it was your right to know, no matter the cost. I did not want to see the sadness on your face that I see now."

"'Tis not sadness you see, except that you did not show me this sooner." So many lonely hours, days, and weeks spent at cross purposes when they could have been learning to care for each other. Hot tears rose in Clarissa's eyes and spilled over.

"Why?"

"Because it would have freed me to love and trust you."

John gaped at her. "It does not pain you that Daniel cared so little?"

"Daniel is already a distant memory. If I shed a tear over him, 'twould be naught but a bit of vanity."

He reached to wipe the fresh moisture on her face. "You are shedding more than one tear."

"Because I was afraid you wanted me no more than he did. That you only wanted to marry me because you needed me to come to Springplace, and that you have regretted your choice since. You speak of your failings, but, after all, I have been no Rosina."

"Thank God!"

When John burst into laughter, Clarissa joined him, startled by his unexpected response. She wiped her cheeks.

"She is a worthy matron, but she is not for me." John picked up the envelope, holding it between his thumb and index finger. "May I suggest we dispense with this missive?"

"Yes." Clarissa spoke firmly and stood. "Allow me." She took the letter and walked to the fireplace, where she dropped it in and watched it burn. The sense of release from that failed dream took her by surprise. She turned to John. "Thank you for telling me."

He patted the bench beside him. "Now come here."

The intensity in his blue eyes made her stomach churn, but she did as he commanded, and John reached for her hand on the table.

"Our marriage may have started as one of convenience, yet we have encountered about every possible inconvenience. And those challenges have meant we've seen about every possible flaw in each other. I say I am glad we've gotten that out of the way. Because now I can see why God put us together."

"You can?" Clarissa laughed on an incredulous breath.

"You amaze me how you understand these people and their

language so fast. And I was wrong to discourage your painting. You have a gift that is meant to be used. Our skills are opposite, our personalities opposite, yet you are strong where I am weak."

"And you are strong where I am weak," she whispered.

John cupped his other hand over hers. "Like two perfect halves of a whole."

Her heart thudding, Clarissa pushed her fingers through his. "If you want me, I am glad Daniel left me."

"Oh, I want you."

A wave of heat swept over Clarissa's face at the low and swift way he said it, with emphasis she could not mistake.

"At first, 'tis true, I did not want a wife. But any time I thought of you ..." He started laughing. "If the elders had pressed me, I doubt I could have come up with another name. Yours was the first face that came to my mind when they asked." John reached out and ran his thumb over her cheek.

"It was?" Clarissa's breath caught in her throat.

"I thought you were beautiful, inside and out. I was not supposed to notice such things then ... but I can now." John's fingers strayed to her day cap. "May I?"

Clarissa nodded. He loosened the ribbons and placed the cap on the table. Then he twirled a loose curl around his index finger.

"Will you take it down?"

"No," she said, and waited only a beat of silence for his stunned expression before adding, "but you can."

He released a quick breath before drawing her onto his lap and pressing his lips to her jaw. By the light of the fire, he found the first couple of pins and laid them on top of her cap, so careful not to lose a one. He pressed his lips to her throat, where Clarissa's pulse beat swiftly. John nuzzled her ear while stealing another pin.

Turning her head with his thumb, he kissed her temple, her eyes, her nose, while removing the metal pieces holding her locks. By the time they tumbled over her shoulders and his mouth met hers, his hands were shaking, and the pins missed the table entirely.

❦ ❦

An hour or so later, Clarissa lay in her husband's arms. They tangled together, wrapped in the quilt she'd packed, atop a corn shuck mattress that may or may not have had bedbugs. She did not care. Outside, the wind picked up, a finger of sound and unseen motion swirling down the chimney, making the sparks pop.

"God's timing is perfect." The breath from John's words stirred the hair by her ear, tickling her sensitive skin. "To be here alone with you, not in a crowded cabin, and to have all night … and all day … and all night …" His voice trailed off as he kissed her shoulder, provoking a small shudder of anticipation.

"May I remind you, you are here to do a job?" Was that her voice, tantalizing, thick and low with repletion?

"Mmmph." The reply got lost in her collarbone.

She caved her shoulders, parting her skin from his kisses so she could think to answer. "But you are right, I appreciate the privacy."

"'Twas the main reason I waited so long, that and knowing your beauty on the inside first would grant me an even deeper appreciation of the outside. Although, had I known the extent of the outside beauty …"

"And here I wondered for a long time if you found me attractive."

"Truly?" John raised up to look at her in the firelight, then parted her lips gently with his and lingered there as he spoke again. "Do you need further convincing?"

Thank goodness he couldn't see her blush. "I am convinced. Your choir helper instructed you well."

"That was not instruction. 'Twas instinct."

It was her turn to bury her head in his shoulder. "Your instincts are very good." Every inch of her glowed with a satisfied warmth, and she longed to melt into him again, but in this new and vulnerable situation, she still needed the affirmation of his words as much as his touch.

"You helped them along a bit. I'm going to have a hard time thinking of surveying these next couple of days." With a sigh, John flipped onto his back and raised a forearm over his temple. His mannerism revealed more unease than his statement warranted.

Clarissa propped her head up. "Is that a bad thing?"

He studied her, swiping her chin with his thumb in that way he had. "No."

"But …?"

"The church does teach that one's wife should not take first place in one's mind."

"Of course, not above God."

"Clarissa, you don't understand. I was never afraid of loving you too little. I was afraid of loving you too much."

She froze, stunned. Did that mean he loved her? His actions indicated he had begun to—in fact, she had felt so cherished but moments ago that she had almost cried out the words herself—though he hadn't told her so. But … loving her too much? Was that possible?

"Some people struggle with keeping those priorities straight more than others." Now John's voice sounded thick, as if he did not want to continue, but forced himself to. "There's something else I should tell you. Another reason I took extra care to guard my emotions. And yours."

A dreadful fear worked its way up from her suddenly queasy middle. "Was there … someone else?"

"In a sense."

Clarissa sat up, clutching the quilt to her. "Had you proposed to her?" The question sounded like a poor warm-up for a soprano part.

"No. Lie back down. Be easy." John pulled her down until her face was cradled on his shoulder. He stroked her back.

She could hardly breathe, so great was her apprehension. And what was this crazy-headed emotion? Something like … jealousy. This woman did not even have form yet, but Clarissa entertained some very uncharitable thoughts toward her. And the fear ... Was this someone in Salem? Someone she had known?

"Stop thinking." John tapped her forehead. "I can hear you."

"Then start speaking."

He sighed. "Daniel and I were not so different as I like to pretend. At least not in youth."

"In what way?" Had John also led someone a merry dance?

"In entering a misguided 'understanding' with a lady. No one you knew," he said quickly when she drew in a breath to speak. Uncanny, as if he'd read her mind. "Just let me get it out. When I took Daniel to and from school in Nazareth and accepted some jobs in the area, I met a young lady named Sadie Benson from an adjoining community."

"Benson. English?"

"Yes, although her mother was German, raised Lutheran and partial to our faith. The father, however, had different ideas. He was a wealthy merchant and wished Miss Benson to wed a 'normal Protestant' with a healthy purse."

"You can call her Sadie," Clarissa muttered grudgingly, then gave a sniff. "And I cannot fathom how people forget that the founder of our church was burned at the stake a hundred years before Martin Luther came out with his ninety-five theses. And that Luther, in fact, found inspiration in Jan Hus."

John refused to digress into a theological defense. The only acknowledgment he gave her indignation before he went on was a brief kiss on her hand. "*Miss Benson* thought she could find a compromise. She imagined my trade would transition nicely to her community. When I showed no interest in that and she thought to lose me, she began to speak of joining our church." He pressed her hand as if steeling her for the admission that came next. "I found myself thinking about her constantly, picturing a life together. She was ... very winsome. Very persuasive."

"Persuasive in what way?" Clarissa couldn't keep the dread of her imaginings from darkening her tone.

"In evoking promises. In making promises. She was supposed to enter the Single Sisters' House while I was away so that I could request her hand on my next visit. But when I returned ..."

"What?"

"She had capitulated to her father's pressure to marry that 'normal Protestant.'"

"Oh, John." Clarissa's heart sank with the same sensation it had upon reading Daniel's letter.

"So, do you see why I was cautious of leading with emotions? Why I wanted to do things traditionally, slowly, with you?"

"I do. I also see how deeply you wanted to spare me that same feeling of ..."

"Rejection?"

"Yes. I never dreamed 'twas you who was spurned."

"I thought I loved her. It took me a long time to remove her from my mind. I never contemplated marriage until ..."

"Until your circumstances forced you to."

"Aye, but I am so glad they did."

She loved how John used the softer "aye" rather than "yes" when the conversation raised deep emotion. "Now we can put all that aside." She sidled closer. Traced her husband's muscular chest with her finger, still shy. She whispered, "I consider this our wedding night."

"It does feel like a new beginning."

Clarissa raised up to look at him. "This weekend is Advent! We will miss the special service at the mission. I had taught the children to sing 'How Shall I Meet My Saviour.'"

"In truth, I would rather be nowhere but here, with you." John bent his head to kiss her deeply.

From the respect and devotion now established between them, not only could passion find safe expression, but love had a place to grow. That would be much easier alone in this cabin than back at the crowded mission, where something would be sure to challenge their relationship almost as soon as they returned.

Clarissa brushed aside the stirring of unease and returned her husband's caress.

CHAPTER EIGHTEEN

Snowflakes swirling down from gray skies added the perfect holiday inspiration for John's outing with Clarissa, the Kellers, and their students to gather greenery at the Conasauga River. Peter had driven the dray wagon from Springplace, while John rode a stallion towing a pack mule.

As Peter returned to the wagon with his axe in one hand and a small tree in the other, John shook his head. "We had better strap that one to the mule unless you want to leave a child here." He eyed the bed of the vehicle, already burgeoning with holly, mistletoe, and magnolia, as well as trees for every cabin at Springplace. "It looks as if we have enough to decorate even the kitchen."

"And maybe the barn." Peter laughed as he lifted the tree to the back of the mule and waited for John to secure it. "But were you not going to put the cornmeal on the mule?"

"Oh yes." John frowned. He'd completely forgotten about the corn they had left at the local mill that morning to be ground. Shrugging, he continued lashing the small evergreen to the mule's pack. "We'll figure it out. But I do hope the women and children are ready to leave soon, especially with that extra stop."

"You think this precipitation will stick? I don't think it is cold enough yet."

"I had hoped to get in a little more work on the cabin." John grinned at Peter, who play-punched his shoulder.

"Eager to leave us for your new abode, huh?" Peter teased.

"I still cannot believe you already had the foundation laid when we returned from our trip. 'Twas the best surprise."

Peter gave a shrug. "I could tell when you brought it up that you felt impatient to have your own space. I cannot say the plan does not benefit me as well."

When he turned red, John laughed. "I daresay!" He couldn't agree more. They had each enjoyed only one evening alone with their spouses in their shared home since their blissful days at Coker's. The taste of privacy had gone to his head, making him all the less enamored with communal living and thankful for Peter's thoughtfulness.

"We would be much further along had you not insisted on half-dovetail notches." Peter's statement had the tone of a grumble about it.

"I cannot sacrifice quality even for … well …" John left the statement unfinished. "Dovetail notches are built to last. If our cabin is to serve as a schoolroom after we leave, you will be thankful that I stood firm on that."

"One day, perhaps." Though his tone belied his admission.

Above the chatter of the children studying the fauna along the riverbank with Sister Keller, Clarissa called John's name.

Peter raised an eyebrow. "Better see what she needs."

"You do not have to tell me twice." John started off through the trees, but Peter's reminder summoned him back.

"Take your axe."

He groaned. "I have no intention of cutting anything else." But he palmed the tool before following the sound of his wife's voice. He found Clarissa standing near a cedar tree with a thick, partially severed branch hanging overhead.

"John!" She pointed upwards. "Could you get this down? 'Twould be perfect for making the *putz*. I want to surprise the children." Her eyes sparkled at the mention of the Moravian custom of creating a manger scene complete with figures, animals, and natural features, but John found her rosy cheeks and lips much more interesting.

Rather than complying, he swept his free arm around her waist. "Do I have the rare good fortune of finding you alone, Sister Kliest?"

She answered on a soft gasp. "Why, I believe you do."

"Do you think 'twill last long enough to steal a kiss?"

Clarissa trailed her lips over his closely trimmed beard, then whispered in his ear. "Best quit talking and find out."

John dropped the axe and drew her in, exploring her mouth in a thorough kiss that left them both breathless. Each time he held her, it seemed they discovered something new about each other. Why had he waited so long to claim such a sweet and yielding wife?

As usual, the moment was interrupted all too soon. Dawnee called out, "Sister Kliest, Sister Keller says it is time to go!"

John released Clarissa with a grudging sigh as the girl came into view. She wasted no time in marching up and slipping her hand into Clarissa's, looking up at her. "When we get back, we do our work?"

Clarissa bent to her eye level and spoke with excitement. "When we get back, we will decorate the trees. Remember all the popcorn we strung?"

"And after that?"

John wasn't sure if Dawnee did not yet grasp the pleasures of the yuletide, or if she simply wanted Clarissa's undivided attention that much. The way she'd followed his wife since their return revealed how much she'd missed her in their absence. He busied himself with cutting the cedar branch while Clarissa replied.

"We shall see. I doubt we will have time before evening prayers."

The girl's voice turned petulant. "You said our work was most important."

John glanced over his shoulder, Clarissa's gaze unveiling her continued uncertainty about the syllabary. They had talked about it a couple of times since receiving Vann's warning. Despite their shared unease, John had reminded her that recording the language was her personal assignment. If Clarissa desired to be released from it, she would need to write to the elders.

His wife looked back to Dawnee, squeezing her mittened hands.

"'Tis very important, but it will keep until after Christmas. We will be very busy for a while." In fact, they already had been. The extra demands of the season, in and out of the classroom, meant they wouldn't be moving into their own place until after the holiday.

"Then ..." Dawnee paused, clearly searching for a consolation prize. "I sit beside you in the wagon?"

"Of course!" Casting John a smile over her shoulder, Clarissa went off through the woods, swinging Dawnee's hand.

John followed, dragging the branch and giving himself a lecture on how much Jesus loved the little children.

After picking up the corn at the mill, they continued south, the bright voices of the children learning the hymn, "Today We Celebrate the Birth," carrying back to him from the wagon.

John reined his horse in with surprise at Springplace. A Cherokee of shorter stature than most but regal bearing with bright red feathers in his cap and silver bangles at his wrists, along with another stern-looking Indian, filed onto the porch next to the Steiners to welcome them back.

Tom A-ca-ru-ca stood up in the wagon so suddenly, Clarissa had to brace him to prevent him from falling over. "*E-do-da!*"

Tom's father, Chuleoa? One of the Indians who had so bitterly opposed the mission in its early days? John had never met the chief, but he knew Chuleoa and one named Sour Mush had written a letter in 1803 complaining that the missionaries had not made adequate progress at the school. They wanted more children fed, clothed, boarded, and taught, and in rapid succession. Only some skillful negotiating had saved Springplace. No one had been more surprised than the Steiners when Chuleoa had delivered his own son into their keeping some time later. Eventually, they had learned that Chuleoa had received the misguided impression that the missionaries had been too proud to have the Indians live with them.

Now, the man puffed a clay pipe and glared at the bounty of greenery in the wagon. His expression told John that he had yet to be fully convinced of the worthiness of their cause.

The Steiners introduced Chuleoa and Sour Mush. Chuleoa had come on business to Vann, who would soon leave to attend yet another treaty negotiation, this one in Washington. John shook hands with both men, getting a strong whiff of something alcoholic from Sour Mush. Probably *ah-me-ge-i*, hominy coarsely beaten, boiled in water, and partially fermented.

"The chiefs will stay with us for a few days," Sister Steiner told them.

"Welcome. You are welcome." John spoke with enthusiasm, although he couldn't help wondering whose cabin they would occupy. They nodded in return. "Brother Steiner, could you give us a hand unloading?"

As Peter directed the greenery to be placed against the porch, the boys pitched in to help. Sour Mush tottered to the step and raised a brown jug to his lips, while Chuleoa waved a hand at their efforts and asked a question in Cherokee. Tom answered in the same language.

"What does he say?" Rosina looked up from arranging her holly cuttings in a pile.

Sam Hicks laughed. "He wants to know why we take the trees out of the forest."

"That is a good question." Lowering his coffee mug, Brother Steiner nodded at the stoic chief. "Tell him we will explain over dinner. We will tell him the story of how God's Son came to earth as a human baby—which we celebrate this time of year—died for us on a tree and rose from the dead."

Chuleoa's brows lowered as he listened to Sam's stumbling translation. He waved a hand as if to erase what had been spoken.

After he answered, Sam shrugged. "He says he has no ears for all that."

John shot Clarissa a wry glance, lowering his voice for her ears only. "Exactly what he said before when he protested the mission."

"And he is hungry," Sam added.

Sister Steiner remained unfazed. An unflappable smile transformed her homely features. "Well, come in, everyone." She gestured them into the cabin. "I will pour the coffee if the sisters will fetch our stew and biscuits from the kitchen."

Later, as the women cleaned up after dinner, the chiefs seemed to be in a better mood. Chuleoa drew Tommy aside for an accounting of his health and his schooling, and when he pulled out his pipe again, seemingly satisfied by his son's enthusiastic report, Sister Steiner suggested he might enjoy hearing the children sing their evening prayers. She did not mention Sour Mush, who'd stretched out next to the fire and begun to snore.

Watching Chuleoa's face soften as the children sang, Clarissa murmured to John, "I think it might please him if I offered to make his sketch. That would give Brother Steiner another chance to talk with him."

John nodded. "He might be willing after this. Shall I fetch your sketchbook?"

She blinked in surprise before a flush stole across her cheeks. His offer of service pleased her, which pleased *him* much more than he had anticipated. Wouldn't she really be surprised when he gave her the Christmas present he'd added to the list Vann sent a servant to Knoxville for? He couldn't wait.

"Yes, thank you. And my charcoal. Sister Steiner has promised the children can decorate before bed—only this cabin. I will help get them started."

When John returned, earning a teasing guffaw from Peter for his trouble, Clarissa and Dawnee were arranging holly in a pewter bowl on the table. Clarissa looked up with a bright smile. "The chief has agreed. I will sketch him from right here."

Next to the fireplace, Chuleoa grunted. He drew himself up and, bracelets jangling, posed with his pipe before Clarissa could even get her sketch pad open. Brother Steiner tugged a chair nearby and opened his German Bible on his lap.

"He's the perfect subject. I can't wait to see how the drawing turns out." John started to lower himself onto the bench next to Clarissa, but Dawnee slid in beside her first. He said a quick prayer to squelch the flicker of annoyance with the girl. She was the reason they were here, after all. Clearing his throat, he stood behind his wife and watched her begin the first strokes. Her hands moved fast, drawing something from nothing.

Apparently equally enthralled, Dawnee laid her cheek against Clarissa's shoulder as she was wont to do.

"My *liebling*, I must use that arm," Clarissa said gently.

Lips drooping, the girl raised her head. When Sour Mush let out an especially loud snore from the ramrod-straight Chuleoa's feet, Dawnee released a quiet breath. "Please, I stay with you tonight?"

When Clarissa hesitated, John cleared his throat again. Sister Steiner picked up on the interchange from across the room. "You are all settled in our loft now, Dawnee. I would hate to lose you."

Dawnee's shoulders slumped. "I no move up there. Things crowding."

Charlie looked up from stringing the tree with a popcorn garland. He held the tail while Rosina held the head. "Come help, Dawnee." He offered her his job. "Here."

Reluctantly the girl acquiesced. He stood close to her and murmured encouragement and direction in Cherokee until she joined in.

Tucking tidbits of holly with bright red berries on the branches, Sam paused. A smile lit his face as he said to Rosina, "I can tell Chief Chuleoa what you told us about evergreen trees. How they remind us of eternal life from Jesus. That will help him understand why we have them in the house."

Sister Steiner gasped. "Why, Sam, 'tis a wonderful idea."

"Yes, it is." Closing his Bible, Brother Steiner gave up his seat by Chuleoa. He approached John and Clarissa with a wink. "Now the little child shall lead them."

Pride shone on Brother Steiner's face as Sam slid onto the chair and started talking fast in Cherokee, using many hand gestures.

When the startled chief swiveled to protest, Clarissa shooed him back into position and reminded him to be still.

"I need more time," she said, even though John could see the sketch was almost complete.

Sister Steiner smiled at them. She leaned down to refill their coffee and whisper, with a wink added in for emphasis. "Words may be our most powerful tool for pushing back the darkness, but sometimes they need the help of a picture."

With a chuckle, John joined his wife on the bench. He gave her shoulders a brief, encouraging squeeze to show that he supported the matron's statement. That earned him a glance of sweet gratitude from Clarissa.

But not everyone was happy. Dawnee caught sight of John leaning close to Clarissa. Her look of admiration for Sam faded into one of dejection, while over the girl's shoulder, Charlie watched her wistfully. 'Twas an awful lot of meaningful staring going on.

❧ ❧

A few nights later, after the contented chiefs departed with promises to return soon for another visit, a crowd again gathered in the Steiners' cabin for the Christmas Eve love feast. Greenery and flowers scented the air, while *fraktur* Scripture writings decorated with colorful embellishments reminded those present of the season. The cheerful pictures of wreaths, hearts, and verses were the gifts of the women to the students and Peggy Vann, who sat with the children from the big house.

Clarissa and the women had spent the night before and the morning in the kitchen, while John had devoted the holy day to prayer rather than roofing the new cabin. He and Brother Steiner had sensed a heaviness this Christmas Eve that he could not explain. Now, as drumming and yelling came from the slave quarters, he began to understand why.

"I am sorry," Peggy said in a low voice when the questioning eyes of the missionaries turned to her. "They do this when ... rest from work?"

John suggested the word she might be searching for. "Holiday?"

"Yes. Holiday."

"Did you tell them they were invited to our service?" After adding another log to the fire, Sister Steiner joined their circle, her prayer book in hand.

Peggy nodded. She glanced at the few faithful servants she had brought with her, who also nodded.

Lips pursed, Rosina jostled Michael on her knee. "It doesn't surprise me. The slaves can't seem to resist those wild orgies. Pleasant went off and left her poor child squalling in his basket in her room off the kitchen. That is why I have him tonight."

That might be so, but Clarissa had told John that Rosina often sent the woman off on chores that left Michael in Rosina's care. He'd responded that hopefully Sister Keller would have her own babe to dote on soon.

"I'll do my best to keep him quiet." Sister Keller pressed a nib of sugarcane to the baby's lips before leaning forward to address Peggy. "We also invited your husband's mother, Wahli. She could not come?"

"She attend big dance at John Rogers' house. Lots people go. Much drinking, eating."

"Oh, that is disappointing. We had hoped she might come here." With a weighted brow, Sister Steiner wrapped her shawl about her shoulders and settled onto the bench next to her husband, forcing John and Clarissa even closer. A fact which he minded not at all. The popping fire warmed his toes, while his wife warmed his side, producing distracting thoughts of holding her later. John had forced his attention back to their meeting when Sister Steiner spoke again. "What of your sister-in-law, Nancy?"

Chief Vann was not happy about Nancy's recent marriage to John Falling, a man he suspected of involvement in the robbery and attempt on his life, so John doubted Nancy had attended a party where her brother was likely to show up.

Peggy lifted a shoulder. "Slaves maybe drum at her house too. Maybe she fear to leave."

"We will go check on her tomorrow. I cannot believe not a single one of the slaves wanted to come, besides you dear house servants." Sister Steiner pursed her lips. "We have spoken with so many in person."

When the slaves lowered their eyes, and the silence stretched to uncomfortable limits, Peggy hesitated, glancing at Rosina holding Michael, then offered a halting explanation. "Your woman, Pleasant … she tell them not to come. Said … your faith not real."

Sister Steiner's hand fluttered to her bosom. "Oh—no."

Rosina gave a murmur of disapproval.

John held his breath as Clarissa swept a glance his way. Pleasant's opinion of the missionaries' hypocrisy was bearing fruit, no doubt taking even the Steiners by surprise, but Clarissa had as good as predicted it.

"Well, 'twould explain why fewer and fewer have come to our services." Brother Steiner shook his head with regret.

When Sally fidgeted at Peggy's feet, Peggy placed a calming hand on her shoulder but kept her dark eyes fixed on Brother Steiner. "They worship ancestors."

"All worship goes to one of only two places." Brother Steiner's reply held the ring of authority. "God or his fallen servant, Satan. Let us begin our remembrance of Christ's birth now, despite what else may be happening on the property."

As Brother Steiner read from the second chapter of the Gospel of Luke, John studied the children. They sat close together, faces downcast. Their earlier excitement about reciting verses and receiving their lit, red wax candles faded as the pounding of the drums vibrated the floor. An occasional shriek curdled above Brother Steiner's deep voice.

Sister Steiner bid the students rise when her husband concluded the story of Jesus' birth. "The children have learned a stanza of 'Morning Star' in German."

As they opened their mouths to sing, a gunshot rang out, far too close to the mission. The women jumped, and the children whimpered.

Were the slaves armed?

John rose. Clarissa reached toward him, no doubt fearing he would go for his own rifle and seek out the origin of the disturbance. But he had a better idea. Without asking, without explaining, he began to sing in German, startling all present with the words of Martin Luther's famous hymn. "*Ein feste Burg ist unser Gott, ein gute Wehr und Waffen.*"

After the first verse, he sang the English translation. Gradually, his fellow workers from Salem joined him, standing one by one, until their voices overflowed the small cabin with power and majesty.

A mighty fortress is our God,
A bulwark never failing:
Our helper He, amid the flood
Of mortal ills prevailing.
For still our ancient foe
Doth seek to work his woe;
His craft and power are great,
And armed with cruel hate,
On earth is not his equal.

Did we in our own strength confide,
Our striving would be losing;
Were not the right Man on our side,
The Man of God's own choosing.
Dost ask who that may be?
Christ Jesus, it is he;
Lord Sabaoth is his name,
From age to age the same,
And He must win the battle.

And though this world, with devils filled,
Should threaten to undo us,
We will not fear, for God hath willed
His truth to triumph through us.
The Prince of Darkness grim,—
We tremble not for him;
His rage we can endure,
For lo! His doom is sure,—
One little word shall fell him.

When they finished, everyone in the room stood in awed silence. A holy hush and a strong presence filled the room. The drumming had lost its power. It continued in the background, sounding hollow. Not even an annoyance.

John sat. Clarissa touched his arm again, getting his attention. She gave a single nod, but the admiration shining in her eyes warmed his heart. There was the look he'd craved from her, and he hadn't had to construct a cabin or start a fire to earn it. At least, not a physical fire.

"Thank you, Brother Kliest. 'Twas just what we needed. Now we will sing 'Morning Star.'" Sister Steiner raised her hands, and the voices of the children mingled in sweet harmony.

Morning Star, O cheering sight!
Ere thou cam'st, how dark earth's night!
Morning Star, O cheering sight!
Ere thou cam'st, how dark earth's night!
Jesus mine, in me shine;
In me shine, Jesus mine;
Fill my heart with light divine.

Clarissa smiled beside him, but something more than the fire created shadows on her face. Her expression had remained troubled since the mention of Pleasant. John reached into the folds of her skirt and squeezed her hand, certain she was thinking of the one person everyone else overlooked. And he loved her for it.

CHAPTER NINETEEN

John's unfaltering voice leading them in "A Mighty Fortress Is Our God" had dispelled the fear of the threat represented by the drumming, but Clarissa's heart ached for those outside their circle of light. Especially Pleasant. The woman acted out of her own pain and loneliness. Would the small gesture Clarissa planned be enough to share the meaning of Christmas with such an angry and unwilling woman?

The beauty of the children's song brought Clarissa back to the moment, her eyes swimming with tears. Their faces glowed as they received their lit candles. Finding Rosina watching her in expectation, she nodded. Time to give the children their presents.

They handed out the painted verses, apples, and sugared nuts and pretzels. While Clarissa tucked an extra painting she had made under her bench to save for later, Peggy Vann admired hers with as much enthusiasm as the young people.

"Thank you. So kind." She flashed them a delighted smile. "Tomorrow, I send gift. Side of beef."

"Oh, Lord bless you." Clarissa threw her hands up before she could think to temper her expression of joy.

Sister Steiner laughed at her enthusiasm and explained to the chief's wife. "Still no sign of the pigs or cows in the woods."

"I understand. Need meat Christmas Day." Peggy gathered her fine wool cloak and beautifully woven Cherokee basket and glanced at Joseph and Sally. "Ready, children?"

John rose. "Let me walk you home, Mrs. Vann."

"Oh, not yet." Her eyes round, Dawnee extended her hand. "We have present too. For teachers."

"What?" Clarissa looked at Rosina, who shrugged.

Dawnee organized the students into a row before the fire. "Isaiah nine, verse six." The others joined in as she continued. "'For unto us a child is born, unto us a son is given: and the government shall be upon his shoulder: and his name shall be called Wonderful, Counsellor, the Mighty God, the Everlasting Father, the Prince of Peace.'" Before the assembly could exclaim over the recitation, the group repeated it in Cherokee.

Clarissa's mouth dropped open. When the children finished, the audience exploded in applause. "However did you manage?"

"We used your book." Sam's white teeth glowed in his tawny face. "You have pictures by the English words you sounded out in Cherokee."

"But, such difficult words!" She clasped her hands under her chin. "I'm quite sure I did not write down words like *counsellor* and *government*!" She glanced at Sister Steiner, who made a face and avoided her gaze. Clarissa cocked her head and grinned. "Someone was very sneaky."

"Really, the children did almost everything," Sister Steiner insisted with a proud smirk. "'Twas Dawnee's idea. She wanted to show you how far they have come with your help."

"Oh, Dawnee." Clarissa gave her a hug.

Arms around her waist, the girl beamed up at her. "Your book made it easy, with the sounds there. We need to take sounds now and—and ..." Her face scrunched in concentration. "Orange-ize."

"Organize?" Sam asked.

"Yes, org-naze. Put letters by Cherokee letters. One day we do lesson in Cherokee! No more confusing English." She flung up an arm, causing everyone to laugh.

"Well, that is the plan, and we can start on it this week." Clarissa beamed, running a hand over Dawnee's slick, dark hair.

Reservations from Vann's warning, the changes in her relationship with John, and her rediscovered pleasure in her art had temporarily diverted her, but tonight—from the spiritual resistance of the local people to the special efforts of the students—

had renewed a sense of calling. She glanced at John, who nodded and smiled. Her heart filled. All the pieces, including her personal involvement at Springplace, were coming together.

Charlie, however, grumbled as he twirled his apple by the stem. "Just more work. Cherokee no need be written."

"You do not have to help, Charlie," Clarissa said, "but I would recommend you stop doing that with the fruit."

She had no sooner gotten the words out than the boy's apple plunked to the ground, bounced, and rolled into the fire. Not just into the ashes, but right into the flames.

"Oh no!" He grabbed the poker but knocked over the whole stand of implements in his haste.

"Never mind." John bent to retrieve the scattered tools. "'Tis a roasted apple now."

Apples they might have aplenty in autumn, but fresh fruit in December was a rarity. Watching Charlie's face crumple, Dawnee held out her apple. "You can have mine."

Sam hastened to step forward. "Take mine instead."

"I don't want yours. I don't need an apple."

"Charlie." A hand going to her waist, Sister Steiner cocked her head and frowned.

Charlie promptly added "thank you," but turned away with his arms crossed.

The boy's recalcitrance brought Vann's similar words about the syllabary back to mind, casting a shadow over the close of the evening. Clarissa walked to the cabin with Peter and Rosina, while John escorted Peggy and the Vann children home. Bright spots from bonfires glowed orange through the trees, the scent of smoke hanging on the crisp air. As they approached the house, the drumming and screaming grew nearer, and Michael's whimpers intensified into full-fledged cries.

"What am I to do with this child if his mother remains over there all night long? I cannot feed him." Rosina's tone tottered on the line between impatience and panic.

Clarissa might have more sympathy if Rosina weren't so selective about when she imparted motherly care, but she didn't relish the thought of a crying baby in their cabin either. Especially when she craved quiet time with John. "Surely, she will return soon. And she will know where to find him." She couldn't keep a twist of irony from the last sentence.

Peter squared his shoulders. "I will go fetch her, or a wet nurse, at the least."

"Wait." Clarissa held up her hand, then pointed. "There, coming from the woods. Who is that?" A dark figure in long skirts broke from the trees. "'Tis Pleasant."

The slave hurried toward them, adjusting her shawl. Rosina's gaze followed the movement. "Doubtless only her own discomfort brings her back to feed the poor child."

Clarissa placed a hand on her arm. "Rosina, you must not assume that."

Shrugging away, Rosina shot her a glare before stepping forward and practically shoving Michael at Pleasant. "About time." She snatched the baby back. "Have you been drinking?"

"No, Sister Keller, I ain't been drinking." Pleasant enunciated each word with emphasis. She kept her eyes down but held her arms out.

"Are you not going to thank me for taking care of your child while you were away, carousing with the slaves you stirred up against us?" Rosina's bitter accusation rang out with the force of a whip.

"Rosina." Now it was Peter who spoke his wife's name, his tone sharp. "Give her the child and come into the cabin."

Rosina did as he instructed, but as he led her inside, she muttered, "'Tisn't fair that those who want children cannot have them, while others who do, do not appreciate their blessings."

"Hush, my dear. 'Twill be our turn soon enough." Peter closed the door behind them.

Clarissa touched the slave woman's arm before she could hurry away. "Merry Christmas, Pleasant." She pulled her painting from beneath her cloak and held it out. "'Tisn't much, but see here in the middle of the holly wreath? 'Tis a mother and baby. You and Michael."

Pleasant took the offering, holding it up in the moonlight. Her lips parted. Clarissa had painted the mother and her child with dark skin.

"You know, Mary felt much as you did. She had not wanted to have a baby. The baby could have cost her everything, but instead, He gave her everything." Clarissa's eyes filled with tears. "The same can happen for you if you soften your heart not only to your sweet son but to a God who loves you very much."

Pleasant stared at the ground. "I hear what you say, Sister Klies'."

"But you don't believe that God loves you?"

"If He do, He have a strange way of showin' it." When Michael fussed and rooted at her chest, Pleasant drew back, shifting his weight.

"We cannot blame God for the evil men do."

"Can't we? I got to go."

"I know. Just one more thing." She spoke rapidly, her words forming an entreating plume on the frigid air. "Your child is yours, not Sister Keller's. If you want her to leave him alone, you must speak up."

"You doan think I've tried?" Pleasant shook her turbaned head. "Naw, Sister Klies', Sister Keller get what she want."

"Except for a baby of her own." Clarissa offered a small smile. "I will help you, next time I see you need it. All right?"

Pleasant's lips firmed. Not exactly a return smile, but an acknowledgment. She didn't thank Clarissa, either, but she nodded before she hastened toward her room adjoining the kitchen.

Inside her own cabin, Clarissa extended her hands to the fire that Peter stoked.

He sent her an apologetic glance and spoke in a low tone.

"Please be patient with my wife, Sister Kliest. I fear her desire to be a mother makes her lose sound reason at times."

A sniffling issued from the Kellers' side of the drawn partition. Rosina was crying? Clarissa's heart softened. If Rosina and Pleasant would look past themselves to the pain of the other, they might find common ground—if only they weren't so stubborn.

"Of course." As much as her feet felt like chunks of ice, she should give the Kellers some space. Making her way to her side of the cabin, Clarissa called out, "Good night, Rosina. Merry Christmas."

The blowing of a nose preceded a shaky but warm reply. "Yes. Overall, it has been a merry Christmas. Good night, Clarissa."

She undressed down to her shift and plunged under the quilt, shivering in deep bone shudders while she waited for the sounds of John's return. After his brisk walk up and down the hill, he would no doubt be colder than she was. But together, maybe they could generate a bit of heat. And maybe if they were very quiet …

Clarissa blushed at the direction of her thoughts. She'd found his singing very appealing indeed tonight. Who knew he possessed such a fine baritone?

A few minutes later, her husband appeared, carrying one of the beeswax tapers from the service. It provided much better light than the fat knots they normally used, showing her a look of mischief on his face as he hung up his hat. Maybe his thoughts ran parallel to hers.

"Hurry and join me," she said around chattering teeth.

"First I have something for you." John placed the candle on the bedside table and went to his trunk. When he sat beside her, fully clothed, he held a brown, paper-wrapped parcel.

Clarissa's stomach sank. "Is that a store-bought gift? I have something for you, but …" 'Twas only a homemade scarf and a silk-on-linen sampler with their names and wedding date.

John misunderstood her reticence. "I don't want you to get up. Mine will keep for tomorrow. But I cannot wait another moment to give you this." He nudged the gift toward her. "Open it, or I won't be able to sleep."

"Very well." Catching her lip between her teeth and attempting to keep the quilt about her shoulders, Clarissa shifted to take the parcel. She unwrapped it to find a walnut box. She pretended astonished pleasure, making her statement in a stunned voice. "You have gifted me with a matching circumferentor."

"No, silly." He undid the brass clasp and flipped the lid up to reveal not two, but three rows of beautiful watercolors.

"Oh, John! Where did you get this?" She scooted toward the candle to get better light.

"Vann had it picked up in Knoxville. It came by way of Boston, I believe."

"All the way from Knoxville! So many shades. I won't know where to start."

"By mixing less to get the color you want?"

"Oh, my love!" Clarissa reached for his jaw to kiss him, then realized what she'd said. Indeed, was she falling in love with her husband? A wave of heat swept her head to toe as John kissed her. The warm pressure of his mouth promised he would be even less content to end on the gesture than she would. In fact, Clarissa trembled as if the very bed shook beneath them.

Yet … the bed *was* shaking. John pulled back with a cry in time to catch the candle perched on the edge of the table. Something on the mantel had no one to catch it and fell with a loud crash. Rosina screeched.

"Another tremor!" Peter called.

Studying Clarissa's face in the shadows, John whispered a joke. "Now, *that* was a kiss!"

She laughed but fell silent when she realized the drumming had ceased. "It would seem God had something to say tonight."

❧ ❧

Two days later, the continuing frigid weather meant the logs of the new cabin remained too cold to hold any chinking. After John finished the math lesson for the students in the children's cabin, Clarissa encouraged him to construct a table for their future home. His restless energy distracted her. Thankfully, Rosina departed to help Sister Steiner in the kitchen.

Clarissa should assist as well. The earthquake had produced another stream of Cherokee visitors anxious to discuss the meaning behind the event—even more so when the water in the springs had turned dark. The guests would be eager for dinner and explanations. But when the Vanns headed home and Charlie and Tom continued with their advanced math assignment, she seized the opportunity to share her ideas with Sam and Dawnee.

Calling them to the side of the classroom, she opened her notebook on the table in front of them. "I need your help making certain I have all the sounds from your language in this list. You see I have put the like sounds together. *Tsa, tse, tsi, tso, tsu, tsv.* And here, *qua, que, qui, quo, quv.*"

Dawnee pointed a slender finger to the column. "You forgot *quu.*"

Clarissa blinked. "So I did! Although I am not certain I am right to use two *u*'s."

"But the sound is long." Sam rubbed his chin as he leaned over the text.

When Charlie looked up from his math lesson and noticed Sam's head right next to Dawnee's, the frown on his face deepened.

Clarissa gestured for him to return to his work. She murmured to her two pupils in a low voice, "You are right. All right, then, two u's it is." She reached for her quill and, bending, attempted to insert the new phonetic, knitting her brows when the addition made her page crowded. "I will leave this list with you for a day or so. You can use my index of words and try to think if I have missed other syllables. 'Tis important we be thorough."

"And after?" Sam's face brightened. "We will begin to make alphabet?"

"Yes." She shared his eagerness, and not because she wanted to leave Springplace. Because she wanted these people to be able to read and write in their own language. The realization made her slightly dizzy, so she sat next to the children.

"Will we use English letters or German?" Sam asked.

"Maybe both."

"What about if we make our own? New letters?"

Dawnee answered in a breathless tone, gazing at Clarissa. "I had dream last night. I see letters, like your big *Q*, but with the—the—"

Sam looked where she was pointing on the page. "The tail?"

"Yes! Tail in different places."

What to make of such a dream? Clarissa, too, was breathless with wonder. They were truly embarking on an undiscovered territory. She finally understood the awe with which John approached wilderness adventures.

She sat forward. "We could use such a symbol for like phonetics, such as these series." The frowns of the children begged further information, but before she could explain, a movement caught her eye.

A strange Indian stood in the door, a colorful turban covering the top of his long, dark hair. He wore wool and buckskin and carried a rifle. The young man's face portrayed disdain for the labors of their schoolroom ... or maybe for the people themselves. Something about that look caused Clarissa to close her book and stand. She stepped to put herself slightly in front of her charges.

"*Si-yu*. Can I help you?"

The Indian's gaze flicked over her, landing on Charlie.

The boy drew in a quick breath. "Iskittihi!"

The man returned no sign of recognition, however, moving past Clarissa and flipping open her language book with one finger. He scowled at the writing there. How much of their discussion had he overheard?

"*U-yo-i*." No good.

Swallowing down a healthy dose of fear, Clarissa closed the cover slowly but firmly, forcing him to withdraw his hand. He glared at her as another Indian entered the cabin. Clarissa's heartbeat quickened. What would she do if these Indians meant harm? She had no weapon, and it would take precious minutes for Peter and John to run from the building site.

Then a woman followed them into the cabin. Charlie jumped up and ran to her. "Kina!" He placed an arm about her waist and turned to Clarissa. "*E-tsi,* Kina." He pointed to the others with what appeared to be pride. "Iskittihi. *Sa-quo u-gi-da-li,* One Feather."

Clarissa frowned but spoke as gently as possible. "I thought your mother was Elisabeth Hughes, Charlie."

He nodded. "Yes. *A-tsi-ye-hi* of Whitetree, my father."

Another wife of Whitetree. And possibly another relative of Doublehead. Forcing herself to draw a slow breath, Clarissa stepped forward to extend a hand to Kina. The woman stared at her hand. Finally, Clarissa dropped it and turned to Charlie.

"Are they traveling through?"

Charlie asked his visitors some questions in Cherokee. After they answered, he turned back to her. "They say Father sent them to check on me. He wants to know my progress. That I am well."

A nervous flutter caused Clarissa to press her hand to her stomach. She wanted to ask why Charlie's parents had not come themselves but knew such an inquiry would offend the stoic trio. "So they will be staying a while?"

"A few days, yes."

"Very well. Children, let us pack up our lessons." Clarissa clapped her hands together, but the gesture produced almost no sound. Wiping her damp palms on her skirts, she managed a smile at Kina. "*Hi-ga?* Would you like to eat?"

The woman gave a brief nod, and the men filed back out the door.

When Clarissa led the group into the Steiners' cabin, Sister Steiner looked up from setting the table with an expression of surprise that quickly faded to resignation, which was then covered with a smile of welcome. Several unknown visitors already stood in front of the fire. Iskittihi pushed in between them, lowering his weapon to lean against the wall. Warming his hands, he studied the picture of Jesus on the cross above the mantel before giving a grunt of disgust.

Sister Steiner murmured to Clarissa as they fetched more tin plates and mugs from the cupboard. "That one seems like a tough character."

In a whisper, Clarissa related the briefest possible summary of the scene in the schoolroom and the unease it had provoked. "I feel as if I should go back there and hide my work on the syllabary."

Sister Steiner glanced over her shoulder. Iskittihi reached for one of their Christmas apples and loudly crunched into it, surveying their yuletide decorations with a narrowed gaze. "I would say, 'twould be wise to do as the Spirit gives guidance."

CHAPTER TWENTY

John stole Charlie from a loud game of Chung-ke after lunch almost a week later. He'd had it with Iskittihi and One Feather monopolizing the boys. Every afternoon, they disappeared for hours on end, returning with no evidence of having hunted or done anything useful. Today they had selected a hill near the mission to roll the concave, five-inch Chung-ke disk down the incline while throwing sticks at it. Knocking the stone over constituted an automatic win; otherwise, the owner of the closest stick triumphed. The boys whooped and hollered as if they were playing stickball—or going off to war. Their commotion had attracted the participation of several adult idlers. They had even drawn in Dawnee. John suspected the game offered an opportunity for Charlie to impress the young lady.

Dawnee looked no happier at being commandeered by Clarissa to join her and Sam in the schoolroom than Charlie did when John pulled him and Tom aside to work on the cabin.

The boys stared at John's moistened mixture of clay, ash, and horsehair with disheartened expressions.

"Why we have do this?" Charlie asked as John placed a trowel in his hand.

"Because I have been waiting for weeks for the weather to warm up enough to chink this cabin."

Peter popped around the corner of the building. "And he needs all the help he can get. So no complaining. Earn your room and board."

"Yes, sir." Tom sighed.

Charlie elbowed him. "At least we not work on stupid word book."

John stifled a wave of irritation. "What was that?"

"Nothing." Charlie knelt and began to apply the chinking mixture with a *schlepping*-scraping sound.

The remark about Clarissa's assignment stuck with him. Working beside Charlie, he attempted a lighthearted tone. "Do your relatives not want you to work on it? The syllabary?"

A protruding lower lip signaled Charlie's reluctance to reply. At last he said, "Father family not want me in school. Here for mother family."

Misgiving curdled John's insides. He'd suspected that the mission of Kina, Iskittihi, and One Feather had been to find some fault with their teaching methods. Had they found it in the syllabary? If so, and if Iskittihi stirred discontent among the Lower Cherokees to the southwest, Springplace stood to lose more than one difficult boy's attendance.

Clarissa had told him she'd put her work away over the last week. This afternoon, she had thought the game provided enough distraction that she could encourage Dawnee to work with her and Sam, but would Iskittihi grow suspicious, especially with the boys gone? Maybe John should have left them in the game.

Then he looked upward at all the rows to be chinked and thought otherwise.

They worked until the light waned and Clarissa called them to wash up for supper. Tom gave a cry of pleasure, while Charlie flung his goopy trowel on the ground and started to dash away.

"Uh-uh!" John called him back, pointing to the tool and then the nearby bucket of water. "Charlie, remember our memory verse: 'Whatsoever ye do, do it heartily, as to the Lord, and not unto men.'"

The boy balled his fists at his sides. "No one ask me. I do not want to do for God *or* men!"

"Life is not about what we want to do. 'Tis about what God wants us to do. And what God wants for you is to learn His ways, which you are doing here. Now, wash the trowel if you want your dinner." Aware of Clarissa's concerned gaze, John hardened his jaw, unwilling to give the rebellious child an inch.

Charlie stared him down a minute before slacking his shoulders and hurrying over to do as John instructed. His movements were quick, distinct. Tom waited in silence until his classmate completed his task.

When they looked at him, John jerked his head toward the Steiners' place. "You can go."

As the boys ran off, he let out a deep breath and shook his head. Clarissa drew near, placing her hands on his forearms and looking up into his eyes. "Difficult day?"

"They did not work willingly."

Her face, rosy in the cold, creased with sadness. "Neither did Dawnee. 'Twas so strange, John. But days ago, she could not wait to help me. Now she seems to only want to spend time with Charlie."

"The boy plays to her loneliness."

"And any progress on his character that had come through seeking her approval has dissolved with the visit of these friends from the west."

"They are a bad influence. Any sign they might be leaving?"

The guests' constant presence, along with that of any other traveling Indian seeking refuge from the cold or answers about the earthquakes, had forced the residents of Springplace to gather in drafty corners of their own cabins while they gave up their fireplaces. He did not think he could abide another night of strangers slumbering on their floor.

Clarissa shook her head. "But at least there were a good many there to witness our New Year's service. Perhaps it will leave a lasting impression on someone. We don't always know who."

That reminded John of something. He tugged her hands. "Come with me a minute."

"Where?"

"You will see." He led her away from the yard, toward the spring. Thankfully, no one was there.

The poplar he'd marked as a witness tree now stood bare, but when Clarissa saw it, she gave a cry of pleasure and rushed forward. John followed, smiling. He could give her little enough—physical, emotional, or material—with so many others and such important work vying for their attention daily. He'd hoped this would be one small, lasting sign of their growing affection.

With her finger, Clarissa traced the heart he'd carved, encircling their initials and the date, January 1, 1806. She gazed back at him with wonder. "You put us on the witness tree."

John grinned. "I wanted to leave a mark that we were here. Long after we are gone, it will remain." His words caused an instant glazing of her expression. "What is it? No secrets, remember?"

"I know you wrote a letter to the elders reporting the conditions in Oothcaloga. Do you think we will be sent there soon?"

"I don't." He reached for her hands again and looked into her eyes. "I wanted to mark a turning point for us. This is *our* witness tree. In the place where I began to court you."

"Oh, John." Clarissa wrapped her arms around his waist and laid her cheek against his chest. "'Twas so thoughtful. Thank you."

He wanted to say more. He *felt* more. But their connection remained so tentative—the stirrings of admiration as they watched their spouse interact with others, subtle smiles, a brush of hands in passing. The crowded conditions at the mission limited true intimacy. John felt lucky to hold Clarissa as they whispered a brief conversation in bed at night. His impatience for much more grew daily. But hopefully soon, having their own cabin would change all that. At least then, when guests arrived, they could take turns hosting with both the Steiners and the Kellers.

John rubbed her back, her wool pelisse rough against his fingers. "I am proud of you. Proud of the work you are doing."

Clarissa lifted her chin. Her bright smile infected him with hope for the future. "That means so much."

John lowered his head. "There is much more I would say if we could ever be alone." He growled the last with frustrated affection.

Then he lightened the mood with a wink. "Perhaps you should start checking the tree."

"Checking the tree?" Clarissa's brow winged upward. A teasing dimple appeared on her cheek.

He jerked his chin in that direction. "There's a notch in the far limb. You might find it bears future messages." Her mouth rounded, and she tried to pull away, but John caught her and brought her back. "I said *future*. I am here in this moment, and I would very much like your attention before Sister Steiner calls us in like naughty schoolchildren."

"Well, you have it." Clarissa ran a hand down his arm, still smiling in that fetching manner. "Say away."

For the next few minutes, there weren't any words at all.

❦ ❧

John reassembled their bed in the new cabin. The scent of freshly hewn logs, herbs, and the tang of the oak fire on the hearth teased his nose. Using the wooden key to tighten the rope in the final opening, he stood to stretch and survey the space.

Clarissa had been delighted with the table and benches he'd made. Sister Steiner had spared a hutch from the kitchen. Both John's and Clarissa's clothes presses sat against the wall, near John's surveying equipment. His rifle hung over the mantel, beneath the wedding sampler Clarissa had made for Christmas. 'Twas beginning to look like home. How was it that John now preferred being here with Clarissa to exploring some distant land?

The chatter of voices preceded his wife, Rosina, and Dawnee. The women entered bearing the mattress and quilt, while Dawnee carried the small bedside table. The girl's appearance surprised John since she'd remained elusive ever since the visit of Iskittihi and company. Finally, the travelers had departed, leaving broken and filthy cooking implements scattered about the kitchen and rumpled blankets in front of the hearths.

Rosina helped his wife position the mattress on the rope bed, then looked around. "Oh, 'tis so homey, I feel quite jealous!"

"'Tis the same size and style as yours." Clarissa giggled as she spread the quilt.

"Well, I suppose so." Rosina put her hands on her hips and pursed her lips. "But yours is new."

Both women laughed, and Clarissa said, "Yours will feel so much more open with the partitions gone."

John smiled. The move already seemed to be improving his wife's relationship with Rosina, which would, in turn, remove any strain between him and Peter.

While they talked, Dawnee scrambled up the ladder to the loft. Her voice drifted down, high-pitched with excitement. "Open up here too! Big! Not full of things like the Steiners'."

"Not yet." John had plenty of equipment he'd like to move from the barn, but that was work for another day.

Dawnee's head appeared over the edge, braids swinging. "No fill it up. Leave room, and I stay here!"

Oh no. John clamped down on his tongue to keep from belting out a protest.

Meanwhile, Clarissa's face twisted in an immediate struggle. "Dawnee ..."

Rosina tried to relieve them of the responsibility of hurting the girl's feelings. "The Kliests need their privacy, Dawnee."

"Privacy?" Climbing down, the girl paused on the ladder, cocking her head.

"Uh ..." Rosina held her hands out, empty, as she searched for the right words. "Time alone."

"Steiners don't need time alone?"

John cringed, glancing at Clarissa, then away. One of these women needed to have a talk with this young lady, and fairly soon, judging from the way the boys followed her around.

"Not as much, no. You know why Brother and Sister Kliest moved here?"

Dawnee braced herself and nodded as her boots contacted the

floor. "To have cabin to work on book."

"And to have a cabin to *live* in. Together. Just the two of them."

Appreciative of Rosina's efforts, John knew he needed to bookend her statement. He stepped forward. "We would love to have you visit us often, Dawnee."

"But not let me stay here? In big, empty up-there?" The girl's moist, dark eyes entreated Clarissa, the person most likely to bend to her plea.

John waited in silence. His wife had to be the one to settle this discussion. He tried not to hold his breath while he prayed she would let the girl down kindly but firmly.

Clarissa twisted her hands together. "I am sorry, Dawnee. Sister Keller is right. Brother Kliest and I need some time alone. But we would love for you to visit, as he ..."

She spoke to the back of Dawnee's dress, then an empty, open door. Clarissa turned and looked at John, holding out her hands as her brow furrowed.

He shook his head. "She must learn she cannot get her way by wheedling."

"She is lonely and misses her mother."

Rosina ran a hand down Clarissa's arm in the manner John wanted to but refrained from in the presence of others. "But you are not her mother."

Clarissa stepped back. "You pluck Michael from his basket to care for him, and Pleasant is right there!"

John winced. So much for the truce between the two women.

Rosina straightened her spine. "I only do so when Pleasant needs to get her work done."

Clarissa pressed her lips together, then responded in a soft but firm voice. "That is not true, Rosina. I have seen you send the woman on chores and grab him up the minute she leaves."

"I do not!" Rosina's face turned red, and she balled her fists in her skirt. When she glanced at John as if seeking support, he took a step back, refusing to meet her eyes. How did he keep getting caught in these feminine squabbles when all he wanted was a quiet home where he could enjoy the company of his new wife?

"Dawnee has no mother here, but Michael—"

"She has all of us, but she prefers you just like Michael prefers me." Rosina's chin wobbled. "Children know when they are loved."

"Michael has a mother." Clarissa raised her voice as she completed her statement, then dropped it to a murmur. "And it doesn't make it right for you to take him away from her, even though you do love him. And even though I know you want your own child."

John touched his wife's arm, whispering her name.

Rosina's mouth fell open, and her eyes glazed over. "How dare you?"

"Rosina, I did not mean to offend you, only to …"

Again, a swish of skirts preceded Clarissa speaking to an open door. Clarissa groaned and dropped her face into her hands. "I was only trying to do the right thing, and I made both of them mad at me."

John pulled her into his arms and rubbed her back. "Sometimes the truth is hard to hear. I am proud of you for speaking up. You did so out of love, though maybe you didn't need to say that about Sister Keller wanting a baby of her own."

Clarissa tipped her chin up, tears standing in her eyes. "I did not mean to rub her nose in her heartache, truly. I just wanted her to finally listen about Michael. How much of Pleasant's rebellion is due to Rosina?"

John nodded. "She heard you."

"Should I go after her?" Two little furrows appeared between her brows.

"No. I think that unwise. Give it time to settle." He dropped a kiss on her forehead as she nodded. "'Tis time for the two of us, eh?" He needed to tell her of his growing feelings, but the moment had to be right. 'Twas not easy for him to speak such things. Maybe tonight.

John lifted her chin again, and with a glance at the open door, bent his head swiftly to hers. His kiss left her flushed and, if he had to guess, decidedly more cheerful.

She looked up at him with a smile. "First, I have a couple of boxes of books and the syllabary I'd like to fetch from the schoolroom. 'Twill free up a good bit of space in there. Will you help me?"

"I will do anything that will get you alone here faster." John winked, running the back of a finger down Clarissa's cheek.

He pulled on a coat to follow her across the clearing, where smoke trailed from the chimney of the children's cabin. His morning arithmetic lesson remained on the slates scattered on the benches, but the room was empty. Clarissa went to sort books on the table under the window.

"Some of these need to stay here. *Word of the Cross*, *Prayers for Every Day*, the dictionary, and the *North American Almanac*. Now, *Something for the Heart*, that is mine." Setting the latter into a half-packed crate, she froze. "John, where is my syllabary?"

He looked around the room. "I don't know. Where did you leave it?"

"I left it right here, on the table."

"You must not have."

"I did! And 'tis gone. Perhaps one of the children took it. Dawnee and Sam did use it to study their Christmas verses. Maybe they are doing so again."

They hastened to rifle through the individual chests of the children's belongings. John even ran a hand under the boys' sleeping pallets, rolled up on the back wall.

Clarissa straightened and pushed her hair off her forehead. "We must also check Dawnee's things in the Steiners' cabin."

"I don't think you will find it there."

"Why not?"

John couldn't bring himself to elaborate, not when two clumps that looked an awful lot like a book binding curled into ashes on top of the fire.

CHAPTER TWENTY-ONE

Clarissa batted back tears, fearing that if they fell, they might freeze on her face the way the water in the wash basin had frozen the night before. Besides, John's breathing had just settled into an even cadence, and she did not want to trouble him. He had done all he could to comfort and encourage her since the syllabary had gone missing the evening prior.

At first, she'd refused to believe someone had destroyed it. She'd insisted they continue their search in the other cabins. They had questioned the children, all of whom protested innocence.

"Sister Kliest's book has helped all of us learn your language better," John had told them with the utmost seriousness when their search yielded no results. "It has helped you learn English better. And, with your help, she was about to begin writing your words down using an alphabet especially for the Cherokees. Is there someone here who thought to put a stop to that?"

"No, sir!" The boys had answered in emphatic unison.

Dawnee had shaken her head but refused to meet John's or Clarissa's eyes.

Remembering, Clarissa sucked in a sniffling breath, and a tear ran down her cheek.

John jostled her shoulder. "Are you crying again?"

"Well ..." She couldn't tell a falsehood. John would see through it, anyway. "I'm trying not to." She fought guilt that her continuing emotion over the syllabary was ruining what should be a time of joy, when they finally settled into their new home.

He drew her tight against his side, but before he could reply, a distant shot rang out.

Clarissa flinched. "What was that?"

"Someone at Vann's. Not near here."

She worried for the people there. "The Steiners said he has been in an ill temper since he returned from Washington."

"I'm sure it does not help that he has the usual houseful of guests. He needed time to unwind from the treaty negotiations." John ran a hand over her hair. "And right now, you also need to try to rest."

"'Tis difficult when things keep happening to make me feel unsafe."

John clutched her close and kissed her forehead. "You are safe. You are here with me." When she nodded, he rubbed her back. "The children have agreed to devote these winter afternoons to helping you reconstruct your book. With all that you have learned and their help, the task will go much faster this time around."

"I know, but I hate fearing that I cannot trust them ... although I still cannot believe 'twas Dawnee who burned it. Not over our refusal for her to live here. 'Tis too petty, John. Unlike her."

"Are you sure? She is very devoted to you. She competes for your attention, even with me." His voice lowered in unveiled displeasure.

"That is just it. I do think she loves me and would not do something she knows would hurt me so badly." Clarissa gasped as a new and frightening possibility dawned on her. She tilted her head up to look at him. "What if it was Iskittihi who burned the book? He could have lingered in the area."

John's mouth twisted to one side. "As much as I want to make you feel better, I can't do so at the expense of common sense. Why burn it? Why not take the evidence back to Doublehead as proof of what we are doing here? And we can't really say some other books might have been in the fire that day, for not only has the syllabary remained missing, but no other books are."

Blinking, she mock-glared at him. "No, you are *not* helping me feel better."

When another gunshot broke the night stillness and she stiffened, he gently massaged her shoulder. "Relax. Anyone intending you harm will have to come through me."

With a sigh, she allowed the curves of her body to sink into his hard muscles. 'Twas true. Their devotion grew daily. Nightly. She had to admit, she rather liked his protectiveness. "Why are you so sure Iskittihi would not burn the syllabary?"

"Because I can picture Doublehead seeking leverage against Vann and his friends. Relations continue to deteriorate between the Upper and Lower towns. More land in Alabama and Tennessee was just sacrificed."

"Did not Vann sign the treaty also?"

"Yes, but I would guess he did so either under great pressure or because he thought the long-term payoff would prove greater than the loss. If he finds out that Doublehead benefited under the table again …"

She squeezed his arm, letting out a soft breath. "There could be trouble."

"Yes. There are many chiefs besides Vann who would want to take action."

"Oh, John! Could we be caught in the middle of a civil war?"

"Surely nothing that serious." But the slight hesitation before John's reply belied his reassurance. He pressed her head down onto his shoulder. "Nothing is going to happen tonight. Try to sleep now."

Horse hooves pounded into the dirt clearing of the mission.

They both bolted upright.

An unfamiliar voice called out. "William Steiner! Come out!"

What trouble brewed now? When John swung his feet to the floor, Clarissa put a hand on his arm. "Please don't go out there. They are calling Brother Steiner, not you."

He gave her a brief, impatient glance as he reached for his pants. "I recognize that voice from my previous time here." He pulled them on and buttoned them. "'Tis Andrew Miller, a white man who was thrown out of Oostanaula for his indecent behavior.

He now lives along the road to Tellico. Wherever he goes, discord follows. I will not leave Brother Steiner to deal with him alone."

As if to verify John's low opinion, the man outside cursed and demanded that Steiner come out, or else he'd beat down the door.

John peeked out between the shutters. "This could be bad. There's a group with him."

While he went to fetch his rifle, Clarissa slipped into her wrapper and moccasins and tiptoed across the frigid boards to take John's place at the window. She could make out five shapes on horseback in the pale moonlight. One of them lay slumped over the bare back of his mount.

Brother Steiner answered from his cabin. Smart man. "What do you want?"

"I have a man here who has been shot. You must take him into your house and lay him in front of the fire!"

Another question came back. "Who shot him?"

"James Vann! Open up and take him in!"

Brother Steiner's head appeared in a crack in his door. "We are all filled up in here." In fact, another party of travelers had claimed the limited space in front of the Steiners' fire just after dinner. Clarissa did not know how Sister Steiner bore the constant inconvenience with patience. She hoped that by the time she reached the woman's age, she might grow into such grace herself. "But we can care for him and offer him privacy in the children's cabin."

Clarissa and John exchanged a glance of wordless communication before John threw the bolt on their own door. She tied the belt on her wrapper, stirred up the fire, and lit another candle. A moment later, John ushered Tom, Sam, and Charlie over the threshold and inside, shivering, blinking, and clutching their blankets like tousled owls. She was not prepared for the middle-aged, weeping woman who trailed behind.

"Oh, my!" Clarissa extended her hand to the distraught newcomer who wore a faded burgundy woolen dress. "I am Sister Kliest. What has happened?"

Grabbing her fingers with her own cold, dry hand, the lady lifted watery, gray eyes. "He has driven us all out."

Recognition hit Clarissa. "Aren't you Mrs. Thompson, the wife of Chief Vann's overseer? I have seen you about, but we have never met."

"Yes. I am the overseer's wife. A position, some would say, affording a small bit of respect. Yet he drove us out like stray cats, and he treated his own wife no better."

Clarissa gasped, pausing as she wrapped a blanket around Mrs. Thompson's coatless form. "Peggy? He drove her away?"

With a bob of her head, Mrs. Thompson clutched the wool around her. "At the point of a loaded gun. He has lost his mind."

"Is she coming here too?"

"She went to Vann's mother's house."

"But that is six miles away, and in the cold and dark!" Clarissa turned entreating eyes on John. "Can you go after her?"

Mrs. Thompson added a discouraging fact. "She left before we did."

"Were the children with her?"

"I do not know. I was hiding in another part of the house, but I heard horse hooves."

"She will be safe on her own mount." John attempted to assure her. "'Tis a good road." Before Clarissa could raise the arguments of ruffians and wild animals, he went on. "Mrs. Thompson will need to stay here with the children while her husband and the other men bed down at the Kellers' and in the children's cabin. Just until we can sort things out."

"That evil man, Miller, is he staying?" Mrs. Thomspon asked.

"I believe he has ridden back to Vann's." John checked the yard one more time.

The woman turned toward the door, throwing off her blanket. "Then we must leave. We cannot stay here. We must go to Wahli's too." When John barred her way, her eyes widened, and her voice grew shrill. "He speaks poison. 'Twas his vile tongue that caused the ruckus at Vann's and led to that poor man being shot, even though he was in a downstairs room minding his own business. Shot him through a hole in the floor, he did!"

"Mrs. Thompson, please. Sit here by the fire and calm yourself." Clarissa turned a chair toward her. "You are frightening the children." She gestured toward the boys, who had lined up in their blankets like a row of caterpillars in cocoons. They were staring at Mrs. Thompson with wide, almond eyes.

"You do not understand! He hates my husband and tried to incite Vann against him. He also hates you and your work here."

Clarissa's mouth went dry. "He ... spoke against us?"

Mrs. Thompson nodded. "He has Vann in his drunken state thinking everything and everyone seeks to take advantage of him. And when we all are gone, he alone will benefit."

John slid the bolt and propped his rifle on the floor. "You will be safe here until morning, Mrs. Thompson. I guarantee it."

Fresh tears filled Clarissa's eyes. Vann needed no one to feed his paranoia. And they hardly needed a further threat to their labors. The comforting traditions of yuletide and the joy of the new cabin faded with yet another reminder that enemies—*the* enemy—still worked on all sides.

❧　❧

Sporadic gunfire continued through the night and into the next morning, robbing everyone of sleep. A mood of short-tempered agitation prevailed. Clarissa and the other missionaries could barely convince the Thompsons to stay long enough to break their fast and discuss their options. Mrs. Thompson begged to depart immediately for Wahli Vann's. Even after Sister Steiner settled her in a chair with a cup of coffee, the woman's nervous fluttering strained Clarissa's already taut nerves. As they partook of biscuits and eggs, however, the men convinced the overseer to accompany Brother Steiner and John to talk things over with James Vann. Peter would stay to conduct the religious instruction of the children, but more importantly, to ensure the safety of the mission.

With the wounded man in the children's cabin, the women decided it best to combine their oversight and instruct the scholars in the Steiners' home.

"We should do something lighter in nature, I think." Rosina curved her finger under her chin, tilting her head. "To lift everyone's spirits."

"Show us how to make the painted verses you gave us for Christmas." Sam threw his hands up in the air.

"Oh yes." Quirking his brow, Tom pointed at him. "With the wreaths and funny swirls around the words."

Clarissa glanced at Dawnee, surprised the idea did not meet with more enthusiasm from her since the girl had often begged to learn the *fraktur* technique. Dawnee's eyes flicked to Charlie, who drew one side of his mouth sideways in derision. When she caught Clarissa watching her, she gave a faint smile, her face drawn. She must have slept little the night before as well.

Most pressing on Clarissa's thoughts, however, were not the children at the mission but those who lived at Diamond Hill. After she and Rosina went to the other cabins to fetch their art supplies, she took a moment to circle by the barn, where the men were saddling horses. In case they needed a quick escape? They normally walked to the plantation.

Clarissa touched John's back to get his attention and leaned close. "Please check on Sally and Joe. We don't know if Peggy took them with her or not."

"She may not have had the opportunity." At Clarissa's look of distress, John hastened to reassure her. "I am sure they would have been quite safe up in the attic."

"With all those gunshots? You heard Mrs. Thompson. The chief shot straight through the floorboards."

Clarissa's comments further agitated Mrs. Thompson, who had followed her husband to the barn to beg him not to go. "Oh, please, let the others go without you. What if Vann shoots you on sight?"

As the overseer tried to reason with his wife, Clarissa angled her back to block out their conversation. "She said even the servants were driven from the house. Who would care for them? We should have gone sooner. They may be alone, frightened. You must bring them—"

"Clarissa." Turning from tightening the girth strap on his horse, John took her hands in his. "You are not helping any more than she is." He cut a sideways glance toward Mrs. Thompson. "God is on our side, and He will go before us. There is no need to fear."

"You are right. I am sorry." Stepping back from her husband, Clarissa filled her lungs with a draught of the cold January air. "I will be praying." And she was glad to see the rifle strapped to his saddle, although she knew John would only use it to defend a life.

His words, spoken with firm confidence, seemed to quiet even Mrs. Thompson. She hushed long enough to watch the men ride off. Was it selfish of Clarissa to wish John's awareness might extend past spiritual confidence to answer her need for words of love? For while he made her feel loved, she still waited to hear it for the first time. Longed to hear it.

Sighing, Clarissa reached over to pat Mrs. Thompson's back about the time a gunshot sounded from Vann's.

"Oh, my heavens! He's shot him, just like I said he would." Only moments had passed. The dust had hardly settled on the trail. But the woman was beside herself. She turned in circles, her palms pressed to her temples. "You must hide me in case Miller or Vann comes for me next."

Clarissa held out her arms to redirect the overseer's wife from fleeing to the back of the barn. "Mrs. Thompson, the men could not have reached the house. They will yet be in the lane."

"Someplace deep, like a potato hole! Have you a potato hole?"

Clarissa spoke over her hysteria. "I am sure the shot was not aimed at them." Otherwise, she might be panicking just as much. She took the woman's hand. "Please, come back to the Steiners' with me now."

"No. No." Mrs. Thompson's eyes fixed on a spot in the back of the stable. "There. I shall hide there. Pull that over me."

When Clarissa hurried into the Steiners' cabin carrying her paints and brushing trash from her skirt a few minutes later, all eyes fixed on her.

Rosina straightened from placing papers in front of each of the children. "Where have you been? And where is Mrs. Thompson?"

Clarissa huffed out a big breath. "She is beneath the pile of Indian corn straw in the barn. She refused to come back with me and says she will remain there until her husband returns for her." She focused on Sister Steiner. "I am sorry, I could not convince her otherwise, so I decided 'twas best to do as she requested."

Hand flying to cover her face, Rosina gave a sudden snort that sounded suspiciously like stifled laughter. The gazes of the students moved from her back to Clarissa, who managed to restrain a smile. 'Twould be such a relief to ease the tense situation with a bit of humor. But they could not teach the children to disrespect a genuinely frightened adult, as Sister Steiner reminded them.

"Poor woman. Brother Keller, will you lead us in a prayer for the safety of our men and Mrs. Thompson's peace of mind?"

The reminder of danger sobered Clarissa immediately.

"Of course." Closing the book of daily recitations they were using to select verses to paint, Peter stood over the table to ask for God's protection. They all concluded with a hearty "Amen."

It seemed to take forever to get through the lesson that day. Even when she helped the children outline their wreaths with black paint, Clarissa struggled to focus. Tom and Sam chattered and applied themselves to their task, while Charlie and Dawnee hung over their papers, closing up like morning glories when struck by the sun's heat.

"What is the matter, you two?" Clarissa finally asked.

Charlie sat back and scuffed his shoe against the leg of the table. "Why do Cherokee boys need to learn to draw?"

Peter knelt next to him. "Because every man should be educated in all areas. Drawing, painting—these are powerful ways to communicate. Sometimes as powerful as words."

Clarissa sent him a thankful glance.

Charlie, however, was not impressed. "Words only have power when spoken. That is how we pass down all we know. Waste of time to write everything."

"I am sad to hear you feel that way." Clarissa turned to the girl beside him. "And you, Dawnee? Do you feel the same?"

"I not feeling good at all."

"Really?" Clarissa placed her paintbrush in a jar of water and crossed to the other side of the table. She pressed her hand to Dawnee's forehead. "Sister Keller, please come check her. I think she is warm."

Biting her lip, Rosina did so. She drew back with a concerned frown. "A bit, perhaps."

Clarissa bent to look into Dawnee's eyes. "Would you like to go upstairs to lie down?"

Dawnee shook her head, her braids sliding across her shoulders. "I finish first. Gift for *e-tsi*."

"Du-a-i will love this," Clarissa agreed with a smile, relieved to see the girl return to her former level of interest. When she heard horse hooves, she straightened and ran to the door. "They have returned!"

"All of them?" Rosina asked.

Clarissa counted the horses and men. "Yes, all of them."

Mindful of the watching children, Rosina turned to her husband. "Brother Keller, will you please fetch Sister Steiner from the kitchen and Mrs. Thompson from the barn?"

They all gathered in the Steiners' cabin a few minutes later, Mrs. Thompson weeping again, this time in relief, and clinging to her husband as tightly as bits of corn husk clung to her woolen dress.

Clarissa embraced John, her hug no less heartfelt for its more circumspect nature. "How are the Vann children?"

"They are fine." He removed his wool overcoat and hung it on a peg by the door. "They passed the night in their attic rooms. The servants have returned and are tending them until Mrs. Vann gets home. Vann always apologizes, and she always comes home."

Clarissa released the breath she seemed to have been holding since the night before. "Praise be. What happened when you arrived?"

"Miller was not there, and Vann had calmed down."

"Although we woke him from sleeping off his stupor." Brother Steiner shook his head. "When he is sober, he knows that Miller is a troublemaker. He promised to not invite him back. He explained that there was another man there last night who insulted him and never needs to return. He started shooting to get this man off his property."

John waved his hat. "He had no idea until we told him that Mr. Rice, the man in the children's cabin, had been shot. He feels badly and will be sending some slaves to help move him into the weaver's cottage this afternoon."

"Thank the Lord." Sister Steiner puffed out a relieved breath. "We can settle the children back in their cabin then."

While everyone else gazed at those same children with tenderness, Mr. Thompson fixed a glaring eye on them, especially on Charlie. "Apparently, Miller gave Vann a bad report that had to do with these boys. When that group of traveling Indians was here last with that Iskittihi, they got into a bag of corn feed. They left a whole sack of it out to ruin in the rain."

Charlie glanced up with round eyes. "Not me!"

Mr. Thompson's eyebrows lifted. "He said one of his men saw you with them."

When Clarissa drew in her breath, John tightened his grip on her hand, urging her to silence. But to her surprise, Dawnee turned toward the boy, her forehead furrowed. "I told you Iskittihi was bad!"

Charlie jumped up and looked around at the disappointed and

accusing faces. "I did not do it! Why you always think it is me?" In anger, he overturned the jar of water in front of him. Then he ran his hand through it, spreading the mess over not only his drawing, but Dawnee's as well.

"Oh no!" Dawnee also leapt up and backed away, brushing dirty water from her skirts. "Shame on you, Charlie Hughes." As Charlie darted for the door, she swayed, and her eyes rolled back in her head.

"Dawnee!" Clarissa barely caught her before her head hit the hearth.

CHAPTER TWENTY-TWO

Had he heard God wrong? Had his own hubris and not the calling of the Almighty summoned him here?

John asked these questions for the first time as he stepped on his shovel and pushed down with all his might. It felt good to do something physical, although he'd far rather be building the church he'd drawn plans for this winter rather than planting apple trees. But with Dawnee lying ill for almost a week now, nothing of consequence moved forward. The children passed the long afternoon hours with handcrafts or endless games of butterbean and marbles, while the women took turns nursing Dawnee in John and Clarissa's cabin. They all remained mystified when, after three days, then five, no spots telling of pox or measles broke out on the Indian girl, yet she remained almost unconscious with a high fever.

After unwrapping the canvas from the bundle of roots, John lowered the tree into the ground. Peter said he should have waited until next week to plant, but John's energy demanded release.

The question rose again ... was he cut out for this? His gift wasn't in theology and evangelism as Brothers Steiner's and Keller's were. John was meant to ride, to explore, to survey, to calculate, to build. None of which he could do while tied to one location.

As the familiar urge to press into uncharted wilderness unfurled within him like a plant breaking out of a seed, he straightened from filling the hole, wiped his brow, and looked to the west. Lots of land to survey there. But he had a wife now, and the church that had trained him expected his allegiance. His best chance to use his gifts lay within its mission work, and that meant Oothcaloga. If Clarissa could finish the syllabary. Right now, that, too, was on hold. Just one more link in a long chain of events that had conspired against them.

John muttered as he started digging again, counting off the remaining obstacles. "Vann. His warning about writing down the language. Pleasant and the slaves. And now Dawnee. What will be—?"

"John?"

He turned toward the voice, hoping to see Clarissa. But Rosina, clad in a mustard-yellow dress, apron, and day cap, stood at the edge of the orchard, waving. "Clarissa needs you."

He jogged toward her, carrying the shovel. "Is there a change in Dawnee?"

She turned toward the cabins, her words as rushed as her steps. "She is awake and agitated. We have tried everything, Brother Kliest." Rosina was nearly breathless from exertion—or worry. "I believe if this were smallpox, we would have seen the signs by now. We treated her with the tea that included catnip, red raspberry leaf, black haw, pennyroyal …"

What was she getting at? "Your point, Sister Keller?" He had little knowledge of herbs, except for those edible or needful for staunching wounds acquired in the wilderness.

She insisted on finishing her list, illustrating her thorough nursing. "And yarrow, which should have sped the disease to the point of producing the blisters of any pox. But nothing. This is beyond our knowledge."

For her to admit that indeed showed desperation, but then … "What do you expect me to do?"

Rosina chewed her lip as they came into the yard. "We were debating sending for her parents."

At last, something useful. "That I can do."

"Sister Kliest wishes to speak with you first."

"Of course."

John opened the door of the cabin to find Clarissa attempting to restrain Dawnee, who thrashed about on her pallet. The girl moaned and tossed her head, resisting Clarissa's ministrations with a damp cloth. His wife glanced up, the frantic expression in her shadowed eyes melting into relief at the sight of him. She had sat with Dawnee most nights, only falling asleep in the wee hours.

"She became restless in the last hour. Her fever is spiking. And look." She pulled aside Dawnee's long, damp hair to reveal a red blister on her temple.

Rosina drew in her breath. She hurried over and pulled up the sleeve of Dawnee's cotton nightdress. "Two more here. This is a pox I have never seen. I will mix a bath of burdock root and goldenseal, but ... I think we must send for her parents."

As Rosina bent over Dawnee, studying her skin further, Clarissa rose to face John. "Can you ride toward Hiwassee?"

"I will leave right away."

Clarissa closed her eyes, and a tear squeezed out. "We cannot lose her. Not after ..." When she swayed, John stepped forward and caught her against him.

"You must pray tonight," he murmured into her hair. "Pray as you never have before."

Her golden curls, escaping from her cap, brushed against John's chin as she nodded.

"Sister ... Kliest?" The raspy summons came not from Rosina, but from Dawnee. John glanced down to see her extending a hand in their direction.

With a soft gasp, Clarissa dropped to her knees again and took it. "Dawnee. I am here."

"This ... my fault."

"No. No, my *liebchen*."

"Yes. I do bad. God send sickness."

Rosina rocked back on her heels and gave them a troubled glance.

Clarissa shook her head, eager to calm the child, but John frowned. They had a word for that in German. *Zuchtkrankheiten*. An illness God gave to teach the error of one's ways.

But he felt the girl was trying to say something more. "What do you mean, Dawnee?"

Dawnee looked back at his wife, and a tear escaped from the corner of her eye. "Burn ... book."

❦ ❧

All John could hope as he rode through the night was that Clarissa could help Dawnee find peace. As he'd packed his haversack and retrieved his long rifle and powder horn, the girl had continued to thrash about and ask for forgiveness that Clarissa gave repeatedly. Yet up to the time that John left, they had been unable to piece together an explanation of why Dawnee had destroyed the syllabary.

When John woke Dawnee's parents from slumber, they readied themselves quickly. The fact that they showed little sign of alarm amazed him. They rode behind him for twenty miles in almost complete silence, not questioning, not blaming, although the light from a partial moon showed tears tracking Du-a-i's face. He found their trust in the missionaries—and in the God they did not yet know—humbling.

But what would happen if Dawnee was not alive by the time they returned? Rosina had said the spots did not look like smallpox. What strange illness gripped the girl, and what was God's purpose in allowing it? How would Little Rock and Du-a-i react if this God took not one, but two, of the daughters they had entrusted to the care of His servants?

The sun splintered across the horizon to their left as they topped the last hill overlooking Vann's plantation. Its pale winter light illuminated a hoary white frost coating the fields and roadside. Thin plumes of smoke drifted from a few chimneys, and a lamp glowed in the kitchen window at Diamond Hill. The horses snorted, weary and sensing the end of their journey near. The riders sat up in the saddles.

John's middle clenched as they rode into the mission. Smoke from his cabin chimney attested to the fact that his wife had conducted another all-night vigil.

The door opened as they dismounted, and Clarissa ran out. She looked around at them, her chest rising and falling rapidly. Tears flowed down her cheeks. She spread her hands, palms up, as if the gesture would invoke elusive words.

Oh God, no. "What is it?"

"She is—she is—" Her mouth moved without further sound as Sister Steiner appeared in the doorway behind her. Then Clarissa broke into loud sobs.

Du-a-i sent up a wail the likes of which John had never heard. But Sister Steiner hurried forward and caught her by the arm.

"No, oh, no, my dear. Your daughter lives." Du-a-i paused long enough to stare at her, clearly as stunned as John at the sister's rapturous exclamation. Sister Steiner's face glowed with blinding joy. "We prayed all night in my cabin, every single one of us, except poor Sister Kliest who was here with your daughter, as she has been without ceasing. Sister Kliest fell asleep. And when she woke …" Now it was Sister Steiner whose words failed.

Clarissa uncovered her face, and a smile broke through. "Her fever is gone. Her skin is clear. She is healed!"

All the air left John's lungs in a single, complete rush of awe and humiliation. Yesterday he had wondered if he had missed his calling. And today he had seen a miracle.

❦ ❧

John sat back from his conversation with Peter and Springplace's latest guest, The Ridge. He'd never felt more alive. Not when he'd scouted this property in the first place. Not when the lot finally gave him approval to return. And not even when Clarissa had agreed to be his bride.

The earth had shaken twice the day after Dawnee's miraculous recovery, but they had not been moved. The occupants of Springplace stood firm in their rejoicing. Now the Cherokees came to them in greater numbers than ever before. Deeply disturbed by the seismic shifts, they brought tales from their communities of massive sinkholes filled with greenish water, of people hiding themselves in cliffs.

Brother and Sister Steiner were drained from talking for two days with two Indians named Uniluchfty and The Trunk. The Steiners had spoken of just about every spiritual topic as their guests listened intently with folded hands. Each time they had gone silent, stealing a sip of coffee or entertaining the unimaginable thought of sneaking off to the necessary, the visitors had demanded that they must share everything, yes, everything they knew about God.

So when The Ridge had shown up with his own questions just as Uniluchfty and The Trunk departed, Brother Steiner had gladly entrusted John's previous acquaintance into his spiritual care. John and Peter had shared how Jesus had willingly died on the cross for the sins of mankind.

Now a furrow settled on The Ridge's broad, tanned forehead as his lips trembled. He looked from John to Peter as if searching for a sign of doubt but finding none. "Oh, how much he must love us!"

Peter lowered his pewter tankard of hot cider. "Yes. He does love us. He loves *you*, Mr. Ridge."

"You do not know what I have done." A cloud of remorse darkened The Ridge's features.

Down John's back, facing away from the fire, a tingle like cold air crept. For a moment, he tried to picture the man younger, a warrior, dressed in buckskin and feathers rather than an English waistcoat and breeches, his now-cropped, gray hair queued, long and dark.

The Ridge had ridden with Doublehead before Cavett's Station when they had violated the Treaty of Holston by attacking two Americans in Kentucky. John knew what had happened after, too, although he'd kept Clarissa from hearing the truth from Goingback that day. Even though The Ridge had been sickened by the act of roasting and eating those men and had afterward broken with Doublehead forever, he'd partaken in one of the most heinous deeds a person could commit. And no doubt countless others.

John caught his breath as the Spirit gave an answer he had to speak. "Yet Jesus died for you. Would have died for you, even if you had been the only one." The awe of that fact, as applied to himself, knotted his throat so that he was unable to continue.

Tears shone in The Ridge's eyes, and he gave a brief nod. "This I will think of deeply. For now"—he sat forward, put a hand on John's knee—"go check on new wife and little girl. She does well, eh?"

John allowed a grin to spread across his face, dispersing the serious moment. "She does well."

Dawnee was recuperating in his cabin, taking all his wife's time, but he found he no longer minded. Well, not much. The girl possessed an irresistible, sweet glow and a cheerful desire to please others, almost as if the touch of angels lingered on her spirit.

Peter put it right when he said, "God's healing of her reminds us all why we are here."

"That it does." John nodded, rubbing his hand over his beard. "In fact, 'tis exactly what Dawnee said."

Peter cocked an eyebrow at him, while The Ridge waited with his customary patience.

The day John had brought Dawnee's parents, expecting to find their daughter on the brink of death, Dawnee had confessed that she had been angry when she burned the syllabary. But not being allowed to stay with them had not been the main reason for her rash action.

Charlie had told her writing down their language went against Cherokee beliefs and that, as Vann had warned them some believed, doing so was as witchcraft. Dawnee did not want them to bring a curse upon themselves, nor did she want trouble from Iskittihi and those like him. When she'd seen the syllabary sitting alone in the empty cabin, she'd thrown it on the fire. But then, she saw she had been wrong to give in to fear.

"She said God told her while she was sick that He was using

both her sickness and the earthquakes to tell the Cherokees about Himself." John did not add it, but Dawnee had also said God would use the syllabary. So she and Clarissa had resumed work on it as soon as she was strong enough.

In fact, he'd find them cuddled up on the bed when he returned, poring over Clarissa's book by candlelight. They would be eager to see him, though. Would jump up to hug him, both of them. Like a family.

Clearing the emotion from his throat, John said his goodnights and stepped into the cold February air. He froze in place, his mouth falling open. In the west, a small white stripe shone on the horizon, while from the east, a red light lit everything almost as bright as a full moon. He threw the door open again, but he seemed to have lost the ability to speak coherently.

"Come! 'Tis incredible! In the sky."

As the occupants filed out, murmuring in confusion, then awe, John raced to his cabin. Sure enough, his girls were scratching away on their syllabary. They jumped at his abrupt entrance.

"John, what is it?" Clarissa stiffened as if bracing for the latest danger.

"You must come out here right now."

"But I have on my nightdress."

"Well, put on a wrapper." He hurried across to snatch up said item of clothing from the chair and toss it at her. "It's an eclipse!"

"An eclipse?" Clarissa gaped and hastened into her robe, then she and John both wrapped Dawnee in a blanket and helped her to the door. The girl stood between them on the threshold, weak with awe, or just weak—he couldn't tell. Clarissa shook her head. "Is this not the strangest season you have ever seen? 'Tis as if the earth is trying to speak."

From across the way, Brother Steiner affirmed her reflection in a loud voice. "'The heavens declare the glory of God; and the firmament sheweth his handywork.'"

"A sign, yes," Dawnee agreed. "This is powerful God." She

turned and looked up at Clarissa, clutching her hand and raising it to her chest. "Your Jesus, He come into my heart too?"

John thought his would shatter with joy. *Thank you, God.* Every single trial had been worth it.

CHAPTER TWENTY-THREE

"See how the first two residence cabins are perfectly in line?" John asked Charlie and Tom on a still-misty March afternoon. He pointed to the buildings, then showed them the likeness he'd sketched in his measurement book. Brows furrowed. Dark heads bent. Nodded. "And how my cabin and your cabin sit perfectly square across from them? We want the entrance of the new church to line up with the middle of the row between."

"Face the kitchen?" Tom's question echoed loud with his excitement. For weeks, the boys had been looking forward to the day John would bring out his surveying equipment. He'd already graded the site and prepared stakes and twine to mark the new building. Today was the day they measured it off. "So we go straight from Brother Steiner's long sermons to dinner?"

Holding the Gunter chain nearby, Peter laughed. "Exactly so, Tom."

Tom hopped on one foot, then made a pounding gesture. "I hit in first stick! I can show *E-do-da* when he come back *go-hi u-sv-hi*."

Tom's mixture of Cherokee and English might have made even less sense to John had he not known Chuleoa had arrived the night before. The chief planned to lodge with them several days while attending a council at Diamond Hill. Naturally, the boy was eager to show his father all he was learning at the mission.

"Aye, you can, Tom." John finished screwing the compass onto its legs and looked up at Charlie, who hung back, trying to act disinterested. John knew better. Even though he'd been reserved since the ruined-feed incident—even more so during Chuleoa's visit—math and spatial relations came easily to the boy. Really, they lit the only spark in his eyes these days. "Charlie, would you come check the mercury in the circumferentor to make sure I've set it up level?"

Thumb hooked on the back of his suspenders, Charlie sidled over. "What?"

John pointed to the instrument. "See here? The little bubble in the liquid? Make certain that it is right in the middle." He waited until the boy nodded before pointing down the detachable arm. "Now look through that sighting vane and tell me what you see."

"Uh ... biggest blueberry bush of Sister Steiner?"

As Charlie stepped back, John double-checked his target. Sure enough, the first of a line of rabbit-eye blueberry bushes, already speckled with small, white, bell-shaped flowers, appeared at the other end of the wire. "Good." He gave an affirming pat between Charlie's thin shoulder blades.

Charlie glanced up and offered a faint smile.

That morning, Tom's father, Chuleoa, had given a speech to the children, reminding them how lucky they were to be well-fed and instructed. He'd encouraged them to be obedient and cheerful and to love the missionaries as their parents. As much as John appreciated the chief's thorough about-face, Chuleoa had looked only at Charlie when he'd spoken of obedience. When Charlie had cringed farther into the corner, John had known this was the day to stake the foundation of the church.

Encouraged by even the tiniest response from Charlie, John sliced the air with the flat of his hand. "So boys, Charlie has given you the direction to walk with the chain."

Peter handed Tom some of the links.

"Too heavy," he complained, pretending to struggle to keep it off the ground.

"'Tis why I have three sturdy assistants today instead of two." John grinned at them.

After a few minutes of "to the right," "to the left," and "stop just even with the edge of the cabin," Peter set down a marker where John indicated. Only after John moved the compass and

Denise Weimer

repeated the process from the corner of the boys' cabin did Peter assist Charlie and Tom in driving the first stake.

John interrupted their victory dance, walking over with his measurement book. "'Tis just the first step, boys. This is our door." He stood flush with the future entrance and pointed. "Now, let's go over our measurements to see how far to each side we have to go to place our corner stakes. If the church will be thirty feet by—"

"Brother Klies', Brother Klies'!"

One of Vann's gardeners jogged toward them, waving. "The chief want you up at the big house."

John cocked his head. "Is not the council meeting?"

Hands on his knees, the man heaved in deep breaths. "Not yet. Jus' the Hicks there now with Chief Vann and Chuleoa, an' they wanna talk to you."

John cut a glance at the dismayed faces of the boys. "What about?"

"Doan know, sir."

"Very well. Tell them I will be right there."

Before John could offer the slave a dipper of water, he took off running again. With a sigh, John closed his book and regarded his helpers. "I dare not keep four Cherokee chiefs waiting."

They answered in perfect unison. "Aw!"

Tom added with a dismissive wave, "They will smoke pipe. No hurry."

Peter grinned at the boy and reassured John. "I can help them finish driving the stakes."

"Thank you, Peter. I will set my things in my cabin and record the measurements later."

"Can we still go get rocks *su-na-le i*?" Tom asked.

John glanced up from packing his compass. "I don't see why not." The hint of springlike weather whetted his wanderlust, making him look forward to the outing to the Conasauga tomorrow in search of fit foundation stones as much as the boy.

Before leaving for the plantation, he found Clarissa in the

❧ 237 ❧

kitchen, clad in her old work dress, cap, and apron. Fetching golden curls trailed down her neck and stuck to her cheek. Even the sniffles and puffiness of eyes and nose brought on by a recent cold could not diminish her charm. He wanted to kiss her on the spot, but all the women, including Pleasant and Dawnee, had turned out to help make candles this afternoon.

"You look awfully nice." She surveyed him, eyebrows lifting. He'd donned his best coat and waistcoat after leaving his equipment in their cabin.

"I have been called to talk with Charles and William Hicks at Vann's."

"To what purpose?" A crease of concern settled between her brows, as it did with any mention of Oothcaloga and its residents.

"That I can tell you when I return. Just wanted you to know where I am bound." John waved from the doorway, having no desire to linger in the space crowded by chattering women.

She leaned out the door behind him, whispering. "In truth, I wish I were going with you. I could use a brisk walk. 'Tis burning up in here."

John frowned. "Have you a fever?" He put his hand to her forehead but felt nothing amiss. "Try to rest a little before dinner. And if you have time, stroll out to the spring."

He winked, and his wife's expression brightened at the hint that another message awaited her at the witness tree.

He took the couple of miles in half the time it would have taken with Clarissa at his side, stopping to sneeze and fussing about getting her skirts in the puddles. As John approached the house, evidence indicated the arrival of extra guests. Smoke poured from all the chimneys. The scent of meat roasting hung heavy and tantalizing on the damp air. Servants dashed to and fro, carrying platters of food, baskets of laundry, and hostelry implements. Watching the activity, John slipped right into one of the many mud puddles himself. He paused on the bricks at the bottom of the steps to wipe his sole on the boot-scraper.

Along with pungent pipe smoke, voices drifted from the open parlor window, low but distinct.

"The paper I transcribe for the colonel show some chiefs got more than the money and rifles received by all those who sign the treaty." Charles Hicks spoke in only slightly broken English, which would provide more privacy from the listening ears of other Cherokees.

"How has the traitor Doublehead seen to benefit now?" Vann asked.

"From what I can tell, he and friends received land in ceded territory."

William Hicks, Charles' younger brother, spoke up. "My brother will watch and listen to see if he attempts to sell these lands to Americans."

Something smashed, reminding John he was eavesdropping, but Vann burst out, "We already know he has done so in the past!"

"Not everyone is convinced of this," William replied as John climbed the steps.

"He cannot continue to break tribal law unchecked," Vann protested. "What example does this set? We must take action."

"The Ridge arrives tomorrow," Charles said. "We will hear what he says about seeking a sentence of execution from the national council."

John's use of the knocker quieted any reply, but not his uneasy awareness that an alignment with these powerful men also meant becoming a target for their enemies.

᜷ ᜷

"Pleasant, can you bring a bit more fat from the boiler?" Pushing aside a damp strand of hair with the back of her hand, Sister Steiner glanced over her shoulder. "My level is getting low."

Clarissa bit back a grimace as the slave poured hot, skimmed beef tallow into the triangular-shaped vessel into which Sister Steiner dipped the candles. Dawnee stirred the mixture, releasing more of the heavy, oily scent that made Clarissa's stomach sour.

With her middle fingers holding the two sticks, or broches, separate but secure, Sister Steiner looked up at Clarissa. "Is something wrong, Sister Kliest?"

"Nothing." Clarissa forced a smile, waiting for the tapers to stop dripping onto the special bench below the sink so she could hang them on the drying frame.

"Hmm. I thought you looked rather bilious just now."

"Only the smell of the fat makes me a little queasy for some reason."

"You can smell that with your stuffy nose?" Rosina cocked her head.

Clarissa nodded. "'Tis nothing." She did not want them to think she was whining. "Probably the drainage making me sensitive."

Sister Steiner pursed her lips as she handed Clarissa the broches, accepting another set from Rosina. "So sensitive you have not wanted your coffee all week. Sister Kliest, how go your courses?"

"My ... courses?" Clarissa thought a moment, then brightened. "Our instruction in reading is off to a good start. Dawnee is especially—"

"Not those courses." Sister Steiner interrupted. "*Your* courses. Your monthly cycle."

"Oh!" Heat engulfed Clarissa's cheeks the same moment Rosina froze and stared at her. "I ... er ... it has been a little while, but that isn't unusual."

"I would say that bears watching." The older woman gave her a smug smile and a wink. "This cold you have may not be just a cold."

As her meaning sank in, Dawnee's head snapped up, and she gasped. "You have *u-s-di-ga*?"

Even Rosina knew the Cherokee word for baby. Her face paled. "I need to get the ..." And she rushed out, the last word lost in the slamming of the cabin door.

Clarissa couldn't focus. She leaned into the counter, staring out the open window at the still-barren landscape. Only the smaller trees had buds, promising new life and color later in the month. New life. Could it be?

Following her thoughts, Sister Steiner pressed her. "Are your gums tender?"

"Well … yes."

"And you get up at night to use the necessary more than normal?"

"I have this week, 'tis true, but surely 'tis too soon for that."

Sister Steiner shook her head. "A woman's body changes quickly when there is a little one inside."

Clarissa placed a hand over her abdomen, but Dawnee gave a cry and tackled her in a sudden, none-too-gentle hug. From her spot laboring over the boiler, Pleasant caught Clarissa's gaze. Nodded in acknowledgment that what Sister Steiner said could be true.

She might be carrying John's child. And he had not even said he loved her yet.

"Oh!" Hot hears sprang to her eyes, and Clarissa covered her mouth as Rosina entered with more firewood for the stove. She turned away so the other women would not witness her emotion.

"We can finish up here without you," Sister Steiner told her. "Go, take a moment."

Thank goodness for the woman's sensitivity. Murmuring her thanks, Clarissa snagged her shawl from the peg and headed outside. The cool air revived her. She hurried along the well-worn path to the mission spring, where the scent of the yellow flowers of the spicebush and the trumpet-shaped blooms of the Carolina jessamine twined around a pine hung honey-sweet in the air. A mourning dove cooed in the distance, calming her with its soft call.

Sure enough, the cleft of the witness tree offered a small, folded paper. In John's thin, looping script, she read: *"Who can find a virtuous woman? For her price is far above rubies. The heart of her husband doth safely trust in her."*

Tears obscured Clarissa's vision as warmth filled her chest, aching as if it might overflow. The truth bubbled up into awareness as clear and sweet as the spring water at her feet. *I love him. Oh God, how I love him.*

And this note, along with the others he'd given her over the past two months—some Scriptures and some compliments that he must have been too shy to yet speak in person—told her, with a courtship far more tender and intentional than Daniel ever had conducted, that John loved her too.

You knew all along what You were doing, marrying me to John and sending me here.

Suddenly, she could see the future, not back in Salem, but right here, with Dawnee and Peggy and yes, even James Vann. *Perfect love casteth out fear.* She loved John enough to set aside her desire to return to North Carolina. If the elders would allow them to remain, she was willing. Yes, willing even to go to Oothcaloga.

Tucking the note away, Clarissa wiped her face, wrapped her shawl tighter, and hurried back to the mission. Not to tell John about her suspicions—no, that should wait until she was more certain—but simply to greet him when he returned from Diamond Hill. To see the face of the man whose child she just knew she carried. And, more practically speaking, they would be wanting her help getting dinner.

John's voice drew her as soon as she entered the complex. And not in a tone she felt eager to hear. Outside the barn, he clutched the neck of Charlie's shirt and bent to look the boy in the eye. "Did you take it?"

"No." Charlie squirmed away from John's grip.

"Don't be afraid to tell me if you did. I just need to know where you put it."

Romantic thoughts scattering, Clarissa hurried forward. "What is going on?"

John straightened and cast her a distracted glance. "When I got back from Vann's, I found my measurement book missing from our cabin."

"Maybe Brother Keller has it." Clarissa ran a hand down Charlie's arm in an attempt to soothe not only his shirt but his feelings, but the boy flinched away from her too.

"I put everything up before leaving. Besides, I already checked with him." John glanced away in an obvious attempt to control his temper. "I must get that back, and right away. I have all kinds of valuable information in there." His gaze flicked back to Charlie, blue eyes like twin lights. "I have told these boys time and again they are not to touch my things without my permission."

"Why you always think it me?" Charlie jerked his fisted hands down to his sides. "Why I want stupid math book? You just like Chuleoa. Just like Vann. Think I bad." His face twisting in anger, he stalked toward the woods.

Clarissa's heart lurched with sympathy. The boy obviously felt as lost at Springplace as she had. "Charlie—" When she made a move to go after him, John put a hand on her arm.

"Leave him for now. He'll return for supper soon enough. I need to talk to you about what I learned at Vann's, and no one else, especially Charlie, needs to hear it."

"Yes? What did the Hicks brothers want?" Clarissa steeled herself for the news.

"For me to come with them after the council to start a new mill. Vann is thinking of going with us, to visit some relatives in the area. Honestly, I think they are lobbying for support. I overheard them say they plan to make a motion at the national council for Doublehead's execution."

"Oh, John." Clarissa's hand fluttered to rest on her stomach. Minutes after realizing there could be a baby there, she already felt the instinct to protect it. "This could bring about so much unrest."

"Which is why I'm not sure I should go."

"Of course you should. There would be no danger yet. The drama between Vann and Doublehead will play out as it will. You should do as you are called to do."

He tilted his head, lowered his brows in suspicion. "Are you that eager to get rid of me again?"

"Just the opposite." Clarissa stroked John's arm much as she had Charlie's, but with better results. His muscles softened under her touch. "I would selfishly keep you here with me all the time, but I know now that staying put is not in your blood. So … the sooner you go, the sooner you'll come back. You said the Hicks' home of Oothcaloga is the best site for another mission, right?"

"I believe the chiefs think so, too, even though they will not bring it up in front of Vann."

"Well, then, the more time you spend with them, the more likely that is to happen."

"I'm sorry, but … are you speaking another language?" John braced her arms with his hands. "The Clarissa I knew …" His sentence trailed off as he shook his head in bemusement.

"Is not the same one who now loves you."

"What?" The question came out whisper-soft, raw.

She pulled the folded paper from under the strap of her chemise. She took a breath, strengthening her resolve. "This says your heart can trust me. I want that. I want you to know that if God is calling us to stay here, or calling you to establish another mission in Oothcaloga, I will stand by your side."

"Clarissa." Taking her hand, John tugged her quickly into the dim, straw-scented overhang of the barn. There he cupped her face. Those blue eyes searched hers, she supposed, for verification that she meant her words. Finally, he seemed to find it, for he dipped his head and let out a breath. "'Tis a certain way to make me *not* want to leave. But … did I hear you say …?"

Clarissa gave a teasing smile, the tender, yearning look on his face wiping away any fear she had about speaking out first. "Brother Kliest. Husband. And now … John. I have fallen in love with you. What are you going to do about that?"

With a deep growl of unspoken emotion, he swooped in to kiss her, hard, then gentle. Against her lips, he whispered, "Love you forever back."

Heart singing, Clarissa wrapped her arms around his neck.

John rubbed his nose against hers. "What have you done to me, *liebchen*?"

"The same as you have done to me." Clarissa leaned in to surrender to his embrace when she heard a scrambling sound. She gasped, drawing back as a figure flew out the back of the barn and disappeared into the trees. "Charlie was hiding there the whole time! He heard everything we said."

CHAPTER TWENTY-FOUR

Clarissa's restlessness demanded an afternoon outdoors. She couldn't focus on linguistics when she had said goodbye to John that morning as he'd left with Vann and the contingent from Oothcaloga. This unease inside—it made no sense. 'Twas like a warning, only she knew not for what. It had been all she could do to stand by her vow to give John the freedom to fulfill his calling, to keep silent about the little life she suspected more every day of growing inside her.

The cloudy afternoon offered the perfect opportunity to transfer fledgling cabbage plants into the garden. Clarissa set them out sixteen inches apart, smoothing the fertilized soil around each one. She loved the smell of the rich earth, the damp loam of spring in the air.

Could her unease have to do with Charlie? Things with him should have been resolved by now but weren't.

After Charlie had overheard her conversation with John, they had returned to the Steiners' cabin to find Tom with John's measurement book, waiting to show his father the drawings from their work that day. When he realized the trouble he'd caused, he'd apologized in tears. He'd even assumed the extra chores John assigned without complaint. Both Tom and John owned their mistakes to Charlie that night. He'd listened to their explanations with an impassive face.

"To be honest, Charlie," John had said, running a hand over his beard with a sigh of regret, "the reason I thought you took the book is that you are the one with the best understanding of it. Your skill in math—well, it amazes me."

Even that admission—which had made Clarissa proud—

had not softened Charlie. When they asked if he had heard their conversation in the barn, he'd denied it. They cautioned him against repeating private information, especially when lacking a full understanding of a situation, but he'd responded with only a blank stare. Ever since, he'd continued to be sullen and withdrawn. Clarissa feared lasting damage had been done. And with John to be away for several weeks now, the gap might not close.

Clarissa breathed a prayer. *Oh God, please help us find a way to connect with him.*

She stood and brushed the dirt from her skirts. White dogwood and purple plum tree blossoms lightened the dark hardwoods and evergreens surrounding the mission, promising warmer weather soon. But today a damp breeze blew down the eastern mountain range. She raised the hood on her cloak. What had possessed her to plant cabbages? The warm kitchen sounded better by the minute.

Before Clarissa could kneel to finish her task, Dawnee ran under the line of dried, hollowed-out gourds strung at the edge of the garden to attract nesting purple martins, which ate insects and drove away crows at planting time. She waved her arms wildly. "Sister Kliest! Sister Kliest!"

Clarissa's throat narrowed as she hurried to meet her. "What is it, Dawnee?"

"You must come, help us look!" Almond eyes huge, the girl grabbed her hand and started pulling her toward the mission.

"Look for what?"

"For Charlie! Cannot find him anywhere. The boys say his things gone. And so is your book of words."

❧　❧

The children cried during the reading about Jesus in the garden of Gethsemane the next day, Maundy Thursday. Clarissa couldn't tell if they did so over the Savior's agony or the absence of Charlie, and now Peter, who had gone after him but had not returned as expected last night. As Rosina cast Clarissa pained looks, her face was as white and strained as the milk Pleasant was pouring the children for breakfast.

She thinks Peter has gotten into some trouble because of the syllabary, so she blames me.

Although perhaps Rosina's fears merely offered an excuse to express the distaste the sister seemed to have developed for her since learning of Clarissa's pregnancy.

Sister Steiner attempted to reassure Rosina. "My guess is that Brother Keller tracked Charlie back to his village and, as it was nightfall, stayed over until today."

"Yes, he should return at any moment." Brother Steiner nodded, his smile in place. "With Charlie in tow. Brother Keller and Whitetree together will talk sense into the boy and send him back."

"Please God, with the syllabary." Clarissa did not even realize she'd spoken until she looked up from her breakfast to find all eyes on her. She cast her gaze back down. She did not need to elaborate on the danger the missing syllabary added to what would have been merely a boy's hurt feelings.

Tom plunked his spoon into his bowl and groaned. "This my fault! I make him look bad to Brother Kliest."

Dawnee shook her head. She'd eaten less of her porridge than Clarissa. "No, my fault. He think I not like him. I just want him to be good."

"'Tis the fault of none of you," Brother Steiner said in his firm teaching voice. "Each person is accountable for their own choices. We all tried to show Charlie the love of God."

"Maybe we had to try harder," Dawnee whispered. She tucked her chin to wipe a tear on the sleeve of her dress.

Brother Steiner's whiskered face firmed at their self-recrimination. "We would do well to focus on our morning verses. Psalm 61:3 and 4: 'For thou hast been a shelter for me, and a strong tower from the enemy. I will abide in thy tabernacle forever: I will trust in the cover of thy wings.'"

Sister Steiner stood. "And to focus on the day's studies, since no one seems to be eating. I will clean up here. Sister Keller, Sister Kliest ..." She made a shooing motion toward the door. "Take the children to their cabin."

When Rosina hesitated, Brother Steiner reassured her. "I will send your husband to you the moment he returns."

Clarissa gathered the students and led them outside, Rosina trailing behind. She would have to start the lesson. Rosina would be of little use in her distracted state of mind. Not that she could blame her. Were John in danger, she would do no better.

As the children settled on their benches, Clarissa had them get out their vocabulary from the day before.

Expecting one of the house servants to deliver Joe and Sally, she did not even look up from helping Sam conjugate a verb when the door opened fifteen minutes later.

Rosina gasped.

Clarissa straightened. Two tall, adult men loomed in the door. Indians carrying rifles. Her vision swam before her, rendering her frozen with shock as Iskittihi strode toward her.

He waved a book in her face. Not just her "book of words," as Dawnee had called it, but the beginning of their Cherokee alphabet, with new letters drawn in both of their hands. Iskittihi spoke in angry Cherokee. "I know this is yours. And now you will answer for it." Stuffing the book inside his hunting shirt, he whirled to bark an order to One Feather. "Bring the girl."

The moment Iskittihi seized Clarissa's arm, One Feather jerked Dawnee from her seat.

"No!" Sam jumped up and threw himself between them, but One Feather shoved him so hard he slid on his backside. The bench fell on top of him.

"Sam!" Rosina started toward him, but a quick motion from One Feather's rifle halted her in a cower.

As shock melted away, a dreadful understanding took its place, and Clarissa's vision cleared. They were going to take them out of here. To where? And what could she do?

A tiny movement near the door caught her eye. Tom, edging along.

Clarissa gave the barest shake of her head. Nothing must happen to him because of her. And nothing must happen to Dawnee either. When Iskittihi propelled Clarissa forward, she twisted to face him. But in her panic-induced state of mind, she couldn't think of a single Cherokee word. "The book is mine! Leave her alone. Sam?" She shrieked the last.

Tears running down his face, Sam chattered off a translation.

Iskittihi held her hands behind her back and leaned over, the smell of grease and leather hitting Clarissa along with his sour breath. "*E-lo-we-hi, s-gi-li.*"

That she understood all too well. *Quiet, witch.*

One Feather half lifted Dawnee. Her feet flailed in the air as if she were running as he bore her toward the door.

"No! Tell him Dawnee is innocent." With a mighty tug, Clarissa broke free of Iskittihi and pulled the girl away from her captor. Arms extended, she attempted to shield her with her body. "Leave her alone. Take me only."

Iskittihi grabbed her arm and bent it behind her back, allowing One Feather to lunge for Dawnee. She whimpered as the Indian jerked her against him. The diversion gave Tom the moment he needed to whisk out the door.

Run, Tom.

On his feet now, Rosina restraining him in a frantic embrace, Sam pled with Iskittihi in Cherokee. But his jaw went slack when the Indian answered.

"What? What is it?" Clarissa asked.

"He said he knows you both wrote in the book, and for a Cherokee to do so is a crime punishable by death."

Clarissa's knees weakened, and she sagged as though someone had punched her in the stomach. She couldn't summon the strength to fight back as, following One Feather with Dawnee, Iskittihi dragged her to the door.

Daylight flooded her vision, along with a whir of motion at the corner of the cabin, accompanied by a woman's battle cry. Something dark slammed into One Feather's head. He stopped. Grunted.

Pleasant retracted her thick chunk of firewood. She never got to swing it a second time, for Iskittihi reached for his gun, allowing Clarissa to break free. She plowed her hip into his and flung herself off the step, knocking Dawnee out of One Feather's grip and to the ground before the Indian could react. Dawnee whimpered as Clarissa crouched over her.

Stumbling from the threshold, Iskittihi misfired into the trees. Horses whinnied from the thicket. The Indians' horses?

One Feather regained his senses enough to swing the butt of his rifle against Pleasant's head. The woman crumpled a few feet from Clarissa. With the alarm sounded, reloading would take too much time. Iskittihi kicked the slave's midriff and snagged Clarissa by the hair. His jerk upward sent her cap flying and fire racing along her scalp.

"No!" She couldn't let these men take them away. Once they were on those horses—

Boom!

A rifle exploded across the clearing. With one hand snapping to his shot bag, Iskittihi shoved Clarissa down with the other. One Feather shouldered his weapon.

"Stop!" Brother Steiner advanced at a run, his rifle leveled. "I will shoot!"

Iskittihi and One Feather exchanged glances. Brother Steiner slowed but kept walking. His steady gaze anticipated any twitch from the Indians.

Please, God. Clarissa couldn't bear for blood to be shed on this mission because of her.

Iskittihi gave a single nod toward the ground. He and One Feather slowly lowered their guns. Brother Steiner's firm steps mingled with Dawnee's weeping and a moan from Pleasant. The minute the Cherokee men raised their hands in a gesture of surrender, Clarissa tugged Dawnee over to Pleasant.

A trickle of blood eased from a small gash on the slave's temple. "Come." She helped Pleasant lift her head, then crawl with them around the edge of the cabin. Clarissa peeked around the corner.

"Back away." Brother Steiner addressed the men in their native tongue. "Leave now."

They did as he said, taking slow steps backward, hands still raised, whether from the possibility that this missionary might actually shoot, or their own reluctance to shoot a missionary, Clarissa couldn't guess. But their faces reflected bitter resentment, and Iskittihi's voice held unmistakable threat as he spat out a string of Cherokee she couldn't decipher. They whirled and ran to their horses.

Clarissa turned back to Pleasant, slipping an arm around her as she propped herself against the stone footer. "Are you all right?"

The woman nodded, holding her head.

"And you, *liebling*?" With shaking hands, Clarissa smoothed Dawnee's hair back and turned up her damp face.

"Yes." Another tear slid down her cheek, but her eyes remained bright. Clarissa pressed a kiss into the part of Dawnee's hair.

As the thunder of retreating hooves shook the ground, Clarissa withdrew her handkerchief from her pocket and dabbed Pleasant's forehead. "Why did you do such a thing, Pleasant? You could have been killed."

Pleasant's one visible dark eye met hers. "Well, I couldn't rightly let them bad Indians take you and the little gal, could I?"

Clarissa's heart surged, and as Brother Steiner loomed over them, she hugged the slave woman with a gentle but fierce affection. "Thank you, Pleasant. I will never forget your bravery on our behalf."

"Youz always been kind to me, Sister Klies'."

Sitting back on her heels, Clarissa broke into laughter. "Where did you even come from with that firewood?"

Pleasant responded with a low chuckle. "I were outside the kitchen when Sam run by. Figured I might get to you before Brother Steiner could."

"And you sure enough did." Brother Steiner crouched down beside them, leaning his rifle against the cabin. "Your delay saved Sister Kliest and Dawnee. Can I help you up, Pleasant?"

The woman stared at him, her eyes wide. The first time she'd found herself the focus of a man's kindly attention? She slipped her dark hand into the thick, white one he held out to her. As he helped her to her feet and Clarissa assisted Dawnee, Rosina rounded the corner with Sam. Sister Steiner approached across the yard, her flying skirts and shawl resembling the ruffled feathers of a goose, with Tom the chick in her wake. Brother Steiner held out a hand to stay the questions forming on his wife's puckered lips. His brows scuttled as his gaze settled on Clarissa and Dawnee. "What did Iskittihi say to you?"

Dawnee answered in a tremulous voice. "He said this not over. They not only ones angry I helped Sister Kliest write down new letters."

Clarissa hugged her close again. "I am so sorry. I never thought helping with the syllabary would put you in danger."

Rosina fisted her shaking hands at her chest. "What did Iskittihi mean, a crime punishable by death?"

"Charlie tell me those who do this witchcraft must die, but I not believe him." Dawnee wiped tears from her eyes. "I thought he just try to scare me."

As everyone fired off further questions, Clarissa's head spun. She pressed Dawnee to her side.

Brother Steiner brought silence with a quick, "That's enough," and directed them all to his cabin. There, Sister Steiner poured Clarissa, Dawnee, and Pleasant cups of water. Rosina prepared a poultice for the slave woman's head while Brother Steiner bent over the table with paper and a quill. "Tom, you did very well today. I need you to do something else."

Punching the air with his fist, Sam burst out with self-condemnation. "I should have beat that Iskittihi!"

"No, Sam." Clarissa touched his shoulder, pressing him back down on the bench. "You could not have beaten them. They were grown men with guns."

His dark brows an angry slash over his eyes, Tom stood next to the older man as he was writing. He asked with breathless eagerness, "How I help, Brother Steiner?"

Brother Steiner folded the paper, heated a glob of wax over a candle, and sealed the edge. He bent in front of the boy. "You run very fast like you did just now. Go to Vann's. Take this to his head man. Tell him he must send his best rider after the chief and Brother Kliest. Dawnee and Sister Kliest are in danger, and we require their immediate return. You understand?"

"Yes." His fingers closed over the missive, and he made to dart for the door, but Brother Steiner stopped him with another admonition.

"You must not be seen. Do not use the lane."

"I run in orchard."

"Good boy. Keep a sharp eye out."

Sister Steiner grabbed Tom and pulled him close to kiss the top of his head. "Jesus, keep him." She murmured the words in a thick voice, then gave him a little shove toward the door.

As soon as it closed behind him, Rosina wrung her hands and burst out. "Where is Peter?" Tears sprung from the corners of her eyes and cascaded down her face. "Did these same men harm him—kill him—then hasten here to do more evil?"

Sister Steiner put an arm around her and spoke in a soothing tone. "We mustn't think like that. My guess is Brother Keller made it to Whitetree, but Iskittihi and One Feather rode ahead early this morning before Whitetree could make peace."

"But that dreadful Indian had the syllabary," Rosina said on a wail.

"That does not necessarily mean anything dire." Brother Steiner rubbed a hand over his graying beard, brows knit in deep thought. "Charlie could have given it to them. But we cannot assume they did not bring others with them, leaving them to wait nearby while they tried to nab Sister Kliest and Dawnee. I also think we cannot wait on Brother Keller."

Still holding Dawnee close, Clarissa looked up. "What should we do?"

"Go to your cabin to pack, and I will fetch you within minutes, once I gather some basic supplies. I will escort you north on Tellico Road to Dawnee's father, Chief Little Rock."

"But will we be safe there?" 'Twas only twenty miles away, an easy ride in a couple of hours.

"Dawnee's parents must be informed of the danger. If they think it best, they could go with you to Tellico."

Hands on her hips, Sister Steiner gave a firm nod. "I will pack food. What Brother Steiner says is wise, and 'twill buy us some time. When Vann gets back here, he can restore order."

Once again, they were relying on the protection of a man who brutalized his own slaves and family members. Her premonition of danger—it had come to pass. Clarissa shuddered, longing for John. If he were here, he would take them to Tellico. But she must trust now in Brother Steiner's assistance.

"Come, Dawnee." Ever since her sickness, the girl had gotten her wish to stay with the Kliests, first on her fireside pallet, then, when she was strong enough to navigate the ladder, in their loft. Only for a short time to work together, John had agreed. Now, Clarissa helped her rise. "Let us do as Brother Steiner says."

"Wait." Sam stood, wavering in place. He lurched forward and enfolded Dawnee in an awkward embrace. He stepped back just as quickly, turning away, face ruddy.

"I cannot go without a hug too," Clarissa told him.

Putting his arms around her waist, he looked up at her with tears standing in his eyes. "Is it gone? The dream of writing our own language?"

She cupped his head. "Not if you hold everything you learned here, in your mind." She tapped his temple. "Remember. And even if evil men succeed in stealing what we have done, a time will come that you can bring forth that dream again ... because God is the author, not us."

"I promise to remember, Sister Kliest."

Her heart in her throat, Clarissa hugged him tight, then approached Pleasant, who sat in the corner with Rosina's poultice to her swelling temple. "Will you be all right, my friend?"

She didn't miss Rosina's quiet gasp.

A jagged smile split Pleasant's dark face. "I be all right, Sister Klies'."

Clarissa bent to hug her as well, whispering, "If I don't see you for a while, remember what I told you at Christmas."

"Yes, ma'am." Without a trace of animosity, Pleasant nodded.

Satisfied, Clarissa held out her hand to Dawnee. Brother Steiner checked to make sure the yard was clear before sending them on their way. She waved to him before she closed her cabin door behind her and bolted it firm.

"Now." She infused a note of cheer into her voice that she did not feel. "Let us pack for a little trip. 'Twill be nice to see your parents, will it not?"

Dawnee's lower lip trembled. "I am afraid, Sister Kliest. What if Iskittihi follow us?"

Clarissa knelt before her, squeezing Dawnee's hands as she quoted Isaiah 41:10. "'Fear thou not; for I am with thee: be not dismayed; for I am thy God: I will strengthen thee; yea, I will help thee; yea, I will uphold thee with the right hand of my righteousness.' We are His children, no? God will go with us."

Swiping a hand across her face to catch another tear, Dawnee gave a tremulous nod.

Clarissa went to fetch a wool blanket they could roll their supplies in. "Only pack what you must. Everything must fit in one saddlebag." She and Dawnee would ride one horse, Brother Steiner the other.

She'd only collected a comb, a small bag of coins, and her cloak when the sound of horses brought her up short. "Brother Steiner was quicker than I expected. Hurry, add your things to the blanket."

The dogs were barking. That wasn't right. Sliding a knife John had left into the top of her boot, Clarissa peeked out the shutters. What she saw stopped her breath. And her heart. Horses—not two, but five—encircling the Steiners' cabin. Iskittihi and One Feather had returned with friends.

God, help us.

"Dawnee ..." What words would properly motivate the girl without scaring her to death? While Dawnee stared wide-eyed, Clarissa snatched the blanket, rolled it, and tied it around her body. "We must climb out the back window and run into the woods. We will be going on foot."

CHAPTER TWENTY-FIVE

"We grow near." Dawnee looked over her shoulder and held a finger to her lips.

Thank goodness. Clarissa sucked in a deep breath in an effort to slow her panting.

For hours, they had trekked mostly through woods to avoid the road, darting even deeper into the forest any time they heard hooves. Greening briars and jagged branches had picked her dress. After she'd tripped on a root and spilled everything she carried, she'd stopped several times to secure the blanket knot on her front.

Now, a stitch in Clarissa's side protested their relentless pace, while her sensitive stomach protested the lack of food. She pinched the offending spot beneath her ribs and tried to emulate Dawnee's stealthy approach to her parents' cabin. The girl crept up behind a massive clump of sweetshrub.

A whisper of dismay passed Dawnee's lips. "Oh no."

Clarissa surveyed the cabin in the clearing, which was surrounded by weathered outbuildings much like those at Springplace. She frowned. "There doesn't seem to be anything amiss."

"Not there." Dawnee gestured from the house with its inviting trail of smoke to the stable. "There. Two horses in corral mean barn is full."

"Your parents don't have that many horses?" Clarissa's heart sank when Dawnee shook her head. "But how can we be sure the extra ones belong to Iskittihi's group?"

She pointed to the edge of the fenced enclosure. "The spotted one. Remember?"

Yes. Clarissa had seen Iskittihi ride that dappled stallion on more than one occasion.

"Oh, Dawnee, I am so sorry." As the safety of their expected haven disintegrated and a picture of Iskittihi and One Feather waiting inside, towering over a frightened Little Rock and Du-a-i—and presumably setting a trap for *them*—took its place, Clarissa wanted nothing more than to surrender to tears. What could they do now? They could never make it to Tellico in the dark, much less cross the Hiwassee on their own.

Dawnee answered her unspoken question. "My *e-du-tsi*, Oocumma."

"Your uncle?"

She nodded. "He live up the road, three, maybe four miles."

Clarissa squeezed her thin shoulder. "Good. We must make haste before dark falls." She did not voice her niggling fear that Iskittihi might have posted a guard there too. They simply must press on.

"Continue on path in trees."

The way they'd just traversed? The girl considered that a path? Clarissa had thought they were picking their way through the forest. Still, she must maintain a brave countenance. She was the adult here, no matter how worried she felt.

They skirted the house and continued through the woods. The faint, reddish light of dusk set the pea-like blooms on the redbud trees aglow, and the whip-poor-will echoed its haunting nocturnal cry. The ground descended to a small creek flowing down from the mountain to their right. They cupped their hands and satisfied their thirst. As Dawnee rose, water dripping from her chin, she pointed to a plant growing in small clumps nearby.

"*So-cha-ni.*"

"Is that good?"

"Good to eat, yes. I not know how you say in English." The girl hurried over to pick the leaves and stems. "And look, onions too."

"Dawnee, 'tis most important to make it to your uncle's. We can eat there."

Dawnee handed Clarissa the *so-cha-ni*, her slanted eyes revealing that the possibility that something or someone might deny them shelter at her relative's home had already occurred to her. "Take one minute. Be safe."

Clarissa squinted at the broad green leaves where Dawnee started to dig. "Looks like lily of the valley."

"No, onion. See? Smell." She lifted her fingers and sniffed them.

Clarissa opened a fold in her blanket to stow the greens, although her middle tied into its own knot at the thought of such a fibrous supper. "Here." She reached into her boot and pulled out the knife. Together they dug into the soft earth until the plant loosened enough for Dawnee to pull up the onion bulb. After they had collected several, Clarissa urged her on. "We must go."

"Yes. Come."

On Dawnee led them, her small form darting sure-footedly under massive hickories and oaks and around dens of mountain laurel and luminescent-blossoming rhododendron. The woods thinned, and they came to the edge of a field. Hope rose in Clarissa's chest, especially when she smelled wood smoke and caught sight of a man burning brush in the clearing.

Clarissa whispered, "Your uncle?"

"No." Dawnee froze, but the farmer in homespun shirt and pants looked their way.

He strode toward them. "Hey! You there."

"Run." Dawnee grabbed Clarissa's hand, but Clarissa tugged back.

"Maybe he can help us."

"*Ni-da-tse-lv-na yv-wi!*" Ugly person. "That … Miller."

The occupation? Or … the surname. The features of the individual now bounding over the tall grass toward them came into sickeningly familiar focus. Stringy gray hair. Bulbous nose. Paunchy belly. He shouted, "Ho! Somebody's lookin' for you."

Dawnee darted back into the deepening shadows, and Clarissa

followed as fast as she could. Miller's heavy breathing, swearing, and crashing through branches sounded close on her heels. She had forgotten the man lived on the way to Hiwassee. Of all the people to encounter when they were already fleeing for their lives! She must keep Dawnee safe at all costs.

Clarissa's hair tumbled loose from her cap. For the second time that day, rough fingers tangled in her long tresses and jerked her back. She snatched free, but when Miller fumbled for her arm, she bent to palm her knife, swiping it blindly in his direction. A yelp indicated the blade had contacted flesh, but she did not look to see where. With a desperate gasp, she tore after Dawnee.

Please, God.

She looked back once more. Miller was pursuing, but his arms flew up, and he went down on a root or rock. Or a gimpy knee. She almost chuckled, her relief was so great.

Oh, thank you. Please let us make it to Dawnee's uncle's house.

They ran in silence until, at last, Clarissa felt safe to gasp out a reassurance. "Dawnee! He's gone."

The girl stopped in her tracks, dropping her arms to her side. She turned and ran to Clarissa, straight into her embrace. Chest heaving, she began to sob.

"Hush, now. 'Tis all right. We lost him."

"We lost him, but I not know where we are!"

Her hand still stroking Dawnee's silky black hair, Clarissa raised her face. Thick underbrush crowded waist-high all around, while the massive shapes of bare, cold hardwoods towered far above. Within minutes, complete dark would fall, bringing wintry cold. Her lips trembled, but she held back her own tears.

Oh God, please help us.

❧ ❧

Exhausted by a day of travel followed by one spent scouting out the mill site with Charles Hicks, John collapsed on the bed in Charles' spare room. One by one, he relaxed his aching muscles under the lavender-scented quilt, convinced of the chiefs' welcome, not only now, but in the future. The Hicks brothers, The Ridge, and Oo-watie had all expressed their hopes that one day the missionaries could start a school in Oothcaloga. Being back here reminded him why locals called this area the Garden Spot. Nestled in a rich valley, a creek burbled past this property—a branch off the Oostanaula River, which snaked around the foot of the western mountain range. Just southwest, on the flip side of the river, lay the famed Cherokee meeting grounds. 'Twas no less beautiful than Springplace. And far more hospitable.

Startled from falling into dreams of rolling, green vistas, John jerked awake when horse hooves pounded outside the cabin. He lay still and waited for Charles to answer the door. But a voice he recognized made him bolt up on the spare mattress. Vann? He'd been staying with The Ridge. What was he doing here in the middle of the night?

Still dressed in his common shirt and breeches, John threw off his blanket and hurried to the front door. Charles stood aside to allow him to address their visitor. "Chief Vann, what is it?"

"Kliest. We must ride." Vann's dark eyes flashed in the moonlight. "Nephew of Doublehead has made trouble. Relatives of his went to the mission and tried to take your wife and the daughter of Chief Little Rock."

Cold washed over John like a plunge in an icy river. "Take …" As his brain fogged with shock, he couldn't complete the question. Why? Where to?

"No time for talk." Vann was already turning back toward the dark yard. "We must reach them before Iskittihi does, or this could go very bad."

❧ ❧

The ache in her legs woke Clarissa as she attempted to shift her weight. Why was her mattress so hard? She must give it a good beating and maybe stuff it again with fresh feathers. She moved her hips and moaned. No mattress lay beneath her, only the cedar boughs she'd cut with her knife the night before. A ghostly rustling from above drew Clarissa's eyes open. Dry brown leaves still clung to the beech tree whose thick yearly canopy provided the clear space she lay in. And her nose felt nearly frozen off in the damp morning chill.

Wrapped in the blanket at her side, Dawnee did not even stir. No wonder. They had spent most of the night shivering, starting at every suspicious rustle. Finally, Clarissa had begun to whisper Scriptures out loud. Every one she could think of, especially those pertaining to protection and comfort. The girl had succumbed to exhausted slumber in the wee hours, Clarissa following her in short order.

Oh God, please help us find our way out of here today. Maybe the morning light would provide a clarity of direction that had been impossible in the dark.

Keeping the blanket tucked around Dawnee as much as possible, Clarissa eased herself into a sitting position. Her sensitive bladder screamed for relief. She took in her surroundings. A dozen yards away, a doe swung her head in their direction, her mouth still full of tender dogwood leaves. She stared. Chewed.

"Dawnee," Clarissa whispered, nudging the girl.

"Mm?" Dawnee raised her head, blinking sleepily.

"Look, a deer. Just there. What is she doing?" Even she knew that deer bedded down for the night.

The doe watched them for a moment, then moseyed away. Dawnee scrambled up, instantly alert in the manner of youth. She pointed. "A deer track."

Clarissa brushed her hair from her face and stood, her gaze following the direction the deer had gone. A path, almost hidden in the rhododendron! "You're right. Should we follow her?"

Dawnee shook her head. "No, ground goes up toward rising sun. We take path the other way. West."

Clarissa brightened at the notion. "Yes, as long as we are

heading away from the mountain, we should be going the right direction. And maybe the path will lead us to a creek."

They took care of necessary needs and quickly braided each other's hair, but having only ingested raw plants the night before, Clarissa was fighting nausea.

As she bent over to roll up her blanket, Dawnee read her face. "You sick?"

Clarissa nodded. She swallowed down the rising bile and secured the bundle around her. "I will be fine."

"My aunt give you bread. Make feel better. Mama ate lots of bread when my little sister in her ..." She rubbed her midsection.

"Tummy?" Clarissa smiled.

"Yes."

Clarissa held a hand out in front of her to indicate that Dawnee should "go ahead"—"*E-gv-yi*." She prayed the deer trail might take them far enough west to intersect the postal road. And that the message had reached John in enough time that he might even now be searching for them in the woods that bordered it.

❧   ❧

Frost glistened on shadowed spaces and along the embankments leading to Vann's plantation. John wanted to ride straight past Springplace in hopes of catching up with Brother Steiner, Clarissa, and Dawnee along the road to Tellico, where the man's note said he planned to take them. But, besides the fact that he needed a fresh mount, he had to stop for a better accounting of what had transpired both before and after Steiner had sent the message.

Perhaps the danger had even abated. Peter might have returned with Whitetree. Local Indians might have rallied around them, ejecting Doublehead's allies from the area. Clarissa and Dawnee might even be home now, waiting for him.

John sat straighter in the saddle.

Then Vann called over to him. "You go to mission. I will go home. We both see what news we can gather. If still needful, I will send my fastest horse for you to ride."

"Thank you, sir." Tears filled John's eyes. For all Vann's personal failings, the man was still a warrior, a rock when needed. He owed much to the Cherokee chief. They parted ways with a nod of understanding at the lane that branched off past the mission.

A crowd ran into the yard when John rode in. He scanned the faces. Tom and Sam. Brother and Sister Steiner, and Brother and Sister Keller. The relief at seeing Peter dissipated as he swept the group again, and his gaze swung back to Brother Steiner.

"Where are they?" As he dismounted, the boys darted forward to take care of his horse.

Brother Steiner shook his head, expression grieved. "Minutes after I wrote the note to you, Iskittihi returned. With friends. They surrounded our cabin—"

"Overpowered him," Sister Steiner said. "Took his rifle."

"But when they searched the other cabins, Sister Kliest and Dawnee were gone."

"We think they went out the window and into the woods." Continuing their back-and-forth recounting, Sister Steiner gestured to the edge of the property. "Thank God they were in your cabin packing when Iskittihi arrived. The Indians were livid. They immediately set out after them."

Peter spoke up, slacking a hip. "That is when I returned."

"Where is Charlie?" John asked him. "Whitetree?"

"Whitetree decided to keep his son at home for a while. He has much work to do to counteract Iskittihi's poison. When we realized that group of dissenters not only had the syllabary but had ridden out for Springplace, I followed right away."

"Brother Keller and I searched in hopes of intercepting the women." Brother Steiner removed his hat and rubbed his head with an agitated motion, his lined face portraying his regret. "But we found no trace of them."

"They would have kept to the woods." John paced, rubbed his jaw. "Did you go to the home of Chief Little Rock?"

"We did." Peter nodded. "By the time we arrived, Iskittihi and the others were already there."

A hot wave of exasperation and fear seared John's body. He let out a cry, raising his face to the sky and dragging both hands down the sides as all the horrible possibilities flashed into his mind.

Brother Steiner laid a hand on his shoulder. "They accosted Du-a-i in the yard. We heard her protesting that she hadn't seen her daughter or Sister Kliest. They barged inside to search. Searched the whole property. Then stayed, making Little Rock and Du-a-i remain inside. We watched the cabin long enough to feel certain that Sister Kliest and Dawnee were not there. If they had been, Iskittihi and his group would have left with them."

"Then, where are they?" Out in the woods somewhere? What if they had stumbled into the trap after Peter and Brother Steiner left? John rounded on the older man, unable to keep the accusation from his voice. "Why did not you stay?"

"We traced the route back, calling and searching the borders of the forest, thinking we might yet find them. We only returned after dark. I am so sorry, John."

John shrugged away, walking a circle in the clearing. He looked toward the lane. "Where is the horse Vann promised? I must go now."

"I will ride with you." Peter gestured for Rosina to fetch his things.

"Wait." Gathering everyone into a circle, Brother Steiner laid a hand each on Peter's and John's shoulders. "Not before we cover this situation with prayer. God is in control. He has Sister Kliest and Dawnee in His hands."

John blinked against the hot tears pricking the back of his eyes. He nodded, but before he could bow his head, Rosina spoke, her eyes glistening. "Before you go, we will bring you drink and food for the journey. You don't know how long you will be, and you must think of Sister Kliest. You will … need to take care of her."

"Think of her? Care for her?" What did Rosina mean? Of

course he would.

"I feel so awful. I have treated her poorly out of vile envy, and I should have done something when Iskittihi came. I should have tried to protect her like Pleasant did. Even Pleasant was more selfless than I. Instead, I just stood there." Rosina's lips wobbled, then she blurted out a confession that rattled John to the bones. "Brother Kliest, Clarissa is with child."

CHAPTER TWENTY-SIX

The creek the deer trail intersected not long after Clarissa and Dawnee started following it flowed downhill. Thick ferns, thorny mayhaws, and orange flame azaleas flourished in the damp environment. Clarissa and Dawnee picked their way along, climbing when the banks narrowed into steep overhangs and stepping carefully through mud and slick rocks when the bed proved broad until the sound of flowing water grew louder. At last, the stream emptied into another body, broader and livelier, but not as wide or deep as the Hiwassee.

Dawnee's face brightened as she held a tree branch back to behold the view. "Ocoee!"

"You know where we are?"

"Yes. Oocumma live beside Ocoee."

Sending up grateful prayers, Clarissa tried to keep up with the re-energized Dawnee as she scrambled down the embankment and hurried along the river. *Please let Oocumma be home … alone.*

When at last a clearing containing a homestead came into view, Dawnee slowed her pace. "Wait here." She pointed to a massive white oak. "If clear, I come back for you."

Before Clarissa could protest, the girl darted toward a small barn. Clarissa held her hand over her mouth as if that would still the frantic beating of her heart. She heard a woman's cry, and she clamped her hand tighter to keep her fear from finding voice. She broke out from behind the tree and fisted her skirts to run to Dawnee's aid. But she'd only gone a half dozen steps when the girl appeared at the door of the outbuilding with an older lady. Silver streaked the woman's braids. Milk streaked the front of her gray linen dress. They were laughing.

Clarissa pressed a hand to her chest, able to breathe again.

"I scare her good!" Dawnee pointed to the milk stain. "Knock over pail."

Tsali, Dawnee's aunt, and Oocumma spoke very little English, but in response to Dawnee's rapid explanation, they welcomed them into their home, where several children Dawnee's age and younger greeted their cousin with squeals and hugs before drawing up to the board. Their bright eyes watched as Tsali served coffee, grits, and—oh, heaven—bacon. As Dawnee related the threat from Iskittihi and the reason behind it, pleasant conversation as well as eating wound to a halt. The faces of Dawnee's uncle and aunt paled, and their eyes widened.

Oocumma cut a hard glance at Clarissa. He asked Dawnee in Cherokee, "Why did this woman make you write down our words?"

Clarissa understood most of Dawnee's reply, filling in the gaps with educated guesses. "She did not make me, uncle. I wanted to. Why should Cherokees not read and write in their own language like everyone else?"

"Many here do not agree. We keep the old ways."

A chill swept over Clarissa. She had not expected resistance from Dawnee's uncle, but he was not incorrect about the mixed opinions of the people. Just before they left, Peggy had related how she and Vann's mother were refuting the beliefs of local residents that the earthquakes occurred as punishment for the Cherokees adopting too many ways of the whites. Many said they should sell their European goods and return to communal living—whereupon the Vann women promptly offered to buy said clothing and equipment, displaying their lack of fear. But they had no such advocates here today. If Oocumma cast them out, they had no way to cross the Hiwassee.

Clarissa sat forward and managed a sentence in broken Cherokee. "Then they are no wiser than the followers of Doublehead, the men who want to hurt us."

Oocumma frowned. His dark eyes snapped back to Dawnee, and she spoke again. "Iskittihi and his friends are at the house of my father. Will you help us get across the Hiwassee?"

"We need to get to Tellico. My husband will meet us there." Clarissa reached into the blanket beside her on the bench and pulled out her bag of coins, separating the drawstrings enough that Oocumma caught the glint of draped-bust, silver half-dollars. "I can pay you."

He put a hand over her open pouch. He spoke, and then Dawnee translated his reply with a quaver in her voice. "I would not let my niece suffer torture or death because of her work with the missionaries. For her to learn their ways is good for her future. But we must leave now. If the bad Indians learn Little Rock has a brother nearby, they could arrive at any moment."

❧ ❦

Spring runoff caused the Hiwassee to roar at a level even greater than its rain-fed fury of the previous fall. Since Oocumma owned only one horse, they had walked to the river. The canoe waited just down the bank—a better option than riding across, no doubt—but Clarissa eyed the foaming rapids with gut-churning unease. She should have passed on that bacon. How could one man ferry them to the other side without being swept downstream in the current?

Dawnee looked at her uncle, her wide eyes suggesting that she shared Clarissa's fears.

"It will be all right." Gaze fixed straight ahead and arms crossed, Oocumma didn't even break his stalwart stance. "I have made it across in worse conditions."

Clarissa added her own encouragement, reaching down to squeeze Dawnee's hand. "Jesus is the master of the wind and the waves, remember."

Dawnee nodded, and they headed for the canoe. They had just settled in the front and Oocumma had given the first push from the muddy bank when pounding hooves and shouts made them glance behind. Five riders approached with rifles cradled against their shoulders.

"*A-le-wi-s-do-di!*" Iskittihi yelled. *Stop!*

Oocumma gave a mighty shove. As the craft shot into the river, he plopped in the rear, bent low, and paddled hard. "Get down."

Clarissa pushed Dawnee onto the bottom of the canoe and grabbed the extra paddle stowed there. She attempted to balance out Oocumma's strokes. The lightweight boat rocked with their movement. Dawnee let out a whimper. Surely, Iskittihi and his friends would not follow them on horseback into such a swollen river. She bent as low as she could while applying her weight to rowing.

Splashing rose above the surging of the water. Clarissa looked back as the men's mounts galloped into the river. Silver geysers sprayed from the horses' legs. One of the Indians lifted his rifle.

"Oocumma!" Clarissa cried.

With a whir like a hummingbird, a bullet zinged across the river in front of them. A warning shot.

Oocumma threw down his oar and reached for his own weapon. Without his added resistance, the rear of the canoe spun into the current. Clarissa paddled hard, but her efforts only seemed to aid the river. Dawnee shrieked as they were pulled downstream backward.

Oocumma aimed, and a puff of smoke exploded from his rifle. A weapon from the bank answered, but whether any of the shots found their mark, Clarissa couldn't tell. The canoe rammed into a rock, spilling them into the icy current.

❧ ❧

A much more practiced marksman than John, Chief Little Rock's aim proved true. A splash of bright red appeared on Iskittihi's arm. The renegade jerked back on his horse's reins with his other hand.

John did not wait to see if Peter and Dawnee's father—whom they had met on the road—faced outright combat in the waters of the Hiwassee. Instead, the minute Clarissa's canoe overturned, he urged his horse down the bank and into the river.

Dawnee's uncle clung to the canoe and had managed to snag the girl. He attempted to right the craft while holding his niece in his other arm. Clarissa, however, bobbed in the current, her arms flailing and a mushroom of olive-colored skirts impeding her efforts to stay on the surface. Her cry for help cut off as water surged over her head.

"Clarissa!" John dug the stirrups into the stallion's sides. Vann's fine black thoroughbred whinnied and tossed his head as the waves licked his withers. "Swim, you beast!" He leaned forward against the neck, and the horse submitted to the water.

His wife's head broke the surface. "John!" Her body smacked against a half submerged boulder and went limp.

"Hold on!" Was she conscious? Fear tasted like metal in his mouth until Clarissa's arm moved, wrapping around the water-darkened rock. His mount found purchase. Keeping hold of the reins, John plunged in, splashing and swimming his way toward her. She turned, held a hand out. The next second, he gathered her in his arms. His body broke the current, pushing him into her as she buried her face in his neck and sobbed.

"All right, now. You're all right."

The stallion scrambled to a ridge of higher ground connecting Clarissa's boulder to another outcropping. Water still sluiced as high as the girth strap as John tugged Clarissa onto the saddle, then mounted behind her. Cradling her sodden shape against his chest, he urged the horse the rest of the way across. They had made it through the worst of the current, and the stallion only had to swim briefly once more.

To his astonishment, Iskittihi's crew was nowhere in sight. Peter, the uncle, Chief Little Rock, and Dawnee waited for them on the other side, the horses dripping nearby. Dawnee's father held her on the bank, examining her limbs for injury.

"Is she all right?" John called.

"I think so," Little Rock said. "Your wife?"

John pushed back Clarissa's wet hair and cradled her face in his hand as they reached the group of soggy survivors. "Are you hurt?" She looked up at him with wide eyes and shook her head, but her crash into the boulder had filled John with a fear he hadn't allowed himself to voice until that moment. *"Der säugling?"*

Her mouth dropped open, her hand moving to her abdomen. "How do you know about that?"

Peter smiled, stepping forward to take the stallion's reins. "I'm afraid my wife is to blame."

John smiled, too, and pressed his lips to Clarissa's forehead. He wanted to say so much more, but that conversation—and the kisses he longed to cover her with—should wait until they were warm, dry, and alone. And after he made certain—preferably by the assurance of the Tellico physician—that she truly was all right.

"Sister Kliest," Dawnee called in a weak voice.

Clarissa lifted her head. "I am fine, Dawnee." She struggled to sit up in John's arms.

Peter reached up to receive Clarissa, but before John let her down, he wanted to make sure no danger remained. He scanned the far bank. "Where did Iskittihi go?"

"Having their leader shot seemed to unnerve the others," Peter said. "They turned tail and fled."

Dawnee's uncle grunted a few Cherokee words, and the girl translated his reply. "They not want to start a war with Upper Town chiefs."

Little Rock lifted his head, glaring. "They should think of that when they try take my daughter. They will now be renegades—*ga-lo-nu-he-s-gi*! Whitetree will cast them out. But many share their views. Had they stirred up such people, danger great." He looked at John. "We should take Dawnee and your wife to Tellico, and from there, you should leave our nation."

❦ ❦

The words of Dawnee's father echoed in Clarissa's head like the tolling of a death knell all the way to Tellico. Clarissa wished she could wring them from her memory as she had the river water from her sodden skirts, but they clung, as chilling as her clothing. The little band found a cabin where a sweet Indian woman allowed Clarissa and Dawnee to dry their garments in front of her fire before they proceeded to the blockhouse. There, they were equally fortunate to find that a diversion of soldiers sent to set up a garrison near Hiwassee—an outcome of the last two treaties ceding even more Cherokee territory—had left an officer's cabin open. After sending word to Springplace of their safe arrival, the captain established them in the small but private dwelling while they awaited a response.

But Clarissa did not feel fortunate. She felt like a failure. And she might have cost the dreams of those closest to her as well. All she could hold onto was the hope that Vann would send word that things had settled down enough in the region for them to return.

They celebrated Easter with their own private sunrise ceremony overlooking the river, but it was hard to rejoice when they kept thinking of those in Springplace. News finally arrived early that next week with one of the chief's trusted couriers. Du-a-i accompanied him on her own pony. She slipped down and ran to embrace her daughter and husband. Clarissa's joy at their reunion plummeted when she noticed the packhorse the courier led. She peeked into the saddlebags while John unfolded a missive from Chief Vann. Their personal effects and books. Her painting supplies. Letters from the other missionaries. She knew before John led them into the cabin to share the contents of the letter that they were not going home.

Home. Her heart pierced through with sorrows. Exactly when had Springplace become home? When Dawnee had arrived? When she and John had become one in body and spirit? When they had hosted the first full celebration of Christ's birth in that spiritual wilderness? Or maybe when the Indians poured into the mission following the earthquakes, eager to hear the truth of God.

Clarissa hugged herself as John read from Vann's letter. "'Whitetree will deal with Iskittihi and his men. I expect they will leave for the Lower Towns. However, they have friends in this area who agree with their views and are angry that Chief Little Rock drew the blood of Iskittihi. It seems the time has not come for the Cherokee boy to make a book. The bad spirits need to settle before such a thing can happen. It is best for Brother and Sister Kliest to return to Salem, and for the daughter of Little Rock not to come back to Springplace this year.'"

Dawnee muffled a wail on her mother's arm. Du-a-i comforted her, but there was no comfort for Clarissa. Tears spilled down her face. "This is my fault. I am so sorry." She glanced at John, yearning for a sympathetic touch or look, but she saw only sorrow in his eyes.

To her surprise, Du-a-i shook her head. Rubbing her daughter's braids, she spoke to Clarissa. "You did no wrong. Only what your people told you to do. What God told you to do. We are not sad we send Dawnee to school."

Chief Little Rock cleared his throat, gestured toward his wife. "We talk, she and me. Dawnee special. We want her learn more."

"But ... how?" Clarissa asked. "I believe the Presbyterians have a mission school near Hiwassee. Perhaps ..."

"Not Hiwassee," Du-a-i said. "Salem."

With a little gasp, Dawnee jerked her head up. "I go to Salem?"

"To the girls' boarding school?" Clarissa met John's eyes. He held her gaze, not rejecting the idea outright. Her heartbeat stuttered at the notion of Dawnee continuing her education in a much more formal fashion, one that could open endless doors for her. "'Twould not be the first time a person of color has attended, but ... have you any idea how far it is? You would rarely, if ever, be able to see her."

Du-a-i nodded, sad but resigned as she played with Dawnee's hair. "I know she want this, and I want best for her."

"Oh, *e-tsi!*" Dawnee threw her arms around Du-a-i's waist. She leapt up to hug her father, who returned her embrace with a stoicism that dammed up any untoward emotion. Then she turned to Clarissa. "You say God turn bad to good. This good!"

One more permission had to be granted. Clarissa looked at her husband. "John?"

Finally, he gave a slow nod. Clarissa opened her arms to the girl, but as she kissed the top of her head, she blinked back tears. Yes, this was good for Dawnee, but how would good ever come out of this for her and John? She had not only failed at her assignment to record the Cherokee language, but she had cheated her husband of his missionary success, at Oothcaloga as well as Springplace. She wasn't sure their marriage could withstand the blow.

CHAPTER TWENTY-SEVEN

One Year Later

"That is lovely, Adelaide." Clarissa bent over her talented blonde student from South Carolina, praising the selection of fruit stencils the young lady had chosen to build her theorem still life. "Those will make a classic painting fit for any grand parlor."

Adelaide beamed with pride. "Thank you, ma'am."

Clarissa straightened and smoothed the striped folds of her cotton gown, once again admiring the light in this room. The addition John had built for her art studio had proved perfect for capturing the late winter and early spring light. She still couldn't believe that after a few months in the cottage they had stayed in after their wedding, they had been able to purchase the very home John had grown up in. The elderly silversmith who had occupied it since the passing of John's father had died, allowing them to move in only a couple doors down from the girls' boarding school. The close proximity had convinced the headmaster that the advanced drawing and painting students could repair to Clarissa's home for their lessons. This studio, with its multitude of long, many-paned windows, had sealed the bargain.

She felt so, so blessed, although a tinge of sadness remained. Clarissa had always been able to neatly tie up every endeavor in her life … until Springplace.

She tilted her head to regard Dawnee. 'Twas difficult not to show the girl favoritism when she thought of her almost as her own daughter. She had blossomed in Salem, though, like the jonquils opening their sunny faces in the garden outside the window. She chattered now with one of her many friends—friends who had first welcomed her as a novelty but quickly been won to permanent appreciation by her sweet temperament.

Clarissa picked up one of the horn paper cutouts she had coated on both sides with linseed oil. "Dawnee, you wanted only apples of two sizes?"

Dawnee glanced up. "Yes, Sister Kliest. I make the apples from the orchards at home. Red and green. Between, I add fall leaves. My mother loves autumn."

"You plan to give this to her when she visits this summer." Clarissa allowed a smile to wreath her face. She couldn't wait for Du-a-i and Chief Little Rock to make their first sojourn to Salem.

"When she goes home, she will think of me every time she looks at it."

Clarissa squeezed her shoulder and whispered. "Your English is coming along beautifully."

"Thank you." Dawnee grinned. With her hair twisted into a neat bun under her cap, only her slightly darker skin tone set her apart from the other girls. "I am doing well in German too."

The tolling of the steeple bell from Home Church jolted everyone to alertness. Clarissa clapped her hands. "Time to return to the school for your dinner. Just leave everything as it is, and we shall continue tomorrow."

She stood by the door for the girls' ritual of retrieving bonnets from the pegs, then gave them a pat and a goodbye as they filed out. Standing tall, Clarissa inhaled a whiff of cool air and growing things. Anticipation filled her. She must hurry so she could feed little William Frederick before dinner. She craved his sweet weight in her arms. She shut the door and applied herself to straightening the tables.

Clarissa entered her parlor from the studio, as fine a parlor as was to be had in Salem. Thankfully, William wasn't fussing yet, though the fullness of Clarissa's bosom told her he would be soon. A noise at the front door stopped her on her way to the kitchen.

"Clarissa?" John called.

He was home early. She hurried to the entry to take his coat and hat and turn her face up for a kiss. Handsome as ever, her husband's appearance always made her heart lurch. He smelled no longer of the wilderness but of crisp air and soap. "How goes it with the sheds for the girls' school?"

Clarissa only noticed John's frown when he pulled back from her embrace. There'd been talk of appointing him roadmaster for Salem. Perhaps he'd learned 'twas not to be? She was about to ask when he drew a stained letter from his waistcoat.

"From Springplace."

Her hand fluttered to her heart and a half dozen questions to her mind. More bad news? Clarissa voiced her foremost concern. "Sister Keller, did she deliver her baby?"

A brief grin broke over John's closely bearded face, and he ushered her into the parlor. "She did, and 'tis a hale baby girl. Named Elizabeth Jane."

"Oh, I am so happy for them." Clarissa clasped her hands under her chin, picturing the little family in their cabin. "I wish I could give them all a big hug." One of her biggest regrets was not having been able to bid everyone goodbye. What she wouldn't give for a good talk with Sister Steiner, and yes, Rosina. She even found that—despite enjoying a home here no less elegant than Dr. Vierling's—she missed their cozy cabin.

And how she wished she'd had more time with Pleasant. Her questions to Sister Steiner about the woman's spiritual progress met with disappointing replies. If Clarissa could return, even for a visit, she could build on the foundation she'd established with Pleasant.

"They could use a hug about now, I would suspect." John drew her down beside him on the sofa.

Reading the concern in his gaze, Clarissa reached for his hand. "What is wrong?"

With every letter over the past year, she'd watched John hope that they might be called back, then be disappointed. Their departure from the mission had in no way eliminated the drama there. In

May, soon after their return to Salem, the ongoing threats from John Falling, husband of Vann's sister Nancy, had culminated in a duel with Vann, who shot Falling dead. A relative of Falling's—a chief—swore revenge. In August, the national council's sentence against Doublehead had been carried out during the Hiwassee Green Corn Festival by The Ridge and another man. But none of the bad news had prompted a call for reinforcements from the missionaries. Now, though, with Rosina having given birth ...?

John interrupted her musings. "It is Vann, Clarissa. He is dead."

"Dead?" Clarissa grasped her throat, where a sudden knot seemed to prevent breathing. The man she had both feared and admired, the larger-than-life force behind Diamond Hill and Springplace—gone? "What happened?"

"It seems he was traveling in a judicial capacity and stopped at Buffington's Tavern near Frogtown. He was standing in the open door when someone fired a shot from outside. It hit him in the heart."

"Do they know who did this?"

John shook his head, separating and stroking her fingers on the settee between them. "Only speculation. It could have to do with Falling—or Doublehead—or the thieves he was rounding up. So many hated him."

"Oh, but the void he leaves! Poor Peggy. Poor Joseph."

"Yes, but they are not the only ones to feel the void. Brother Steiner writes that chaos has broken out. The slaves are confused and fighting. Wahli has accused the missionaries of having designs on Vann's fortune and is denying them entrance to the house. Rumors are spreading that the school will close, and parents are withdrawing their children. They are down to the number they had when we left."

"John!" Clarissa scooted closer and leaned her head against his shoulder.

He stroked her hair. "They are not certain they *can* remain open, without Vann's patronage."

She sat up and looked at him. "What can we do to help?"

He shrugged. "Pray. And I thought I would go to the elders and ask if we might raise a special offering."

Clarissa nodded. "And would you ... deliver this special offering?"

"There is no *you*." John ran the back of his finger down her temple, his gaze gentling as he traced the curve of her face. "Now there is only *us*. And I cannot see how it would serve to drag you and the baby to the Cherokee Nation when they may be hard-pressed to feed us when we get there."

Clarissa lowered her lashes, picked at a fold in her skirt. "If it came to that, I would not oppose you going alone."

"Clarissa, I thought I told you I had let go of that dream."

"But you shouldn't have to on account of me."

"I also told you that I don't blame you. None of us knew that many Cherokees considered writing their language witchcraft, a crime punishable by death—least of all you, who were practically coerced into participating."

Her eyes swept up to meet his. "I do not regret it. All my life, I have striven to control my own destiny. Despite my faith, I wanted what I wanted. God used Springplace to show me I had to give up *my* dreams. To die to myself in order to really find my life."

John squeezed her hand but tucked his chin, seeming unable to respond.

She continued. "I am content in the fact that, while I went because of duty, I found true love. Ours, as well as a love for those people. My only regret is leaving a task unfinished."

"Remember what you told Sam?" John waited for her to nod. "You planted a seed. Those boys can water it. Maybe even Dawnee. And look how well she is doing."

"Yes, I do tell myself that, but that is not what I meant. I meant your task. Your calling."

John sat back, sighed, and rubbed his hand over his beard. "You know what you said about dying to self? Well, it might have taken me longer to realize this than it did you, but I, too, went to Springplace for the wrong reasons."

Clarissa raised her brows. She had always looked on John's calling as the noble one. "How so?"

He cleared his throat and shifted. Chewed his lip. "I did love the people when I went. And I loved God and wanted them to know Him. But I loved my own ambition more."

"John—"

He held up a hand, hushing her. "No, 'tis true. Achievement, adventure, and purpose ... I'd say those had been the three pillars of my life up until our time in the Cherokee Nation. And I'm ashamed to say, I've been mourning them. But through this time, God has been teaching me to seek Him and find contentment in the blessings He has given me ... which are bountiful." He smoothed back her hair, twisting a loose strand around his index finger.

Clarissa captured his hand and kissed his knuckles with a passion she normally reserved for his lips. She buried her face in his rough palm, mostly to cover the tears that had sprung to her eyes. "You are a good man. The best man. I am honored beyond words to be your wife."

John reached for her, but a throat clearing jolted them apart. Mary Ellen, the single sister whom they paid to watch the baby while Clarissa taught her classes, stood on the threshold, jostling a red-faced William on her hip. "Pardon me, ma'am, but he's getting a mite testy."

"Of course, Sister Krause. How remiss of me. You must be getting back home for supper." Clarissa held out her arms, but John stood and took the baby. He thanked the nursemaid and sent her on her way.

The five-month-old cooed at his father as John bounced him in the air. "He does favor my father more by the day."

"And in temperament is very like his first namesake, Brother Steiner."

"As long as he doesn't sprout a gray beard anytime soon." John frowned when William stuck his fist in his mouth and started sucking fiercely. He lowered the child in his long gown onto Clarissa's lap. "I think he'll be more ready to see me after he's seen you first."

※　☆

While Clarissa fed the baby, John wandered into Clarissa's studio. He liked to see what the students were getting up to. Observing Clarissa so fulfilled with her lessons—and her own drawing—took the edge off his wanderlust when it reared its craggy head.

Frames holding silk backdrops scattered with weighted stencils filled the work table. Fruits in various stages of creation glowed with brilliant hues in the evening light. He picked out Dawnee's right away, with those bright, plump Georgia apples. Nice.

But where were the paintings Clarissa herself was working on? Sister Krause said she came in here every morning for a couple of hours before her students arrived. Whenever John had inquired how she spent that time, however, she'd given a vague reply.

A dressing screen that could serve as a backdrop for portrait-painting blocked one end of the room. Behind it, a riot of supplies overflowed from boxes and crates. But a covered easel held a canvas. John lifted off the muslin and dragged in a soft breath.

'Twas a stunning likeness of Diamond Hill backlit by the setting sun. Horses, corn fields, and hardwoods in their autumnal splendor dotted the hills, while in the hollow, smoke rose from the cabin chimneys at the mission. A pain stabbed his breastbone. 'Twas almost as if he were there.

John's foot nudged a canvas on the floor, a leaning stack of paintings. Kneeling, he came face-to-face with The Ridge in his fierce dignity. The hair raised on the back of John's neck. Behind him was Chief Chuleoa with his red feathers and silver bracelets. Peggy Vann, gracious and serene, with her hands folded on her Bible—just as she had so often reposed during their meetings. Pleasant held Michael, her face beneath her turban reflecting a secret tenderness only Clarissa had observed. John's heartbeat stuttered as he beheld the familiar faces of Tom, Sam, Sally, Joe, Dawnee … and even Charlie as they sat at their lessons.

All drawings from Clarissa's sketch pad, fleshed out in vivid watercolor. Each person one he missed with deep longing but was unable to embrace or speak with, probably ever again. Like looking back on a chapter of his life closed forever, and perhaps closing for those still at Springplace now as well.

Tilting the paintings back against the wall, John covered his face with his hand. He did not try to stop the tears that spilled from his eyes.

The questions poured out too. "Oh God, why would You allow so much to be accomplished only to be lost? Not just the syllabary, but maybe now the entire mission." He placed his hand on the painting of the students, as though he could transfer a blessing to them as he prayed aloud. "These children, they are precious in Your sight. They are the next generation of a noble people who so desperately need You. Please don't leave them to the darkness."

His hand trembled on the canvas. The connection faded, but a voice he did not expect spoke. He heard it in his spirit as clearly as if Brother Steiner stood over him booming out a sermon. In fact, the voice sounded strangely *like* Brother Steiner.

I have raised up a helper.

John tilted his face. A cardinal sat on the blooming cherry tree outside the window. "Who, Lord?"

When no answer came, he rose, brushing off his cheeks and tugging down his waistcoat. Then he stopped. Stared at the paintings. He wasn't the helper, but he could help.

❧ ☙

On a glorious Saturday in April, Clarissa came home from the bakery with her basket full of sweetbreads. Removing her bonnet, she unloaded her bounty in the kitchen and set the water to boil on the German ceramic stove. The pale pink of its tiles matched the dogwood blooming in her yard. Perhaps she would call John to enjoy their coffee and rolls on the bench under its spreading branches, where they could watch the plump spring robins hop about. Now that would be romantic if William would stay quiet in his crib for another half an hour.

But where was John?

A scrape on the floorboards overhead and she looked up. A speck of dust fell in her eye. She grumbled. Blotted with her handkerchief. What was the man up to?

Going to the foyer, she lifted her voice a notch above normal. "John?"

When no one responded, Clarissa tiptoed up the stairs. At the top, though, she almost yelled when a figure stepped in front of her. Not John, but Mary Ellen, her face red and a finger held up to her lips.

"Shh. You'll wake the baby."

"*You'll* wake the baby, with all that racket." Clarissa craned around her for a glimpse into the nursery. "Whatever are you up to, and whatever are you doing here on a Saturday, anyway?"

Mary Ellen propped her hand on her ample hip. "Brother Kliest sent for me to sit with William and said to get out the trunks while I was at it. I was moving them as quiet as I could when I heard you below. Brother Steiner said he left you a note on the kitchen table you should read right away."

Clarissa released a puff of breath, fighting indignation at this strange deviation from the norm. And her tea plans. "Very well."

In the kitchen, a paper sat folded and propped against her candlesticks. She picked up it and read. *Come back to where it all began.*

She puckered her lips and tapped her toe. What did that mean? Their romance? He must refer to their first meeting. On the square? No. Before that, she had come upon John after he had taken Daniel's letter from the witness tree. Was he waiting for her there? Irritation dissipating like the steam coming from the tea kettle, she smiled.

Clarissa removed the whistling kettle from the stove before snatching her bonnet and tying it on again. She grabbed a sweet bun, too, and stuffed a bite in her mouth as she set out the door. She was always hungry these days, and it was no trifling walk up that hill to the corner of Salem.

By the time she reached the tree, she was puffing from exertion. She paused, bending forward to catch her breath. Finally, she was able to hear the twittering birds over her own inhalations. She straightened and surveyed the scene. No one in sight. Nothing but the greening forest, the road, and the tree. And a paper-wrapped parcel peeking out of the knot.

Clarissa hastened over and retrieved it. It was tied with twine the way Bagge's secured special purchases, and her name was written on the outside. She opened it and let out a cry. She held a beautiful cameo brooch in her palm, the overlay of shell intricately carved with a lady's profile on a peach background, set in delicate gold filigree.

A deep voice spoke from behind her. "Excuse me, ma'am, but what is such a beauty as yourself doing unaccompanied on this road?"

She whirled to face John. "And what are you doing, leaving me such expensive presents in the crook of a tree?"

"I had it—and you—in my view the whole time." He approached, lifting his hat. Winking.

She wouldn't let him off that easy. "*Buying* me such expensive presents? John ..." Clarissa held up the brooch, running her finger over its cool surface. "Oh, John, 'tis so lovely, but 'tis far too fine for Salem."

"But not, I dare say, for Philadelphia."

Did the woods go silent of scampering squirrel feet and chirping birds, or did a flood of stunned silence fill her whole head? "Did you say ... Philadelphia?"

"I did." A smirk danced on John's lips, teasing her with laugh lines. His eyes held steady on hers.

She took a tiny step toward him, breathless all over again. "Have you been called there to do a job ... and I get to go along?"

"No, my dear." John's reply contained a sudden solemnity.

She drew back with uncertainty.

"*You* have been called there, and I get to go along." When Clarissa only blinked at him, he produced an envelope from his pocket and handed it to her.

Her eyes focused on the writing, but the name there made no sense. "Thomas Sully?"

"Remember him? I believe you once had a great desire to visit said gentleman before I swept you off your feet."

Clarissa could only stutter, the letter suspended between them.

John leveled a stare with those blue eyes of his. "Your paintings. The mission. God gave me an idea, so I wrote to my brother in Philadelphia and asked if his mentor could arrange a showing for you. Mr. Sully is beyond himself at the notion of displaying artwork depicting real Cherokee people. He is more than willing to invite all the wealthy Germans he knows in the area to help raise money for Springplace."

"Oh ... my paintings ... to be seen ..." She still couldn't talk right.

"Are you upset with me?" John cocked a brow at her. "Perhaps I should have asked you first, but I did not want you to be disappointed if it did not work out."

"Upset? No. Overwhelmed. Yes." That was better. Sentences, although they were short. She slid the letter into her waistband, to be read when her brain worked.

"My dear, this is your chance." John took hold of her hands, bounced them up and down. "A tremendous opportunity."

Absorbing that truth, Clarissa sucked in a deep breath, and it seemed joy instead of spring air spiraled through her. Reviving her. Inspiring her. "If we can raise money for Springplace, I am ready to go this minute. I know you said Charles Hicks has promised to represent the mission's interests before the national council, but I am sure they have immediate need of funding. Imagine what they could buy, John. New books. Testaments. *Beef*."

Now that she was rolling, John had to hold up a hand to stop her. "All this is true, but that is not all I meant."

"What did you mean?"

"I mean we will be staying a while. Mr. Sully has agreed to tutor you."

"He will … teach me?"

"Yes."

"For how long?" This couldn't be.

John shrugged. "Two, three months."

"But my teaching here…" Even as she said it, sending an anxious glance down the lane at an approaching gentleman on a horse, Clarissa knew her protest sounded weak.

"Is almost at the end of the term. A substitute will be found. We will be back in time for Chief Little Rock and Du-a-i's visit." John tugged her off the road, closer to their tree.

"But what will you do? Surely you will not leave me in Philadelphia alone."

He threw back his head on a scoff. "With all the trolls there? Hardly! No, I have arranged a job surveying an estate outside town for a Lutheran with padded pockets. I will only leave you with Sully and his wife during the days. We will take Mary Ellen to help with William if you approve." He paused to tip his hat to the rider, who nodded an acknowledgment. After the man passed, John squeezed her hands again, leaned toward her. "What is it, Clarissa? You don't seem happy."

"I am terribly happy. Beyond myself. Beyond words. But also … afraid."

He chucked her chin. "Of what, *leibchen*?"

She had to think a moment. Finally, she seized on the edge of the truth. "Of turning my focus back to myself again. I don't want to lose the ground I gained."

John pulled her to his chest, where the sound of his heartbeat stabilized her, and murmured into her hair. "Clarissa, your talent deserves to be nurtured, not so it can become an idol, but so you can use it for God."

"But ..." When he put it that way, she could see it. Grand vistas opened in her mind. God was giving Clarissa her heart's desire.

"I once thought your paintings a distraction from your work, when they *were* your true calling. Who knows what your future may hold."

Tears ran down Clarissa's face as she tucked her hands against John's chest. "You would do this for me?"

He pressed his lips to her forehead. "I would give my life for you, the same as you were willing to do for Dawnee. That is love. I thought I had to find adventure among the dangers of the frontier, but I'm willing to face this new challenge—even if it is in a city." John offered her a rueful grin.

Laughing, Clarissa swung their joined hands between them. "Yes. This time, we will do it together."

AUTHOR'S NOTE

When I set out to write about the Cherokees and Moravians during the Federal period of Northwest Georgia, little did I realize I'd chosen my most challenging setting ever. Not only was this a new time period for me as an author, but I had combined two very unique people groups with their own customs and languages. Two groups that could hardly communicate with each other when they first met!

Let me start by saying that while almost all the major incidents in *The Witness Tree* actually happened, I drew those incidents from an approximately ten-year timeframe. While I typically prefer sticking to exact history, in this case, I felt the modern reader would benefit most from a "slice of life" overview of what it was like to live at Springplace during this period. I used *The Moravian Springplace Mission to the Cherokees: Volume 1, 1805-1813* as my base reference.

My Moravian characters were fictional but at times inspired by the real missionaries, such as Anna Rosina Gambold, whose work as a teacher and botanist influenced the creation of Rosina Keller. The backgrounds for the Kliest brothers also resembled those of real-life Salem residents: Daniel Wohlfarth (1796-1841) for Daniel and Frederick Christian Meinung (1782-1851) for John. Though also fictional, the boarding scholars represented composites of the real students who lived at Springplace. As documented in the Moravian diaries, there really was an incident where an all-night prayer vigil proceeded the recovery of a female student from a mysterious illness.

The name of the captured slave, Solomon, was changed from Peter to avoid confusion with my missionary character. I did use the real names and general histories of Pleasant and her son

Michael, enslaved servants to the Moravians of Springplace. As far as history bears out, both resented their masters and never became Christians.

When creating characters as well as plot elements in a historical novel, I ask, "Is there a historical precedent, or would this have been realistic or likely to have happened?" For instance, in the real history of Salem, the elders decided that a couple of the men who felt called to the Cherokee mission should take wives first, resulting in hurried marriages approved by the lot. Thus, the basis for John and Clarissa's marriage of convenience.

Several incidents I condensed into the novel's shorter timeframe bear further comment. The mission at Springplace was established in 1801. Doublehead was executed in August of 1807; James Vann was murdered in February 1809. Charles Hicks stepped into the gap he left as local advocate for Springplace. Cherokee Agent Colonel R. J. Meigs also secured a hundred-dollar annual government grant for the school, and a wealthy Philadelphia merchant indeed helped finance the mission in 1811. Thus, the idea of Clarissa's paintings opening the door to donations.

The workers at Springplace labored until June of 1810 before the first Cherokee—Margaret "Peggy" Vann—made a profession of faith. Severe seismic disturbances and an eclipse marked the years 1811 and 1812, prompting many others to inquire about God.

Many people know that George Gist/Guess, or "Sequoyah," wrote the first Cherokee syllabary. A syllabary consists of symbols that correlate to syllables rather than a symbol for every word or a standard set of letters based on speech sounds. While the man's name and life, as well as the origins of the syllabary, are robed in contradiction and speculation, several sources confirm that Captain John Ridge (son of The Ridge, who was called Major Ridge only after leading the Cherokees alongside General Andrew Jackson during the Red Stick War of 1814) rushed a troop of Georgia Cherokee Lighthorse to North Carolina to save Gist from slow death by torture for witchcraft. An 1811 Cherokee law mandated a civil trial before execution, allowing Sequoyah to prove the legitimacy of the syllabary.

This lesser-known, surprising part of Sequoyah's story led me to posit: "What if the missionaries at Springplace had attempted to create a syllabary first?" After all, the Salem congregation had consulted Apostle to the Northern Indians David Zeisberger in 1797 for advice on establishing a mission to the Cherokees. He wrote in response, "My advice would be, if one or several Brethren are willing, first to learn the language of the Cherokees. The Indians are always agreeable to a desire to learn their language and like to see it written down."

While we might assume that such an endeavor would have been doomed to failure, I wondered … what might God have wanted to accomplish through that failure in the story of our missionary characters? We all face failure at some point in our lives, and often we mistake the role of seed planting or watering for failure just because we don't get to see the harvest. In this case, I hinted at the future harvest of a written Cherokee language through the boys Clarissa leaves behind in the Springplace school. These boys could have influenced others who came later.

The residents of Oothcaloga indeed considered establishing a mission in their community but ended up sending their sons to Springplace. The Ridge sent his son John, and The Ridge's brother Oo-watie (later David Watie) sent his son Buck (the brother of Stand Watie, the last Confederate general to surrender). Both finished their education at the Congregationalists' Foreign Mission School in Cornwall, Connecticut, and married local white women (creating quite a scandal—possible fodder for a future novel). Buck Watie took the name Elias Boudinot after his sponsor. Boudinot returned to the new Cherokee capital of New Echota, where he worked with missionary Samuel Worcester in altering Sequoyah's syllabary for printing the *Cherokee Phoenix* newspaper, the Bible, and Christian hymns.

Only the greatest respect has been meant to all the people

groups represented in *The Witness Tree*. The more I study history, the more I am convinced that every race consists of both good and bad individuals. Or more accurately, all peoples are in need of a Savior ... thus the driving force behind the Moravian outreach. Whatever strengths and weaknesses they brought to the corner of the Cherokee Nation that is now Northwest Georgia, they left a far-reaching impact of education and faith among the Cherokee people.